Maryanne O'Donnell
May 13, 1985

Elliott O'Donnell's

GREAT GHOST STORIES
OMNIBUS EDITION

Elliott O'Donnell's

GREAT
GHOST STORIES
OMNIBUS EDITION

Edited by

HARRY LUDLAM

ARCO PUBLISHING, INC.
New York

Published 1984 by Arco Publishing, Inc.
215 Park Avenue South, New York, NY 10003

Library of Congress Catalog Card Number: 83-72572

ISBN 0-668-06077-8 cloth edition
ISBN 0-668-06080-8 paper edition

First published by W. Foulsham & Company Limited, England, as
Casebook of Ghosts (1969) and
The Screaming Skulls and Other Ghosts (1964)

Copyright © 1964 & 1969 Elliott O'Donnell

Printed in Great Britain

CONTENTS

INTRODUCTION

Elliott O'Donnell as a boy was afraid of being alone in the dark—horribly and painfully afraid. The ghost stories told him by his sister and the family's sewing-maid made his fear all the stronger. Yet the dark fascinated the parson's son and he longed to explore it though he dared not.

It was not until he had ranched in the Far West of the U.S.A., where he rode cattle, sat at the camp fires and listened to Indians and backwoodsmen talking about eerie lights they had seen on Wizard Island in Crater Lake, and stories of haunted trees no horse would go near, and ghost dances; not until he had freelanced as a writer in San Francisco and New York, trained for the stage in England, acted on tour and in London, and then settled in St. Ives, Cornwall, that he first seriously thought of becoming a ghost-hunter. This was at the turn of the century.

Since then Elliott O'Donnell, who was born in Bristol in 1872, has been novelist and ghost story writer, lecturer and broadcaster, radio playwright and criminologist. But it is in the realm of the supernatural that his most exhaustive work has been done.

He has written more books on ghostly phenomena than anyone. He has investigated countless cases of reputed hauntings, alone and with many notable people including the late Duke of Newcastle, Lord Curzon of Kedleston, Sir C. A. Smith, and Sir Ernest Bennett. He has documented many authentic accounts of supernatural appearances and seen much phenomena himself.

The true stories he now tells, together with some compelling legends, are among the most enthralling gathered in more than half a century of ghost-hunting. Only in some of the true tales, for various reasons, have names of people involved been changed.

H.L.

Let me state plainly that I lay no claim to being what is termed a scientific psychical researcher. I am not a member of any august society that conducts its investigations of the other world, or worlds, with test tube and weighing apparatus; neither do I pretend to be a medium or consistent clairvoyant—I have never undertaken to " raise " ghosts at will for the sensation-seeker or the tourist. I am merely a ghost-hunter. One who lays stake by his own eyes and senses; one who honestly believes that he inherits in some degree the faculty of psychic perceptiveness from a long line of Celtic ancestry; and who is, and always has been, deeply and genuinely interested in all questions relative to phantasms and a continuance of individual life after physical dissolution.

Elliott O'Donnell

THE VEILED GHOST OF HIGHGATE

THERE was standing when I was young in the vicinity of Highgate, north London, a quaint, rambling red-brick house with a moss-grown courtyard in front. Inside were large gloomy rooms and dark staircases and passages.

The owner of the house resided abroad. No one lived in it for long and the following traditional story was associated with it.

Towards the end of the eighteenth century there were living in the house a Mr. Bruce, his wife and daughters. Charles, the only son of Mr. Bruce and a wild and reckless youth, had been living in Paris for two years when he suddenly returned home, so ill that he had to be put to bed and Miss Black, a nurse, engaged to attend him.

On her arrival Miss Black was shown into the invalid's room. The furniture was of the handsome, heavy kind characteristic of those times. The panelling on the walls was black with age, the fireplace supported by massive buttresses. The large curtained bed in which Charles lay stood in the centre of the floor, and an oil lamp glimmered on a table.

Miss Black replenished the fire, which was low, and sitting down at the table started to read the Bible. She had been instructed to keep very quiet. Now and again blasts of wind shook the leafless branches of the great trees in the garden, while snow spluttered on the embers as it was wafted down the wide chimney.

Curious to see her patient, Miss Black gently pulled aside the curtain round his bed. Contrary to her expectation he was not asleep but lay motionless on his back, his bright blue eyes glaringly fixed on her face, his underlip fallen, mouth apart, cheeks a perfect hollow, his long white teeth projecting fearfully from the shrunken lips, whilst a bony hand, covered with wiry sinews, was stretched on the bedclothes. He was not a pleasant sight. Miss Black quickly returned to the table, leaving the curtain still drawn aside.

About midnight the patient began to breathe heavily and seemed to be very restless. Turning to look at him, Miss Black was greatly surprised to see a closely veiled woman seated in a chair near the head of the bed. Miss Black was about to move when the woman motioned to her to keep her seat.

Miss Black could not see the woman's face, owing to the veil, but she got the impression that she was young and good-looking. She was slender and rather tall, and wore a light green dress. She had gold earrings, a large gold locket and chain and a massive gold, bejewelled bracelet of curious workmanship, all of which sparkled in the lamplight. Miss Black concluded that the woman was a relative.

Charles Bruce, who had become more than ever restless, heaved and sighed and seemed in great distress. Miss Black was rising to go to him when the woman again motioned to her to remain seated. The heat from the fire made Miss Black drowsy and she dozed for a few minutes. When she awoke, the woman had gone.

At the same hour the next night the same thing happened. Miss Black was reading at the table when, on looking at the bed, she saw the veiled woman seated beside the patient. She got up and, undeterred by the repellant action of the woman, approached the bed, whereupon the woman rose and moved slowly and noislessly towards the door.

The face of her patient terrified Miss Black. Deep drops of sweat were on his brow and his lips quivered as if in agony. His glaring eyes followed the receding figure of the woman, who mysteriously vanished just before she reached the door.

The strain she had undergone watching the sick man and the strange woman was so great that Miss Black told the Bruces she could not stay another night in the house. It was only after the doctor implored her to remain that she very reluctantly yielded.

The next night was Christmas Eve. It was bitterly cold but dry. The wind moaned and sighed and rattled the ill-secured shutters, generating dismal echoes in the gloomy passages of the old building.

At the same hour as on the previous nights the veiled woman suddenly appeared by the bed of the invalid. His gasping and heaving made Miss Black's heart sicken and when, in spite of the warning hand of the strange woman, she approached the bed, the corpse-like features of Charles became horribly convulsed, his eyes starting from their sockets. Miss Black spoke but there was no reply. She touched him very gently. He was cold with terror and unconscious of any object but the mysterious woman.

Thinking her patient was going to expire, Miss Black was about to go for assistance when the woman bent over Charles, who made a feeble effort to keep her away. Miss Black ran at once to the woman, whose clothes were very wet although the weather was dry, and, obeying a sudden impulse, raised her veil. There was no face under it, only a blank.

The shock Miss Black received was so great that she fainted. She was found in the morning lying on the floor only half conscious.

Charles Bruce lay stiff and lifeless, one hand across his eyes as if to shade them from some object he feared to look on; the other hand gripped the coverlet.

That same morning, it was later discovered, the body of a foreign woman, young and beautiful, in a green dress, with gold earrings, a gold locket and chain and a massive bejewelled gold bracelet of curious workmanship was washed ashore on the Kent coast. She had been in the water three or four days. Her identity, if known to certain people in England, was never divulged.

The Bruces left the house soon after the death of Charles and never returned. It was shortly after their departure that the house was rumoured to be haunted by the ghost of a young man, supposedly Charles Bruce, who was seen and heard wandering disconsolately in the dead of night from room to room, along passages and up and down staircases, ever seeking companionship and sympathy, and finding none.

11

THE SCREAMING SKULLS OF CALGARTH HALL

In the vicinity of Lake Windermere there stood in the early seventeenth century a small farm occupied by Kraster Cook and his wife Dorothy. They were a hard-working, thrifty couple, who loved their cottage and their few acres, which had been handed down to them through many generations.

The land all around their holding was owned by Myles Phillipson, the head of a rich and influential family, and who, though not titled, was that type of English country squire who had long met the nobility on terms of equality. Myles Phillipson had an attractive young wife and they planned to build a new manor house upon their estate. Of all the many acres that were theirs, none seemed so desirable to the Phillipsons as the little farm of their humbler neighbours.

But Kraster Cook would not sell. Time after time Phillipson went to him, offering inducement after inducement, but all to no purpose. He could not shake the stubborn farmer's decision.

One day Myles Phillipson returned from the Cooks' cottage with a brow as black as thunder, vowing he would have the land if not by fair means then by foul.

There is a story in the Old Testament of King Ahab, how he coveted the vineyard of his subject Naboth, and how his wife, Queen Jezebel, counselled him wickedly as to how he might secure it. Whether Myles Phillipson's wife had gotten her inspiration from this story cannot, of course, be known, but as wickedly as Jezebel counselled King Ahab, so did Mistress Phillipson counsel her husband.

Next morning Phillipson rode over to the cottage. Smiling, he offered his hand, telling Kraster Cook that he had given up all idea of buying his land and that he had decided to build the new house upon his own acres. He hoped that bygones would be bygones, and that all the harsh words he had spoken would be forgotten. And further to show his changed spirit, he asked the farmer and his wife to be his guests at the manor house on Christmas Day, which was then a little more than a week away.

The Cooks were relieved and glad that their powerful neighbour had changed his mind about their farm. They hesitated about accepting the invitation, however, for they knew that at the great house the event would be a gay one, and that to it would come the gentry of the county and their wives, all in silks and satins, and furs and flashing jewels. They felt that they would be out of place and uncomfortable—yet Myles Phillipson had asked them, and they did not feel that they should refuse and thus seem to turn aside from the hand of friendship he had offered.

So when Christmas Day came around, Kraster Cook and his wife mingled with the Phillipsons' other guests, looking in their homespun clothes like a pair of timid country mice. Their host and hostess tried to put them at their ease, but when they sat down at the long table for dinner they were bewildered and silent, and during the greater part of the meal they sat stiff and uncomfortable, hardly venturing to glance away from their plates.

Opposite Kraster Cook was a small bowl of pure gold and its glitter attracted his attention; he seemed to find relief from his embarrassment in staring steadily at it. There came a lull in the conversation around the table which was broken by the clear voice of Phillipson's wife saying:

'I see that you greatly admire that bowl, neighbour Cook. Well, it is worth any man's admiration.'

Naturally this attracted the attention of all at the table both to the farmer and the bowl. Cook reddened under the scrutiny and stammered some reply. Other guests commented upon the treasure and the incident ended. Ended for the time—but the fact that Cook had paid unusual attention to the article was fixed in the mind of those present. With dinner over, the farmer and his wife waited about for as long as they

13

thought was etiquette, then, thanking their host and hostess, they hastened home.

The next day soldiers came to the home of the Cooks. They carried man and wife away to the jail, and there they separated the couple, thrust them into cells, and refused to tell either the reason for their arrest.

A week later the Cooks were taken out of their cells and brought up for trial. It was only when they were in the dock that they found that they were accused of stealing a gold bowl, the property of Mistress Phillipson, their neighbour.

Mistress Phillipson stepped daintily into the witness box and sat and told her story. It was to the effect that the bowl in question had been on her table during the Christmas feast. It had been close to the prisoner, she said, and she was so struck by the manner in which he had insistently gazed upon it that she had spoken to him about it. She narrated the conversation that had taken place, which was confirmed by the testimony of several of those who had been her guests. Two servants then came forward and swore to having seen both the prisoners in the great banquet hall while the other guests were dancing. Finally the bowl itself was produced and two soldiers swore that on searching the cottage of the Cooks they had found it hidden away in one of the bedrooms.

In the face of all this, the amazed and frightened denials of the farmer and his wife were useless. They could do little but shake their heads feebly and stammer incoherently when the judge asked them if they had anything to say.

So, according to the cruel laws of the time, sentence of death by hanging was passed upon them. It was not until the sentence had been delivered that Dorothy Cook found her tongue. Leaning forward with wild, dark eyes, and in a voice that rang through the room, she pointed at Myles Phillipson and his wife and said:

'As there is a just God, you and your wife, Myles Phillipson, have damned yourself forever for our land! Neither you nor your breed will ever prosper. Whatever cause that you support shall lose. Your friendship shall be fatal, and all those that you and your breed shall love will die in pain and sorrow. You shall have no happiness in old house or new, for my husband and I will be with you night and day. You and all your breed and all your household shall be tormented by us. Never, as long as life lasts, shall you be rid of us!'

The soldiers silenced her and dragged her back to prison. A few days later she and her husband were hanged by the neck until dead.

While the bodies of the two were still swinging in chains at the crossroads, the Phillipsons seized the old farmstead, had the house pulled down and began the building of Calgarth Hall in its place. By the time next Christmas rolled around it was built and they were in it.

Again the gentry and their wives came in their silks and satins, furs and jewels. Merriment ran high, the Cooks and Mistress Dorothy's curse forgotten.

In the midst of the dinner Mistress Phillipson slipped away from the table to go to her room to bring back a jewel she wished to show. There was no gas in those days and the great hall was dimly lighted by sconced candles. The wide stairs were filled with shadows, but Mistress Phillipson, candle in hand, paid no heed to them. She turned a curve. Ice seemed suddenly to run through her veins. She stood frozen with terror.

For there, perched upon the balustrade, so close to her that she could have reached out her hand and touched them, were two grinning skulls. One was a woman's—long, dark hair hung from it. The other was as clearly that of a man. And in the flickering light of the candles the two skulls grinned and seemed about to open their ghastly mouths to speak to her.

Mistress Phillipson shrieked and fled to the dining room where, white and trembling, she poured forth her story to her husband and guests. The whole party, armed with rapiers and candles, followed up the stairs.

The skulls had not vanished. They were just as she had described them—only now instead of being perched on the balustrade they were resting on the top step of the bend.

15

The boldest of the party approached the objects and thrust at them with his sword. They were no phantoms—they were very real skulls indeed, and the blade clanged against their bones.

'It's a trick—a jest by some scurvy knave!' someone exclaimed. Suspicion fell upon a certain page, and he was taken and tied to a pillar in one of the cellars, and left there in the darkness to force confession. The skulls were ignominiously hurled into the courtyard. In due course the whole household retired.

But it was not the trembling page, imprisoned below, who was guilty—the Phillipsons soon had evidence of that.

It was about two o'clock in the morning that the household was brought out of bed by a succession of high-pitched, agonized screams. Instantly all was confusion at Calgarth Hall. Doors opened, and women with frightened faces peered out and half-dressed men came pouring into the halls. They followed the screaming. It led them to the staircase and there, to their unbounded astonishment and terror, perched again the two grinning skulls.

An instant before the searchers had turned the corner and laid eyes upon the grim objects, the screaming had abruptly ceased. But not one among those who stood there had any doubt that the sounds had emanated from or been caused by the skulls.

There was little sleeping done the rest of the night. The things remained where they were. But in the morning Myles Phillipson himself took them out and threw them into the pond.

Now the curse of Mistress Dorothy Cook was remembered, indeed. Silently the guests left Calgarth Hall, and all that day when Myles Phillipson and his wife looked at each other it was with white faces.

That night they heard from behind tightly-barred doors the weird screams once more echo throughout the manor. And next morning there again were the two skulls perched upon the staircase.

Now began for the guilty pair an intolerable existence. No servants would stay overnight and, indeed, few servants would stay at all. Guests became fewer and fewer, and only the oldest, most courageous friends dared to visit the Phillipsons or to invite them to their own houses, for everyone recalled that part of the curse promising friends sorrow and misfortune. Yet the Phillipsons had courage, too, for they would not abandon the house. They stayed there, defying their implacable visitants.

It was the reality of the skulls that added the most complete touch of horror to the manifestations. If they had been ghostly, mere wraiths, it would not have been so bad. But they were sinisterly real, and back in the mind of each of the Phillipsons was the thought that some night they would awaken to find the grinning teeth at their throats.

In the meantime misfortune followed close behind Myles Phillipson. His business dwindled; every venture into which he went met with loss. At last, shunned by practically all, the two died, leaving little except Calgarth to their son.

When the new heir took over the house the skulls screamed menacingly all that night. But it would seem that with the deaths of the man and woman who had sent the Cooks to the gallows their fury was lessened. At any rate, from the reports that exist, it is indicated that their manifestations took place only on Christmas Day, the anniversary of the fatal dinner, and also upon the anniversary of the day the Cooks were executed.

Apparently, however, there were two other restrictions which they imposed. Any attempt to remove them from the house was sure to be followed by a long period of unrest when the screams rang out night after night. Nor could young Phillipson give any dinners at the nearby Manor House. There is record that he tried this once—but only once.

His guests, so the story runs, were at the table when the screams rang out close to the great doors; then the doors swung open and the skulls rolled in and leaped upon the cloth. The whole company sprang to their feet and fled out into the night.

17

Sorrow was the constant lot of the heir. When he died he was poorer than his father had been when he passed away. And so it went through the succeeding generations until the Calgarth estate passed out of the hands of the family altogether, and the last Phillipson of the line died literally by the wayside, an outcast and a beggar.

Thus the curse was fulfilled in its entirety.

THE FIFTH STAIR

ONE morning early in the 1900s Guy Vance, a free-lance journalist, enquired at the office of Baine, Pell & Co., Kensington, if they knew of any small house in the S.W. district of London that was to be let unfurnished at a moderate rental.

'There is one in Ricket Road,' Mr. Pell told him. 'It is a two-storey house, and the rent is only fifty pounds a year.'

'That is certainly moderate,' Vance said. 'Why is the rent so low? Is anything wrong with it—drainage, dampness, cracks in the walls due to settlement?'

Mr. Pell shook his head. 'No, sir, there's nothing wrong with it. The last tenants remained in it for the full term of their seven years' lease.'

'When can I view it?' Vance asked.

'Any time you like,' Mr. Pell replied.

Accompanied by one of the estate agent's clerks, Vance went to number thirteen Ricket Road, Kensington, the next day and liked the house so much that he took it for three years, with the option of remaining in it for another three years at the same rental.

He engaged Mrs. Camp, a middle-aged woman, as his housekeeper, and Emma Larkin, a younger woman, as a general servant. They slept in the house. Jane Bolt, a girl of about twenty years of age, was a daily. The household was completed by Pop, a bull-terrier, and Eve, a grey cat.

It was not until Vance had been in the house several weeks that things began to happen. He was in his sitting-room writing one evening when Pop growled and ran to the door, his hair bristling. Puzzled at the dog's odd behaviour Vance opened the door, and saw a strange woman in black emerge from a cupboard under the stairs, cross the little hall and enter the kitchen. He could only get a side view of the woman, and what he saw of her face startled him, it was so white.

Wondering who she was he went to the kitchen. Only Mrs. Camp was there. She was getting his supper, as it was Emma Larkin's night out. Mrs. Camp stared in astonishment when Vance asked where the strange woman had gone.

'What strange woman?' she queried.

'Why, the one who entered the kitchen just now,' Vance replied.

'You must be dreaming, Mr. Vance,' Mrs. Camp said. 'No one has been here.'

It was Vance's turn to stare at her. 'I most distinctly saw a woman in black with a very white face come out of the staircase cupboard and come in here,' he said.

He told Mrs. Camp about Pop. They were both mystified. But that was only the beginning of the disturbing happenings.

The following day Mrs. Camp, going upstairs, had reached the fifth stair, which was directly above the cupboard, when she was suddenly overcome with the utmost horror. She felt there was something very dreadful underneath her. She was a strong-minded, practical woman, very sceptical regarding the supernatural, but it was only with the greatest effort that she pulled herself together and went on upstairs. She did not say anything about it to Vance, and tried to persuade herself that her spell of horror had been due to imagination.

Pop showed a strong aversion to going up the staircase, and it was noticed that Eve confined herself apparently to the ground floor.

Some days passed, then one morning Emma Larkin ran screaming into the kitchen, sank into a chair and had hysterics. When she had recovered sufficiently she said that when she was going up the staircase to make the beds, something heavy whizzed through the air past her and fell with a thud in the hall. She did not see anything but she felt most acutely that it was very ghastly and horrible.

Mrs. Camp did her best to calm and assure her that it was just her fancy, but Emma declared she could not stay in the house an hour longer, and left.

That evening about nine o'clock Vance was in the sitting-room reading by the fire. Mrs. Camp was out, and he was alone in the house. Everywhere was still except for the ticking of the clock in the hall and the pattering of heavy raindrops on the window-panes.

Suddenly the hush was broken by a scream, so piercing and full of terror that Vance was appalled. It was followed by a heavy thud. Vance nerved himself to open the door, but nothing was to be seen, nothing to account for the sounds. He shut the door and returned to his seat by the fire, and was glad when Mrs. Camp returned.

He decided that the house was badly haunted, especially the staircase. He had already made a note of the ghostly happenings and now added to this list the cry that he had just heard.

The next day a new general servant, Mary Pring, took the place of Emma Larkin, and for a time all was quiet. Then, one day about a week after Emma had left, Jane Bolt came to Mrs. Camp and said: 'One of the rods on the staircase is out, and every time I try to put it back my fingers go numb—I can't manage it.'

Mrs. Camp went to the staircase. As her instinct had led her to expect, the stubborn rod was on the fifth stair, the very stair on which she had experienced the sudden wave of horror. She tried to put it back but her fingers, too, became numb. Just then Vance, who heard her talking to Jane Bolt, opened the drawing-room door and asked if there was anything the matter. The moment he spoke Mrs. Camp's fingers ceased being numb, and she replaced the rod in its socket without any difficulty.

Again there was a lull of several days, and Vance and Mrs. Camp were hoping that there would be no more disturbing happenings when Mary Pring, looking very pale and scared, came to Mrs. Camp one morning and asked the name of the strange lady in black.

'What strange lady?' Mrs. Camp enquired, not knowing what else to say.

'Why, when I was about to go up the staircase just now,' Mary said, 'I got a bad start. I suddenly saw a rather tall woman with a very white face and forbidding expression coming down it. She was in a black dress. She passed by me, and when I looked to see where she went, she had vanished. I don't want to see her again.'

Mrs. Camp guessed that the woman who had startled Mary was the mysterious person in black that Vance declared he had seen cross the hall one evening and enter the kitchen. The housekeeper was not at all curious to see that woman.

But she did. One evening about a fortnight after Mary Pring's experience, Vance was talking to Mrs. Camp and Mary in the sitting-room, the door of which was wide open, when he heard someone coming down the staircase. As there was no one in the house except the three of them—the daily had left—they stared at one another, wondering who it could be. They then looked and saw crossing the hall the woman in black.

She was clutching by its long grey hair with one hand a human head that appeared to have been just decapitated. Dangling from its ears were gleaming gold drop-earrings. A weird light surrounded the woman and the head. The woman went to the cupboard under the stairs, turned slowly round, revealing a face that was the incarnation of everything bad, stepped into the cupboard and abruptly vanished.

The shock of what they had witnessed had been so great that it took Vance and the two women some moments before they could even partially recover. Mrs. Camp was the first to compose herself. Both she and Mary declared their inability to remain in the house any longer, and left the next day. Vance, not caring to stay in the house alone lest he should see the woman with the head again, or something even worse, put up at an hotel until he could find another house.

Before he left the neighbourhood he made many enquiries, and eventually learned that about sixty years before he went to number thirteen Ricket Road a dreadful murder had been committed there. A woman named Kate Murphy had murdered her mistress, Miss Delia Brown, an elderly spinster, in a manner too awful to describe, and after dismembering her body on the flat roof of the house had distributed her remains in various parts of the district. Miss Brown's head was the only part of her body that was never found.

The owner of thirteen Ricket Road, after listening to Vance's account of the ghostly occurrences that he had experienced there, had the floor of the staircase cupboard excavated. Under it was a skull with long, matted grey hair. The doctor who examined it was of the opinion that it had been there for many years; so that although there was no actual clue regarding its identity, it seemed not unlikely that it was the missing head of poor murdered Miss Delia Brown.

THE FATAL PHANTOM OF ERINGLE TRUAGH

ONE of the most interesting cases of hauntings in the annals of ghost-lore is that of the old churchyard of Eringle Truagh, in County Monaghan, Ireland. According to a traditional story many centuries old the churchyard was haunted during the whole time people were buried there by a spirit fatally attractive to young men and girls. It only appeared in the churchyard after the funeral of a native of Eringle Truagh.

To girls it assumed the form of a very handsome young man, and to young men that of a very beautiful golden-haired maiden comparable with the Elle Maids of Scandinavia and the Lorelei of the Rhine. The manner in which the phantom contacted its victims was this:

A young man who had been present at the burial of someone very dear to him, in spite of the priest's warning lingered in the churchyard alone after everyone else had left. He was bewailing the death of the dear one when he suddenly saw approaching him a provocatively lovely girl. Her face full of sympathy, she bade him mourn no more for the loved one he had lost and assured him that she was far happier now than she would have been had she lived. Comforted by the girl's words the youth entered into conversation with her. They sat close beside one another on the low wall of the churchyard and the young man became more and more enthralled by her wondrous beauty. Never in his life had he beheld either in actuality, or in dreams, anyone so beautiful. So enchanted was he that he never thought of questioning her identity or whence she came.

He made desperate love to her. She reciprocated his sentiment, and bade him promise to meet her in the churchyard four weeks from that day and seal his promise with a kiss.

This he did. Directly their lips met in a kiss she vanished; and then, and not till then, did he recollect the traditional

24

story of the haunting of the churchyard and realize that she whom he had embraced so fervently was the much dreaded phantom.

Overcome with horror he rushed home and implored his relatives and the parish priest to save him. But prayers proved to be of no avail. The shock he had sustained resulted in a fatal illness, and in exactly four weeks he was, on the very date he had pledged to meet the phantom, brought to the churchyard in his coffin.

The phantom did not invariably appear in the churchyard, there are instances of it being present at dances and weddings, where it never failed to secure a victim. The fatal kiss and promise were always given, and the final meeting with the phantom was always in the churchyard on the pledged day.

William Carleton, the Irish novelist (1798 to 1869), was so intrigued by the traditional haunting of the old churchyard that he visited the place. Writing about it afterwards he said: 'I have been shown the grave of a young person about eighteen years of age, who was said about four months before to have fallen a victim to the phantom, and it is not more than ten weeks since a man in the same parish declared that he gave a promise and fatal kiss to the ghost and consequently looked upon himself as lost. He took a fever and was buried on the day appointed for the meeting, which was exactly a month from the time of his contact with the spirit.

'Incredulous as it may seem the friends of these two persons declared, at least those of the young man did, to myself that particulars of the meetings with the phantom were detailed repeatedly by the two persons without the slightest variation. There are several other cases of the same kind mentioned, but the two alluded to are the only ones that came within my personal knowledge.'

I was so interested in the haunting that in 1926 I wrote to the postmaster of Monaghan about it and asked if he could tell me where I could get photographs of the old churchyard. In his reply he mentioned Carleton's ballad and said the church of Eringle Truagh had been dismantled many years previously and only two ivy-covered gables remained of it. But, he said, belief in the story of the Phantom of Death still lingered.

I later obtained several photographs of the old churchyard in which are to be seen the graves of the alleged victims of the much dreaded phantom.

THE GREY HORROR

IN the summer of 1894, when on my way out West in the U.S.A., I stayed for a week at an hotel in Denver. There I met William Smith, an elderly minister who was well versed in the traditional ghost stories and legends of some of the American States. One evening when we were alone he told me about the dreadful grey ghost that had formerly haunted Grenburg Valley, on the eastern shore of the River Hudson. This is his story.

One afternoon in the seventies of the last century two young men, Herbert Hall and Walter Wren, arrived at a little village near the eastern shore of the Hudson, the inhabitants of which were mostly of Dutch extraction. After they had had a meal at the village inn they asked the landlord to tell them the way to Grenburg, a small port on the Hudson where they intended to stay the night.

'There are two ways,' the landlord said, 'the one a good deal longer than the other but preferable when it is getting dusk.'

'What difference does that make?' Wren asked. 'Is the road very rough?'

'It is very rutty and rocky in places,' the landlord said, 'but that is not what I had in mind.'

'What did you have in mind?' Hall queried, eyeing him keenly.

The landlord hesitated. 'There is a valley a mile from Grenburg which has a bad reputation.'

'Robbers?'

The landlord shook his head.

'What then?' Wren asked impatiently.

'Well,' the landlord said, 'the folk around here say it is haunted.'

The young men burst out laughing.

'You don't mean to say you believe in ghosts!' Hall said.

'I have long wanted to see a ghost. What is the story associated with the valley? I'll be bound there is one—a murder?'

The landlord shrugged. 'There are all sorts of stories but you would only ridicule them.' He proceeded to give them directions as to both ways of getting to Grenburg.

Thanking him and declaring their intention of bearding the lion, or rather ghost, in its den, they selected the road through the valley, and with their knapsacks once again strapped to their backs they set off at a brisk pace.

At last the travellers reached the summit of a hill and, deep down beneath them, they saw, spread out for some considerable distance, a thickly wooded valley, all dark and mysterious in the uncertain twilight. As they descended into it they became aware of the funereal-like silence that greeted them on all sides.

The dale was in fact so deeply situated that even the wind, which for the last half hour or so had been blowing with great force along the surface of the hill, was scarcely to be felt there. Occasionally a fitful blast could be heard among the lofty trees, when the pale Fall leaves gave out a curious husky crackling. Otherwise all was absolutely, wonderfully still.

The two men were so impressed that neither spoke until they had arrived at the bottom of the decline, and were standing in almost Stygian darkness amidst the shadows of the foliage on either side of them. Hall was the first to break the silence.

'This must be the haunted glen,' he said. 'Pretty cheerful, isn't it?'

'It is that,' Wren replied, looking around him trying to pierce the gloom, 'but come on. I vote we get out of it as soon as possible.'

Further on they came to a wide open spot where there were crossroads. Here the shadows lay very thick—so thick, indeed, that they had to curb their pace and proceed very slowly lest they should take the wrong route.

It was while they were thus engaged, straining their eyes and peeping around them apprehensively, that they became impressed with the certainty of some object moving slowly

28

ahead of them through the gloom. At such an hour, for it was now getting late, and in such a dreary place, this was calculated to challenge attention, and Wren and Hall found themselves gazing at the object with an intensity that had in it something not very far removed from fear. By and by they were able to see it a little more clearly, and they perceived it was a very tall figure, apparently a man walking at an even pace, but with immensely long strides.

He was going in the same direction as they were and was only a few feet in front of them, but to their astonishment they found that although they accelerated their pace with the idea of overtaking him, they did not approach the least degree nearer; without seeming to increase his speed, he yet maintained invariably the same distance away from them.

They had now struck off along a road they believed to be the right one and were walking tolerably fast. The figure preceding them, however, was seemingly in no way aware of their proximity, for without once turning its head towards them, with the same measured stride, it steadily advanced. At length Hall, more perhaps to relieve his feelings than anything else, called out:

'Hullo there! Who are you?'

There was no response. The figure did not show by any gesture the slightest consciousness that it had heard, but continued pacing on at the same rate and at the same distance. The two friends now suddenly realized that their sense of hearing, which the strangely emphasized silence of the place had rendered abnormally acute, had not caught any sound of footsteps coming from the figure. They could readily decipher the echoes of their own, but the figure seemingly trod with absolute noiselessness.

This came as an unpleasant surprise, and soon they became poignantly aware of the advent of novel and distinctly uncomfortable feelings. Pride prevented them admitting this and they were striving to rally their faculties and, at all events, to simulate unconcern, when the unexpected happened. The figure abruptly swerved off the road and, making for a large wooden gate leading on to a gravel drive, came directly into the moonlight.

Both Wren and Hall at once emitted an involuntary cry. Instead of being clothed, the figure was nude! It gleamed a horrible, sinister grey. It had very long arms and legs and a peculiarly small and rotund head, and when it suddenly turned and looked at the two travellers it revealed a strange and startling countenance.

The features were more or less human, but the expression in the big, deep sunken, light-green eyes was not. So frightful was it, so indescribably exultant and devilish, that Wren and Hall shrank back appalled, too petrified with fear to utter a sound.

Fortunately, however, the figure showed no inclination to dally. Moving onward, still with the same peculiar lengthy and measured stride, it advanced up the drive, eventually disappearing from view round a rather abrupt curve. A few seconds later there was a faint sound in the direction it had taken, resembling a human cry, and a moment or so later, still from the same direction, there was a repetition of the noise, but much more prolonged and bearing with it a tone of suffering quite beyond the ability of words to describe.

There was another pause, and then, apparently nearer, a yell of the most piercing intensity, the animal element in it seeming to strive for mastery with the human; and its final echoes had scarcely died away before the whole valley became alive with appalling sounds, with moanings, plaintive and yet horribly menacing, and with whoopings, interspersed with harsh, discordant cries and queer, hollow-sounding, long-reverberating laughter.

This went on for about a minute. It then quite suddenly ceased and was followed by a silence unbroken save for the gentle rustling of the fast-dying foliage and the melancholy sighing and soughing of the night breeze.

Wren and Hall waited for a few minutes, until they could sufficiently pull themselves together, and then continued their tramp, eventually reaching their destination without further mishap.

(William Smith stopped here and said that was enough for one night. The following night he went on with his story).

An Irishman named Patrick O'Rourke, hearing about the ghostly experience of Hall and Wren, went to the village inn where the two men had stopped on their way to Grenburg and prevailed upon the landlord to tell him anything he knew about the grey ghost and haunted valley. And this was what the landlord said:

'Four years ago last April I was going through the valley in the early hours of the morning. The dawn had only just broken and the track in places was still dark. Well, when I was pretty nearly opposite the large wooden gate leading into the White Grange, as we call it, my horse (I was riding a brown cob that I had not had in my possession very long) suddenly shied, and I saw sitting by the wayside, up against the trunk of an elm, a tall figure. In the uncertain light I thought it was a man, some tramp who was either having a nap or was ill. I called out to him and, as he did not reply, I called again and was considering dismounting to see what was the matter with him, when he suddenly and with amazing agility sprang to his feet. I then got a fearful shock.

'It was no man at all, but a grim and ghastly caricature of one!

'It was gigantic, ten or twelve feet in height it seemed. It was nude, its skin being seemingly a glistening, uniform grey, and its face like that of a death's head; a death's head, however, with something frightfully lurid and evil in its big, round eye-sockets. I had not time to observe more because my horse bolted, but when I eventually reined it in and looked around I saw the thing, whatever it was, cross the road with enormous bounds and disappear through the gateway leading to the White Grange.'

Here the old man paused for a moment, then, clearing his throat, he went on again:

31

'There were two travellers that the great grey ghost actually touched—or at least, one of them. They were walking through the woods when they heard footsteps behind them. They turned and saw following them a great grey shape, whose unearthly long arms trailed along the ground. It was of unearthly height, too. Its head seemed to tower up into the trees, and that head was a grinning skull.

'The men began to run, but the thing covered at one stride ten times the ground they could. Closer and closer it came—the gigantic grey shape that pursued the fleeing travellers. And suddenly a soft, incredibly repugnant something like a cloudy hand half turned to flesh covered like a mask the face of one of them.

'He shrieked once and fell. The other, crying with horror, ran on. The thing did not pursue him. Next morning a searching party from the village sought the other traveller. They found him wandering in the woods half insane. He never quite recovered his mind.'

Here the old man paused again.

'And there is no accounting for the haunting?' O'Rourke asked.

'There are theories,' the old man said.

O'Rourke then enquired of him the name of the present owner of the White Grange, and having obtained it he went on his way. A week later and he was back again in the same neighbourhood. In the interval he had written to the owner of the property and, somewhat to the owner's astonishment, had obtained leave to stay a night there.

The night chosen for the expedition proved to be exceptionally wild and stormy. O'Rourke had invited three friends of his living in the county to go with him to the Grange. He had chosen them because they were very stolid, matter-of-fact athletes, not in the least degree likely to give way to nerves.

Having first assured themselves no one was hiding anywhere in the house, they looked for a spot to commence their vigil and finally selected the room O'Rourke believed, from the description given to him, was the haunted chamber. It was

32

situated at one end of the corridor and possessed two doors, the one leading into the corridor and the other into what in earlier days was styled a powder closet. It was an oddly constructed apartment, for across the middle of it were two pillars, and on the wall between them hung a grotesque looking piece of tapestry.

The four friends sat on the floor in a row right across the room, O'Rourke facing the corridor, Moor and Ross facing the tapestry, and Ventry facing the entrance to the powder closet. At first, every now and then, they fancied they heard soft footsteps tip-toeing up and down the corridor—once they seemed actually to be in the room—but after a time these sounds all died away and there was nothing but silence, unbroken save for the occasional rattling of doors and windows and the beating of rain against the panes of glass.

One by one the quartet fell asleep to be awakened by hearing the church clock sonorously boom out three. Moor at once rose to his feet.

'Look here,' he said, 'it's morning. Nothing will happen now and I have to be at—' Then he suddenly changed his tone and with a wild cry of 'Oh, my God, there it is!' he staggered back against the wall.

The other three looked and in the dim light of dawn that struggled to get in through the crevices of the shutters, they saw, standing erect between the pillars, a luminous something. Nothing more at first. By and by, however, while all were gazing at it in open-mouthed wonder and excitement, it suddenly became hideously and alarmingly vivid, and they saw an immense form, streaked, so it seemed to them, a lurid black and grey.

Moor and Ross glanced at its face, and they said afterwards it was like the face of a corpse, only a corpse that was nearly in the skeleton stage, the skin being drawn tightly over the bones, and the mouth devoid of flesh and grinning. The impression it gave them was that it was intensely hostile. O'Rourke and Ventry contented themselves with peering at the body only, they did not dare raise their eyes to the head.

33

They stared at it for some moments, until in fact it began to approach them, when Moor gave way to panic and shrieked out: 'Strike a light, one of you!'

O'Rourke then lit a candle, and the thing at once vanished. The four men did not stay to talk the matter over. They made for the corridor immediately and hurriedly left the house.

A week or so later came a kind of sequel. O'Rourke was again in the neighbourhood. Indeed, the spot so fascinated him that he paid a flying visit to it. When he was in the valley looking around him, a stranger suddenly came in sight and accosted him. He said that on the very night O'Rourke and his friends were in the big house looking for the ghost he had seen it.

'It crossed from there,' he said, pointing to a tall isolated tree on one side of the road, close to a pit with a wide, dark, gaping mouth. 'Watch that pit closely tomorrow night between twelve and three o'clock. It is the pit that causes the White Grange and the valley to be haunted. It goes right down into the bowels of the earth. There are holes like it in Peru and Brazil. They attract and harbour a foul and dangerous species of elemental spirits.'

Precisely at the time he mentioned O'Rourke went to the haunted valley. The night was fine, but dark scurrying clouds suggested the possibility of rain. The pit made his flesh creep. There was something so eerie and menacing about it.

He approached it cautiously and was gazing at it apprehensively when he got a terrific start. Rising out of its reputed fathomless depths was a luminous ghastly grey head. The only live thing about it was a lurid, baleful light in the depths of its fleshless eye-sockets. It was the same horrible phantom that O'Rourke and his friends had seen in the White Grange.

O'Rourke stared at it aghast, and when grisly shoulders gradually appeared he did not wait to see any more, but took to his heels.

He was quite satisfied that what the stranger had told him about the pit was true. He never went to the valley again.

34

Some years later the supposed fathomless pit was filled in, and when that was done Grenburg Valley ceased to be haunted.

Thus ended the strange story that William Smith so kindly told me in Denver City more than seventy years ago.

THE GHOST OF FRED ARCHER

In the early summer of 1927 a considerable sensation was caused in Newmarket by a report of the appearance of a ghost in the Hamilton Stud Lane. Two local people, a mother and daughter, declared that they saw a phantom horseman emerge from a copse, gallop noiselessly towards them and when near, mysteriously vanish.

The older woman had a vivid recollection of Fred Archer at the time he was a familiar personality in Newmarket, and she was certain the apparition she had seen was he. The horse of the phantom rider was grey, and that had been the colour of Archer's favourite steed. There had long been a rumour in Newmarket that the Stud Lane was from time to time haunted by Archer's ghost.

Fred Archer, the second son of William Archer, a well-known jockey, was born at Cheltenham in 1857. Between 1870 and 1884 he won more than 2,000 races and achieved world-wide fame. His was a household name. Archer suffered a terrible blow by the death of his wife, to whom he was devoted, in 1884, within a year of their marriage. For a time he abandoned riding. The attraction that it had for him proving too great he again appeared on the racecourse and was as successful as ever.

In 1886, worried about his increase in weight, he tried to reduce by taking less food. He would sometimes hardly eat anything for three or four days, his only diet being a few water biscuits and a small glass of champagne. Never very robust, this treatment told on him, and when he had an attack of typhoid fever he had little strength to cope with it. During the absence of his nurse from the sick room one day he shot himself. He was only twenty-nine years old.

Archer was buried in the cemetery at Newmarket in the same grave as his beloved wife.

36

On June 3rd, 1927, at the request of the northern newspaper for which I was working at the time, I went to Newmarket with the express purpose of spending a night in the Hamilton Stud Lane on the chance of seeing the alleged ghost. I visited Archer's grave and made numerous enquiries relative to the haunting. On the heath I entered into conversation with an old man seated on the ground beside a wheelbarrow.

'Have I ever seen or heard anything about Archer's ghost?' he said in answer to my interrogation. 'Well, yes, I have often seen what I thought might be his ghost when I was a youngster. On one such occasion I had been to Six Miles Bottom, and was returning home along the road leading past the Green Man and what is known about here as The Two Captains. It was between one and two o'clock in the morning, the moon was high overhead, no one was about, and all was so still that you could catch the slightest sound.

'Well, I had just passed the junction of the London and Cambridge roads, and had almost got to the cleft in the Devil's Ditch, through which the main road runs, when all of a sudden I saw on the white roadway alongside me what resembled the black shadow of a horse and rider. Wondering where the material counterpart of the shadow could be, I at once looked around but there was nothing to be seen, only bare space on either side of me, nothing, I thought, that could in any way account for the shadow. Yet it was still there, and it continued to move along by my side for some little way, when it suddenly vanished.

'The rider, judging by the shadow, seemed to be of a fair height and to be wearing a kind of hat, which might have been what we used to call a deer-stalker or it might have been a jockey's cap; at any rate it seemed to have a sort of peak. My impression was that it was Fred Archer's ghost, which I had been told was sometimes to be seen on the heath, but when I spoke about it to an old friend of my father, a man who had lived in these parts close on eighty years, he said that it was far more likely it was the ghost of one of the highwaymen that used to rob and murder people on the heath.

'I still believed, however, that what I had seen was the ghost of poor Archer. But there, it might have been just my fancy.'

I made my way back to town, and later returned with the intention of spending some time in Hamilton Stud Lane. Passing once again by the cemetery I turned down a seemingly interminable straight road, flanked on either side by neatly trimmed hedgerows, having in their background fields and, here and there, solitary trees. On at last reaching the end of this stretch I came to a slight dip with a building on either side of it, and just beyond, three buildings and gates, also on either side of the road a collection of trees forming a kind of miniature spinney.

Feeling somewhat tired after what was to me an unusual amount of walking I looked around for somewhere to rest, and at last spotted a suitable spot up against the hedgerows and under the shadow of the trees. Making for myself as comfortable a seat as the nature of the ground allowed I sat down and began reading a little book on Cambridgeshire that I had bought in the Charing Cross Road the previous day.

The waning daylight, however, soon put a stop to my reading. I dozed, and awaking with a start got up and was stretching myself when I suddenly became conscious of a sensation of eeriness. A moment or two later I sensed something large flash past me. The spot became so uncanny that I left it.

I was trudging along the road with no particular goal in view when I encountered a cyclist, and asked him if he could tell me whereabouts in the lane it was that Archer's ghost was alleged to have been seen.

'Why, yes,' he said, with a smile, 'in this lane.' And he thereupon described to me the spot where I had had the eerie sensation.

Without realizing it, I had been in the haunted Hamilton Stud Lane. I returned to the spot, and after being there for some time I again experienced the odd sensation and heard sounds like those made by a horse rapidly approach me. I saw nothing. When the sounds were close to me they stopped abruptly, receded and gradually died away in the distance.

Nothing further happened. Whether what I experienced was due to poor Fred Archer's ghost I cannot definitely say. As to why his spirit should have haunted the lane and neighbourhood, that must be left entirely to speculation. None of us is sufficiently acquainted with the laws and ways of the unknown to decree. We can only surmise.

THE HAUNTING OF THE GORY HOTEL

I WAS having a discussion one day in my London club with Sir Roland Melville, Bart., about ghostly phenomena, and he told me the following experience which he had had some years previously.

He was travelling one day from Paddington to Penzance in an express. On the way the train was held up when the line was blocked through the collapse of a bridge, and he was obliged to seek a room for the night in Plymouth. After much hunting he at last found one in an hotel not far from the Hoe.

The room was a back one on the first floor. It smelt fusty. The bed was in the middle of the floor and on one side of it was a large cupboard. There was a gas fire in the room and Sir Roland sat by it to warm himself, for it was a very cold night. Tired with his journey and made drowsy by the heat of the fire he went to bed and dozed fitfully, being awakened by a laugh, loud and mocking. He sat up indignantly and saw an eerie spherical light on the door of the cupboard.

As he stared wonderingly at the door it began to open very slowly. Little by little the aperture increased and an object appeared. It was a luminous head, the head of a negro. The mouth was bared in a ferocious grin, and the dark glittering eyes suffused with diabolical hatred.

The aperture kept widening until a whole body appeared. In one hand it held a carving knife. Stealing stealthily out of the cupboard the negro, crouching down, crept towards the bed. Petrified, Sir Roland watched him as he drew nearer and nearer. After what seemed to him years, the negro reached the bed and, bending over it, raised the knife. As it was about to descend the spell which had chained Sir Roland ended and, tumbling out of bed, he made for the door. He stayed on the landing till he could not stand the cold any longer.

Ashamed of his fear he then went back into the room. It was in darkness. There was no sign of the phantom negro. He slept till morning.

The line not being quite cleared Sir Roland had to spend another night in the hotel. As on the previous night he sat for a time by the fire in his room, and then got into bed. He fell asleep, and woke with a start to feel a cold, clammy, bare body lying by his side.

He sat up and made to spring out of bed but found he could not. He was again limb and tongue tied, and again an eerie light appeared on the cupboard. As before the phantom negro emerged from the cupboard and crept to the bed. His eyes, glowing with malicious joy, were fixed not on Sir Roland but on the man by his side, as he raised his gleaming knife. The chain which had held Sir Roland spellbound broke as before, and springing out of bed he got to the landing. This time he did not return to his bedroom but sat in the coffee room till morning.

He angrily related his experiences to the landlord of the hotel, who was full of apologies for putting him in the room, which he admitted was haunted. According to the tale he told Sir Roland, about a hundred years previously the hotel had been a private house owned by Mr. Jasper Stevens, a widower, who had made a fortune in the West Indies. His only companion in the house was his negro servant Tom, whom he had brought from Jamaica. Tempted by the money Mr. Stevens foolishly kept in the house, Tom murdered him, and disappeared. The police failed to trace him.

Sir Roland suggested that the cupboard out of which the negro ghost emerged should be examined. This was done. At the back of it was a spring which, being opened, revealed a secret chamber. Crouching on the floor of the chamber, a bloodstained knife by his side, and a heap of gold coins in front of him, was the skeleton. Apparently the negro, discovering the spring, had got into the cupboard but been unable to get out of it, so starving to death.

Hence the haunting by his ghost. Efforts to exorcise it proved futile, and the haunting continued until the hotel was demolished—a year after Sir Roland Melville stayed in it.

THE LONDON VILLA OF GHOSTLY DREAD

In a by-road not far from the old Crystal Palace there was standing prior to 1914 a small villa known locally as the Mystery House. It was often to be let, as no one ever stayed there for long.

After it had stood empty for a considerable time, a family named Trent took it. Mrs. Trent thought there was something strange about the house almost the moment that she crossed the threshold. However, nothing unpleasant happened till they had been in it a fortnight.

On entering her bedroom in haste one morning Mrs. Trent drew up sharply on seeing the bedstead shake and one of the pillows move. Wondering if some pet animal was in the bed she went to it and very cautiously raised the pillow. There was nothing under it. She removed the bedclothes, but there was nothing under them. She peered under the bed; there was nothing there.

Mystified but thinking it was probably just her imagination, or maybe some kind of an illusion or hallucination, she thought no more of it.

The following night Mr. Trent was awakened by a spine-chilling scream coming from his wife's room, which was next to his. In a terrible fright he jumped out of bed and dashed to her.

In the moonlight, which flooded the room, he saw his wife trying to push away a pillow which was over her face. Something seemed to be pressing it down. He seized the pillow and found himself struggling with an invisible thing that smelt horribly. The struggle seemed to him to last interminably but more likely it was only for a few seconds. To his relief, whatever it was desisted, and the pillow fell on to the floor.

His wife had been too exhausted to help him, and it was not until she had fully recovered that she was able to talk.

42

She said that all she knew was when she awoke from a nasty dream, the pillow had been removed from under her head and was over her face, and she felt that someone was trying to smother her.

Mr. Trent persuaded her to change rooms with him. She did, and nothing further took place for a week. Mr. Trent was then alone in the house, his wife, children and the maid having gone for the afternoon to Hampstead.

Fancying he heard a noise in the basement he went down to inspect the place but found nothing to account for it. Having satisfied himself that the doors and windows were all securely fastened he was mounting the kitchen staircase when he heard footsteps following him. He looked round but there was no one there.

Thinking it must have been his imagination he went on again, but he had not mounted more than a couple more steps when he again heard the footfalls behind him. He abruptly swung round, and for a moment the sight of his own shadow, which stood out very black on the cream coloured wall beneath him, made his heart beat with unusual fierceness, but there was still no one to be seen. He stamped his feet and mounted a couple more steps, but everything was quite still, and he had gained the hall and was halfway up the flight of stairs leading to the first landing when the same mysterious footfalls were again audible.

In spite of his scepticism for ghosts and the like he now felt a ghastly fear stealing fast upon him, and with these uncomfortable sensations he continued his ascent. There was no repetition of the steps now until he had arrived on the top landing, when they came running up behind him, very fast, as if someone was making frantic efforts to overtake him.

This time it was with an effort he turned round, but as on the former occasions, there was no one to be seen. The unaccountable nature of the occurrence filled him with vague and almost horrible sensations, and yielding to the excitement he felt gaining control over him he leaned over the banisters and shouted sternly, 'Who is there?'

The sound of his own voice, thus exerted in the utter solitude of the house, and followed by the most death-like silence, had in it something so unpleasantly thrilling that he now experienced a degree of nervousness which he had never felt before.

A week later and the place was once more to let. Then an ex-actress of the name of Cattling took it. She arrived with a whole retinue of dogs—poms and dachshunds. The first week of her tenancy passed uneventfully enough. The dogs were very restless at night, growling and whining and keeping very close to one another, but she attributed that to their being in new surroundings and never for one moment gave it serious heed.

Then one evening one of the poms suddenly cried out as if it had been hurt. She ran upstairs to her bedroom where she had left it, and found it lying on the floor. At first she thought it was asleep, but on examining it more closely she discovered it was dead.

She was puzzling this over when something attracted her attention to the bed, and to her surprise she saw one of the pillows was standing on end. She approached it, and then came to a sudden halt. The pillow had assumed the most extraordinary and wholly unaccountable shape. It was like a face, the face of some very bizarre animal with a monstrously long nose and two deep-set eyes that gleamed horribly, and with apparent devilish merriment.

It so fascinated her that for some minutes she simply stood staring at it, and then, yielding to a sudden paroxysm of fury, she rushed at it, and catching hold of it, straightened it out and flung it on the ground.

'You killed the dog,' she shrieked, 'and want to harm me. You won't! You won't!'

There now followed a fairly long spell of comparative quiet. Then one night the unexpected happened. Mrs. Cattling, as per habit, went for a walk accompanied by her pets, and did not return home till late. The house was in pitch darkness and she was in the hall, groping about for matches for the gas,

44

when a box was quietly slipped into her outstretched hand. As might be expected she was terribly taken back, and for some seconds she stood stock still, not knowing what to think or do.

If it was a burglar, she tried to argue, why had he not struck her? And yet, if it was not a burglar, who could it possibly be? The suspense at length became so unbearable that, resolving to learn the worst and see whatever it was face to face, she struck a light, and then very cautiously peered around.

There was no one, nothing to be seen. Mystified, she now went upstairs to bed, and having locked and barricaded the door after her, she speedily undressed and crept in between the sheets.

She slept till morning, and was in the act of dressing and laughing at her fears during the night, when close to her elbow she heard a long protracted sigh. She immediately turned round, but there was no one there, nothing to account for it.

A week or so after this she had some friends round to spend the evening with her. They played cards and were in the middle of an exciting hand of bridge when one of them, who was merely a spectator, uttered a loud exclamation and pointed to the wall.

'Look at that picture,' she said. 'What is making it behave like that?'

They all glanced in the direction she indicated and were greatly astonished at seeing an old coloured engraving in a frame swaying violently to and fro, without any apparent cause.

They all sat quite still and strained their ears, but there was absolute silence, not the remotest sound of any kind, either from within or without. One of them then went to the window which, though open at the top, was closed at the bottom, and peered out.

'The night seems very calm and still,' she said. 'It would take a good deal of wind to make that picture move.'

Then, suddenly it was still, and absolutely motionless, like all the other pictures in the room, and everyone present felt a curious sensation of relief. Nothing of further moment occurred during the rest of Mrs. Cattling's short tenancy, and after she had left the premises they stood empty for another long period.

It was during this interlude that an adventure in connection with the house is said to have befallen two people living in the neighbourhood. They were a young man and girl, sweethearts, who, strolling out together one evening, chanced to pass the 'mystery house'.

'Strange that house never lets, isn't it?' the young man remarked as they paused in front of it and gazed up at the windows. 'I wonder what's wrong with it.'

'Why, they do say as how it's haunted,' the girl replied, 'but ghosts is all nonsense, ain't they, Reg?'

'I reckon so,' Reg laughed. Then, fired with a sudden inspiration, 'I say, supposing we sit for a while in the back garden. It will be nice and quiet there.'

From the garden the couple commanded a complete view of the back of the house, and they were commenting on the appearance of it, how peculiarly neglected and deserted it looked, when they simultaneously gave vent to a deep 'Oh!' Exactly opposite them on the first floor was a window, and up to the present it had been bathed in gloom.

Now, however, quite suddenly it became illuminated with a dull, glimmering light of an unhealthy bluish colour which appeared to originate from within the building.

They fled precipitately and on future occasions took very good care to give the 'mystery house' a distinctly wide berth.

The next recorded happenings at the house occurred quite late in its life. A Mrs. Eveley took it for six months, and her household consisted of herself, grown-up daughter Barbara, and two servants, Matilda and Phyllis. The disturbances began the very first night of their tenancy. Going to bed somewhat early, as she was very tired, Barbara awoke with a violent start to see in the white moonlight a very tall form in black bending over her, and the next moment the bedclothes were snatched violently off her. The bed was then shaken vigorously to and fro.

This went on for some seconds when at last, to her infinite relief, the figure left the bedside, and she heard the door give a loud slam.

Barbara's terror was so great that for some minutes she dared not stir. As soon, however, as her faculties had somewhat recovered from the shock, she sprang out of bed and rushed into her mother's room. Mrs. Eveley was a very strong-minded woman, not in the least degree afraid of burglars, and rousing the servants she bade them search the house with her.

They did so, going into every room and examining the cellar and cupboards, but they found no one, and could discover nothing which would explain in any way the remarkable occurrence.

About a week later the whole household was aroused in the middle of the night by the sound of hammering, coming apparently from the basement of the house. As the servants refused point blank to accompany Mrs. Eveley downstairs to see what it was, she lit her candle and went alone.

When she arrived in the basement she found the kitchen door wide open, while on the table, in the centre of the floor, she saw what appeared to be an enormous black coffin. The shock at encountering such a ghastly spectacle was so terrific that she at once fainted.

Hearing her fall Barbara and the maids hastened to her assistance, and on reaching the basement all three saw the shadowy outlines of something they could only describe as infinitely alarming and grotesque come out of the kitchen, run past them and ascend the staircase with gigantic bounds. This came as the climax, and within a week the house once again stood empty.

The house had been standing empty for some long time when the landlord, happening to visit it one day, fancied he could detect a smell of gas. He sent for a plumber, and prior to the man's arrival waited in one of the rooms. After a while, hearing, as he thought, a noise on the top landing he ran upstairs to ascertain the cause of it, and not discovering anything to account for it came down again, and was surprised to find the plumber had arrived and was already engaged at his job.

'How on earth did you get in?' he said to the man. 'I made sure I had shut all the doors.' The man made no reply, however, and the landlord, concluding he must be deaf, watched him in silence for some minutes, and then hearing a knock at the front door went to see who was there.

Rather to his astonishment it was another plumber.

'Why, how is this?' he said. 'One of your men is already here. Surely there is no need for two.'

'It can't be one of our men, sir,' the plumber responded, 'for I am the only man available. He must have come from somewhere else.'

'You are from Smith's, are you not?' the landlord asked.

'Yes, sir,' was the reply.

'Well, the other man must have come from them too,' the landlord answered, 'for that is the only firm I sent to. You had better come inside and see.'

Bidding the man follow him he went to the room where he had left the workman, but there was no sign of him. Remarking that it was very odd he called out, but there was no response. He then searched the premises, but there were no traces of the workman anywhere. And when Smith's man examined the gas pipes he quickly found the leakage. There were no evidences whatever of any attempt having been made at a repair.

The landlord, of course, knew the reputation the 'mystery house' had acquired, and he could only conclude that what he had witnessed was another of its already long list of ghosts.

The original owner of the house, who had committed suicide, had been a man of very bad reputation, and it was thought that the hauntings might either be due to his earthbound evil spirit, or to something that occurred on the site of the house before it was built.

AN UNSOLVED MYSTERY

NOT far from St. Shepherd's Grove, Dublin, there is an isolated house dating back to the days of Dutch William. For years it stood empty, no one caring to stay in it for long, and Mrs. Valentine, the owner, was despairing of letting it when Colonel Ward took it furnished for a year.

His wife and children moved in shortly before Christmas, he being unable to join them as yet. The first few days passed uneventfully. It was not until Mrs. Ward had been there a week that anything disturbing happened.

She was in the sitting-room reading when there was a rap on the door; it sounded as if it was made with bare knuckles. Wondering who it could possibly be as the servants had gone out, Mrs. Ward went to the door. Confronting her was an old woman in a mob-cap and old-fashioned dress. She was very ugly. Raising a skinny hand she shook it menacingly at Mrs. Ward, leered, and turning sharply round she ran across the hall and up the stairs, remarkably nimble for one of her age.

Considerably startled Mrs. Ward tried to persuade herself that the old woman was a friend of the maids. She resumed her seat by the fire, and had barely sat down, when, much to her relief the maids returned.

The next day Colonel Ward came. That night he sat up late. It was close on one o'clock when, candle in hand—there was no gas in the house—he went into the hall. The fluctuating light from the candle was not enough to dissipate the gloom. Fancying he heard a noise he turned, and found himself face to face with the old hag his wife had seen. An odd light enveloped her and illumined her pale eyes, which glowed maliciously as they met the Colonel's startled gaze.

'Who are you?' he stammered.

She did not reply but, leering at him, she ran across the hall and ascended the staircase. When near a bend she paused and, looking down, shook her fist. Then, turning, she vanished quickly out of sight.

At breakfast that morning Colonel Ward said, 'My dear, I have seen your old woman. I do not wonder that you were scared. I was too. She is not pretty.'

In the afternoon Jack Deane, Mrs. Ward's brother, who had just left Sandhurst and was waiting for a commission, came to spend Christmas with them.

He was in the boot-room when he saw a woman standing in the doorway.

'Here, mother,' he exclaimed, 'take this boot to be cleaned.'

Picking up one of his boots he threw it across, and to his surprise it passed right through her. Thinking that it must be his fancy, he threw the other boot, and the same thing happened. He rubbed his eyes to make sure he was not dreaming. The woman was still there, and for the first time he saw her face illumined in the gloom. It was that of a very ugly old woman.

He took a step towards her, and she disappeared.

Much concerned now Deane sought his sister and told her that he must have been working too hard, and, as a result, was having hallucinations.

'It was no hallucination,' Mrs. Ward said. 'What you saw was a ghost. Paul (her husband) and I have both seen the old woman.'

The three of them, Colonel and Mrs. Ward and Jack Deane were standing in the hall talking that evening, when they heard the clinking of glass and rattling of china. The sounds came from the dining-room where the table was loaded with glass and china ready for the party they were having the next day, Christmas Eve.

They at once went to the room. The moment they opened the door there was a tremendous crash, and all the glass and china fell upon the floor.

Lying on the floor was the bleeding body of a boy of about twelve years of age. Bending over him, a look of fiendish glee on her beautiful face, was a young woman dressed in a costume

50

of a bygone age, her white arms and breast gleaming with gold and jewels.

By the side of her crouched the old hag, who leered at the intruders, an expression of devilish malice on her puckered up face. A weird light enveloped the three figures.

As the appalled intruders stared at the scene before them the room darkened, and there was an eerie silence.

The Wards left the house the next day.

THE HAUNTED BUOY

PAGET HICKMAN was one of my father's old friends. Like my father and myself he was greatly interested in the supernatural.

He was at a resort in Kent one summer when he had an extraordinary experience. He was on the beach on very hot day, and was looking for a resting spot when he saw an old buoy high and dry ashore. He went to it, sat down, and rested his back against it.

Overcome with the heat and tired with walking about, he presently dozed. How long he was in that state he did not know. When he came out of it he found himself standing in front of a garden gate on which was a nameplate: Dr. Horace Crawley. He opened the gate, walked up the path, and knocked at the door. A young and very attractive woman opened it.

'Oh, I am so glad that you have come, Ralph,' she exclaimed. 'You are very prompt. He is dead.'

Hickman found himself smiling, and said, 'When did he die?'

'Two or three minutes before I rang you,' the woman replied. 'I want you with me when the doctor comes.'

She took him to a back room on the first floor, where a grey-haired man, who looked many years older than the woman was in bed. Hickman was looking at the man when the woman backed out of the room, turned the key, and locked him in.

'You are cooked,' she cried, 'really caught! You poisoned him with that drug you got in Brazil. There is some of it in your clothes in your wardrobe. I put it there. Now for the police.'

It was all so sudden that for some moments Hickman stood as one stunned; then, realizing his danger, he tiptoed softly to the window and looked out of it. It was a deep drop to the back garden below. Raising the window with as little noise as possible, he swung over the sill, and, trusting to luck, dropped.

The woman cried, 'Eustace, Eustace, he's getting away—stop him!' A tall, strongly-built man rushed out of the back of the house and gave chase to Hickman, who, shaken by his fall, had only just picked himself up. He at once fled.

The tall man, shouting 'Murderer!' pursued him. Round to the front of the house Hickman spurted—he had been a fast sprinter at school—and made for the sea front.

A party of picnickers were in a field. Hearing the tall dark man crying 'Murderer! Stop him!' they joined in the chase. Panting and nearly worn out Hickman got to the beach. Several men who were there tried to stop him, but dodging them he got to the buoy, scrambled into it and tugged at the lid that was open. It came down and closed with a click.

He heard his pursuers shouting, banging on the buoy and trying to lift the cover, but they could not. It was automatically locked. He chuckled. By and by the air felt close and he perspired. There was no ventilation. Which was the worst, to be hanged for murder or suffocated? The air grew closer and closer. There was a tight feeling in his chest. He gasped and tried to swallow. His throat was dry—parched.

Hickman suffered from claustrophobia—always had a great dread of being confined in a narrow space. He was now. He beat the sides of the buoy. He would rather be hanged than endure more of what he was undergoing.

He cursed Mrs. Crawley, cursed the day that he was born, even cursed the Creator. His tongue seemed on fire. To quench his awful thirst he licked the sweat on his hands and body. It felt as if his eyes were protruded yet they saw nothing. A stopping in one of his teeth seemed molten.

Then suddenly something was happening—there was motion. Dimly his senses grasped it. Slowly, very slowly he was being borne to the sea. A churning and rolling about produced nausea. He was on the seas. He lost consciousness.

When Hickman came to he was lying on the baking hot beach with his back against the buoy. It took him some time to realize that his dreadful experience was but a dream. He made enquiries about the buoy, and learned that it was well known to be haunted, and that there was a probable explanation of the haunting.

It was this: —

Several years before Julian Harper, a married businessman in the resort, had been one of Mrs. Crawley's clandestine lovers. He was rung up one day by her and asked to come quickly as her husband was very ill. He went, and had in actuality experienced all that Hickman had undergone in the dream—the accusation of poisoning, the escape from the house, the pursuit, the getting into the buoy and the awful suffering when in it. But, fortunately for Harper, a workman who had been repairing the buoy had left his wallet in it, which brought him back to the beach. The workman found Harper unconscious, overcome by the lack of air.

No action was taken against Harper; apparently Mrs. Crawley and her accomplice afterwards had no desire to substantiate their accusation.

THE MAN IN BOILING LEAD

In Liddesdale, about five miles off the highway from Carlisle to Jedburgh, stands the ruin of Hermitage Castle, traditionally reputed to be one of the worst haunted castles in Scotland. It is situated in a valley amid green hills with Hermitage Water, a lovely babbling stream, coursing along over a rocky bed at the foot of it.

The oldest part of the castle, grey and hoary with age, was probably built by Nicholas de Soulis in the thirteenth century. It functioned as one of the great, immensely strong fortresses on the Scottish border. It was added to in or about the fifteenth century. After the ownership of it by the family of de Soulis, the castle passed into the hands of the Douglasses, and afterwards became the property of the Earls of Bothwell.

It was to Hermitage Castle that Mary Queen of Scots rode one day from Jedburgh to visit Bothwell, who had been wounded in a fight with a robber.

The eerie reputation earned by the castle is largely due to William de Soulis, who was regarded by the local inhabitants as a sorcerer, and believed to practise black magic in a castle dungeon. With his followers, who were as cruel and savage as himself, he pillaged and ravaged not only Liddesdale but territories far beyond it.

No one resented Soulis' conduct and detested him more heartily than the young chieftain of Keilder, a land on the other side of the Scottish border, who for his great strength and agility, was popularly known as the Cout (colt). The two had always been sworn enemies. Great therefore was the Cout's astonishment one day when a messenger bearing an olive branch, as an emblem of peace, came to Keilder with an invitation to a banquet at Hermitage.

In spite of the entreaties of his beautiful young wife not to accept the invitation, and a warning by the Brown Man of the

Moor, a local seer and prophet, the Cout, fearless of danger, went to Hermitage Castle accompanied by a score of his friends and retainers.

Soulis greeted him cordially with many professions of regret that they should ever have been on bad terms. The fare was sumptuous, the wine, probably obtained in a marauding expedition, excellent.

During the meal Soulis cunningly contrived to cast a black magic spell over the Cout's followers; the Cout, who was immune from it owing to a charm given him by the Brown Man of the Moor, sprang up from the table, knocked down the men who tried to seize him and sped out of the castle. He was pursued by Soulis and a troop of armed men.

In trying to leap over Hermitage Water the Cout fell into a deep pool and was held down in it till he was drowned. The pool is still called the Cout's Linn, and in the castle grounds is a gigantic grave alleged to be that of the murdered Cout.

The foul murder of the Cout and the continued depredations by Soulis at last roused all Liddesdale and the surrounding lands against him. A petition was presented to the King asking his permission to destroy Soulis. The King, tired of hearing constant complaints about Soulis said, 'Oh, boil him if you please, but let me hear no more of him.'

He was taken at his word. The enemies of Soulis attacked Hermitage Castle, overcame its defenders and seized Soulis. As he was being led away to his doom, he managed to throw the key of the black magic dungeon to his familiar spirit 'Redcap', with the injunction to keep the dungeon ever afterwards locked.

He was taken to the Nine-Stane Rig, a Druidical circle, and thrust head-first into a cauldron of boiling lead.

'In a circle of stones they placed the pot
On a circle of stones but barely nine
They heated it red and fiery hot
Till the burnished brass did glimmer and shine.
They rolled him up in a sheet of lead

A sheet of lead for a funeral pall
They plunged him in the cauldron red
And melted him lead and bones and all.
At the Skelf-Hill the cauldron still
The men of Liddesdale can show
And on the spot where they boiled the pot
The spreat (water rush) and the deep-hair
       (coarse pointed grass) ne'er shall grow.'

The cauldron is said to have been preserved for very many years at Skelf-Hill, a hamlet between Hawick and Hermitage.

The King, soon after the petitioners left him, fearful lest they should take what he said to them literally, tried to stop them before they got to Hermitage but was too late.

'Redcap' did as Soulis bade him and kept the door of the black magic dungeon locked. Ever afterwards it was haunted by the earthbound ghost of Soulis and the evil spirits he had evocated. People passing by the castle at night testified to hearing blood-curdling yells and demoniacal laughter.

Nor was that the only haunted dungeon in the grim old castle. In 1324 Sir William Douglas, the then owner of Hermitage, becoming jealous of his friend, the gallant and popular Sir Alexander Ramsay, who had been appointed Sheriff of Teviotdale, a post that he, Sir William, had long coveted, treacherously seized Ramsay and starved him to death in a dungeon; for several days the wretched captive existed on grains of corn that dribbled down from a granary overhead.

For years after Ramsay's death heart-rending cries and groans could be heard at night coming from the dungeon in which he had been confined.

THE CREEPING HAND OF MAIDA VALE

A SOMEWHAT impecunious family named Newman, attracted by the remarkably low rental of a house in Maida Vale, London, took it on a three-year lease. They moved into it in December, and for the first few months of their tenancy nothing occurred to suggest even remotely that the house was haunted.

Then, in March, shortly after the advent of Maisie Newman, a buxom girl of about twenty years of age, to take up her abode once more with her parents, things began to happen.

Coming home one afternoon Maisie went into a room in the basement to take off her boots, and, while there, suddenly saw an old woman wearing an old-fashioned black gown, a white cap, the somewhat crumpled border of which fitted closely to her head, and a white handkerchief pinned across her bosom, standing in the doorway looking at her.

Thinking it was either a new servant or a daily, Maisie called out casually: 'Here, Mary, or Jane, or whoever you are, take these boots like a dear and dry them for me.'

They were very high 'lace-ups' and Maisie tossed them carelessly, one after the other, at the old woman. To her unmitigated surprise and horror, the boots went right through the aged dame, who, turning slowly round, disappeared in the gloom of the narrow stone pavement outside.

As soon as she could pull herself together Maisie ran upstairs, and, meeting her mother in the hall, was explaining to her what had happened when she suddenly stopped short, pointed excitedly at the staircase and exclaimed, 'There she is—that is the woman!'

Looking in the direction Maisie indicated, Mrs. Newman saw to her astonishment the figure Maisie had just described in the act of ascending the stairs.

Remembering a test for hallucination that had been explained to her a short time before by a medical man, Mrs. Newman now quickly determined to try it. Pressing one eye, so as to throw it out of parallel focus with the other, she stared hard at the figure, which immediately appeared double.

Convinced now that what she saw was objective, for had it been merely the result of hallucination it would have undergone no change from the test applied to it, Mrs. Newman at once proceeded to follow the figure upstairs.

Moving absolutely noiselessly, it had gone about halfway up the second flight when it abruptly vanished, and Mrs. Newman and Maisie found themselves staring into empty space.

This was the Newmans' first experience with the unknown. The second occurred a few days later. Mr. Newman, who never finished in the City very early, and who had, as a rule, much correspondence to attend to when he got home, was in the habit of sitting up late, and on the night in question it was close on twelve before he put down his pen and rose to go to bed.

Switching the light off and gently closing the study door, for everyone else had long since retired, he crossed the hall on tiptoe and began to ascend the stairs. The intense and unusual (so he thought) silence of the house struck him forcibly. The window on the landing overlooking the garden in the rear of the house was open, and the tapping of the ivy against the glass sounded so strangely loud that Mr. Newman was for a moment quite startled. He could almost have fancied it was someone outside rapping. And then a draught of cold air rustling past him set the shabby, weather-worn front door rattling on its hinges, and the rattling was so pronounced that it really seemed as if someone was turning the handle and trying to gain admittance.

Step by step Mr. Newman mounted the stairs. He had arrived on the middle step of the second flight leading to the first floor, when he suddenly felt himself collide with something that was apparently obstructing his way.

Wondering whether he was asleep or awake, he rubbed his eyes vigorously, and again attempted to ascend. The same thing happened. He came right up against some invisible object, and this time he drew back with a violent shudder.

He was still standing on the edge of the stair, shivering and not knowing what to do, when something cold and clammy seemed to fasten round his throat, and in another instant he began to choke.

He tried to free himself, but though he could distinctly feel the thing round his neck throttling him, he could grasp nothing with his fingers. He threw out his arms and beat the air wildly, he stamped on the ground and kicked, but it was of no avail. He could feel or touch nothing, and all the while the sensation of being strangled intensified more and more.

At last, just as he was on the verge of losing consciousness, and the buzzing in his ears had developed into thunderclaps, a door from somewhere overhead opened and a voice that might have come from several houses away, it seemed so remote, called: 'Father, Father—whatever is the matter?'

In a moment Mr. Newman experienced a great sensation of relief. The thing, whatever it was, relaxed its hold and he was able once again to breathe freely.

Up to that time he had not felt as much actual fear as repugnance. There had been something in the touch that had repelled and shocked him, but now that it was gone reaction set in, and Maisie, for it was she who had called out, found him standing on the stair, looking ghastly white and trembling.

The next experience of the haunting concerned the Newmans' tortoiseshell cat, which soon showed she was just as much in possession of the psychic sense as any dog or human.

To begin with, although Julie, as the cat was called, was decidedly fond of wandering about the upper part of the house during the daytime, nothing would induce her to remain there after dark. The moment it began to grow dusk, she was invariably seen hurrying downstairs to the ground floor or kitchen, and no amount of coaxing would persuade her to go upstairs again till the following morning. Also, for no apparent reason, she would sometimes in the evening exhibit signs of panic, and if the door of the room she was in happened to be shut, she would claw it frantically in her efforts to get out.

One day, early in April, Mr. Newman's married daughter, Violet, accompanied by her only child, Delia, came on a visit to the house. Like most children, Delia was very fond of playing with animals, and she soon struck up a friendship with Julie.

One evening, shortly after tea, her mother, hearing a commotion in the breakfast room, where she had left Delia playing with Julie, ran to see what was the matter. To her relief, Delia was all right, and on being asked what all the noise was about, replied, 'Why, Julie has behaved so badly, I didn't know she was such a naughty, jealous old thing. While I was playing with her a few minutes ago, another animal came into the room and wanted to join in.'

'Another animal!' Delia's mother exclaimed in great astonishment. 'What animal?'

'Well, I don't exactly know what is was, Mummy,' Delia replied, 'for somehow I couldn't see it very plainly. It seemed to be all misty, but it wasn't a cat or a dog, for it had long, funny ears and moved about ever so fast. I tried to touch it, but it wouldn't let me, and it jumped about so I couldn't get very near it. Julie gave up playing with me the moment it appeared, and she kept scratching at the door so hard that I let her out, for I was afraid Granny would be angry. Just look at what the naughty thing did,' and Delia pointed at the marks of Julie's claws on the door.

'I see,' her mother said, shaking her head severely, 'but tell me, Delia, what happened to the animal you talk about? Where is it now?'

'In that cupboard!' Delia cried, pointing to a small cupboard near the fireplace. 'It ran in there when I was chasing it; that is what all the noise was about, and as soon as I had it nice and safe inside I shut the door and bolted it.' The child clapped her hands gleefully.

'And it is there still?' her mother asked anxiously.

61

'Oh, yes,' Delia laughed. 'It couldn't possibly get out. See!' and, tiptoeing gently to the cupboard, she shot back the bolt and threw open the door.

There was nothing whatever inside.

The last experience the Newman family had with the unknown in this house occurred a night or two later. The married daughter, Violet, slept with Maisie in a room on the first floor. On this particular night they both retired to bed somewhat earlier than usual; Maisie fell asleep almost as soon as her head touched the pillow, while Violet lay propped up with pillows reading. At length, growing weary, she fell asleep too, but soon afterwards awoke suddenly and completely, with a vivid sense of some extra unlooked-for presence in the room.

She sat up hastily and looked at the candle. She had left it burning, and very little of it remained. Feeling extraordinarily awake she took up her book and recommenced reading. By and by, however, the feeling that this extra unlooked-for presence was still in the room, close to her, grew so strong that she put down her book and glanced cautiously around. There was nothing and no one to be seen, saving Maisie, who lay sleeping peacefully by her side, and Delia, who was in a small bed beside them, also fast asleep.

But still Violet was not satisfied: she felt unquestionably that there was an additional something or someone in the room with them. Peering round her furtively, for the extraordinary stillness in the atmosphere generated fear, a fear to which she had hitherto been a total stranger, she suddenly received a shock.

On the wall facing her, about midway between the floor and the ceiling, was a strange and sinister-looking shadow. It was the shadow of a hand with fingers stretched out, as if in the act of clutching something. Violet moved her own hands at once, but that made no difference—the shadow still remained there. Then she shifted the pillow and various other objects around her, but the shadow still retained both its shape and position. Seized with a horrible fascination, she now sat bolt upright and stared at the hand.

It did not seem, somehow, to be a man's hand; it was scarcely large enough. It was more like the hand of a coarsely-made woman. The fingers were long, with bony protruding knuckles and very square tips. There were no rings on any of them, and the top of the little finger was missing.

It was not merely an ugly hand; it was hideous and repellent, and Violet, as she sat staring at it, felt just the same feeling of loathing well up within her as she would have felt had she been staring at some venomous and repulsive insect.

And now to her horror the shadow suddenly began to move. Rising slowly, it crept stealthily up the wall, till it eventually reached the ceiling. There for a moment or two it paused, and then with a furtive, spider-like movement it cautiously advanced over the ceiling, nearer and nearer to the bed, till it finally halted exactly over Maisie's head.

A terrible fear now seized Violet. She tried to cry out, to utter any sound, but she could not. She was tongue-tied and helpless, and in this condition she was compelled to witness all that followed. She saw the shadow slowly leave the ceiling and descend the wall, always with the same horrible insect-like movements, till it came to about on a level with Maisie's head.

Then, quite suddenly, it vanished, and immediately afterwards Maisie moved, while an expression of fear, speedily followed by one of loathing, which in its turn was supplanted by one of pain, convulsed her features.

Violet, still unable to move a hand or foot or utter a sound, was now compelled to watch her sister undergoing physical as well as mental torture, for she appeared to be labouring for breath, precisely as if she was being very gradually but surely throttled.

When she awoke she told Violet that she had just had the most horrible dream. She had dreamed that someone had tried desperately hard to strangle her, and so realistic had it all been that she could still feel the fingers pressing with hideous ferocity on her windpipe.

Violet then told Maisie about the hand, and for the rest of

the night the two sisters lay awake, talking, with candles burning by the bedside.

In the morning they told their parents what had occurred, and insisted on them leaving the house at once.

Mr. Newman now thought it high time to make enquiries, and as, on doing so, he learned that the house had long borne a reputation for being haunted, he straightway interviewed the landlord, the interview resulting in his being let off the remainder of the lease on payment of what amounted to little more than a nominal sum.

Mr. Newman made enquiries about the house but learned nothing more than that it had been rumoured to be haunted for a long time, and that some very queer people were said to have once lived there.

THE MAN ON THE LANDING

A VERY strange case of complex hauntings occurred, and I believe even yet occurs, in a fine old country mansion, once the home of the Rickard family, near Weymouth.

It is a queer, rambling building, full of winding oak staircases and long narrow corridors. Some of its windows look down on a gloomy courtyard and others on the even more gloomy burial ground of a very ancient church. Viewed in the daytime, even, the atmosphere of the place impresses one with a sense of loneliness, and this sense deepens as the day progresses.

After sunset, when the shadows from the great elms and firs clustering around the house darken its walls and windows, the effect is ghostly in the extreme, and it would be a matter of positive surprise to a believer in the superphysical if the place did not contain a ghost.

Actually it is said to contain at least two. One of them appeared some years ago to a Mrs. Walters, who was on a visit to the then tenants of the house.

Towards dusk one afternoon Mrs. Walters left her children in the nursery to dress for dinner, and on the landing outside met her daughter-in-law, also a visitor.

While they were standing talking Mrs. Walters suddenly heard footsteps, and on looking down the staircase whence they came she saw a tall man with iron-grey hair in the act of ascending.

Struck with his appearance, for there was something strange about him, she watched him mount to the top of the stairs and then cross the landing some few yards from where they stood. Advancing towards a door leading into what was at one time an oratory, but which had for some years past served as a kind of a box-room, he opened it very stealthily, and, entering, closed it gently to.

Convinced now that he was a thief, Mrs. Walters at once ran to the door and flung it open. To her amazement, however, no one was there.

Around her lay a pile of trunks and miscellaneous pieces of funiture, but of the grey-haired man there was no trace.

Mrs. Walters at once told her daughter-in-law what had happened and asked if she could in any way account for it. To add to her mystification, however, her daughter-in-law denied ever having seen the grey-haired man and tried to persuade her it was sheer imagination.

They were still discussing the matter when their hostess, attracted by their voices, which were raised somewhat high, appeared on the scene, and, on hearing Mrs. Walters' story, at once exclaimed, 'Why, that was the ghost!'

She then went on to explain that the house was haunted by the ghost of an old man, popularly believed to have been murdered in it centuries ago, in a manner too horrible to describe.

On another occasion Sir C. T——, the tenant of the house, entertained two judges who were on their way to the assizes at Dorchester.

During the meal one of the judges was very talkative and cheerful, while the other hardly said a word but sat wrapped in gloomy abstraction. Afterwards, when they were driving together to Weymouth railway station, to catch the train for Dorchester, the gloomy judge suddenly observed to the cheerful one, 'I say, do you know why I was so silent at dinner?'

'No,' said his friend. 'Why?'

'You will laugh at me, I dare say, when I tell you,' replied the other. 'It was because I saw, standing behind our hostess's chair, all the time we were at the table, a figure that was the exact counterpart of herself.'

'Nonsense,' laughed the cheerful judge.

'It's as true as I'm sitting here,' the gloomy judge said, 'and you may depend upon it, we shall hear bad news of her before long!'

What he said proved only too true, for within an hour after

they had left Sir C. T.'s, Lady T. retired to her own apartment and hanged herself.

Still another haunting. One summer evening some years ago two girls were standing at one of the windows of the old house, drinking in the sweet-scented air and admiring the effects of the soft white moonbeams on the beautiful old ivy-covered church, that stood only a little distance from them.

The night was very still—scarcely a whisper of the wind, nor a rustle of leaves; and in the fields that lay alongside the church the cattle were standing dumb and motionless. Indeed, the only sign of life and movement were the bats that whirled in noiseless flight in and out of the trees and bushes on the lawn.

The girls, who had been silent for some minutes, were about to interchange remarks, when suddenly a bell began to toll.

'Good heavens,' one of them exclaimed, 'why that's the Passing Bell! Who can be dead?'

'Does it never ring excepting on the occasion of a death?' said the other.

'Why, no,' her companion replied, 'and I have never heard it so late at night as this before.'

There was something in the sounds that fascinated them, and they stood listening till the bell at length ceased and silence once again reigned. Then they went to bed.

In the morning one of them—the daughter of the then tenant of the house—received a telegram saying that her grandfather, who lived in the country, but at some distance along the coast, had died suddenly, at the very time she and her friend both heard the Passing Bell.

Much puzzled to know why it had rung, however, for it seemed hardly likely that the news of his death could have travelled so quickly, she went to the church and inquired of the sexton.

'The Passing Bell?' he exclaimed, looking at her in amazement. 'And of this church? Miss, you're mistaken. No one died in this village last night and no bell rang.'

'Oh, but it did,' the girl insisted, 'for I and my friend both heard it. Someone must have got into the belfry.'

67

'Impossible,' the sexton said emphatically, 'for the key of it has never been out of my possession; no, not for an instant.'

Greatly mystified, the girl then inquired of the vicar, and with the same result. No one had died in the village, he informed her, and no bell had tolled. And there the matter ended, to this day a puzzle.

THE LEGEND OF COOKE'S FOLLY

ABOUT the year 1673 there was living in a large mansion close to the Durdham Downs, Bristol, a merchant named John Cooke, who had made a vast fortune trading overseas. He was one of the city sheriffs, and greatly esteemed on account of his wealth. The day came when there was much rejoicing owing to his wife having given birth to a son. To celebrate the event a grand banquet was given in the Cookes' house.

Many rich Bristolians were invited, including Mr. Griffith, the mayor, Mr. John Hicks, a former mayor, and other local celebrities. No money was spared to make the occasion a great and memorable success. There was music and dancing, games and amusements of all kinds.

One incident alone marred the pleasure of the day. It occurred during the banquet. In the midst of the general gaiety a gipsy astrologer, who was known locally as the Wizard of the West, suddenly entered the dining hall. Full of wrath at not having been invited to the banquet he stalked through the long lines of tables and, halting by the host, with a dreadful scowl on his face, solemnly spoke these lines:

> 'Twenty times shall Avon's tide
> In chains of glistening ice be tied
> Twenty times the Woods of Leigh
> Shall wave their branches merrily
> In Spring burst forth in mantle gay,
> And dance in summer's scorching ray.
> Twenty times shall Autumn's frown
> Wither all the green to brown.
> And still the child of yesterday
> Shall laugh the happy hours away.
> That period past, another sun
> Shall not his annual circle run

Before a silent, secret foe.
Shall strike the boy a deadly blow.
Such and sure his fate shall be;
Seek not to change his destiny.'*

The guests listened to this harangue in amazement. They did not know what to make of it.

The awful malevolence in the gipsy's eyes as they glared at the host sent a cold chill down Cooke's spine. He sat appalled till the gipsy had finished speaking and then in tremulous tones begged him to relent and offered him gold if he would not predict anything so fearful for his son.

Rejecting his offer with scorn and repeating the last two lines of his oration, the gipsy marched out of the banqueting hall.

His departure was as mysterious as his advent. No one saw him enter the grounds, no one saw him leave, or knew what subsequently became of him. Mr. Cooke was very superstitious, he lived in an age when credulity in witches, ghosts and necromancers was universal. He believed fully in what the gipsy had said. Nor did the passing years diminish his fear of the fulfilment of the gipsy's prediction.

The greatest care was taken of the young Cooke who became a fine, handsome youth. One day when he was in a street in Bristol, he chanced to see a beautiful girl looking out of a window. Their glances met and it was a case of love at first sight with both of them. He obtained an introduction to her, and after he had seen her several times, he told his father that he wished to marry her.

His father wanted him to marry someone else, not considering the girl his son loved good enough for him. She was a tradesman's daughter. They had many heated arguments but in the end John Cooke gave way, and his son become engaged to the girl he loved. John Cooke would not, however, consent to his marriage until he was twenty-one.

When that time was drawing near, John Cooke, fearful lest

* 'Wild Oats' by Albert Smith.

the predicted secret foe should get within striking distance of his son, had a tower built on his ground and made it as safe as possible against any undesirable intruder. In this tower, provided with every comfort, John Cooke insisted on his son remaining till his twenty-first birthday was past. The eve of that day found the Cookes in a fever of anxiety. The most careful watch was kept in the grounds lest anyone should try to enter them without permission.

The weather being very cold, the imprisoned youth was provided daily with faggots for a fire. He let down a rope from his windows, and the basket was attached to it. This was done as usual on that particular eve. John Cooke and his wife gave sighs of relief as they saw their beloved son draw the basket of faggots up to his window and take them into the room.

Only a few more hours and the limited time of the prediction would be passed. And as yet no sign of the secret foe. Midnight came, still no sign, and the Cooke parents retired to rest rejoicing. The much dreaded enemy had failed to put in an appearance.

Early in the morning John Cooke went to the tower and gleefully shouted to his son to come down from his bedroom and open the front door. There was no reply. Again and again he shouted, and still no reply.

A ladder was procured, and a servant climbed it and got into the bedroom.

John Cooke's son was dead, bitten on the right arm by an adder that had been in the basket of faggots. So the gipsy's prediction had been fulfilled after all. The adder was the secret foe.

John Cooke did not long survive his son. After his death the tower he built was ever known as Cooke's Folly.

THE MAUTHE DOOG

To those who are under the impression that ghosts invariably appear in the form of some human being, it may come as a surprise to learn that there are quite a number of well authenticated cases of hauntings by the ghosts of domestic and wild animals. One of the most widely known hauntings by an animal ghost is that of Peel Castle, in the Isle of Man.

Peel Castle is one of the most beautiful and picturesque ruins in Great Britain. The animal ghost that has haunted it intermittently for many centuries is called the Mauthe Doog. According to Waldron, a famous authority on the Isle of Man, the Mauthe Doog used to confine its visitations to two parts of the castle, which was then garrisoned by soldiers and sometimes inhabited by the Lord of the Isle himself, namely, the guard-room and a subterranean passage connecting the guard-room with the ancient Cathedral of St. Germain.

It used to be the custom for the sentry who was going off duty and had charge of the keys of the castle, which he had to deliver to the captain of the garrison, to be accompanied to the latter's apartments by the soldier forming one of the new guard or relief. To him the keys were to be next entrusted.

On one occasion, however, the sentry coming off duty had a little too much to drink, and in a fit of bravado declared he would go alone to the captain, even if he met the devil himself. For some seconds the soldiers in the guard-room could still hear the reverberations of his heavy footsteps on the flagstones of the passage and the clinking of his sword and armour; then all was quiet, till the silence was suddenly broken by the most spine-chilling screams, like those of a man taken by surprise and thrown into almost indescribable paroxysms of terror, intermingled with the most unearthly and terrible sounds. No one dared move or even speak, but

72

all sat cowering over the guard-room fire, gripped with such dread they did not even venture to glance around.

By degrees the sounds ceased. Once again the well known heavy footsteps and clanking of metal were heard, and presently into the guard-room walked, or rather, tottered, the sentry. He was ghastly pale, his eyes stared wildly and he was shaking all over.

Those were not the symptoms of drunkenness but of terror — abject terror. Three days later he died. Shortly before he died he said that on entering the captain's room he had seen the Mauthe Doog in the captain's chair, and he had never recovered from the shock it gave him.

The impression the Mauthe Doog gave to all who saw it was that it was not the ghost of any material dog, but a diabolical spirit in the form of a dog. It was furthermore thought that it only had the power to harm people who said and did wicked things, and for that reason the soldiers when on duty in the castle took care never to use bad or blasphemous language.

The origin of the haunting by the Mauthe Doog is supposed to date back to pagan times when, according to tradition, black magic was practised in the Isle of Man. There is no authentic record of the last appearance of the Mauthe Doog.

In Hood's Magazine of the forties of the last century another dog haunting is mentioned, not in Peel Castle itself but in its immediate vicinity. Strange noises were for a time heard at night coming from the rear of the castle. Some of the occupants of the castle, being curious to ascertain the cause of the noises, kept watch one night in the grounds. After they had been there for some time they heard the most unearthly cries and howlings, and a huge dark four-footed creature with fiery eyes rushed past them, plunged into the stream that flowed in the grounds and made for some trees in the near distance.

In a few moments there were harrowing screams and diabolical laughter. The sounds lasted for some minutes and then gradually died away, to be succeeded by an eerie silence. Utterly appalled, the watchers lost no time in returning to their quarters in the castle.

There is yet another traditional haunting associated with Peel Castle. Its origin dates to the reign of Henry VI. That unfortunate king incurred the animosity of the proud and lovely Eleanor, wife of Humphrey, Duke of Gloucester. She was an adept in the black art and, aided by her paramour, Roger Bolinbroke, and Margery Jourdemain, the notorious witch of Eye, she made a wax image of Henry.

At midnight the three conspirators took the image to crossroads, and, pronouncing maledictions on the King and uttering black art incantations, they pricked it with their knives. They then heated it in a fire and watched it gradually melt, begging Satan to inflict Henry with a wasting away malady. As a result of their evil deed the King was suddenly seized with a mysterious and very painful illness. The Duchess was suspected of being the cause of it. She, Bolinbroke and Margery Jourdemain were arrested.

Jourdemain was burned at Smithfield, Bolinbroke was horribly tortured and hanged, and the Duchess of Gloucester was imprisoned for life in Peel Castle. She died there after fourteen years, and ever since her death her ghost is rumoured to have haunted the castle and its vicinity.

The writer in Hood's Magazine credits Peel with yet another haunting. In the old days, beyond the cathedral there were ponds overgrown with weeds. A mother and her child had, it was said, suddenly disappeared from the neighbourhood, and mouldering skeletons believed to be theirs were found close to one of the ponds.

After their discovery the spot where they had been was for many years haunted by the phantom of a tall woman holding in her arms a ghastly pallid infant. No horse would pass the spot at night or any dog go near it.

THE PHANTOM DRUMMER OF CORTACHY

ACCORDING to the traditional story of the haunting of Cortachy Castle, in Angus, a former Earl of Airlie numbered among his retainers a very handsome and engaging drummer, of whom he became exceedingly jealous.

The legend does not inform as to the cause of the jealousy, but one naturally infers that it had something to do with a woman, and who more likely than the Countess! Anyhow, one day the unfortunate drummer, taken unawares, was seized, bound hand and foot, thrust into his own drum, and hurled from one of the top windows of the castle on to the flagstones of the courtyard beneath. The result was instantaneous death.

It appears that the drummer had been threatened by the enraged Earl several times previously, and that he had been heard to say that, if his life was taken, he would never cease haunting the Airlie family. If this were so—and there seems to be no more feasible explanation of the hauntings—he has certainly been as good as his word, for whenever a member of the Ogilvie Clan, to which the Earl belongs, dies, the beating of a drum is heard, either in Cortachy Castle itself or somewhere on the estate.

In 1849, for example, a young lady of the name of Dalrymple went on a visit to Cortachy and, whilst dressing for dinner the night after her arrival, was greatly astonished to hear, close underneath her window, the sound of music. At first it was very faint, but it gradually grew and grew, until it finally resolved itself into the distinct beating of a drum.

Leaning on the window-sill she listened attentively, for there was something about the sounds, quite apart from their novelty, which fascinated her. On they went, louder if anything than before, and yet their loudness had a certain hollowness about it that Miss Dalrymple could not liken to anything she had ever heard hitherto. She was still listening, immeasurably interested, when a rap came at the bedroom door, and the tattooing immediately ceased. It was the maid come to help her dress for dinner.

Miss Dalrymple casually inquired of the maid who the drummer was, and her astonishment was further increased on the servant replying that she had never heard of him, and was quite sure he was no one in the employ of his lordship. Determined to find an elucidation of the mystery, Miss Dalrymple waited till they were all seated at the dinner table, and then, turning to the Earl, she asked, somewhat abruptly:

'My lord, who is your drummer?'

Her remark produced an extraordinary effect. The Earl turned deadly pale, and an expression of terror swept over the face of the Countess, while everyone at the table suddenly broke off their conversation and appeared extremely embarrassed. Miss Dalrymple, at once seeing she had made a mistake, adroitly changed the subject and no further allusion was made to her experience till dinner was over and the company had retired to the drawing-room. She then mentioned the incident to one of the family, who looked very surprised, and said:

'What! Have you never heard of the drummer?'

'No,' Miss Dalrymple replied. 'Who in the world is he?'

'Why,' her companion responded, 'he is the family ghost of the Airlies, and is always heard beating a tattoo, either in the house or the grounds, whenever a death is impending in the family. The last time he was heard was just before the death of the Earl's first wife; and that is why the Earl turned so white, and the present Countess looked so frightened when you enquired who the drummer was. The subject is an extremely unpleasant one in this family, I can assure you.'

Miss Dalrymple was of course very much upset. The knowledge that her remark, made with all innocence, had caused such pain and alarm distressed her, while the idea of having to pass the night in the room whence she had heard those ominous sounds filled her with the grimmest apprehensions. It was not without considerable misgivings that, later on in the evening, she said goodnight to her host and hostess and retired to rest.

Isolated and lonely as her quarters had seemed to her before, they appeared to be infinitely more so now, and as she glanced round the apartment at the massive four-poster, with its sepulchral-looking canopy, and the ebony wardrobe, the door of which swung suspiciously open on her approach, her heart failed her, and she paused irresolutely on the threshold. Her eyes then wandered to the cupboard by the fireplace, and she fancied she heard a slight movement in it, a surreptitious shuffling, as though some person was concealed within. Her hair rose accordingly and her heart gave a series of tumultuous pulsations. Nothing further happening, however, and all being quite still, she gradually recovered her self-possession and, trying to assure herself that there were absolutely no grounds for her fears, she walked boldly up to the wardrobe and, finding no one in it, next approached the cupboard, and that being empty too, she proceeded to undress and, getting into bed, soon fell asleep, not waking till the maid came to call her for breakfast.

The day passed quite uneventfully, and once more it was time to dress for dinner. Miss Dalrymple was before the mirror arranging her hair, when to her terror faint strains of music again arose from the courtyard beneath. Unable to tear herself away from the spot, she was compelled by some restraining influence to listen and, as before, the sounds grew and grew until they at last swelled into the loud, reverberating roll of a drum, which, although coming from apparently just beneath the window, had nevertheless a curious, far-away sound about it that was even more noticeable than it had been the previous evening.

Miss Dalrymple wondered now how she had ever associated those tattooings with anything earthly, they seemed to emanate so unmistakably from something supernatural, considerably accentuated by the fitful muttering of the wind, the rustling of the creeper round the window, and the black, swiftly scudding clouds.

Unable to endure the thought of spending another whole

day in the castle, Miss Dalrymple left early the following morning, and, calling on her way home at the house of some friends, told them what had happened.

Five months later the Countess of Airlie, though absolutely well at the time the phantom drumming was heard, was taken suddenly ill at Brighton and died within a few days. In a diary, subsequently discovered among her possessions, a note in her handwriting was found to the effect that, on hearing Miss Dalrymple mention the drummer, she intuitively felt the prognostication was intended for her—the Countess—and that her doom was irrevocably sealed.

The whole circumstances of the case were made known at the time to Mrs. Crowe, who published them some years afterwards in her book 'Night Side of Nature'.

Five years after Miss Dalrymple's experience, the drumming was again heard.

A certain young Englishman, whom I shall call Mr. Lovell, was on his way to the Tulchan, or shooting-lodge of the Earl of Airlie, where he had been invited to spend a few days by the Earl's eldest son and heir, Lord Ogilvie. He was riding a stout pony and had as a guide one of the Earl's keepers, also mounted, a typical Highlander, dour, tough and wiry. For two solid hours they had threaded their way across a bleak and desolate moor, with the wind from the mountain tops whistling in their faces and at times almost forcing them to a standstill. For the most part it was pitch dark, but occasionally a rift in the black, stormy clouds enabled them to catch a glimpse of the scenery through which they were passing. It was horribly inhospitable and monotonous—a wild expanse of brown sodden soil, interspersed at intervals with thick growths of gorse and bracken and big tarns and swamps, whose dark surfaces glittered ominously wherever they caught the straggling moonbeams. Here and there were the white trunks of decayed trees that lent an additional dreariness to the aspect, and brought with them a sense of isolation and depression. Lovell, strongly affected by it all, felt chilled both physically and mentally.

At last, to his relief, twinkling lights, which his guide informed him were those of the Tulchan, were seen some little distance ahead. Visions of hot drinks and a roaring fire now rose refreshingly before Lovell's eyes, and he was congratulating himself on having got so far without mishap when, from a low ridge of ground just in front of him, came the soft strains of music.

'Hulloa!' he exclaimed. 'What's that?'

The guide made no reply, but urged his pony to go faster. The music grew louder, and the clouds, suddenly parting, let through a broad belt of moonlight, which illuminated the whole landscape and threw into strong relief all the outstanding features. There was not another habitation of any kind, saving the Tulchan, visible for miles round, and no cover for anyone to find concealment in, excepting a few very low gorse bushes; consequently Lovell felt he must be mistaken, and that the music must after all emanate from the shooting-lodge. As they advanced it became louder and louder, until presently it developed into the unmistakable beating of a drum, a steady and continuous roll, that conveyed with it an extraordinary feeling of uncanniness.

Lovell again asked his guide the meaning of it, but the latter, pretending not to hear him, urged his pony into a furious gallop. They were soon level with the ridge and the few gorse bushes that lay scattered along it, but there were no signs of anyone in hiding there, and the drumming followed them.

On their arrival at the door of the Tulchan it abruptly terminated, nor did Lovell ever hear it again.

To his surprise Lord Ogilvie was not there to welcome him, and he was informed that his lordship had been unexpectedly summoned to London on account of the illness of his father. The following day news was received that the Earl had passed away in the night and Lovell was then informed that the drumming he had heard—and which the keeper now admitted having heard also—had been for many generations a sure prognostication of death in the Ogilvie family.

THE GHOSTS OF THE BEECHES

MAJOR Horace Wyndham, R.E. (ret.), was looking for a house in the country. A firm of estate agents in Upper Norwood, to whom he went, gave him the names of a number of houses without success as the rent was too high, or he did not like the situation, and he was beginning to despair when they at length found The Beeches in Lancashire, with a very low rental. The estate was within thirty miles of Manchester.

Wyndham trained to Wrington, the nearest station to The Beeches, and from there took a taxi to Saxby, a large village on the outskirts of which The Beeches lay. It was a building shaped like two unequal sides of a rectangle. The walls were overgrown with ivy and tall trees sheltered it on either side. A winding carriage drive led up to the house, which was faced by a lawn, at the far side of which was a lake spanned by a long wooden bridge.

The bridge had a curious fascination for Wyndham. He leaned over the railing on one side of it, and peered into the water. wondering what secrets the dark depths might contain. The house was very old and had changed hands repeatedly.

He liked it, and took it on a three-year lease, returning to see the furniture moved in. His family, consisting of his wife, his son Robin, a cadet at Sandhurst, and his daughters, Nora and Lilian, were to follow him in two days.

After all the furniture had been assigned to their proper places and he had had supper, Wyndham sat for a time in front of a fire in the sitting-room, and then went to his bedroom. Besides himself in the house there was Mrs. Bird, the cook, and Gertrude Wise, one of the maids; the rest of the servants were to come with the family. He thought as he sat before the fire, prior to getting in between the sheets, how incongruous the furniture looked amid the old world settings

—the oak panelling on the walls, the ingle and the ancient cornices.

He got out of his easy chair and was about to cross the floor when he stopped short, and rubbed his eyes to make sure he was not dreaming.

He was certain the pillow had been flat on the bed, had it not been he would have noticed it. But now it was upright, and no longer smooth. Its shape was changing, changing very gradually into the resemblance of a face, the distorted face of a man—eyes staring, mouth gaping and distended. Wyndham went to the bed and put the pillow in its place. The desire to get into bed had now gone. He resumed his seat by the fire. The bed, however, had a strange fascination for him. He felt obliged to look at it. The bedclothes moved and seemed to be in a state of convulsion. Presently they rose pyramidally higher and higher and assumed a figure like that of a mal-formed person, with a peak-shaped head. The now sinister fashioned eyes suggested malicious amusement, and the mouth leered mockingly. The size and malignity of the figure appalled Wyndham and for some moments he sat petrified.

At last, pulling himself together with an effort, he walked to the bed, and as he did so the figure subsided, and the clothes fell into their proper place.

'Absurd!' Wyndham muttered. 'Perfectly ridiculous! I must have been dreaming.' But he knew it was no dream and that there was something devilish funny about the bedstead. He did not relish the idea of sleeping in the dark but forced himself to do so, and slept soundly till the morning.

Nothing more of note occurred till after the family had moved in. Robin, who had finished his first term at Sandhurst, was the next to have an experience.

He was approaching the lake one afternoon when he saw two men, one tall, the other short, on the bridge. The tall man suddenly caught hold of the other, and, in spite of the smaller man's struggles, hurled him over the railings and into the lake. Full of anger at such a cowardly attack Robin rushed to the bridge, but on reaching it saw no sign of the tall man.

81

Yet he had been in the centre of the bridge—and there was nowhere for him to hide. Robin then peered down into the dark water. It was perfectly calm and undisturbed—nothing to be seen of the short man. Completely mystified he retraced his steps to the house, not mentioning the incident to anyone.

It was Nora's turn next. She was in the orchard taking down apples one morning when someone touched her shoulder. She turned round and was not a little startled to see a tall, shrouded figure in black confronting her. It remained stationary for some moments, and then, walking away, was lost to view among the trees.

Hastening to the house she told Lilian and Robin about the shrouded figure. Lilian laughed and said it must have been a monk from a neighbouring monastery. Robin thought of the man he had seen on the bridge, but still said nothing.

Mr. and Mrs. Wyndham occupied separate bedrooms, close to one another. Mrs. Wyndham was preparing to undress one night when the shaking of the heavy curtain covering the oriel window made her look wonderingly at it. There was no wind. It was a very calm night. She was still gazing at the curtain when it bulged out as if someone was standing behind it.

To utter a sound might make whoever was there emerge and attack her, so she stole as noiselessly as possible to the door, opened it, then sprang out to the landing and ran to her husband. He called Robin, and the two of them went into Mrs. Wyndham's room and searched everywhere. There was no trace of an intruder. The mystery of the bulging curtain remained unsolved.

Then, one of the maids told the cook that she had been awakened in the night by an icy hand on her forehead. She was so terrified that she buried her head under the clothes, and did not stir till the morning. She said if it occurred again she would leave.

The butler told Wyndham in confidence that the house was haunted—he had seen a shrouded figure in black bending over him in the night. It had been a dreadful shock.

But Lilian scoffed at the butler's account of his ghostly experience. 'It was a nightmare,' she said. 'He had eaten too much at supper.' He was a big eater.

Lilian's room was isolated at the end of the corridor. She had just got into bed one night when she heard footsteps in the corridor. They halted at the door of her room, and through the closed and locked door something crawled in. It looked vaguely like a person on all fours, and yet there was a non-human element about it—a semi-animal appearance. It had a scaly body and bald, bulbous head.

It came with a crab-like motion, stealthily towards her. Compelled by a force she could not resist, she sat up and watched the thing getting slowly nearer and nearer to her. Reaching the bed it crawled, to her terror, under it, and she felt the bed heave up.

Tumbling out of it, all her scepticism now gone, she rushed out of the room, down the corridor, and into Robin's room. He roused her father, and, armed with revolvers, they went to Lilian's room and not without some reluctance and apprehension looked under the bed and searched everywhere.

To their relief there was no sign of the thing Lilian claimed to have seen.

The Wyndhams were now in a very unsettled and perplexed state. They did not know what to do—stay or leave.

Another ghostly happening furnished them with an answer. They were sitting in the hall shortly before supper one evening, when there were screams from the servants' quarters and presently through the hall rushed the spectral form of a short man, his face convulsed with terror. Close on his heels came the figure of a tall man holding what looked like a meat chopper or axe in one hand. A gruesome light surrounded both figures. They passed through the wall of the room opposite their entrance.

Their exit was succeeded by the entrance in a body of the servants, who very excitedly informed Mrs. Wyndham that they could not stay another day in the house.

As the house could not be managed without servants, and it

was very doubtful if new ones would remain long, the Wyndhams were obliged to sacrifice money and leave.

The estate agents who had obtained the house for them now admitted that they were not surprised at their departure, as no tenants had remained in it for long. According to a traditional local story, about a hundred years ago a young brother had murdered his elder brother in the house in order to inherit a fortune, and had thrown the body into the lake.

It was this diabolical murder that was supposed to furnish an explanation for the haunting of The Beeches by the phantoms of the two brothers; but for an explanation of the other ghostly happenings one would have to look much further back, probably to black magical rites and acts practised on the site of The Beeches estate in very remote days.

THE PHANTOM CLOCK OF PORTMAN SQUARE

THE idea that hauntings are invariably due to troubled and unhappy spirits of the dead ever seeking the prayers and consolations of the living is, of course, as any genuine psychical researcher knows, entirely erroneous. In many cases of hauntings, perhaps even in the majority, the nature of the phenomena suggests they are due to some species of spirit that has never inhabited a human body, and one which, far from pining for the society of mankind, desires nothing better than to be left rigorously alone.

Such spirits are, as a rule, entirely antagonistic to all human beings. An example of this is the haunting of a house in Upper Gloucester Place, Portman Square, in the heart of London.

A few years prior to World War I the house, which had stood empty for some time, was taken by a Mr. and Mrs. Strawn. One night Mrs. Strawn could not, try as she would, go to sleep. She was reviewing in her mind, probably for the umpteenth time, the incidents of the day, and planning and arranging certain little jobs for the morrow, when she suddenly became conscious of an extraordinary stillness. It seemed forced and unnatural, the prelude, in fact, to something which her instinct told her would be alarmingly unpleasant.

A few minutes later, when her suspense had become well nigh unbearable, the hush was abruptly broken by the sonorous striking of a grandfather clock, the sounds apparently coming from the landing close to their bedroom door. But the Strawns had no such clock in their possession.

Although almost fainting with fright, Mrs. Strawn felt constrained to count the strokes. One, two, three, on and on it went till it struck twelve, and then, to Mrs. Strawn's astonishment, it struck once more. Thirteen. After that there was a short interval, and then once again the clock commenced striking, and this time very slowly and with a curiously menacing intonation it struck five.

There then followed a heavy silence, which was eventually broken by Mr. Strawn whispering, 'Did you hear that, my dear? I wonder what it means.'

They were of course unable to say then, but Mrs. Strawn knew soon enough, for exactly five days later her husband met with a fatal accident while roller-skating at a rink in London.

After such an experience one might have thought that the first thing the widow would do would be to vacate the house, but for some strange reason she stayed; and for several years she was in no way disturbed. Then, suddenly, all kinds of queer noises, such as knockings on the walls and doors, and crashes, as of cartloads of crockery being dashed on the floor from a great height, were heard in the house. The noises, commencing as a rule at about midnight and lasting till two o'clock, continued night after night.

Mrs. Strawn, acting upon the advice of a friend, called in a medium, who, after staying in the house only a few minutes, took her departure, declaring she had seen and conversed with the spirit of a former occupant, and that there would be no more disturbances in consequence.

The disturbances continuing, however, Mrs. Strawn called in another medium. But the result was the same, and although the spirit who was responsible (a different spirit this time, by the way) was again said to be laid, there was no abatement of the trouble.

It was not until these futile attempts at exorcism had taken place that Mrs. Strawn thought of communicating with me. I then went to see her, and after hearing her story of the clock and other phenomena she had experienced, I told her that, in my opinion, the influence at work there emanated from some spirit that wanted her out of the house—a spirit that was inimical, if not actually evil. I also told her that it was, in all probability, an elemental—elementals being quite distinct and apart from the earth-bound spirits of the dead.

Even as I spoke, a feeling that it would be dangerous for her to remain in the house any longer came over me so strongly that I urged her to leave the place without delay.

I did not see her after that for several weeks, and then, quite by chance, I found myself sitting next to her at a theatre performance.

'Well,' I said, 'have you left the house?'

'No,' she replied. 'Somehow I couldn't tear myself away, and, do you know, I heard that phantom clock again last night. It struck thirteen first of all, just as before, and then very slowly it struck three. I have a relative who is very ill, and I cannot help feeling that it predicts death. What do you think?'

I could not say what I thought, for while she was telling me of the incident I had a strong presentiment that the ghostly clock had foretold her own death. I again urged her to leave the house at once.

Two days later—that is to say, on the morning of the third day after hearing the phantom clock striking—she was killed in a taxi-cab collision in Portman Square. The piece of glass that was the instrument of her death (it severed the jugular vein, and she died in exactly three minutes from the time she was struck) came from the window that was farthest from her, while the woman, an intimate friend, who was with her and sat next to the window was untouched, as also was a small dog that had sat on Mrs. Strawn's lap.

I heard nothing more of No. —— Upper Gloucester Place for about a year. I then met a man at a friend's house one afternoon, who, happening to hear me tell a friend about Mrs. Strawn and the phantom clock, remarked, 'Oh, I know that house well. It has been haunted, so I have heard, for a very long time now and apparently by a variety of ghosts, as your clock ghost is quite new to me.' He then told us the following story.

'About thirty years ago an uncle of mine, hearing that the house was to be let at a very small rental applied for it to the agent.

' "I think I ought to tell you," the agent observed, after

87

my uncle had announced his desire to take it, "that the house bears a reputation for being haunted. Indeed, that is why we are offering it at such a low figure."

' "Oh, that won't worry me," my uncle laughed, "for I don't believe in ghosts. They are all bunkum. But, tell me, has the house a history? I mean, has anything happened there, for although I don't care two raps about ghosts, I do not altogether relish the idea of living in a house where a notorious murder has been committed."

'The agent smiled. "You can make your mind quite easy on that point," he said, "there has been no murder in it and, as far as I am aware, not even a suicide, though what may have happened on the site of the house before it was built I cannot, of course, say. The haunting is, I understand, confined to one room, the large back bedroom on the second floor, and I should advise you to convert it into a store-room."

'My uncle laughed again. "Why, what nonsense!' he exclaimed. "I will sleep in it myself."

'Finally my uncle took the house and within a few days moved into it. He was absolutely well at the time. Three months later he called to see me one morning, and I was appalled at the change in him. He must have lost a stone in weight, and, instead of having a healthy complexion, he had no colour at all; his face was all white and drawn and haggard. He had in fact altered to such an extent that I hardly knew him.

' "Why, Uncle!" I exclaimed, after I had helped him off with his coat and handed him one of the brand of cigars I kept especially for him, "how ill you look! What's wrong with you?"

' "Everything," my uncle groaned. "You won't believe me perhaps when I tell you, my boy, but I'm lost, lost body and soul. You can't conceive a more hideous fate."

'He spoke so despairingly that I looked at him in amazement. Was it possible, I wondered, that he had become deranged since last I saw him?

' "No," he replied, interpreting my thoughts, "I'm not mad, Jack. I wish I were. I'm horribly sane. You haven't seen me since I took up my house in Upper Gloucester Place, have you?" I shook my head.

' "I thought not," he went on. "Well, you may recollect my telling you that the agent said the house was haunted and strongly advised me not to sleep in a certain room. Well, like the fool I was, I only laughed at him and slept in the room he warned me against. For exactly a week nothing happened, and then one night I had an experience so hideous that I have never been able to dismiss it from my mind—not for a day, or an hour, or even a minute. Listen.

' "Shortly after I got into bed I fell asleep and had the most singular dream. I thought, as I was lying there in bed, that the door of my room suddenly opened and a man in evening clothes, with a very white face, looked in at me and whispered, 'Come.' Well, I got up. Frightened though I was, for there was something about the man that was undoubtedly terrifying, I nevertheless felt constrained to obey, and followed him.

' "Down the staircase he led me to the cellar under the pavement, where, to my astonishment, I saw a flight of stone steps going right down, down into, apparently, the bowels of the earth. I shrank back in horror, whereupon my guide turned round and once again whispered, 'Come,' and, as before, I was compelled to follow.

' "He took me down countless steps till we finally arrived at a stone passage, along which we went till we suddenly found ourselves in a vast vaulted chamber. The centre of the floor was occupied by a long table, at which were seated a number of men and women, all with faces the same startling white as my guide.

' "On my entrance a man sitting at the end of the table nearest the passage looked round and motioned to me to be seated, and though I would have given anything to retreat, I again found it impossible to do other than obey.

' "When I had taken my place near him, I looked round at the company, who were conversing together in semi-whispers, and was at once struck by the mingled expression of furtive fear and utter hopelessness in their faces. They seemed to be in a constant state of terror, of terror at each other, at their surroundings, and over and above all, at the form seated at the end of the table, that I had at first taken to be a man but which now seemed to me to be a strange and horrid cross between a human being and some particularly grotesque kind of animal.

' "The horror with which the whole scene inspired me at length became so unbearable that, unable to endure it any longer, I sprang up, and was on the point of rushing out of the chamber when a woman seated at my side caught hold of me and, with the most surprising strength, pulled me back.

' " 'It's no use,' she laughed, 'you can't get away. We are all of us here for Eternity.'

' "For the love of God, let me go," I cried, turning to the thing seated at the end of the table. "I haven't done anything."

' " 'Oh, yes, you have,' was the reply, uttered in a strangely far away and hollow voice. 'You have slept in the room you knew we haunted, and everyone who sleeps in that room is bound to come here sooner or later. Mr. Robert Percival slept there, and he is here now, so are Miss Sarah Hackett, Mrs. Emma Freeman, Colonel William Sacherell, and others.

' " 'They all slept in that room and were drawn here by our atmosphere, which in a similar fashion drew you. We will let you go now, however, on one condition, and that is you promise us you will return here some time or other on June 21.'

' "Well," my uncle said with a groan, "I promised, and no sooner had I done so than everything became a blank, and I awoke to find myself in bed."

' "It was nothing more than a dream, Uncle,' I reassured him.

' "Wait," my uncle said. "It had all been so hideously vivid that I made enquiries and finally elicited the fact that a Mrs. Emma Freeman, a Miss Sarah Hacket and a Colonel Sacherell had actually lived in this house and died there. So you see I am lost. I have promised those fiends that I will return to them on June 21, and if I don't go of my own accord they will find a means of making me."

90

'I tried to laugh him out of it, but it was of no use, and finally I suggested he should leave the house and go abroad for a change. He wouldn't agree, however. The house seemed to have some extraordinary fascination for him—I have subsequently discovered it has for everyone who once stays there—and he remained.

'I called to see him on the afternoon of June 21. He was apparently well then, though terribly nervous and restless. When I called again the following morning he was dead. He had died, so the doctor said, in his sleep, from heart failure.'

HORROR IN SKYE

IF you are anxious to contact people who are gifted with second sight and are born mediums, you should go to the Isle of Skye. There you may still find people who are genuinely clairvoyant and clairaudient.

The following is a true story of a strange happening in a Skye cottage.

A lady, who for convenience sake I will call Mrs. Grant, was staying for a time in Skye. She was much annoyed by hearing from Elspeth, one of her servants, that a shepherd had been telling her about a ghost he had seen in a cottage on the bank of the river Rhundunan. Mrs. Grant sent for the shepherd and rebuked him for frightening her maid.

'Indeed, ma'am, I am very sorry that you should be vexed with me,' he said, 'but were it to cost me my situation, I cannot sleep in that cottage after what I have seen there.'

'And what have you seen?' Mrs. Grant asked, greatly impressed by the serious manner of the shepherd.

'You may laugh,' he said, 'at what I am about to tell you, but it is absolutely true. During the last three nights I have been roused from my sleep by a queer noise in the room, and on looking around me I have seen the figure of Mary, one of your maids, all dripping wet, standing by my bedside. She has had her handkerchief tied round her head, and her arms folded over her breast. After gazing at me for a few moments, she has kissed me on the forehead and then glided across the room and stood for a few moments by the door. While I have been looking at her, she has suddenly and unaccountably vanished.'

'She did not harm you in any way?' Mrs. Grant said.

The shepherd shook his head. 'No, ma'am, but she scared me.'

Mrs. Grant tried to persuade him that he had either been

dreaming or someone had played a trick on him, but he maintained that what he had seen was supernatural.

Soon after Mrs. Grant had this conversation with the shepherd, she was with Mary getting linen out of a cupboard in Mary's room, when there was a sudden report as if a firearm had gone off in the cupboard.

'Oh, ma'am,' Mary exclaimed in horrified tones, 'there will be grave-clothes taken from that chest before this week is over.'

Mrs. Grant laughed at her.

The next day Mrs. Grant sent Mary with a message to Portree, which was a good distance from her house. It rained incessantly during Mary's absence, and the river she had to cross, which flowed at the foot of the park near Mrs. Grant's house, was very swollen.

As Mary was a very long time away, Mrs. Grant grew extremely anxious about her, and sent several people to search for her. Mary's body was found in the river. In attempting to cross the river at the ford she had missed her footing and had been drowned. What seemed so strange was that her arms were folded across her breast, and she had bound her head round with a handkerchief, just as the shepherd said he had seen her appear on three successive nights in his room.

The pistol report she and Mrs. Grant had heard in the linen cupboard in her room had been a portent of her own death.

GHOSTS AND MURDER

ALTHOUGH ghosts, in spite of popular belief, do not as a rule appear with any definite purpose, there are plenty of well-authenticated cases in which they have played a very material part in the detection and prevention of crime.

One of the best known cases of this kind is that of the Cawood Castle murder. The story of this crime is as follows:

About noon one Tuesday in April, many years ago, a man named Thomas Lofthouse went into a field near Cawood Castle to water some quickwood. He had used one pail of water and was hurrying off to get another, when he suddenly saw, walking a few paces ahead of him, a young woman whom he at once recognized as his wife's sister. Very much astonished, as the woman's husband, William Barwick, had given him to understand she had left home on a visit the previous afternoon, he quickened his steps to overtake her, but no matter how fast he went, she kept the same distance ahead of him, although she apparently never altered her pace.

They continued in this fashion, he exerting himself to the utmost and she moving along calmly and without effort, till they came to the banks of a dreary-looking pond, where she sat down and began to dangle something white in the water. The object appeared misty and obscure, but his instinct led him to believe it was a baby. Mrs. Barwick had a child a few months old.

Lofthouse was about to advance to speak to her and ask what she was doing there, when she unexpectedly vanished, and he found himself merely staring into space.

Convinced now that what he had seen was a ghost, and feeling very alarmed in consequence, he hurried off and at once sought William Barwick.

'William,' he said, 'what has happened to your wife and child? I saw them both a few minutes ago by the side of the

94

pond near the castle, and it's my belief that they have met with foul play, and you know all about it!'

Barwick turned as white as a sheet and, looking horribly guilty, mumbled out something to the effect that as far as he knew his wife and child were still away on a visit.

Convinced from the man's demeanour that he was lying, Lofthouse now went to the authorities, who promptly had the pond dragged, with the result that the bodies of Mrs. Barwick and her child were found there.

Barwick was arrested and, on being charged with their murder, he confessed to having taken them unawares while out walking with them the previous evening, and to having thrown them both into the pond.

It is satisfactory to note that he was very quickly executed, but it is extremely doubtful whether the deed would ever have been brought home to him had it not been for the ghosts.

Another remarkable instance of ghostly intervention in connection with crime is that relating to the Guilsborough murder of 1764. Guilsborough is an ancient village in Northamptonshire about midway between Northampton and Market Harborough.

At the beginning of 1764 one of the most familiar figures in the neighbourhood was an old pedlar known as 'Scottie'. For many years he had visited the village regularly at intervals of about six or seven weeks, and when, after his last visit, about February or March, several months passed without his again being seen, people began to wonder what had become of him. Then an incident of a very startling nature occurred, which threw a sinister light on the mystery.

A boy named Seamark was overheard by the village schoolmistress to say to a play-fellow with whom he had had a quarrel that he would serve him as his father had served Scottie.

Her suspicions being aroused, the schoolmistress demanded of young Seamark what he meant, and on his refusing to explain, she shut him up in a cupboard and called in several of the leading lights in the village. They cross-examined the boy, and eventually succeeded in extracting from him the following information.

It seems that on the evening of the day Scottie was last seen in the neighbourhood he had called, on leaving Guilsborough, at the Seamarks' house, which lay in a very lonely valley, just outside the village. Seamark had with him at the time two friends, John Croxford and William Butlin—both of whom bore a bad reputation—and on ascertaining that Scottie had done a very good day's business, the three men determined to put him out of the way. Plying the unfortunate pedlar with liquor till he was more than half drunk, they suddenly threw him on the ground and murdered him in the most barbarous fashion, subsequently cutting up the body and burning it in a brick oven.

This was the gist of young Seamark's story, and he furthermore declared that he and his brother had witnessed the entire transaction from a hole in the floor overhead, but were far too terrified to do anything.

On learning all this, certain of the local authorities at once went to the Seamarks' house, and, taxing Mrs. Seamark with a knowledge of the crime, received from her a full corroboration of everything the boy had said. As a result, Croxford, Butlin and Seamark were arrested, tried, and eventually hanged, all three, however, protesting to the last that they were innocent.

One evening shortly after the execution of these men, the chaplain of the Northampton gaol, where they had been confined, was sitting in his study, wondering if after all the trio had actually murdered Scottie. Not a few people in Guilsborough believed that the story of the murder was trumped up by Mrs. Seamark, who was known to have been not on the best of terms with her husband, and that circumstance, coupled with the fact that none of the trio had confessed, filled the chaplain with a certain amount of doubt as to their guilt.

He was leaning back in his chair, still thinking of the matter, when he suddenly felt he was no longer alone in the room and, raising his eyes, saw to his amazement someone standing facing him on the opposite side of the table.

The light from the candles having for some inexplicable reason sunk very low, he could not at first distinguish who the stranger was, but on leaning forward and scrutinizing him, he saw with a thrill of horror that it was Croxford, the man whose execution he had attended some twenty-four hours previously. The chaplain tried to say something, but his terror was so great that his tongue clave to the roof of his palate and he could not articulate a syllable. He felt on the verge of fainting, when his visitor suddenly began to speak.

'I am John Croxford,' he announced, 'and I have come to tell you, so that you can afterwards inform the world, that I and my two companions, Butlin and Seamark, were alone responsible for the death of the pedlar. We murdered him exactly in the manner described by Mrs. Seamark and the boy, and if you desire a proof that it is in very truth the spirit of John Croxford that is now speaking, and that you are not dreaming, go to the field exactly behind the Seamarks' house and dig up the ground immediately behind the pump. There you will find a box, and in it the ring I took from Scottie's body. You can identify it because it bears this inscription, "Hanged he'll be who steals me", and never did a warning come truer.'

With these words he stepped back and seemed to amalgamate with the gloom, eventually becoming absorbed completely by it. The candles then suddenly burned again brightly, and nothing out of the ordinary was to be seen.

The chaplain, much mystified and strangely impressed, went on the morrow to the field at the back of the Seamarks' house, and, digging in the spot indicated, found there a box and in it the ring described.

An extraordinary case of what may be termed psychic intervention to prevent crime occurred at the beginning of the last century. A Mr. Thornton, of Fulham, dreamed one night he was in the garden at the back of his house, waiting for something, he did not know what, to happen. After a while he heard voices, and in the moonlit space opposite him there appeared two people, his gardener and the kitchenmaid. They appeared to be engaged in earnest conversation, when suddenly the gardener, seizing the girl round the neck, threw her down and began to murder her.

Overwhelmed with horror, Mr. Thornton was endeavouring to go to her rescue when he awoke, bathed in sweat. He was so upset by the vision that it was some time before he could settle down again to sleep, and when at length he did doze off he dreamed exactly the same dream as before, waking up just as the climax was reached.

This time, feeling more than ever disturbed, he got up and, lighting a lamp, prepared to visit the spot where, in two successive dreams, he had witnessed the tragedy.

On reaching the kitchen, through which he had to pass, he saw to his surprise the kitchenmaid, dressed exactly as she had been in his dream, in a hat and cloak, as if prepared for a journey. He asked her why she was up and in her outdoor clothes at such an early hour, for it was not much after three o'clock, and, much abashed, she replied that she was about to meet Mark, the gardener, who was waiting for her at the garden gate with a horse and trap to drive her to the neighbouring village, where they were to get married.

Mr. Thornton told her he had no objection to her marrying the gardener, but he did not like her leaving the premises in so stealthy a fashion, and he bade her wait and not do anything rash till he had first of all interviewed her intended spouse.

He then hurried down the garden path as far as the gate, but could see no sign of any horse or trap or man, and he was about to return to the house when he fancied he heard someone digging. Following the direction of the sound, he drew up under cover of some bushes and saw the gardener hard at work, turning up the soil with feverish haste.

Feeling absolutely certain now that his dreams were intended to warn him that a horrible crime was about to be perpetrated, Mr. Thornton suddenly sprang out on the gardener and caught him by the shoulder. The man started violently and, seeing who his assailant was, promptly fainted.

We are not told whether the marriage ever came off, but we presume the gardener did not remain long in Mr. Thornton's service, and that the girl at least was appraised of what had taken place.

Ghosts are not credited as a rule with any liking for courts of law, at any rate whilst proceedings are in progress, but according to T. Charley, a writer on supernatural lore during the last century, there is at least one instance of a ghost having put in an appearance at the assizes.

Charley states that a man was once placed on trial in an English court charged with murder, but so slight was the evidence against him that it was soon a foregone conclusion that he would be acquitted.

When the court had, as they thought, examined the last of the witnesses and were about to prepare for their recommendation of 'Not Guilty', the prisoner suddenly electrified everyone by leaning forward and pointing wildly to the apparently empty witness-box.

'My lord,' he exclaimed, 'it's not fair; it's not according to law. He's not a legal witness.'

The judge was about to rebuke him, when an idea seemed suddenly to flash across his mind, and he said in those gentle tones which none could assume at times better than he:

'Why is he not a legal witness? I believe the court will allow his evidence to be quite good, when he begins to give it.'

The prisoner, however, shook his head and, trembling violently all over, cried: 'No, no, it cannot, it must not be. No man can be allowed to be a witness in his own case. He is a party, my lord—he cannot stand where he is.'

Everyone present was now becoming intensely interested, though greatly perplexed as to what it all meant.

'You are mistaken,' the judge replied calmly. 'Every witness who comes here has a perfect right to speak. It is for us to determine the legality of his evidence when he gives it.'

Upon hearing this the prisoner was so overcome that for some seconds he could not utter a sound. He then exclaimed in a voice of the greatest agony: 'My lord, my lord, if you allow him to speak, I am a dead man!' And, repeating over and over again the words 'a dead man', he swayed, and would have fallen had not a chair been given to him.

The judge then told the prisoner that he believed a guilty conscience was tormenting him, and begged him to say what it was he had on his mind. The prisoner hesitated at first but, after appearing to undergo the most terrible struggle with himself, finally confessed he was guilty of the crime charged to him. He declared that he now confessed and told the truth for no other reason than that he was afraid to do otherwise in the presence of the man he had killed. He had seen him, he said, enter the court and with noiseless steps proceed to the witness-box, where he was still standing, pointing to the ghastly wound in his throat that caused his death.

Charley states that although no one saving the prisoner saw the ghost, by far the greater number of those present believed it to be actually there, and stoutly refused to accept the theory that the accused was merely the victim of an hallucination. Anyway, his confession was accepted, and he was forthwith found guilty and duly executed.

It is not, however, invariably the case, as the following will show, that the unknown powers are successful in their endeavours to frustrate the designs of those who contemplate crime.

Some years ago there lived at Portlaw, a small village nine or ten miles from Waterford, an innkeeper called Adam Rogers. One night Rogers dreamed he was standing in a very barren and deserted spot on a mountainside. It was daylight, but although the sun was shining very brightly, it did not seem in any way to diminish the awful feeling of loneliness and depression with which the place inspired him. Everything about it, the colouring, conformation, and even the soil, suggested something hideously evil, while the very atmosphere was impregnated with a sense of impending tragedy.

While he was standing still and taking all this in, voices suddenly fell on his ears and he became aware of two men coming along, side by side, towards him. The one was very tall, with broad shoulders and a curious, slouching kind of walk. He had a swarthy complexion and strongly marked features, with something about them that was decidedly sinister and alarming.

His companion, on the other hand, who seemed to belong to a superior class, was a puny little man with a singularly mild and benevolent countenance.

Neither of them apparently noticed Rogers, but continued talking with much animation till they arrived at a ditch. Here they paused, and the little man was in the act of stepping across the ditch when his companion suddenly picked up a big stone and struck him violently on the head with it.

Rogers tried to cry out and rush to the rescue, but he found himself unable to make a sound or move a limb, and in this state he was compelled to witness a most horrible and cruel crime, which was enacted with the most extraordinary vividness. He awoke only on its completion, and when the murderer was rising from his knees with a dreadful grin of satisfaction.

The dream impressed Rogers so much that he narrated it to his wife, and they were still discussing it when the door of the inn opened and two men entered. To Rogers' dismay he saw at once that these two strangers were absolutely identical with the two men who had figured in his dream.

They asked for luncheon, and appeared to be on the best of terms; but Rogers, observing them closely, was now even more convinced than he had been in his dream that a great social gulf lay between them.

The big, burly, sinister-looking man, whose name was Caulfield, was rough and uncouth, while the smaller of the two, whom his companion addressed as Mr. Micky, had both the speech and manners of a gentleman.

Rogers was so greatly perturbed that, when Mr. Micky came into the parlour to pay the bill, he tried to persuade him to stay the night there and let Caulfield continue his journey alone. Instead, however, of telling Mr. Micky why he was so anxious on his behalf, Rogers, for fear of being laughed at, made no mention of his dream at all and merely succeeded in mystifying his visitor, who failed to see any rhyme or reason in his endeavours to detain him.

The strangely assorted pair went off together, and that very night the news reached Rogers that the body of a man, horribly mutilated, had been found on the mountainside a few miles from Portlaw. Full of the gravest apprehension, Rogers, accompanied by his wife, went to view the body, and they both identified it at once as that of Mr. Micky. They then told the authorities of the visit of Mr. Micky and Caulfield to their inn, expressing it as their opinion that Caulfield was the murderer. In consequence, Caulfield was arrested at Waterford just as he was about to embark for Newfoundland, and, bloodstains being found on his clothes, he was formally charged with the murder of Mr. Micky.

At the trial Rogers not only proved that Micky was last seen in company with Caulfield but described every article of dress the two men had been wearing on the day of the murder with such exactness that the accused, who had hitherto maintained an air of the utmost indifference, was at last roused out of his lethargy and, turning to Rogers, cried excitedly:

'How is that you, an innkeeper, used to all kinds and conditions of people visiting you, should have paid such particular attention to what two more or less ordinary customers wore on that particular day? Does it not strike you and everyone else here that it is most extraordinary?'

'Maybe,' Rogers replied, 'but I had a particular reason,' and he then described his dream. During Rogers' recital the prisoner remained absolutely silent and in an apparently dazed condition, in which he continued whilst his namesake, Sir George Caulfield, who at that time was Lord Chief Justice of the King's Bench in Ireland, pronounced sentence of death.

Before his execution, however, Caulfield admitted that he was guilty, and declared that every detail in the dream which Rogers had narrated in court was absolutely true. He added that as soon as he set eyes on Rogers he felt, somehow, that they had met before, and that Rogers would, in some remarkable manner, play a fateful part in his destiny.

A HAUNTED HAMPSTEAD HOUSE

Had I not known a friend of an intimate friend of the senior partner of a firm of estate agents in Haverstock Hill, I feel pretty certain I could never have obtained the keys of No. —— Church Walk, Hampstead, for the purpose of conducting there a midnight vigil.

As it was I had some difficulty since, according to the rules of the firm, the keys of all the houses on their list had to be returned to the office before it was closed for the night, and I, of course, wanted to keep them overnight, in order to watch for the ghost which was reputed to haunt the place.

I had heard, on pretty reliable evidence, that the house in question was one of the worst haunted houses in London. I chose a night in September for my investigation because, in my experience, ghostly demonstrations occur more often in this month than in any other. I had no idea what form the manifestations took; whether they were merely auditory, or visual, or both. All I knew about them was that they were reputed to be most alarming.

I arrived there, alone, about eleven o'clock. In most empty and long-deserted houses there is a feeling of loneliness; and certainly in this house there was a feeling of intense loneliness. I was conscious of it directly I crossed the threshold—and I was conscious also of a sensation of acute depression. That thoughts and emotions poignant enough to permeate the atmosphere linger, to influence and affect certain super-sensitive minds is, I think, now recognized by most serious students of psychical search.

'How someone must have suffered!' was my first thought on entering, and hardly had I conceived it, when from close beside me came a curious sound, half a sigh and half a shudder.

With the aid of my torch I looked sharply round. No one was there.

103

I examined the rooms on the ground floor and basement, and everywhere I went I had the uncomfortable feeling of being followed and closely watched.

It was when I had finished examining the kitchen and was in the hall that I first heard footsteps—distinct pattering footsteps, that at once conjured up mental visions of a child. They came down the stairs towards me, halted and then abruptly retreated, as if panicked.

As I went up the stairs after them I again heard that queer shuddering sigh, this time just in front of me.

Having gone into all the rooms, I decided to hold my vigil on the staircase leading from the top landing to the floor immediately beneath it. A staircase is often the most haunted place in a house, and I instinctively felt it was so in this house.

Again and again as I sat there in the dark, listening and watching, I heard the stairs below me creak, as if someone was creeping very stealthily and surreptitiously up them; and several times I heard that harrowing half-shudder, half-sigh; but I saw nothing.

About three o'clock, tired of sitting on the hard stairs for so long, I got up and was crossing the landing beneath when I bumped into someone or something.

I flashed my torch. No one, nothing was to be seen, but as I stood there staring around my eyes became focused on the handle of a door facing me. It was the door of a room I had been into, and I remembered closing it after I left it. It was still closed, but the handle was turning, and presently the door very slowly commenced opening. . . .

It took a very great effort on my part to go to the door, throw it wide open and look into the room. No one was there, but as my light played over the bare boards and walls I very distinctly heard a door on the other side of the landing gently open and as gently close.

Someone or *something* was undoubtedly moving about.

Startled by this realization, I let my torch fall. As I was stooping to pick it up it was thrust into my hand!

That such an apparently considerate and, on the face of it,

ordinary act should have produced a paralysing effect on me may seem to some people extraordinary, but I can only say it did, and that for some moments I was utterly demoralized.

When eventually I recovered sufficiently to switch on my light, to my relief I saw nothing. I was seemingly alone, and yet I had the very uncomfortable feeling that a presence of none too pleasant a nature was standing close beside me.

I spent what remained of the night on the staircase leading from the first storey to the ground floor.

The darkness of the night had for some time given way to the grey early morning when the front door opened and a red-haired woman, carrying a carpet bag in one hand, entered. I wasn't sorry to see that charwoman. She made me realize that the horrors of the night were at last over.

It was futile to remain there any longer, so I came away.

'And you actually saw nothing?' my friend remarked when I narrated my experience to him.

'Nothing,' I replied, 'and I stayed there till the charwoman or caretaker arrived in the morning.'

'Char or caretaker!' he said, with growing interest. 'What was she like?'

I told him.

'Why, my good man,' was his answer. 'Then you did see something after all. That was the ghost!'

He went on to tell me that, according to rumour, many years before a red-haired woman had murdered and dismembered a a child in the house and carried away the remains in a CARPET BAG.

THE HAUNTED QUARRY

I HAD never been in Galway till I went on a visit to my friends the Dillons. They were having a house warming, having only just come to the house, Ballybrig Castle. The castle was really a castellated house, quite new. Indeed, the Dillons were the first occupants.

It was built on virgin soil, no other house nearer to it than a mile. Fronting it was a newly fashioned terrace lawn, and beyond that a rugged field with sparse trees, a hillock, and a quarry. In the rear of the house was a yard enclosed with high walls, and a pool, said to be fathomless.

The Dillon family consisted of Mr. and Mrs. Dillon, three girls, Nora, Sally and Deirdre, and two sons, Daniel, an architect, and Christopher, a sailor in the Royal Navy. He was home on leave.

I had the feeling that there was something very queer about the house the first night I was in it. Something I had never experienced before, too subtly unusual to explain.

Tired after a long journey I went to bed earlier than usual, and soon fell asleep. Something woke me sharply, and I had a feeling that something startling was about to happen. The window magnetized me. I got up and went to it. The night was fine, and very still; every object in the landscape stood out very clearly. A big dark Galway hare scurried across the ground and a night bird hooted dismally.

Looking in the direction of the quarry I saw a misty shape emerge from it, and come slowly towards the house. It was tall, and gave me the impression of something human in form but with unusually long spidery arms and legs, and a rotund head—something not unlike a giant Dutch doll. It came striding along in the moonlight, its arms hanging loosely by its side.

Fascinated I watched it drawing nearer and nearer, till it reached the house, when it swerved, swung round and strode in the direction of the yard and stabling. The house dogs whined and growled for a few seconds, and were then silent. I sensed that they were very frightened.

I could not drag myself away from the window for some time. Eventually I released myself from the magnetic chain that bound me, and went back to bed.

I did not say anything about my experience to the Dillons.

The following morning Nora came down to breakfast looking pale and as if she had not had a good night. She then told us that she had had a very jarring experience. It was similar to mine.

Deirdre was the next to have a queer experience. She was on the lawn throwing a ball to Pickle, one of the dogs. She threw it further than she intended, and it went into a bush. She told Pickle to go after it, but on getting near the bush he stopped, his hair bristled, and he whined and growled.

Deirdre looked behind the bush. There was a whizzing sound, the ball was thrown back over the bush, but she could not see who or what threw it. It left her somewhat disturbingly thrilled.

Then Sally, while standing on the hillock one morning felt a hand clutch hold of her ankle and deliberately try to trip her. She screamed and the hand let her go. It was a big bony hand with long fingers.

Without daring to look around her she ran to the house.

The boys now regarded the haunting seriously. Daniel had a friend, Herbert Ranger, who was a member of a psychical research society, and he invited him to the castle.

Ranger came and listened very attentively to the accounts of the haunting, including mine.

'I don't know what I can do,' he said. 'I am just a researcher and more or less a sceptic. I can't exclude the possibility of it being a case of nerves and imagination with Nora. She saw what she thinks is a ghost. Fear is infectious, and Sally and Deirdre and you, Mr. O'Donnell, fancy you saw a ghost too.'

'It was no fancy,' Sally said. 'Had I not screamed I should have fallen. Mr. O'Donnell is not neurotic. He saw the ghost.'

Ranger smiled. 'He thought he did. I will have a look at the quarry, as it is from there your ghost apparently comes.'

After supper he sat talking till after eleven, and then set off alone to the quarry.

'I hope to goodness he will see the ghost,' Sally said, 'and be damned well scared.'

'It will take a lot to scare Herbert,' Daniel laughed. 'He is very tough.'

'Just the sort to get scared,' Christopher said. 'I know the type. Cocksure and supercillious.'

We all waited anxiously for Ranger's return. At last he came.

'Did you see anything?' we cried.

'I saw something,' he said.

'What?'

'I imagine it is what Tylor,* the authority on nature spirits, calls an elemental. He believes that everything has a spirit — trees, stones, rocks; and they live harnessed to the things to which they are so closely allied till something happens to detach them. In this case it was the making of the quarry. When that was effected a nature spirit became loose and wandered abroad. Such nature spirits are harmless, or the reverse. In this case it is the reverse, and I strongly advise you to have the quarry filled in, or sell your house.

'To fill it in would be a hard job,' Christopher said.

'I don't think so,' Daniel said. 'The Galway Corporation might be glad to have an additional place to pitch their rubbish. I'll get in touch with them.'

He did, and the quarry was gradually filled in.

When the filling was completed — the quarry was not so very deep — the haunting of Ballybrig Castle ceased.

*Prof. Tylor was a well-known nineteenth century animist.

THE SPECTRES OF THE GABLES

FROM time to time I have come in contact with what I have believed to be entities from another world. One such occasion happened when I was living in a village in the Midlands.

There was a man named William Roberts, who was a builder. He was a widower and lived alone in a cottage. There was rather a mystery regarding the death of his wife, who was drowned in a pond.

In appearance William Roberts was far from prepossessing. He was about five feet eight inches in height, stocky and hunch-backed. He had a large head, big, mal-shaped ears, very light blue eyes under shaggy eyebrows, and a blotchy complexion. The ground on which he lived belonged to a Mr. Reginald Cliff, who occupied The Gables, a picturesque house about two hundred yards from Roberts' cottage.

The Gables was at one time a small house. Roberts had lived in it and without the permission of Mr. Cliff, who was the landlord, had added to it, and for that reason he actually had the audacity to think The Gables belonged to him. Mr. Cliff naturally opposed any such claim, had him ejected, and lived in The Gables himself. He kindly permitted Roberts to rent the cottage near him.

Roberts nourished a bitter animosity against Mr. Cliff for denying his right to The Gables. I never liked Roberts and always tried to avoid him out-of-doors. On one occasion, however, I was obliged to meet him. He at once started his usual harangue against Mr. Cliff, and said that when he died he would haunt The Gables and drive Mr. Cliff and his family out of it. I was shocked at the venom in his voice and the malign glitter in his light eyes.

He had a stroke soon after my encounter with him, and died from the effects of it. Shortly after his death I left the village and returned to London.

A year or so later the Cliffs asked me to spend a weekend with them. The night of my arrival at The Gables I occupied a room at the end of a corridor on the first floor. Tired from my journey and much walking before I embarked on it, I fell asleep almost before I was between the sheets.

I awoke with a start and a feeling that something was about to happen. Fancying I heard a sound close to me, I sat up. It was a fine night—I had not drawn the curtains as it was very warm—and the moonlight flooding the room rendered every article in it clearly visible. There was nothing to account for the noise.

I was still glancing around when two figures—those of a man and a woman—emerged from one of the walls. Their white faces showed no animation, they were those of the dead. In spite of his dreadful corpse-like appearance I recognized the male apparition at once. It was William Roberts. The female phantom did not resemble Mrs. Roberts nor anyone I had ever seen.

In the course of very many nocturnal vigils in houses and places reputed to be haunted, sometimes alone and sometimes with other people, I have been badly jarred, but seldom if ever more so than on this occasion. There was something so indescribably evil and sinister about the figures, and when they came towards me I scrambled out of bed and on to the landing.

However, I quickly pulled myself together and went back to the room. To my great relief the apparitions had gone, and there was nothing more ghostly than the white pillows gleaming in the moonlight.

In the morning I related my experience to the Cliffs, who said they had frequently been disturbed by noises at night but had never seen anything. When the Roberts lived in the house there had been one large room at the end of the corridor. After they left Mr. Cliff had made a partition in the room, dividing it into two, a fact of which I was unaware. This, the Cliffs thought, might account for the apparitions seeming to emerge from the wall, which actually was the partition.

Contrary to their wish, I slept another night in the same room but did not see the ghosts again.

William Roberts failed in his design to drive the Cliffs from The Gables, for they lived in it for many years, long after the ghostly disturbances ceased.

PEARLIN JEAN OF ALLANBANK

A TRADITIONAL tragic story is associated with Allanbank, a seat of one of the several lines of Stuarts.

About the middle of the eighteenth century Sir Robert Stuart, the youthful owner of Allanbank, went one summer to France to study the French language. While there he chanced to meet a very pretty Sister of Charity named Jean and become infatuated with her. At first she repelled his advances, reproving him severely for venturing to make love to one who had so entirely given herself up to a life of self-denial and unworldliness. He was however so persistent and pleaded his cause with such apparent whole-hearted earnestness that she yielded at last to his entreaties and agreed to marry him.

The courtship seemed to run smoothly for a time; then, suddenly tiring of the trustful girl but not daring to break off the engagement openly, Stuart wrote to her saying he had to return to Scotland on urgent business.

He made preparations very covertly for the journey, and was seated in the coach ready to start for the nearest port when Jean appeared and begged to be taken with him. A painful scene ensued, Jean eventually climbing on to the forewheel of the coach in a vain endeavour to get into the vehicle, while the callous Stuart ordered the coachman to start off. The coachman obeyed, with the result that Jean slipped from the wheel on to the ground and was driven over and crushed to death. Quite unmoved, the inhuman Stuart drove to the coast and sailed thence to Scotland.

It was late afternoon when he got to Allanbank and the shadows of night were already blackening the roadside. There was an ominous stillness about the place, a sense of some impending uncanny happening.

On approaching the lodge archway leading to his ancestral house, the horses of his carriage shied, and it took all the skill and coolness the driver possessed to steady them. Wondering what was the matter with the horses, Stuart looked out of the carriage window and received a terrible shock.

Peering down at him from the top of the stone archway was a luminous white face. As he stared at it, too spellbound with terror to utter a sound or even stir, its eyes suffused with an expression of fiendish glee, while a white hand moved slowly upward and pointed to the forehead, which bore the marks of a ghastly wound.

For a moment he did not recognize the face, and then suddenly he realized it was the face of the dead Jean, but that in it there lurked a something that he could not associate with the gentle, affectionate creature he had so wantonly made love to in France.

He was still gazing at it in horror when the carriage horses plunged suddenly forward, tore through the archway and along the avenue leading to the house. Above the clatter and rumble of the wheels, however, he could hear a loud mocking laugh, which followed him for some distance and then gradually died away in a long, plaintive wail.

That night strange things happened at Allanbank. The inmates of the house were awakened by the opening and shutting of doors and the pattering of high heels on the stairs and in the passages.

A young footman, curious to discover who was disturbing the household at so late an hour, crept out of his room and downstairs on to one of the landings. He was about to tiptoe along a corridor when the sound of footsteps ascending the staircase at the far end of it made him hurriedly conceal himself in an alcove. As he crouched there, fearful lest he should be discovered, the footsteps left the stairs and he could hear them in the corridor—the regular, measured tap, tap of high heels on the polished oak floor—coming his way.

Nearer and nearer they drew, accompanied by the rustling of a silk dress. Just as they were close to the alcove the moon, which had hitherto been obscured by a dark cloud, suddenly showed, clear and bright, through an oriel window near at

113

hand and illuminated the whole corridor with its white, penetrating rays.

The young footman gave himself up for lost and was ransacking his mind for some plausible excuse for his presence in the corridor when the steps drew level with the alcove, and to his unbounded astonishment he saw—no one. How he got back to his room he never quite knew, but he arrived there some way and hid under the bedclothes, quaking, until daybreak.

From that time onward hardly a night passed without uncanny happenings. Sir Robert Stuart, who had lost all his former gaiety and light-heartedness, went to some place in either a border county or actually in England, and returned after several months with a bride.

On the night of their homecoming no one slept. Doors continually flew open and closed with loud bangs; light, tapping footsteps were heard running to and fro, as if someone was in a state of great agitation; and sighings and moanings sounded first in one part of the house and then another, though more particularly on the landing outside the room in which the young laird and his newly-wedded wife slept.

No less than seven ministers were sent for simultaneously to lay the unhappy spirit, but Jean would have naught to do with them or their prayers and continued her ghostly disturbances the moment they were gone.

Seized with a sudden inspiration, Stuart got a portrait of Jean and hung it on the wall of the dining-room between the portraits of himself and his wife. There was then comparative peace at night for some weeks.

But the sight of Jean's face reposing tranquilly on the wall next to her husband became at length so intolerable to Lady Stuart that she insisted on having the portrait placed somewhere out of sight. That night Jean was back at her old ghostly pranks and was more disturbing than ever.

Sir Robert Stuart, realizing the futility of trying to get rid of Jean, resigned himself to being haunted by her, which he continued to be incessantly till his death. When that happened the haunting of Allanbank ceased.

A certain Mr. Charles Kirkpatrick Sharpe, who lived in Edinburgh during the eighteenth century, numbered among the members of his household Jennie Blackadder, a nurse, and Betty Norrie, a housekeeper, both of whom had formerly been servants at Allanbank.

Jennie affirmed that she often used to hear the tapping of high-heeled shoes along the corridor in the Stuart mansion, but although the sounds sometimes passed close to her she never saw anything. Betty Norrie, on the other hand, affirmed that she and some of the other maids used to see the ghost of Pearlin Jean so often, that in the end they got quite used to her and were never scared, except when she emerged suddenly from some dark nook or corner and took them unawares.

THE HAUNTING OF ALLUM COURT

RALPH ALDRUM, a keen psychical researcher, hearing reports of the haunting of Allum Court, a country mansion not far from Taunton, wrote to Mr. Walter Smith, the owner of the house, asking permission to spend a night or two there with a friend.

Mr. Smith, who was in Paris at the time, gave his consent and expressed his desire to accompany Aldrum and his friend. 'I hardly know the place,' he wrote, 'as my uncle who left it to me has only died recently.'·

A date was fixed for the three men to go to Allum Court, but owing to Smith being unexpectedly detained in London he was unable to travel to the house with Aldrum; consequently Aldrum and his cousin, Jack Dean, went there without him.

It was about six o'clock in the evening when they arrived at Fairland, the nearest station to Allum Court. There they were met by a dog-cart and an old groom—it was before the days of motor-cars. The Court, which was in a slight hollow, was a rambling old building covered with ivy up to the chimneys. A great hall, in the centre of which was a large round table, faced the travellers on entering. A wide black oak staircase led to a gallery connecting the two wings of the house, the East and West.

No one was living in the house. The caretakers, Mr. and Mrs. Brown, lived at the lodge. Mrs. Brown had prepared a hot meal for the two visitors in the spacious dining-room, and after it Aldrum and Dean went for a stroll in the grounds.

It was a fine night, deliciously fresh after the stuffy atmosphere of London. A gravel path circled a picturesque lake at the far end of the wide, well-kept lawn, and a belt of larches and fir trees threw black shadows over the deep, dark water. The two men had just reached the gravel path when they saw coming towards them a woman in a white or light dress. She was carrying a bundle in her arms. When about twenty yards from them she stopped. There was a glorious yellow moon, and the light from it focusing on her revealed her face with quite startling clearness. It was very pale. She appeared to be young with dark hair and eyes.

The bundle was a baby. Raising it in her arms, with an expression of the utmost loathing and hatred in her face, the woman hurled the baby into the lake. Then, turning, she walked swiftly away, disappearing from sight in the gloom and shadows of the trees.

For some moments the two men were too overcome with horror to move or speak. The ghastly incident had been enacted in absolute silence, neither the woman nor the child uttering a sound. There had been no sound of a splash when the child entered the water, and the woman had gone as noiselessly as she had come.

The realization of this came to the two men simultaneously, and they intuitively felt that what they had witnessed must have been the ghostly re-enaction of a horrible crime. The eeriness of the spot affected the men to such an extent that they made quick tracks for the house.

They were tired and soon went to their respective bedrooms. Aldrum was warming himself by the fire in his room, for the night had become chilly, when Dean entered. He said that after what had taken place in the grounds he felt too shaken to remain alone. The two decided that instead of going to bed they would sit all through the night by the fire. For some time they talked and smoked, then gradually their conversation waned and they both dozed.

Aldrum was the first to wake. The sound of a distant clock striking twelve fell with startling distinctness on the stillness that reigned everywhere. Dean was still fast asleep. Aldrum experienced a curious sense of expectation, a waiting for he knew not what. Presently he heard the tap, tap, tap of light hurried footsteps coming along the corridor outside the room. Hardly had they passed the door when there was an awful wailing scream followed by the slight sound of a struggle.

Dean was awake in an instant and sprang to his feet. 'Good God!' he cried. 'What was that?'

Aldrum threw open the door and they both peered apprehensively up and down the corridor. Nothing was to be seen but a long spray of ivy that waved and swayed in the breeze, beating gently against the window at the end of the corridor nearest to them. They were far too scared to sleep again and sat in the room with two candles burning till daylight. They said nothing about what happened to Mrs. Brown.

During the afternoon Smith arrived. He was very interested to learn of their experience.

'The uncle who left me this place and seldom stayed here told me there was a ghostly legend associated with it,' he said. 'In the reign of Charles II one of his and my ancestresses lived here. She was very beautiful—her portrait was painted by Lely. Even in that dark age of immorality she was conspicuous for her wickedness, and for her many evil deeds was doomed after death to haunt for ever this house and grounds.

'To all people but the heir of every third generation she appears as she was in life, young and lovely. To him she is in a form as hideous as her soul was bad.'

And he added: 'Unless I marry and have a child my line of Smiths ends with my death.'

'Are you not scared lest you should see the hideous ghost?' Dean asked.

Smith laughed. 'No! I have never seen a ghost and never shall. I am not psychic like you two must be.'

After their evening meal all three men went into the grounds. It was a glorious moonlight night, hardly a breeze and very still. Occasionally an owl hooted and a far off dog barked.

They had got to the gravel path by the lake when Dean clutched Aldrum by the arm. 'There she is!' he cried. Coming along the path was the same woman carrying the baby wrapped in a dark cloth in her arms. As she drew nearer and came into the moonbeams every feature in her face was thrown into strong relief against the dark background of nearby trees and bushes. There was a half frightened, half resolute look in her lovely expressive eyes. She had got to about twenty yards from them when she halted, her face suddenly convulsed with an expression of loathing and fiendish hatred. She raised her arms and hurled the baby into the lake; then, as on the preceding evening, she turned sharply and walked quickly away.

This time, however, there was a certain indistinctness or something shadowy about her as she went that they had not noticed before. Aldrum and Dean asked Smith what he thought of the dreadful drama they had just witnessed, and he replied: 'I have not seen anything. I told you that I would not as I am not in the least degree psychic.' But he did not doubt that they had really seen what they described. He thought that the lovely phantom woman might well have been his wicked ancestress, and the child she threw into the lake the product of her alleged incest. He suggested that they should all sit in the corridor that night and await the advent of the tapping ghost.

So at about three minutes to eleven the three men sat, a few feet apart, outside Aldrum's room. Their only light was from the moon which was visible through the end window. They were half asleep when the house-clock struck twelve. They tensed immediately, their ears strained to catch the anticipated tapping. But no sounds were heard, everywhere was still. After a few minutes had elapsed Smith yawned. 'The ghost won't come,' he said. 'Ghosts never come after midnight.'

Aldrum lit a candle and looked at his watch. He had taken the precaution to set it by the church clock that morning. The church clock was fast—it was not quite twelve. He blew out the light and was about to say something when the door at one end of the corridor opened and closed. The silence that followed was soon broken by the tap, tap, tap of high heels on the hard boards. It was a measured tread, light yet determined, accompanied this time by a sound between a swish and a rustle, like the brushing of a silk dress against the walls of the corridor. Nearer and nearer the tapping came, yet still nothing was to be seen.

As the invisible feet passed Aldrum he could feel the boards quiver under them. Dean was sitting a little distance behind Aldrum. Hardly had the sounds passed Dean when Smith suddenly rose from his seat.

'Take the thing away!' he shouted hoarsely. 'Take the cursed thing away! Oh my God!' He gave a gasping cry of terror and fell.

The next moment there was the awful spine-chilling wailing scream that Aldrum had heard the previous night; and then a death-like silence. And it *was* death, for when Dean bent over the prostrate Smith and felt his wrist, there was no sign of life.

The doctor whom they summoned said Smith's death was due to shock and excitement, that he had had heart disease.

Remembering what Smith had told them about the heir of every third generation seeing the phantom of his evil ancestress in an inconceivably hideous form, Aldrum and Dean believed that Smith had at last seen a ghost.

THE GHOSTS OF THE WHITE GARTER

THAT haunted inns should be far more frequently met with than haunted houses of any other kind seems only natural when one considers that in bygone days so many inns were nothing more or less than death-traps—dens into which travellers were lured and surreptitiously butchered.

Then again, even those who died a natural death at an inn would in all probability be earth-bound, the strong desire to communicate with far-away friends or relatives chaining them to the spot where sickness and death so unexpectedly overtook them.

Perhaps one of the best authenticated inn hauntings is that of a hostelry in Portsmouth called The White Garter. In the last century Mr. Samwell, an officer in the Royal Navy, had a very remarkable experience there. He was travelling by horse-coach from London to Portsmouth and had almost reached Guildford when an accident occurred to the coach which caused a long delay. Consequently he did not arrive in Portsmouth till long after midnight, when, to his consternation, he found every inn in the town full. After wandering about for a considerable time, he at length found himself in a very narrow thoroughfare on the outskirts of the town, leading to Portsea. He was threading his way carefully along it, for there had been much rain of late and the ditches on either side of the roadway were full of water, when to his intense satisfaction he suddenly saw a little way ahead of him a faint glare of light. Quickening his steps, he soon found that the light came from a low, white, straggling building, standing some yards back from the road. After he had rapped several times the door was answered by a woman who, not without a certain hesitation, agreed to let him have a bed and breakfast.

Always interested in and observant of women, Samwell took careful stock of his hostess while she was speaking, and noticed that, although she was somewhat negligently dressed and was by no means as spick and span as most of the young women of his acquaintance in London, her clothes were nevertheless good and expensively made. This impressed him a good deal, because from her voice and appearance he had concluded that she belonged to the working classes. She was attractive in a dark, gipsy-like fashion, but there was something in her eyes that repelled him. She also exhibited a curious snake-like movement of the limbs when she walked, which struck him as singularly odd..

Nor did he like the look of the house. It was unusually dark and gloomy, and the silence that greeted him as he walked across the stone-flagged hall and mounted the broad black oak staircase at the heels of the woman, seemed peculiarly emphatic.

The room to which Samwell was conducted was on the first landing. It was low and irregularly built, full of deep, inlet cupboards and recesses, which the waving, uncertain light of the rush candle that the woman handed him barely penetrated. Samwell, however, was far too tired and accustomed to dangers of all kinds to trouble much about his surroundings. He gave a hurried glance round to see that no one was in hiding, and then, shutting the door and locking it, flung off his clothes and got quickly into bed.

How long he slept he could not say, but he awoke with a violent start and with the peculiar sensation that he was no longer alone. Half opening his eyes, he saw something bright by his bedside. He at once sat bolt upright, and was astounded to see standing in front of him the tall figure of a man, wrapped in a shaggy overcoat, wearing a slouched hat, and holding a lantern in one hand.

For some seconds Samwell stared at the intruder, too dumbfounded to say anything, but his power of speech at length returning, he sternly demanded of the stranger who he was and how he dared venture into the room with permission. Not receiving any reply, and seeing the figure raise an arm as if about to strike him. Samwell sprang from the bed and hit out with all his might. To his astonishment, however, his fist encountered no resistance, so that, overbalancing, he fell on the floor, and when he picked himself up and glanced around for his antagonist, he found he was alone.

Thoroughly alarmed, for he could only conclude that what he had seen was an apparition to warn him of some impending danger, Samwell resolved to get out of the place as quickly as possible. In rousing the landlady to pay her he would incur the danger of bringing on to the scene other inmates of the house, who would doubtless try to prevent him leaving, but, he reflected, he was very fit and strong, and though he possessed no firearms, he had with him a stout cudgel, which in his powerful grip would be a weapon of no mean order, and at any rate it would be better to be awake and prepared, and to die fighting, than to get back again into bed, go to sleep and probably be done to death without the opportunity of resisting.

Having thus made up his mind, Samwell opened his door cautiously and, walking on tiptoe across the landing, crept as noiselessly as possible downstairs, not pausing till he had gained the ground floor. He then quickly unbolted the front door and, having set it ajar, so that he could make a hurried exit if necessary, he called aloud to the landlady. Once or twice during his descent of the stairs he had fancied that he heard someone moving about, and he was constantly under the impression that he was being stealthily watched, so that it was hardly a surprise to him when the landlady, accompanied by a dark, squat, sinister-looking individual whom she addressed as 'Charlie', very shortly made her appearance, fully dressed.

As the pair of them came downstairs into the hall, Samwell distinctly caught the clicking of several door handles from somewhere overhead, and the very subdued whispering of harsh, uncouth voices. On his telling the landlady why he was leaving, both she and her companion pressed him to stay, declaring that what he had experienced could only have been a dream. There was something in their voices, however, which Samwell did not like, they sounded hollow and insincere; and that, coupled with the expression in their eyes and general appearance, put him on his guard. He hurried from the inn and spent the rest of the night walking the sea front.

In the morning he recounted his experience to several of the townspeople, who told him that a mystery had for a long time hung over that particular inn, more than one stranger putting up there having mysteriously disappeared, whilst pedestrians, passing by it at night, had complained of hearing startling noises and seeing strange, unaccountable lights.

Sir John Carter, who was at that time Mayor of Portsmouth, was induced to take the matter up, but when the authorities went to the house it was found that the proprietors had decamped. The affair was then allowed to drop and, according to report, the premises were shortly afterwards pulled down, when a number of remains, unmistakably human, in all stages of decomposition, were found under the flooring and in the back garden.

Another house, also a hostelry, was soon erected on the same site, but despite an altogether different signboard, this inn was never alluded to locally save by the familiar name of The White Garter; and the sinister reputation which had been associated with the former building was to a certain extent speedily acquired by the new one. Horses passing by its entrance late at night were said to shy at strange and inexplicable shadows that silently emerged from the gateway and took up their stand by the wayside, whilst cries and groans, and occasionally sounds of frenzied, hurried digging, were only too plainly heard coming from the ground in the rear.

The disturbances this time, however, were entirely attributed to the supernatural, as the owners of the establishment were highly esteemed people who ran the house on most excellent lines, and whose conduct of it seemed above suspicion. Things went on in this way for some years, and then a story got into circulation which once again brought the house into bad repute and led to another speedy change, both of proprietorship and signboard.

A Mr. Harrison, on accepting an appointment in the Naval

Dockyard, left his home in London and journeyed to Portsmouth with the intention of taking up his new duties without delay. On his arrival in the town he set to work at once to look for lodgings, and, finding every apartment house in the place full, he finally succeeded in getting a room at the White Garter Hotel. The landlady had only a double-bedded room left, and this she did not wish to let to a single person. However, when Harrison offered to pay the double fee she somewhat reluctantly consented, and he engaged the room, stipulating that he should have it to himself and not share it with another man, as she had at first suggested.

Having a good many letters to get off by the night mail, it was late before he turned in, and, being of a somewhat shrewd and cautious disposition, and remembering that Portsmouth was said to be the happy hunting ground of rogues of all kinds, he first of all carefully locked his door. He then undressed hastily, for the room was none too warm, blew out the light and scrambled into bed. Harrison went to sleep almost immediately, to be aroused about two o'clock by a curious moaning sound from somewhere beneath his window. Unable to make out what it could be, he was about to get up to look when his eyes fell on the spare bed by his side, and he received a violent shock. Confronting him, in a half-sitting, half-lying posture, was a man. The moonlight being very strong and fully focused on the bed, every detail in the stranger's appearance stood out with the most startling distinctness. He was a young fellow, to judge from his jet black hair and whiskers, evidently in the prime of life, but his head was bent low and consequently Harrison could not see his features. He was only partially undressed, having his trousers, shirt and vest still on, and his attitude suggested he was fast asleep.

At first Harrison, who was furious at the trick his landlady had played on him, contemplated rousing the stranger and telling him to leave the room instantly, but the man kept so quiet that, on second thoughts, Harrison decided to leave him alone and say nothing till morning. Thus resolved, he lay down again in bed, and was soon fast asleep.

125

This time Harrison slept undisturbed, and did not wake till a neighbouring church clock informed him it was seven o'clock. The room was then aglow with sunshine, and the hum of voices in the yard and grounds outside announced the fact that the day's work had already begun. Harrison looked at the bed alongside his. The semi-dressed individual, whom he now took to be a sailor, was still in the same position, asleep, but Harrison saw with a thrill that whereas there had been nothing on the man's head before, it was now swathed in bandages. What puzzled him most, however, was to think how the stranger could have got into the room, as the door was still locked on the inside; the only window was bolted, and there was no other apparent entrance.

Still pondering over this Harrison slowly began to dress, and, fetching in the hot water which the maid had left at the door, he had his shave. This done he turned away from the dressing-table, and, his glance travelling in the direction of the two beds, he saw to his intense surprise that the sailor was no longer in the room. Utterly mystified as to how the man could have left without his either seeing or hearing him, and feeling for the first time since his arrival in the house a sensation closely akin to fear, Harrison hurriedly completed his toilet and hastened downstairs. After he had finished his breakfast he summoned the landlady, and angrily demanded what she meant by breaking her promise to him and letting someone share his room.

'Share your room, sir!' she cried. 'Whatever are you talking about? There was no one in your room last night but yourself, and you know that as well as I do.'

'No, I don't,' Harrison retorted furiously. 'Here, take your money, but you will never catch me crossing your threshold again.' And, throwing the money to her, he clapped on his hat and was stalking out of the house when a curious, half-frightened look on her face made him pause.

'It must have been "Whiskers" you saw, sir,' she said faintly. 'I feared he would never rest.'

126

What the deuce do you mean?' Harrison remarked, his curiosity now thoroughly aroused.

'Tell me,' the landlady replied, 'had the man who stayed in your room all night very black hair and whiskers?'

'Nothing could have been blacker,' was the response.

'And was he dressed as a sailor?'

Harrison nodded.

'Well, then,' the landlady observed emphatically, 'that was no man but a ghost, and I might as well make a clean breast of it. Some days ago we had a party of sailors staying here, and two of them, one a young fellow with curly black hair and whiskers, the other a much older man going bald, occupied your room. They sat up very late drinking and playing cards, and the bald-headed man accused "Whiskers", as we called him, of cheating. There was a fight, and "Whiskers" received a blow on the head from a glass bottle. Of course I did all I could for him, but he died before morning in the bed alongside the one you slept in. I ought, of course, to have told the authorities, but the bald-headed man begged me so hard not to do so, as it would mean for certain a charge of manslaughter against him, that I kept quiet—you see, I had the reputation of my house to think of too, and in the end they, the bald-headed fellow and his mates, secretly buried "Whiskers", with my sanction in the garden.

'The servants, I believe, knew nothing of what had occurred, but the day before yesterday Polly, one of the chambermaids, came to me with a scared face and told me she had seen "Whiskers" looking out of the window of the room he had slept in, with something very queer fastened round his head. I told her it was sheer fancy and that she must have been dreaming, but now I know that "Whiskers" does really haunt the place, and if the story leaks out I shall be ruined.'

Not wholly convinced that the woman was speaking the truth, Harrison went away fully intending to report the matter to the local police, but on arriving at the dockyard he found that his appointment there had been cancelled; another post had been allotted to him in the Colonies and he was requested

127

to leave for abroad almost immediately. In these circumstances he could do nothing but make a few hurried arrangements for his departure, and it was not until his return to Portsmouth several years later that he thought again at all seriously of the strange adventure he had had in the double-bedded room at the old inn.

Thinking there must be some mystery attached to the place, he set out to look for The White Garter, and, arriving at the well-remembered spot, found a new signboard hanging out where the old one had been. The house, so he was told, had been partly pulled down and rebuilt, and was now under a different name and an entirely new management.

Years have elapsed since then but, if there is any truth in rumour, the place is still in existence and still badly haunted.

Taunton and York both have old inns with certain rooms said to be haunted by vicious ghosts, people who have spent the night in them undergoing all the painful sensations of choking and strangulation. Bristol has an hotel with an underground passage connecting it to a house on the other side of the road, and this passage was long reputed to be haunted by strange-coloured lights flitting to and fro and the figure of a woman with a very white face, and clad in garments which were very tattered and torn. She was seen usually peering round corners with a grim and evil smile.

In the Chilterns there is an inn, once a farmhouse, that stands close beside crossroads, and there all manner of startling things are said to happen periodically. For years the place may go unmolested by any kind of supernatural disturbance, and then, quite suddenly, the hauntings may break out and continue night after night for weeks and sometimes months. One of the phenomena alleged to occur there is the sound of a loud grunting and snuffling which is heard about midnight, coming from waste ground behind the building. People have, it is said, occasionally gone out to ascertain the cause of these strange sounds, and all who have done so invariably come back declaring, with terrified faces, that they have seen a herd of enormous black hogs gnawing and tearing at some white and ghastly-looking object on the ground. However, the moment any attempt is made to interfere with these animals, they instantly and inexplicably disappear.

A suggested explanation of this phenomenon is that, many years ago, a former proprietress of the place, tiring of her husband, who was a great deal older than herself, and desiring to marry someone else, gave him drugged wine to drink and then, carrying him into the pig pen, left him there for the voracious animals to eat.

Yet another ghostly manifestation witnessed outside the inn is that of a shrouded figure which is from time to time seen, on nights when the moon is full, suspended to a phantom gibbet at the junction of the four roads. On these occasions guests in the inn have been awakened by the rattling of chains, and on looking out of their windows have seen the form dangling gently to and fro in the still night air. Once someone fetched a shotgun and fired at it repeatedly, but with no effect; for it still continued its slow and solemn oscillations, vanishing only at dawn.

There is still one more ghostly phenomenon apparently attached to the place, and that a white face with long, straggling locks of grey hair blowing all around it, and big dark eyes full of the most heartrending despair. It is generally seen at twilight, and always peering in at one of the windows on the ground floor. As a rule, those who have seen it have been far too terrified to attempt to address it; but on the rare occasions when people have summoned up the courage to speak, it has invariably vanished instantaneously without making any kind of response whatever.

Of this phenomenon there is no explanation at all. Possibly the spirit may be that of some murderer or suicide buried at the crossroads, and chained to the spot through the enormity of his or her vices.

In London there are a number of hotels reputed to be haunted. There is one, for instance, in a quiet side-street not far from Southampton Row, where guests have been aroused about two o'clock in the morning by the mad galloping of horses. The sounds come from very far off in the first instance, and, growing gradually louder and louder, eventually seem to be actually in the house itself, and so close to the beds of the listeners that they can actually feel the rush of wind in their faces as the phantom steeds tear wildly past them. Nothing, however, that I know of, has ever been seen there.

Lastly, there is a hotel close to the Strand where the haunting is of a more remarkable nature. A man staying there not long ago awoke in the night feeling a cold air blowing up from beneath him all around his bed, and with the sensation that he was lying suspended over a funnel-shaped pit of the most prodigious depth and terrifying appearance. It was all so absolutely realistic—he could even hear the steady drip, drip of the water from the reeking earthen sides, and detect the faint smell of fungus and decaying vegetable matter peculiar to such places—that the sweat burst out all over him and he clung on to the mattress in an agony of terror till the morning.

He spoke to the hotel proprietor about it, and finally succeeded in extracting an admission from his host that the experience he had had in the room was by no means an uncommon one, nearly everyone who slept there at that time of the year complaining of the same sensations. The proprietor could only account for it by the rumour that where the hotel now stood there had once been a pit into which the dead, and sometimes the living too, were flung indiscriminately during the Great Plague.

THE NUN OF DIGBY COURT

RALPH MARLOW received a letter one morning in December, 1820, from his friend Dick Holloway. 'Dear Ralph,' Holloway wrote, 'If you are not fixed for Christmas stay with me at Digby Court in Warwickshire. I have inherited the house and lands from my great-uncle Sir Arthur Holloway but I have never been there. Do come.'

As it happened Marlow had not fixed on anywhere to spend Christmas, so he was glad to accept the invitation. He and Holloway were old Harrow boys and had shared the same study there.

He packed his portmanteau and took a hackney coach to the Peacock Inn at St. Pancras, where he got a seat in the stage-coach for Warwick. On arriving at Warwick he found a carriage waiting for him, and was driven to Digby Court. A drive through an avenue of stately old trees led to the house, a long building of two storeys at each end of which was a gabled tower covered with ivy. Fronting the house was an extensive lawn, and at the end of this a lake bordered by trees and bushes.

On entering the house Marlow was led by Mrs. Hay, the elderly caretaker, across a wide hall, overlooked by a gallery connecting the East and West wings. A broad oak staircase led from the hall to the gallery.

A good supper was laid for him in the dining-room, the walls of which were adorned with portraits of the Holloways. Marlow did full justice to it, for the drive along the frost laden high-road had made him very hungry. Mrs. Hay asked if there was anything she could do for him before he went to bed, and then left the house. She lived at the park lodge, and seemed in a hurry to get back to it. Holloway was not to come till the next day. Marlow sat before the cheerful wood fire in the dining-room for some time before he went to bed. He then experienced his first shock.

As he was ascending the staircase to his room a figure covered with what looked like wool rushed past him, leaving behind it a dreadful smell, like that of a charnel house. What the figure was, whether male or female, or anything at all human he could not tell, and it was only with a desperate effort that he recovered from the fright that the thing gave him, and continued to ascend the stairs.

His room was in a corridor in the East wing, and there he found a bright fire in the wide, old-world grate. He locked the door, sat before the fire for some minutes, and then got into bed, sleeping till Mrs. Hay brought him a cup of tea in the morning. He did not mention his experience to her.

Holloway and a party of people, with servants and luggage, arrived at noon. A more merry party had seldom, if ever, sat down to lunch. They then spent the afternoon wandering about the house and grounds.

Marlow, Holloway and some of the guests were approaching the lake along a path flanked on either side by bushes when a woman in the garb of a nun passed quickly by them.

'A nun!' Holloway exclaimed. 'How did she get here, I wonder? There is no convent near here.'

They watched her receding form till it vanished round a bend in the path. When they returned to the house Mrs. Hay was still there and Holloway asked the caretaker who the nun was. Looking very taken back and nervous she said, 'I don't know, sir. I have never seen a nun here.'

After supper and coffee in the drawing-room, the women chatted for a while, and then went to bed. When they had gone the men sat in the big hall, smoking and drinking. It was close on twelve o'clock when one of them uttered an exclamation of surprise, and pointed to the gallery. Standing in it were three people, two men and a woman. They appeared to be talking but made no sound. Suddenly a nun rushed into the gallery and, falling on her knees in front of the trio, raised her hands in a supplicating gesture. Her face was that of a long buried corpse, and a ghastly stench accompanied her. Appalled by her appearance and the smell the men in the hall stared in spellbound silence at the gallery. They did not speak or stir until as suddenly as they had appeared the phantom figures vanished.

'My God! Horrible! Ghastly! What does it mean? Don't tell the ladies,' were the exclamations that succeeded the disappearance of the apparitions.

'I'm dashed if I know what it means,' Holloway said. 'I had no idea this place was haunted. My great-uncle never complained of ghosts.'

They kept very near one another when they went to bed.

In the morning two of the women declared that nothing would induce them to stay another hour in the house; they had been visited by a dreadful figure covered with wool, and smelling horribly, in the night, and had been obliged to sit huddled close together in the corridor for a time.

Their departure saw the departure of all the women and some of the men; those that remained out of bravado saw the same phantoms again that night.

All the servants having panicked and left, Holloway, Marlow, and the other men who had stayed left too, and Digby Court was abandoned to cobwebs, stillness and ghosts.

THE PHANTOM LADY OF BERRY POMEROY

ROMANTICALLY situated amid some of the most beautiful scenery in Devon, the picturesque ruins of Berry Pomeroy Castle, near Totnes, date to two main periods. The older part is said to have been built by Ralph de Poerai (Pomeroi), one of the followers of William I, who for his valour in battle was given much land in the vicinity of the river Dart. The later portion of the ruins date from the mid-sixteenth century, when the estate of Berry Pomeroy, comprising the village of that name, castle premises and territory passed into the possession of the Duke of Somerset, who shortly afterwards became Lord Protector.

Either before or during the feudal wars the castle was made into a fortress, considered practically impregnable because of its standing on an eminence, with one of its sides on the brink of a cliff, and the only approach to it being through a wood, which in those days was very dense and extensive.

There is little doubt that during its long history many a dark and tragic incident was enacted within its massive and grim walls.

One violent scene that lived long in the memory of those who witnessed it occurred towards the latter part of the reign of Richard I. That monarch having learned, on his return from captivity, that Henry de Pomeroi, lineal descendant of Ralph de Pomeroi, founder of the castle, had been disloyal to him, having sided with Prince John against him, ordered his arrest. On the approach of the king's pursuivants, de Pomeroi, rather than surrender, mounted his favourite charger and, with a shout of defiance, made it leap from the battlement of the castle into the gorge beneath.

Henry's is one of the ghosts rumoured to haunt, periodically, the castle ruins and the nearby banks of the river Dart.

The castle remained in possession of the de Pomeroi family

from the days of the Conqueror to about the year 1549, when the last of its owners was accused of taking part in a rebellion against the Government, and only saved his life by making over his estate to the wily Edward Seymour, Duke of Somerset. The castle was dismantled during the Civil Wars of the seventeenth century but was restored to all its pristine splendour by Sir Edward Seymour in the reign of James II. After his death it fell into a state of decay, the process of destruction being quickened, so it has been asserted, by a thunderstorm of the most unparalleled violence.

The more widely known of the castle hauntings concern either two phantom ladies, or, if only one, an apparition whose purpose and significance is not always the same. In her one role she is merely the presager of death to a member of any family intimately associated or connected with the castle, while in her other role she deliberately lures to death or serious accident any person who has the misfortune to see her.

At the International Club for Psychical Research in 1913 Mr. Taylor, an elderly member of the club, related an authentic story told him in his youth by a Mrs. King of Torquay. Mrs. King said that her brother, who was an officer in a line regiment, while spending his leave at home, went one day to Berry Pomeroy village to see the castle. Not believing in ghosts he paid no attention to the rumour he had heard of the castle being haunted. Having obtained the keys, on payment of a small gratuity to the lodge-keeper, he was wandering about the ruins, when he saw a young and beautiful girl, wearing a very becoming albeit somewhat quaint costume, beckoning to him, as if in distress, from the summit of one of the lofty, ivy-clad walls.

Supposing she was afraid to move lest she should fall, and wondering who she was and how she got there, he searched for a means to get to her, and, having found what appeared to be the only way, he had nearly reached her when the masonry under his feet subsided, and it was only by a miracle that he saved himself from plunging to a great depth. Clinging desperately to a narrow ledge he was all but spent when luckily he was seen and rescued.

On mentioning the lovely damsel and her predicament he was informed that there was no need to worry about her since she was not of this world but the much dreaded phantom of a long defunct member of the Pomeroy family, who took a fiendish delight in luring people, especially men, to their destruction.

Mrs. King's story of the haunting of Berry Pomeroy Castle by this phantom is one of many told of the apparition. Regarding the death presaging phantom, the following account is taken from the memoirs of the eminent physician, Sir Walter Farquhar.

When Sir Walter was a general practitioner in Torquay, he was summoned one day to the wife of the Steward of Berry Pomeroy Castle, who was seriously ill. On arriving at the castle, a portion of which was occupied, he was shown into a gloomy room, a curious feature of which was an old staircase in one corner leading to an apartment overhead.

He was becoming impatient at being kept waiting when the door opened and a woman entered. Owing to the dull weather and the window being stained the light was so poor that he could not see the woman's face very distinctly, but he got the impression that she was young and good looking, and that her dress was of some very rich material. Her bracelets jingled as she walked across the floor and the jewels in her ears and on her breast emitted a faint glow.

Without seeming to notice Dr. Farquhar she made for the staircase, halted at the foot of it, as if hesitating to go on, and then slowly began to ascend. When she was nearly at the top she again paused and looked down and round at the doctor. At that moment the sky seemed to brighten and, the light from the window over the stairs focusing on her face, she was then for the first time fully revealed to Dr. Farquhar. She was strikingly beautiful but her attractiveness was in a large measure marred by the reflection in her features of the obvious struggle that was taking place within her, a struggle between passions of the most vicious kind and utter despair.

That she belonged to a wealthy and highly aristocratic class was depicted in the delicate moulding of all her lineaments, in the exquisite shape of her hands, with their long tapering fingers, in the richness of her dress and in her costly jewellery. Immeasurably shocked but horribly fascinated, Dr. Farquhar stood rooted to the floor, wholly unable to tear his gaze from her face, so wicked and so pitiably despairing.

The was an indescribable eeriness about her that infected the atmosphere of the room, and he felt, as he looked at her, that he was seeing a soul damned without a particle of hope.

Continuing her ascent the woman vanished from view overhead. Sorely perplexed and not a little jarred the doctor was debating in his mind who or what she could have been when he was summoned to the bedside of his patient.

He visited the patient again the following morning and was pleased to find a great improvement in her. After he had left her and was alone for a few minutes with the Steward, he told the latter about his strange experience in the castle the previous day. To his consternation the Steward was much upset. 'I would rather anything had happened but that,' the Steward exclaimed, and on Dr. Farquhar asking what he meant, the man told him that the beautiful figure he had seen on the staircase was not of flesh and blood but the ghost of the daughter of a long ago Pomeroy owner of the castle, doomed for many sins and crime, one of which was the murder of her child, the outcome of an incestuous intercourse, to haunt the castle, always appearing in that particular room prior to the death of someone living in the building.

'The last time she was seen here,' the Steward said, 'was the day my son was drowned, and her appearance to you yesterday can only mean one thing, the death of my poor wife.'

Dr. Farquhar told him there was really no need for alarm as his wife was no longer in any danger. The Steward, however, refused to be comforted; and that very day, a few hours after the doctor's visit, his wife died.

Many years later, when Dr. Farquhar, no longer a general practitioner, was living in London and had achieved fame in his profession, a woman came to see him one day about her sister who, she said, was becoming very ill over nothing more than a persisting hallucination. The woman said that she, her brother and sister, while staying a few weeks in Torquay, had driven one morning to Berry Pomeroy to see the castle. While she and her brother were in conversation with the lodge-keeper her sister was alone in the room with the corner staircase, and when they returned to her they found her in a very agitated state. The sister declared that a woman had passed through the room, wringing her hands and with an expression on her lovely face that she would never forget.

'We laughed at my sister,' the woman said, 'and told her she must have been dreaming, but she persisted, and still persists that she saw such a person.'

'Do you know if anyone closely associated with the castle died soon after your visit to it?' Dr. Farquhar asked.

'The Steward died the same day,' his caller said.

'Your sister is suffering from no hallucination,' Dr. Farquhar exclaimed, 'for I, too, saw that woman.' He then described his experience in the room with the corner staircase, expressing his wish to see the sister. 'Whatever you do,' he added, 'never again ridicule her or cast any doubt on what she told you.'

The following day the woman's sister came to him as a patient, and under his treatment she rapidly got well.

THE HAUNTING OF ST. GILES

HOSPITALS, like gaols, are sometimes haunted. Bethesda is haunted by the ghost of a girl, Rebecca, and a hospital near Buckingham Palace Road, London, by an eerie black mist which is seen in one of the wards before a death; but no hospital has been so badly haunted as a hospital near Edinburgh, which we must call 'St. Giles'.

My old schoolfellow Bruce Carnegie met with an accident some years ago in Edinburgh, which necessitated his going to St. Giles. He was put in Ward D, and had a cubicle to himself.

The third night he was lying in bed in a state of semi-wakefulness when two nurses entered the room with a moveable couch. The older of the nurses gave him an injection. They then put him on the couch and took him to a room where there were two doctors in white hoods and white robes—their faces muffled. One of them bent over him. Carnegie sensed that it was a man with a dark beard and dark, gleaming eyes full of fiendish hatred. The man was intent of doing something to him.

'Why don't you begin?' he found himself asking.

'It's all over,' a voice then said, and Carnegie was conscious of the most excruciating pain. He asked for something to relieve it, and the nurse gave him a pill. He asked for another, but she shook her head—'I cannot give you more.'

'Oh, hell, I can't bear it,' he pleaded. 'You must,' she said. 'Be patient.'

Her voice weakened and faded away. His brain cleared. He recognized his surroundings—the cubicle. He was still in it. The pain had ceased but he retained a vivid, none too pleasant recollection of it.

He later spoke about the incident to one of the nurses, and she asked, 'Was this in Ward D?'

'Yes,' Carnegie told her.

'I thought it was,' she said.

He asked her why, but she would not tell him, and he did not find out until he had left St. Giles. He then heard that Ward D in the hospital was well known to be haunted.

He discovered that about twelve years before he went to St. Giles there were two doctors, Mackie and McGowan, an anaesthetist. Both men were in love with Hilda Reid, a very pretty, petite blonde. They had been friends but rivalry made them foes. When Mackie was knocked down by a car and seriously injured, he was put in Ward D at St. Giles, and an important operation was found to be necessary. A surgeon in the hospital named Warren undertook it. McGowan administered the anaesthetic. He overdid it purposely and deliberately murdered Mackie—the perfect crime. He then married Hilda Reid and left St. Giles with her.

It was after McGowan's death—he met with a fatal accident several days after his marriage—that all came out, and that Ward D, which Mackie had occupied, began to be haunted.

THE PHANTOM TRUMPETER OF FYVIE

FEW castles have figured as often in the ghost-lore of Scotland as Fyvie Castle in Aberdeenshire. Of the ancient Scottish baronial type of architecture, it was built during the latter part of the fourteenth century, probably on the site of a much earlier castle, in a wooded valley encircled by undulating hills.

It passed eventually into the possession of Sir Henry Preston of Craigmillar, who distinguished himself at the battle of Otterburn. Sir Henry, in order to enlarge his domain, demolished a neighbouring monastery and used the stones he took from it to add a tower, known afterwards as the Preston, to Fyvie Castle. During the transference of the stones from the monastery ruins to the castle three of them fell into the nearby river.

It was about this time that Thomas the Rhymer, Scotland's most prolific prophet and curser, came to the castle one day and solicited a night's shelter. Sir Henry would not admit him, and had the great gate of the castle shut in his face. From all accounts Thomas was very hasty tempered and quick to take offence. Full of indignation at being treated so inhospitably he stood in front of the castle and pronounced one of the curses for which he was so renowned.

A violent storm of rain and wind burst over the castle and grounds while Thomas was speaking, but round the spot where he stood there was a dead calm and the ground remained perfectly dry. This was regarded by the awed spectators as sure proof that Thomas was under supernatural protection and that no harm would or could befall him.

Thomas declared that until the three stones had been recovered the Fyvie property would never descend in the direct line for more than two generations.

Two of the stones were recovered, but the third was never found. Owing to a quantity of moisture being constantly found on one of the recovered stones, no matter how dry and warm the weather, the castle was sometimes styled the Castle of the Weeping Stone, weeping on account of the missing stone.

The curse Thomas pronounced is said to have worked until comparatively recent times.

Sir Henry Preston had only one child, a girl. She married a Meldrum, and on Sir Henry's death Fyvie passed into the possession of the Meldrum family. They did not own it long, for in 1596 they sold it to Alexander Seton, third son of George, Sixth Lord Seton. He was created Lord Fyvie and Earl of Dunfermline.

The Setons had an exceptionally honourable family history and were renowned for their loyalty to their sovereign, but, like Sir Henry Preston and the Meldrums, they would seem to have been under some kind of a blight while they remained in Fyvie Castle. This was believed to be owing to Thomas the Rhymer's curse.

The estate was forfeited when the fourth Lord Fyvie espoused the Jacobite cause and fought for the old Pretender. It was sold in 1726 to William, the Second Earl of Aberdeen, who bequeathed it to his son by his third wife, Lady Anne Gordon, sister of Lord Lewis Gordon. I understand that their descendants in the direct line died out some years ago.

There would seem to be some doubt as to when the traditional haunting of Fyvie Castle by the famous Phantom Trumpeter actually began, though it was during the eighteenth century. There are several versions of the tragic happenings that are popularly thought to have occasioned the haunting.

According to one of these versions, Andrew Lammie, a trumpeter in the service of the then owner of Fyvie, fell in love with Agnes Smith, daughter of a well-to-do local miller. Owing to the parents of Agnes strongly disapproving of her marrying a poor trumpeter, she and her lover used to meet clandestinely.

Unfortunately for Andrew he had a formidable rival in the Laird of Fyvie, who wanted Agnes for his mistress. The Laird, who was informed of the clandestine meetings of the lovers,

142

had Andrew seized, taken on board a ship and transported as a slave to the West Indies.

After several years Andrew luckily effected his escape and came back to Scotland. He at once sought Agnes, but was told she had died of a broken heart. The shock of her death proved too much for Andrew in his enfeebled state of health and he died too. On his death bed he cursed the Laird of Fyvie and swore that always before the death of a Gordon of Fyvie his trumpet would be heard either within or immediately without the castle walls.

According to another version of the story, the parents of Agnes Smith, angry with her for loving Andrew Lammie and rejecting the advances of the Laird of Fyvie, caused her death. But in spite of the harsh measures adopted by them, she put love and poverty before wealth and position and ever remained faithful to her poor despised sweetheart.

The story of her love for Andrew is immortalized in the well known Aberdeenshire ballad, 'Mill O' Tifty's Annie'. The poet has substituted the name Annie for that of her real name, Agnes. The following verses are taken from the ballad:

'Fyvie lands lie braid and wide.
　　And oh, but they be bonny!
But I wadna gie my ain true-love
　　For a' the lands in Fyvie.
'But mak my bed and lay me down,
　　And tarn my face to Fyvie
That I may see before I die,
　　My bonny Andrew Lammie.
They made her bed, and laid her down,
　　And turned her face to Fyvie
She gave a groan, and died or morn,
　　She ne'er saw Andrew Lammie.
The Laird of Fyvie he went hame,
　　And he was sad and sorry;
Says 'The bonniest lass O' the country-side
　　Has died for Andrew Lammie.'

143

Oh, Andrew's gane to the house-top
   O' the bonny house O' Fyvie;
He's blawn his horn baith loud and shrill
   O'er the lowland lass of Fyvie.
'Love pines away, loved wines away,
   Love—love decays the body;
For the love O' thee, now I maun dee;
   I come, my bonny Annie.'

And with those words he died.

A stone effigy on the summit of one of the castle's turrets is thought to represent Andrew Lammie, whose trumpet points in the direction of a monument erected in Fyvie kirkyard in memory of Agnes Smith.

It was soon after the death of Andrew Lammie that the haunting of Fyvie by a phantom believed to be his is said to have begun. For many years before the death of a Gordon of Fyvie the harrowing blast of a trumpet was heard in the dead of night, and the tall, menacing, shadowy figure of a man clad in a picturesque tartan was seen either within the castle walls or in close proximity to them.

Andrew's ghost was not, however, the only phantom that periodically visited Fyvie Castle. The ghost of a lady wearing a green dress was rumoured to appear at various times.

Issuing from a room known as the Haunted Chamber, she walked or rather glided through the winding passages and panelled rooms, ascending and descending the winding staircase, and, returning to the Haunted Chamber, disappeared in it with alarming abruptness. Who she was in her lifetime is not definitely known.

THE PHANTOM RIDER

QUEER, inexplicable things occasionally happen in the hunting field. They happened on the famous Dingborough Hunt. My friend Harry Martin, when he was living in Blankshire, joined the Dingborough. Harry, who was not quite thirty, held a commission in the Yeomanry, and though a good rider, was inclined to be a little too risky at times.

It was when he was with the hounds one day in February that a strange thing happened.

The pack met at Gilsby. It was fine when they started, but after they had run a fox down it became foggy, and they decided not to go on. One by one all the members of the hunt rode off, and Martin found himself alone. In clear weather he would not have minded, but in a fog and in a locality he did not know too well, he anticipated difficulty in getting home — a distance of twelve miles or more.

He was riding along disconsolate but trying to be cheerful, when he saw a little way ahead of him, riding in the same direction, a misty figure on a black or dark horse. He followed the rider, glad to have a companion in distress. By degrees the fog cleared, until he was able to see the rider very distinctly. It was a woman, a brunette, but to his surprise she was dressed in the picturesque costume of ages past.

Wondering who on earth she could be in such outlandish clothes he called to her, but there was no reply. Looking around him he could not see any familiar objects, and he realized with no little annoyance that he had lost his way. On and on rode the woman ahead; he shouted, and she must have heard him, but she still made no response, never once turning her head.

An eerie feeling came over him. She did not seem real, and the stillness and sense of isolation was so acute.

It was growing dusk. The woman quickened her speed, and Martin did the same, but without getting any nearer to her — always they were the same distance apart. Ahead of him the ground sloped, and the speed of both riders increased. Martin tried to rein his horse in but could not, it was as if the other horse magnetized it.

They were tearing now, the wind whirring in his ears, when ahead of them he saw to his horror a gaping pit. The woman rode straight for it. On reaching it she looked round, and for the first time he saw her face—white and lovely. She smiled at him, waved, and, signalling him to follow, leaped on horseback into the yawning chasm.

With a frantic effort he tore himself free of the saddle and crashed to the ground as his horse, never pausing, plunged madly forward over the brink, into the depths below. Dazed, Martin picked himself up—a few more feet and he would have been over the edge. He peered down but could see nothing—only blackness. He hurried away, and after some hours finally got to his destination, more dead than alive.

His story awoke interest, and he learned an explanation of what he had experienced. The locality of the pit was traditionally reputed to be haunted.

In the seventeenth century, living in the vicinity of the Dingborough Hunt were the Leeches, a new rich family. They had only very recently come to that part of the country. They had one child, Emily, a dark haired beauty, and among her many admirers was Robert Hunt, the only son of a widow. Robert, an unsophisticated youth of twenty, first saw Emily at a meet of the Dingborough, and fell violently in love with her. She encouraged his affections; his country manners and rawness amused her. But he was just her plaything, someone with whom to pass the idle moments till Lord Hartley, the man she wished to marry, returned from abroad. When he did, she gave the cold shoulder to Robert, and laughed in his face when he stammered that he loved her.

Bitterly grieved, Robert threw himself into the pit and was fatally injured. Before he died he cursed Emily, and declared that she would haunt the locality of the pit till Doomsday.

It was her ghost that Harry Martin must have seen; an apparition as beautiful as she was evil.

MY NIGHT IN OLD WHITTLEBURY FOREST

WHEN about to begin one of my nocturnal investigations I am not infrequently asked if I am feeling psychic—if I feel that I may see or hear something supernatural, or sense something hypernormal in the atmosphere of the place. Well, on the Thursday night of my arrival at Black House, some thirty miles from Northampton, I neither felt or sensed anything untoward.

The weather conditions, however, struck me as being distinctly favourable for a psychic manifestation of some kind. In my experiences in a variety of climates I have found that it is on nights when the weather is disturbed, as for example, when there is a thunderstorm, or it is very windy and raining hard, or at the other extreme when it is exceptionally fine and still, and the moon is full, that ghostly phenomena are most likely to occur. Also, I believe ghostly manifestations are largely dependent on the time of year, the late summer and early autumn being rather more conducive to them than any other period. Hence the conditions on that September night at Black House, when a strong wind moaned and whistled through the tree tops and set all the windows and doors jarring, were certainly in favour of my visit.

I had been told that the phantom of a man had been seen in various parts of the house, sometimes smoking a phantom pipe, when the smell of tobacco was distinctly noticeable, but beyond that I had heard little or nothing; consequently no stories about the place were running in my mind and I could rule out all possibility of suggestion.

Soon after my arrival at the house, while my two hostesses stood talking with my companions from the local newspaper, I got my first impressions. I suddenly sensed very strongly the presence of oak trees and stags. I mentioned this and learned for the first time that the house stood on ground that had once formed part of old Whittlebury Forest, which had abounded in oak trees and harboured many stags.

As the night was well advanced we began our sitting.

None of us being orthodox spiritualists we did not form a circle but individually found the first convenient seat. We sat in darkness and in silence. The outdoor conditions kept favourable; every now and then gusts of wind howled like a host of lost souls round and round the house.

Suddenly I was conscious of a curious change in the atmosphere of the room. A new element seemed to have entered it and intermingled with it, one that was very eerie. I was trying to diagnose this change when I felt a strong psychic current sweep past me in the direction of the door leading into the garden, close to which one of our hostesses, Miss H, was sitting. The change in the atmosphere at once became clearer; there was with us some elemental presence, something of the semi-human, semi-animal species that is associated with trees and forests.

At my request, one of our party had brought a dog with him, as dogs, in my opinion, are sure psychic barometers, invariably making some kind of demonstration when anything supernatural is at hand. My companion's dog now started to bark aggressively, as if there was something near at hand that it very strongly resented.

Through the window overlooking the front garden facing me I saw a leadenish blue light, or rather glow. It lasted a few seconds then gradually faded away. Other members of the party also saw luminary phenomena, but through a glass door that led to another part of the house. Some of these lights were in the form of a crescent and others a triangle.

During the whole time that these phenomena were manifesting intense excitement prevailed, a general thrill shared not only by my friend's dog but by several dogs belonging to the house, and located in various parts of it, for one and all began to bark savagely. When the lights eventually disappeared and the dogs became silent we relit the lamps.

We then related our respective experiences. Some of us

had heard ghostly footsteps moving about the premises, others had heard uncanny whistling; while there were those who had seen and heard nothing. I asked Miss H if she had been conscious of the psychic current that had swept past me, and she said she had. She had felt something very unusual and unpleasant suddenly approach her. She was quite sure that it was not the spirit of the smoker; she had seen him in the room directly afterwards but he was friendly. She thought that the phenomenon must be one of the numerous psychic entities that sometimes haunted the immediate vicinity of the house but which rarely entered it.

One of the other sitters told me afterwards that she was holding one of Miss H's hands at the time and could feel Miss H trembling violently.

After a short interval we sat in the darkness again. This time I, too, heard the uncanny whistling; it was just as if someone was standing by the window whistling to an animal and it was followed by the sound of faraway horse's hooves. The sounds drew rapidly nearer and seemed to pass through the room, dying gradually away in the distance. Directly afterwards I heard mutterings and whisperings. Then silence.

After a time Miss H relit the lamp and asked if anyone had heard the sounds of a horse in the room. I and several others told her that we had. She then informed us that she and Miss D had often heard the sounds of a horse tearing through the room, always at the same hour, namely two o'clock in the morning, the very time I had heard the sounds.

The sitting, which ended as dawn broke, had been successful in that it corroborated the statement of the two women, Miss H and Miss D, that Black House was really haunted. I afterwards looked up the history and traditions relative to Whittlebury Forest and found that the locality has throughout long centuries borne the reputation of being haunted.

One of the apparitions is that of a headless horseman, whose appearance is regarded as a portent of misfortune, even death. Happily no one saw the horseman that night. It is said to be more often seen in the lanes and fields in the neighbourhood of Black House.

A phantom lady is also said to haunt the site of old Whittlebury Forest as a punishment for her cruel treatment of one of her lovers. She is nocturnally hunted by a phantom huntsman and a pack of spectral hounds. It is this particular haunting that is said to have suggested to Dryden his poem of Theodore and Honoria.

THE FOURTH TREE IN THE AVENUE

ONE autumn evening four men sat in a room in a house in the Midlands. They were all members of a psychical research society, and among them was my friend Dr. Leonard Smyth. All they knew about the house was that it was rumoured to be badly haunted; they knew nothing specific.

It was eleven o'clock when they began the sitting, and it was not until nearly one o'clock that anything occurred. Smyth's dog Prince growled, and drew close to his master. A board in the room creaked and quivered, and there was a swelling on the floor.

The swelling grew and presently an aperture appeared. The four men gazed at it in fearful anticipation as something dark showed in the hole. It rose very slowly out of the floor—a head, the head of a woman with long, dishevelled dark hair, big, glossy dark eyes, and a corpse-like face, grey and drawn. The face of the long dead.

The four men gazed at it in horror, but more was to follow. Little by little the body of the woman rose to view, holding in her arms a dead baby. Rising completely out of the hole, the woman, carrying her ghastly child, glided noiselessly out of the room. From the distance came the banging of a door—then silence.

The four shaken men rose, took a sip of brandy, and left the house, feeling that they had had enough of ghostly horrors for one night.

They breathed freer in the open air. Outside the house a carriage drive led to an avenue of magnificent old trees. The four men entered the avenue and stopped at the fourth tree. Something made them halt there, a compelling sense, and they all experienced a wave of evil well from the tree. Although it was a calm night with no wind, the branches of

151

the tree were moving restlessly to and fro, and a vague shadow dangled momentarily from one of the branches.

When it was gone, the spell that had glued the men to the spot in front of the tree released them, and they went on to their respective destinations, satisfied that there was decided truth in the rumour that the house and grounds were haunted. The traditional story of the haunting they ferreted out afterwards.

They learned that in the eighteenth century, Squire Arnold had lived in the house. He engaged a housekeeper, Mary Anne Giles, young and attractive, and had no difficulty in seducing her. She then had a child. Tiring of her, the squire murdered both mother and child and buried the bodies under the floor of the room where the four men had sat.

The disappearance of the woman gradually became known, and a party of people set out to search the house. Arnold learned of their coming and, full of terror and remorse, hanged himself from the fourth tree in the avenue.

A NIGHT VIGIL AT CHRISTCHURCH

MANY people will remember the sensation caused in the neighbourhood of Bournemouth by the murder of Mr. Rattenbury, and the subsequent suicide of his clever and beautiful widow in a pool of the River Avon.

It was the hearing of rumours of ghostly happenings, supposedly arising from the widow's death, that led to my holding a vigil on a night in October, 1935, at the scene of her unhappy ending.

The morning of the day I selected for the vigil was very wet, but the weather improved later in the day. I arrived at Christchurch about noon and at once made inquiries concerning the rumours. The evening was well advanced when I eventually set out on my errand, armed with nothing more formidable than a thick stick and a torch. The spot where Mrs. Rattenbury had destroyed herself the previous June was a kind of backwater of the Avon, in a lonely meadow about 300 yards from a lane and close to some railway arches.

One of the stories I had heard was that a woman cycling along the lane one evening a few weeks before had heard a series of cries coming from the direction, so she thought, of the arches. There was something so unearthly and altogether unusual about the cries that she got off her bicycle at once and stood by a wooden gate leading into a meadow skirting the lane and facing the distant river.

By the railway embankment and arches was a shed, and as the woman stood listening she saw a blue light suddenly appear over this shed and then come towards her. As it drew nearer it took the form of a very tall person, wearing a shroud. No face was visible, but there was something so awesome about the figure, especially in the long strides it took, that the woman became terrified and, jumping on her cycle, pedalled frantically away.

153

Another story was said to have originated with a railway employee, who, when walking along the embankment one night, saw something very bright on the river bank. He climbed down to get a closer look, and to his surprise saw that it was a knife. On his approaching, the knife vanished, and he then noticed a commotion in the water. In one spot the water was whirling round and round, like a miniature whirl-pool. Then, suddenly it grew still, and out of it rose a hand. It was a very white hand with rather long, slender fingers, on one of which flashed and sparkled a ring. For some seconds the fingers clutched the air convulsively, and then the hand sank out of sight. The railwayman, who had all this time stood rooted to the ground with shock, now took to his heels, convinced that it was no human being he had seen in the whirl-pool.

These were not altogether nice stories to remember when I was padding the lane alone, but they would keep coming back to me; and I remembered also a third, the story of a cyclist who, when riding along the lane one night, soon after the Rattenbury tragedy, had, on getting near the embankment, seen a woman, young and smartly dressed, walking alongside him. Although he increased his speed, it made no difference; she still kept abreast of him, apparently without increasing her pace, and this continued for some little distance, when suddenly she quite inexplicably vanished. Three nights following he had the same experience, and always in that particular part of the road; but on none of these occasions could he ever see the woman's face with any degree of clearness. It always seemed to be hidden by a mist, though the rest of her, her arms, legs and body, stood out with startling distinctiveness. After the third night he is said never to have seen her again. I thought of this story whenever a cyclist came along.

As the night lengthened and the traffic grew less and less, till it practically ceased, a feeling of intense eeriness came over me. Later, as I came to a halt by a gate, which I imagined was the gate from which the woman had seen the shrouded

154

figure. I was conscious of a feeling of intense sadness. It came upon me quite suddenly, a terrible sadness that seemed due not to anything hitherto associated with me in any way, but to the surroundings—to something connected with what I saw; the long, lone railway embankment, with three gaping arches, the solitary hut, the great stretch of unkempt grass, flecked with stunted and oddly fashioned trees and the dikes of water, whose surface gleamed in the starlight.

I suddenly felt that something was coming along the lane. I say felt, because I saw and heard nothing, yet I was certain, as certain as I have been about anything in my life, that something had entered into the darkness of the night and was drawing near me. Nearer and nearer it drew, a nameless presence, one that brought with it increasing sadness. It came right up to me. I was conscious of it standing by my side looking at me, trying to read my innermost thoughts. I sensed beauty appertaining to it, beauty and youth, but not happiness or goodness; yet I felt it was not wholly evil. It passed on and left me, and with its departure I was no longer sad.

I left the gate and walked towards Rotten Row, but I had not gone far before I stopped—I felt I had to. I was near an isolated tree growing close to the laneside. A black mist rose out of the ground near a tree—I have never seen anything so unpleasantly black. I had not felt afraid when I had the experience near the gate, but I felt uneasy now.

The mist crept slowly towards me, indescribably sinister. I felt impelled to go back to the gate. When I got there a feel came over me that I must drown myself. The river had suddenly become a magnet. No longer dark and cold, it seemed now to give out light, a light that was most alluring and seductive; the light drew me on and I had to fight desperately to keep where I was and prevent myself succumbing to its fatal influence, which I instinctively associated with the mist. Then suddenly all desire to drown myself ceased.

Feeling that nothing further would occur, I now came away, to learn later that others had experienced some of the strange things I experienced there, in particular that terrible desire to drown oneself in the spot where Mrs. Rattenbury ended her life.

Is her spirit at rest? Some think not. I keep asking myself, was that sad presence hers? Did something draw her to the riverside as something tried to draw me, and was it that sinister black mist?

You must form your own conclusions on these strange happenings which are described exactly as they occurred.

THE HAUNTED STREAM

In Warwickshire there is a stream, deep in places, which in former days supplied a mill long disused with water.

In the nineties of the last century there was a family named Burton living in a house about half a mile from the stream; Mrs. Burton, an elderly widow, and two girls, Rose and Phoebe. Mrs. Burton, who had married late in life, was attractive at fifty and both the girls were very pretty, Rose being dark and Phoebe fair.

Rose was secretary to a rich man, and Phoebe a manicurist in a beauty salon. They were very fond of dancing and went on Saturday evenings to a dancehall in Birmingham about ten miles from Camly, where they lived. They went by train, as there were no motor vehicles in those days.

It was at the dancehall that they met a young man named Renton, the son of a brewer. He was tall, handsome and wealthy. The girls fell in love with him, and became rivals.

Renton preferred Phoebe, and they were engaged, but a dreadful tragedy prevented them marrying. Phoebe was drowned in the stream. How she got in the stream was a mystery; it was supposed that she fell in when returning from the dancehall—possibly she had drunk a little too freely.

It was two years after the tragedy that my friend Brian Richards went to live in Camly.

Mrs. Burton was dead. Rose had married Renton, sold the house, which her mother left her, and gone to live in France after divorcing her husband. The Waverley, the house where the Burtons had lived, had become a boarding house. Brian stayed there. It was kept by Mrs. Wills, a widow, and there were three servants who slept in the house: Mabel, the cook, and Emma and Lucy, the maids. Lucy Hart came daily, and a youth named Percy to clean shoes and do various outdoor

157

jobs. It was a very well run house. Everything had to be done as Mrs. Wills wished, in strict order, no idling.

All went smoothly with Brian the first week he was in the house. It was on the following Monday that something strange happened. He was on the landing of the first floor when, thinking that someone was calling him, he leaned over the balustrade and looked down. A girl in a pink dress was in the hall, a very pretty girl with flaxen hair and blue eyes. She was carrying a bunch of flowers, and he noticed a gold ring on one of her fingers, Her cheeks were very pale. Crossing the hall she entered the sitting-room.

Brian, who was strongly attracted by the girl, entered the room immediately after her, but she was not there, the room was empty. Yet there was only the one door and the lofty window was open only at the top.

Much puzzled he asked Mrs. Wills who the girl was. She did not know; there was no such person in her house, she said.

The next day about the same time Brian and Mr. Taylor, a fellow boarder, both saw the girl in pink cross the hall and enter the sitting-room. They told Mrs. Wills and she then confessed that the house was haunted. She begged them not to mention the ghost to the servants, or they would all leave. The two men had little choice but to promise not to say a word to anyone.

That evening Brian was brushing his hair at the dressing-table in his room when he saw reflected in the mirror a girl open the door and peer into the room—a girl with dark hair and eyes, who would have been very good looking but for her pallor and expression, which was clouded with hate. The reflection only lasted a few moments and he then saw only himself again. But the look of hatred in the girl's eyes haunted him, it was so diabolical.

Nothing further happened for some days. Then, one evening after dinner, he had another strange experience. He was walking along a lonely lane leading to the river, a distance of nearly half a mile from the house, when someone went by him.

It was the girl in pink. This time, however, she wore a green dress, and as she walked ahead of him he noticed something filmy and unreal about her that he had not observed before. She kept ahead of him to the stream. Close to the bank of it was a bush. She had just reached the bush when an invisible someone jumped out of it on to her. There was a cry of surprise and terror, followed by sounds of a desperate struggle between visible and invisible; a splash and the girl in green was in the water. As she sank, a white hand wearing a gold ring appeared above the surface of the stream clutching the air.

Throughout the swiftly enacted incident Brian felt as if he was witnessing something in a dream, yet his senses told him that it had actually happened—that he had been present at a battle of hate which had ended in murder.

What happened to Rose Burton, in France, was never known in Camly. The stream by the bush is still haunted.

THE CASTLE TERRORS

IRELAND is traditionally and primarily the land of the O's and Mc's, and most of the reputed haunted castles have belonged to one or other of those clans.

The picturesque ruins of Dunluce Castle, on a cliff in Ireland, are said to be haunted by the spirit of the original owner, who for his crimes was doomed to remain earthbound. Dunseverick Castle in Antrim is similarly haunted.

The old O'Neills of Tyrone, one of whose descendants is the Count O'Neill of Portugal, have, like my line of the O'Donnells, a banshee, which used to appear at Shane Castle. She was very lovely, and confined her advents to one room. Should she be seen merely pacing silently to and fro, her appearance boded no ill, but if she was seen wringing her hands or heard singing, her presence was a portent of some grievous catastrophe to a member of the clan. One of the O'Neills heard her voice prior to setting out on a long journey. A few days later he was killed.

The ancient Shane Castle was destroyed by fire in or about 1816.

An O'Flaherty of Galway was marching out of his castle one night on a foraging expedition, when he heard his traditional banshee singing sadly on one of the castle turrets. The following night his wife heard the banshee, and a few days later her husband's followers brought back his body; he had been killed by a member of a clan with which he had a feud.

On another occasion more than one banshee was heard singing at the castle of the O'Flahertys prior to the death of the wife of the clan chief.

The ruins of Ross Castle, Killarney, are rumoured to be haunted by the ghost of the O'Donohoe. Every few years in the dead of night he emerges from Ross Castle on his famous white horse, accompanied by his male and female followers, and rides three times round the lake of Killarney. That done, he returns with his retinue to the castle, and is seen no more for another decade.

Moving to Wales, in Brecknockshire are the ruins of Builth Castle. According to a traditional story, Llywelyn II of Gruffydd, the last actual Prince of Wales, came to Builth as a last resource, supposing it to be held by his friends. He rode there in the snow, having taken the precaution to have his horse shod backwards, so as to mislead any of his enemies who might be on his track. But he was refused admittance to the castle, and the blacksmith who shod his horse gave information to the English.

As Llywelyn returned, dejected and sore at heart, he was set upon and killed by Adam Francton, who was ignorant of his rank. Learning whom he had slain, Francton obtained permission to cut off the prince's head, and it was sent to Edward I at Rhuddlan, to be afterwards carried through the streets of London, while the body was buried at crossroads near the spot, which still bears the name of Cefynn-y-Bedd Llywelyn— 'The ridge of Llywelyn's grave'

The ruins of Builth Castle and the crossroads are both rumoured to be haunted, from time to time, by some of the spectres and unearthly sounds peculiar to Wales.

No counties in England or Wales are more haunted than Glamorganshire and Pembrokeshire. St. Donat's Castle in Pembrokeshire is reputed to have been haunted for many years by a phantom in white, believed to be the ghost of a Lady Stradling. And Gideon Shaddoe wrote in the last century about a castle in Glamorganshire that numbered among its several ghosts the phantom of a mail-clad hand and arm, which he saw one day thrust out of a window far beyond the ivy-clad wall of the ancient building. The bell of a church near the castle had been heard to toll 'of itself' on Hallowe'en.

Many wrecks have taken place off the rocky coast of Glamorganshire; after one of them, in which an evil local landowner was drowned, a black coach with four spectral horses was seen to drive from the seashore to his mansion. The coach was believed to contain the spirit of the drowned man, who for his many crimes was doomed to haunt the mansion and neighbouring countryside till the Day of Judgment.

A weird story is told of Linlithgow Palace in Scotland. One night in 1539 King James V cried out for torches, and on his attendants rushing into his chamber, he told them he had seen the ghost of the Laird of Balvearie. 'He came to me,' James said, 'and addressed me thus: "Oh, woe to the day that ever I knew thee or thy service; for serving of thee against God, against his servants, and against justice I am adjudged to endless torture." '

The laird died that night in his home, and the people who were with him affirmed that he had said those very words as the king had heard them in Linlithgow.

Dumbarton Castle has a much later ghost. During the seventies of the last century the two daughters of a captain, who was for years in command of the staff division stationed at the fort, were standing one moonlight night at the window commanding a view of the terrace, above which the sentry on duty had to walk. Suddenly one of the girls exclaimed: 'See, the sentry out there is pacing to and fro but he has no head!' The other sister looked out and saw a tall, headless man in an old-world uniform.

The next day, on the girls mentioning to friends what they had seen, they were told that the headless sentry at Dumbarton Castle had been a known fact in the county for hundreds of years.

The Castle of Duntulm was at one time reputed to be haunted by the ghost of Donald Gorm, who used to terrify the inmates by slamming doors, tramping up and down staircases, and making unearthly groans and cries. The disturbances did not cease until a young man sat up alone in the castle one night and, when the ghost of Donald Gorm appeared, arrayed in the tartan of his clan, the Macdonalds, spoke to it and learned the reason for it haunting the castle.

Dunstaffnage Castle, long in ruins, is said to have been haunted by a glaistig that, before the death of a member of the clan owning the place, used to wail in the building and tread along the passages and rooms, pulling the clothes from the beds of some of the sleepers, with dismal moans and cries.

Unlike the banshees of Ireland, the glaistigs of Scotland not only attach themselves to certain families but also to caves and streams and beaches. They vary in appearance, as do the Irish banshees. Some of them are old and withered, others very lovely, with long, golden hair and blue eyes. Sleat Castle, Breacacha Castle, the ruins of Mearnaig Castle and several other castles are all reputed to have been haunted at times by glaistigs.

A weird true story is told of a castle in the Hebrides. It is situated on a cliff and close to a mansion. Both buildings belong to a branch of the M——s. The castle is in ruins. One Christmas in the seventies of the last century the M——s gave a ball, and among the dancers were a Miss Ross and young M., the second son of the laird, who was in the Royal Navy.

When the dawn had broken Miss Ross and young M., who had been dancing together, walked to the castle ruins. Miss Ross was suddenly startled on seeing a girl, whom she took at first to be one of the other guests, gazing at her through what appeared to be an inaccessible window.

'Do look at that silly Maud Grey,' she said, 'she will be killed if she does not take care,' and she ran towards her, pulling her companion with her.

When she got close to the girl she saw she was not Maud Grey, but a young girl dressed entirely in white, with long fair hair falling over her shoulders, and having on her right arm a broad silver bracelet of curious design. The girl regarded Miss Ross fixedly for a moment, and then disappeared.

'Good heavens!' Miss Ross cried. 'She has fallen over the rocks.'

She ran to the window and looked out, but no traces of the girl were visible: indeed, no human being could have scaled the steep, precipitous crags on that side of the ruins. Miss Ross looked at her companion; he was very pale and silent.

On their way back to the house they met Maud Grey. She had never been near the ruins.

'Who could the girl have been?' Miss Ross asked young M.

'Don't mention her to any of the family,' M. replied. 'I will tell you who I think she was, but first let me ask if you noticed the bracelet on the girl's arm.'

'I did,' Miss Ross exclaimed, and described it to him.

M. became even paler and said: 'You have seen our evil family ghost. Her history is this: one of my ancestors and the heir of the M's fell deeply in love with a beautiful peasant girl. They became engaged and were about to be married, when the girl suddenly disappeared and was never heard of again. It was supposed she had been murdered by one of his relations, who was furious at the thought of him marrying a girl of such humble birth. For very many years there were preserved in our family two silver bracelets, such as you describe, with which our chiefs betrothed their brides. One of them had shortly before disappeared, and it was believed that the infatuated youth had given it to the poor girl whom he intended to marry.

'Ever since, we M——s have always been warned of an approaching death by a fair-haired girl with this bracelet on her arm.'

Young M. died soon after Miss Ross had seen the ghost.

THE HOUSE IN BERKELEY SQUARE

PROBABLY no case of haunting in England has ever attracted more attention than that which was alleged to take place at No. —— Berkeley Square. Berkeley Square lies in the very heart of Mayfair, and consequently, when it was rumoured that a house in such a fashionable and highly aristocratic surroundings had a ghost and a very terrible one too, all society at once become interested.

Lord Lyttelton wrote in 'Notes and Queries' for November 16, 1872: 'It is quite true that there is a house in Berkeley Square (No. ——) said to be haunted, and long unoccupied on that account. There are strange stories about it, into which this deponent cannot enter.'

And seven years later 'Mayfair' magazine stated: 'The house in Berkeley Square contains at least one room of which the atmosphere is supernaturally fatal to body and mind.'

For years the house continued to stand empty because of the dreadful, uncanny things said to occur there. Few people dared to pass it alone late at night.

Among the stories told me about the haunting is the following:

One bitterly cold night in December two sailors, named Stephens and Carey, who had come from Southampton to London on a week's furlough, having squandered all their money found themselves penniless with nothing to eat and nowhere to sleep.

After rambling forlornly along street after street, seeking in vain an archway or alcove where they could rest and find shelter from the icy wind, they came at length to Berkeley Square, silent and deserted.

They were leaning against the railings of the Square garden when Stephens suddenly said: 'Do you see that house over yonder, matey? It's to let. Why shouldn't we get in and do a night on the boards?'

Carey at once agreed. He was desperately tired, and the prospect of being able to lie down in the quiet somewhere, even if it was only in a coalhole, appealed to him.

Biding their opportunity, when no one was about the two seamen cautiously approached the house and slipped back the latch of one of the windows, which to their joy and surprise was not barred, and climbed into the house. Groping their way along a dank, dark passage they bumped against banisters and after a brief pause decided to venture aloft.

On reaching the second floor they decided to spend the night in one of the back rooms. It was a trifle more dismal and seemed in rather a worse condition than the other rooms they had seen, but on the outside wall near the window there was a pipe which could easily be got at should they be disturbed.

Feeling that a fire would be comforting they stole downstairs, careful lest their footsteps might be heard next door. Not finding any stray wood anywhere they broke up two or three fixed drawers in the kitchen dresser and, returning to the room they had chosen for the night, they soon had a fire. The heat from it gradually made them drowsy and presently they fell asleep.

They were abruptly roused by sounds in the lower part of the house. As they sat up and listened, the sounds likened to footsteps and began to ascend the stairs.

The footsteps might have been made with bare, fat feet, there was a curious shuffling stealthiness about them. They crossed the first floor landing and began to climb the stairs to the second floor.

A great terror gripped the sailors. The steps at length came on to the landing, approached the room and halted at the door, the handle of which began slowly to turn. After a period of agonizing suspense the two men saw the door slowly open and something of indescribable horror, neither human nor animal, appear on the threshold. As it moved stealthily towards the men the spell that had held them broke.

Stephens made a dash to the window, but so great was his terror that in grabbing at the water-pipe to climb down it he missed and crashed to the ground. The injuries he received were so severe that he died, but not before he was able to explain what had happened. Carey was found by a policeman early in the morning, roaming round and round the Square quite insane.

There is another story of the haunting of No. —— Berkeley Square.

A family whom I will call Jarvice, on coming to London one autumn took up residence in the house. After they had been in it for some weeks one of the maids, happening to go into the room in which the two sailors had suffered their harrowing experience, was shortly afterwards heard screaming for help. Fearing she was ill, Mrs. Jarvice ran to the room and found the girl lying on the floor in a fit.

The maid never properly recovered, but from her rambling statements it was inferred that her lamentable condition was solely due to something very dreadful that she had seen in the room. After this the room was kept locked, and no one ever ventured within its precincts, till a friend of the Jarvices, a Captain Raymond, who was engaged to one of the daughters, hearing what had happened, begged to be allowed to sleep there. He was so persistent that Mr. and Mrs. Jarvice finally gave in to him, on condition, however, that some arrangement was made by which he could summon aid if needed.

To this Raymond agreed, and it was decided that, in order to let the family know that all was going well with him, he should ring the bell by his bedside once every hour between midnight and dawn; if, on the contrary, something amiss should happen, and he should suddenly need help, he gave his most solemn assurance he would ring the bell twice.

The chosen night arrived, and as the captain retired to the room, the rest of the family, unknown to him, assembled together in the hall, no one daring to go to bed.

Very slowly the minutes passed away until midnight drew near. Then from afar off came the slow and measured chimes of the church clock. Simultaneous with the third stroke a bell gave a single, solitary tinkle, and everyone expressed themselves immeasurably relieved.

Again there came a wait, and the minutes crept tediously by with the family's nerves full stretched. Reassurance came from one of the Jarvice boys, who disclosed that the captain had in his possession a big service six-shooter; he had asked that no one be told about this in case they should be scared and fancy he might shoot someone with it.

Then suddenly all heard the bell. This time a clang, as if it had been pulled violently, then a slight pause, a very faint tinkle, and the loud crack of a revolver, after which silence.

Amid frenzied cries from the women a wild rush was made for the stairs, Mr. Jarvice leading the way, candle in one hand and poker in the other, to be joined en route by the servants, who came running down from their quarters on the top landing, with white and terrified faces.

On bursting into the room the family found Captain Raymond shot dead by his own revolver.

What terrible thing had forced his hand?

WILL-O'-THE-WISP AND CORPSE CANDLES

ONE of the most familiar of 'ghosts' to us all, perhaps, is Will-o'-the-wisp or Jack-a-Lantern.

Descriptions of this phenomenon vary. It is usually described as resembling the light of a lantern, varying in colour; sometimes leadenish blue, greenish or reddish, sometimes of no distinct colour at all. It is said sometimes to hover about, keeping close to the ground, while at other times it flits and bounces about in the air, occasionally following people at a distance.

According to one theory, Will-o'-the-wisp's 'haunting' is confined to marshy places, but this cannot be true. I have spent nights on marshy ground on Exmoor and Dartmoor and have never seen it; nor have I met any people in those localities who have seen it, so that the idea of it being just a marsh gas is erroneous.

Will-o'-the-wisp has also been said to be similar to the Welsh Canhywllau Cyrch—Corpse Candles—but this is incorrect. The corpse candles are invariably a portent of death, whereas Will-o-the-wisp is of no specific significance.

Will-o'-the-wisp has also been likened to Ph3, phosphorescent hydrogen, a gas exuding from decaying vegetable and carnal matter, said to be seen at times in cemeteries, to which it is apparently chiefly confined. This gas is seemingly sometimes the colour of Will-o'-the-wisp, but that is about the only peculiarity that the two have in common.

All gases have some heat and a characteristic smell but, according to accounts of Will-o'-the-wisp, it is entirely without heat or odour. In short, it is a baffling mystery, a phenomenon that has up to the present time never been satisfactorily explained.

Turning to the traditional corpse candles of Wales, when in various parts of Wales I have questioned people about these phenomena but have never met anyone who has seen them, though some have known people who have testified to seeing them. Belief in the candles is still strong in certain localities. The following account of them by the Rev. Mr. Davis is taken from 'News from the Invisible World' by T. Charley, published during the last century.

'We call them (the Canhywllau) candles because that light doth resemble a material candle-light; saving that when one comes near them they vanish; but presently appear again. If it be a little candle, pale or bluish, then follows the corpse either of an abortive, or some infant; if a big one, then the corpse either of someone come of age; if there be seen two or three or more, some big, some small, together, then so many such corpses together. If two candles come from divers places, and be seen to meet, the corpses will do the like; if any of these candles be seen to turn, sometimes a little out of that leads to the church, the following corpse will be found to turn in that very place.

'When I was about fifteen years of age, living at Llanylar, late at night, some neighbours saw one of these corpse candles hovering up and down along the bank of the river until they were weary in beholding; at last they left it so, and went to bed. A few weeks after a damsel from Montgomeryshire came to see her friends who lived on the other side of the Istwyth, and thought to ford it at the place where the light was seen; but being dissuaded by some lookers on (by reason of a flood) she walked up and down along the bank, where the aforesaid candle did, waiting for the falling of the waters, which at last she took and was drowned.'

In a wild and retired district in North Wales the following occurrence took place, to the great astonishment of the mountaineers (reported in 'Frazer's Magazine').

'We can vouch for the truth of the statement as many members of our own Teutu, or clan, were witnesses of the fact. On a dark evening, a few years ago, some persons with whom we are well acquainted were returning to Barmouth on the south or opposite side of the river. As they approached the ferry-house at Penthryn, which is directly opposite Barmouth, they observed a light near the house, which they conjectured to be produced by a bonfire, and greatly puzzled they were the reason why it should have been lighted. As they came nearer, however, it vanished and when they inquired at the house respecting it, they were surprised to learn that not only the people there displayed no light, but they had not even seen one; nor could they perceive any sign of it on the sands.

'On reaching Barmouth the circumstance was mentioned, and the fact corroborated by some of the people there, who had also plainly and distinctly seen the lights.

'It was settled therefore by some of the old fishermen that this was a "death-token"; and sure enough, the man who kept the ferry at that time was drowned at high water a few nights afterwards on the very spot where the light was seen. He was landing from the boat when he fell into the water, and so perished.

'The same winter the Barmouth people, as well as the inhabitants of the opposite banks, were struck by the appearance of a number of small lights, which were seen dancing in the air at a place called Borthwyn, about a mile from the town. A great number of people came out to see these lights and after a while they all but one disappeared, and this one proceeded slowly towards the water's edge, to a little bay where some boats were moored. The men in a sloop, which was anchored near the spot, saw the light advancing—they also saw it hover for a few seconds over one particular boat and then totally disappear. Two or three days afterwards, the man to whom that particular boat belonged was drowned in the river, while he was sailing about Barmouth harbour in that very boat. We have narrated these facts just as they occurred.'

I have several other accounts of these phenomena, all of them asserted to be authentic. Those who have seen them are convinced they are prophetically supernatural, omens of coming ill, only experienced by people of genuine old Welsh extraction.

Then there is the phenomenon of the churchyard ghost.

Herbert Mayo, M.D., in his book 'Popular Superstitions' published more than a hundred years ago quotes several cases of phenomenal lights appearing in churchyards and other places where people have been buried.

Here is one of the instances taken from 'Archives', a reliable German book by P. Kieffer. The story was sent to Kieffer by Herr Ehrman, who was told it by Herr Pfeffel, his father-in-law.

A youth named Billing, who was a candidate for Orders, had experienced sensorial illusions and was particularly sensitive to the presence of human remains, which made him tremble and shudder in all his limbs. Pfeffel, who was partly or wholly blind, was in the habit of holding the arm of Billing when taking a daily walk in his garden near Colmar.

At one spot in the garden Pfeffel felt Billing give a sudden start, as if he had received an electric shock. He asked Billing if anything was the matter. 'No, nothing,' Billing replied. But on their going over the same spot again the same thing happened. Billing, now being pressed to explain the cause of it, said that it arose from a peculiar sensation which he always experienced when in the vicinity of human remains; that it was his impression a human body must be interred there, but that if Pfeffel would return with him at night he would be able to speak with greater confidence.

Accordingly, they went together to the garden when it was dark, and as they approached the spot Billing said he could see a faint light over it. At ten paces from it he stopped and would go no further, saying that he saw hovering over it, as if self-supported in the air, its feet only a few inches from the ground, a luminous female figure nearly five feet high, with the right arm folded on her breast, the left hanging by her side. When Pfeffel stepped forward and placed himself about where the figure appeared to be, Billing declared it was now on his right hand, now on his left, now behind, now before him. When Pfeffel cut the air with his stick, it seemed as if it went through and divided a light flame, which then united again. The experiment was repeated the next night, in company with some

172

of Pfeffel's relatives, and gave the same result. Only Billing was conscious of the apparition, the others did not see anything.

Pfeffel then, unknown to Billing, had the ground dug up, when was found at some depth, beneath a layer of quick-lime, a human body in progress of decomposition. The remains were removed and the earth carefully replaced. Three days afterwards Billing, from whom this whole proceeding had been concealed, was again led to the spot by Pfeffel. He walked over it without experiencing any unusual impression whatever.

Mayo, who was partly if not entirely a materialist, was seemingly in accordance with Prof. Von Reichenbach, a German scientist, who believed in what Mayo termed the Od force; that is, a gas which is said to make itself visible as a dim light or warning flame to highly sensitive subjects. Such persons, according to Mayo and Reichenbach, see flames issuing from the poles of magnets and crystal, one of the causes which excites the evolution of the gas being chemical decomposition: in other words, decaying bodies of human beings.

Von Reichenbach experimented with a Miss Reichel in a cemetery near Vienna. Wherever Miss Reichel looked she saw masses of flame, which manifested mostly about recent graves. She described the appearance of the lights as resembling less bright flames than fiery vapour, something between fog and flames, the lights rising to four feet above the ground. Miss Reichel did not apparently feel any heat exuding from the flames when she put her hand in them.

Von Reichenbach, who had learned about Pfeffel's experiments with Billing, concluded that the luminant phenomena Billing declared he had seen in Pfeffel's garden were due to the same cause as those Miss Reichel said she saw in the cemetery near Vienna. Pfeffel and Von Reichenbach apparently believed that all ghosts said to be seen in churchyards were due to this natural gas.

But were they? Are they? If due to a.natural gas, how is it more people have not seen them? It is more credible to believe that these alleged luminary phenomena in cemeteries may be

173

due to the supernatural. I have seen no satisfactory explanation yet stated as to why these ghostly lights should be apparently restricted to places where dead humans are buried. Why not dead animals? What hosts of these mysterious lights would appear if they too were included!

Another luminant phenomenon is St. Elmo's Fire, a light said to be seen at sea, especially in southern climates, often during thunderstorms. Of a light resembling a kind of star, it has appeared at the top of masts of ships, spires, other pointed objects, on the tops of trees, on the manes of horses, even occasionally on human heads.

Scientists, who of course believe all luminant phenomena are due to a natural cause, believe that St. Elmo's Fire finds an explanation in a rapid production of electricity. If this is so, surely expert electricians could produce a St. Elmo's Fire on any of the aforesaid objects. But have they ever done so?

I do not doubt that such lights have been seen, there is ample evidence to prove that; but the theory that electricity is the sole explanation of the phenomena does not seem to me to be wholly satisfactory.

Like in the other true tales and legends we have seen, science has so much to explain before we can even begin to enter the province of the unknown.

THE HOUSE OF THE BLOODY CAT

I CAN see Mrs. Hartnoll in my mind's eye as distinctly as if I were looking at her now. Hers was a personality that no lapse of time, nothing could efface; a personality that made itself felt on boys of all temperaments.

She was classical mistress at the dame school in Clifton, Bristol, where for three years I was well grounded in all the mysticisms of Kennedy's Latin Primer and Smith's First Greek Principia.

I doubt if Mrs. Hartnoll—we never knew her first name— got anything more than a very small salary, for governesses in those days were shockingly remunerated and the poor soul had to work monstrously hard. Drumming Latin and Greek into heads as thick as ours was no easy task.

But there were times when, the excessive tension on the nerves proving too much, Mrs. Hartnoll stole a little relaxation; when she allowed herself to chat with us, and even to smile—Heavens! those smiles! And when she spoke about herself, stated she had once been young—a declaration so astounding, so utterly beyond our comprehension, that we were rendered quite speechless— and told us anecdotes.

Of her many narratives there is one in particular that remains

175

as fresh in my mind as when she first recounted it. I give it now as far as possible in her own words, as we all heard it then, in that hushed classroom :

"Up to the age of nineteen, I lived with my parents in the Manor House at Oxenby. It was an old building dating back, I believe, to the reign of Edward VI, and had originally served as the residence of noble families. Built, or rather faced with split flints, and edged and buttressed with cut grey stone, it had a majestic though very gloomy appearance, and seen from afar resembled nothing so much as a huge and grotesquely decorated sarcophagus. In the centre of its frowning and menacing front was the device of a cat, constructed out of black shingles and having white shingles for the eyes. The effect of this was curiously realistic, especially on moonlight nights, when anything more lifelike and sinister could scarcely have been conceived. The artist, whoever he was, had a more than human knowledge of cats—he portrayed not merely their bodies but their souls.

"In style the front of the house was somewhat castellated. Two semi-circular bows, or half towers, placed at a suitable distance from each other, rose from the base to the summit of the edifice, to the height of four or five stairs; and were pierced, at every floor, with rows of stone-mullioned windows. The flat wall between had larger windows, lighting the great hall, gallery, and upper compartments. These windows were wholly composed of stained glass, engraved with every imaginable fantastic design—imps, satyrs, dragons, witches, queer-shaped trees, hands, eyes, circles, triangles and cats.

"The towers, half included in the building, were completely circular within, and contained the winding stairs of the mansion. To ascend the stairs when a storm was raging was to feel that you were being risen by a whirlwind to the clouds.

"In the upper rooms even the wildest screams of the storm were drowned in the rattling clamour of the assaulted casements. When a gale of wind took the building in front, it rocked it to the foundations, and at such times threatened its instant demolition.

"Midway between the towers there stood forth a heavy stone

176

porch with a Gothic gateway, surmounted by a battlemented parapet, made gable fashion, the apex of which was garnished by a pair of dolphins, rampant and antagonistic, whose corkscrew tails seemed contorted—especially at night—by the last agonies of rage convulsed. The porch doors stood open, except in tremendous weather; the inner ones were regularly shut and barred after all who entered. They led into a wide vaulted and lofty hall, the walls of which were decorated with faded tapestry that rose, and fell, and rustled in the most mysterious fashion every time there was the suspicion—and often barely the suspicion—of a breeze.

" Interspersed with the tapestry, and in great contrast to its antiquity, were quite modern and very ordinary portraits of my family. The general fittings and furniture, both of the hall and house, were sombre and handsome : truss-beams, corbels, girders and panels were of the blackest oak, and the general effect of all this, augmented, if anything, by the windows, which were too high and narrow to admit of much light, was very similar to that produced by the interior of a subterranean chapel.

" From the hall proceeded doorways and passages, more than my memory can now particularize. Of these portals, one at each end conducted to the tower stairs, others to reception rooms and domestic offices.

" The whole of the house being too large for us, only one wing—the right, and newer of the two—was occupied. The other was unfurnished, and generally shut up. I say generally because there were times when either my mother or father—the servants never ventured there—forgot to lock the doors, and the handles yielding to my daring fingers, I surreptitiously crept in.

" Everywhere in that unused wing, even in daylight, even on the sunniest of mornings, were dark shadows that hung around the ingles and recesses of the rooms, the deep cupboards, the passages, and the silent, winding staircases.

" There was one passage, long, low and vaulted, where these shadows assembled in particular. I can see them now as I saw

177

them then, as they have come to me many times in my dreams, grouped about the doorways, flitting to and fro on the bare, dismal boards, and congregating in menacing clusters at the head of the staircase leading to the cellars. Generally, and excepting when the weather was particularly violent, the silence here was so emphatic that I could never feel it was altogether natural, but rather that it was assumed especially for my benefit —to intimidate me. If I moved, if I coughed, almost if I breathed, the whole passage was filled with hoarse, reverberating echoes.

"Once, when fascinated beyond control, I stole on tiptoe along the passage, momentarily expecting a door to fly open and something grim and horrible to pounce out on me, I was brought to a standstill by a loud clanging noise, as if a pail had been set down very roughly on a stone floor. Then came the sound of rushing footsteps and of someone hastily ascending the cellar staircase. Fearful as to what I should see, I stood in the middle of the passage and stared. Up, up, up they came, until I saw the dark, indefinite shape of something very horrid. It was accompanied by the clanging of a pail. I tried to scream, but my tongue cleaving to the roof of my mouth prevented me, and when I tried to move I found I was temporarily paralysed. The thing came rushing down on me. I grew icy cold all over, and when it was within a few feet of me, my horror was so great I fainted.

"On recovering consciousness it was some minutes before I summoned up courage to open my eyes, but when I did so they saw nothing but the empty passage—the thing had disappeared.

"On another occasion when I was guiltily paying a visit to the unused wing, and was about to ascend one of the staircases leading from this same passage to the first floor, there was the sound of a furious scuffle overhead and something dashed down the stairs past me. I instinctively looked up, and there, glaring down at me from over the balustrade, was a very white face. It was that of a man, but very badly proportioned, the forehead being low and receding, and the rest of the face too long and narrow. The crown rose to a kind of peak, the ears were pointed and set very low down and far back. The mouth was very cruel and thin-lipped; the teeth were yellow and uneven. There was no hair on the face, but that on the head was red and matted. The eyes were obliquely set, pale blue, and full of an expression so malignant that every atom of blood in my veins seemed to congeal as I met their gaze.

" I could not clearly see the body of the thing as it was hazy and indistinct, but the impression I got of it was that it was clad in some sort of tight-fitting, fantastic garment. As the landing was in semi-darkness and the face at all events was most startlingly visible, I concluded it brought with it a light of its own, though there was none of that lurid glow attached to it, which I subsequently learned is almost inseparable from spirit phenomena seen under similar conditions.

" For some seconds I was too overcome with terror to move, but my faculties at length reasserting themselves, I turned and flew back to the other wing of the house.

" One would have thought that after these experiences nothing would have induced me to have run the risk of another such encounter, yet only a few days after the incident of the head I was again impelled to visit the same quarters. In sickly anticipation of what my eyes would alight on, I stole to the foot of the staircase and peeped cautiously up. To my great relief there was nothing there but a bright patch of sunshine, which, in the most unusual fashion, had forced its way through from one of the slits of the windows near at hand.

" After gazing at it long enough to assure myself it *was* only sunshine, I continued on my way down the vaulted passage. Just as I was passing one of the doors, it opened. I stopped— terrified. What could it be? Bit by bit, inch by inch, I watched the gap slowly widen. At last, just when I felt I must either go mad or die, something appeared—and to my utter astonishment, it was a big black cat! Limping painfully it came towards me with a curious gliding motion, and I saw with a thrill of horror that it had been very cruelly maltreated. One of its eyes looked as if it had been gouged out, its ears were lacerated, and the paw of one of its hindlegs had either been torn or hacked off. As I drew back from it, it made a feeble and pathetic effort to reach me and rub itself against my legs, as is the way with cats, but in so doing it fell down, and uttering a half purr, half gurgle, vanished—seeming to sink through the hard oak boards.

" That evening my youngest brother met with an accident in the barn at the back of the house, and died. Though I did not then associate his death with the apparition of the cat, the latter shocked me very much, for I was extremely fond of animals. I did not dare venture into the unused wing again for nearly two years.

" When next I did so, it was early one June morning, between five and six, and none of the family, saving my father, who was out in the fields looking after his men, were as yet up. I explored the dreaded passage and staircase, and was crossing the floor of one of the rooms I hitherto regarded as immune from ghostly influences, when there was an icy rush of wind, the door behind me slammed so violently, and a heavy object struck me with great force in the hollow of my back. With a cry of surprise and pain I turned sharply round, and there, lying on the floor, stretched out in the last convulsions of death, was the big black cat, maimed and bleeding as it had been on the previous occasion. How I got out of the room I don't recollect, I was too horror stricken to know exactly what I was doing; but I distinctly remember that as I tugged the door open there was a low, gleeful chuckle, and something slipped by me and disappeared in the direction of the passage. At noon that day my mother had a seizure, and died at midnight.

" Again there was a lapse of years—this time nearly four— when, sent on an errand for my father, I turned the key of one of the doors leading into the empty wing, and once again found myself within the haunted precincts. All was just as it had been on the occasion of my last visit. Gloom, stillness and cobwebs reigned everywhere, while permeating the atmosphere was a feeling of intense sadness and depression. I did what was required of me as quickly as possible, and was crossing one of the rooms to make my exit, when a dark shadow fell athwart the threshold of the door, and I saw the cat.

"That evening my father collapsed and died as he was hurrying home through the fields. He had long suffered from heart disease.

"After his death we—that is to say, my brother, sisters and self—were obliged to leave the house and go out into the world to earn our living. We never went to Oxenby again, and never heard if any of the subsequent tenants of the house experienced similar manifestations."

So ended Mrs. Hartnoll's story. But the sequel to it came, for me, years later, when as a young man I stayed for a few weeks near Oxenby and met, at a garden party, a Mr. and Mrs. Wheeler, the then occupants of the Manor House.

I asked if they believed in ghosts, and told them I had heard their house was haunted.

"Well," said Mrs. Wheeler, "we never believed in ghosts till we came to Oxenby, but we have seen and heard such strange things since we have been in the Manor House that we are now prepared to believe anything."

They then went on to tell me how they—and many of their visitors and servants—had seen in one wing of the house the phantasms of a hideous and malignant old man, clad in tight fitting hosiery of medieval days, and a maimed and bleeding black cat, a big creature that seemed sometimes to drop from the ceiling and sometimes to be thrown at them.

In one of the passages, said the Wheelers, all sorts of queer sounds, such as whinings, moanings, screeches, and the clanging of pails and rattling of chains, were heard, while something that no one could ever see distinctly, but which they all felt to be indescribably obscene, rushed up the cellar steps and flew past, as if engaged in a desperate chase. The disturbances grew to be so frequent and so harrowing that the wing had to be vacated and was eventually locked up.

But the Wheelers, being more resolute than earlier tenants, did not leave the situation at that. They decided to excavate in different parts of the haunted wing, with grim results. In the cellar, at a depth of some eight or nine feet, they found the skeletons of three men and two women. And in the wainscoting of the passage they discovered the bones of a boy.

The remains were taken away and given decent burial in the churchyard.

Everything now seemed to bear out local tradition, which had been handed down through centuries by word of mouth. This was to the effect that the Manor House originally belonged to a knight who, with his wife, was killed while out hunting. He had only one child, a boy of about ten who became a ward in chancery. The man appointed by the Crown as guardian to this child proved an inhuman monster, and after ill-treating the lad in every conceivable manner, eventually murdered him and tried to substitute a bastard boy of his own in his place. For a time the fraud succeeded, but on its eventually being found out, the murderer and his offspring were both brought to trial and hanged.

During the guardian's occupation of the house many people were seen to enter the premises but never leave them, and consequently the place got the most sinister reputation. Among other deeds credited to the murderer and his offspring was the mutilation and boiling of a cat—the particular pet of the young heir, who was compelled to witness the whole revolting process. Years later, a subsequent owner of the property had a monument erected in the churchyard to the memory of this poor abused child, and on the front of the house constructed the device of the cat.

Mr. and Mrs. Wheeler invited me to visit the now quietened and reopened wing at the Manor House, and as I paced the old rooms I vividly recalled Mrs. Hartnoll's experiences there; and wondered whether news of the later remarkable events at her former home ever reached her.

MY FIRST GHOSTS

I HAD seen my first ghost long before Mrs. Hartnoll told us her story of Oxenby. This was as a young boy in Ireland, in the old house where I was born, in the 'seventies, the son of a Church of England country vicar.

I was just five years old and had been put to bed at my usual hour, but on a long summer's day. The sun was still shining, and the light came through the drawn blinds, preventing me from going to sleep. As I lay on my side, trying to relieve the boredom of my own company by counting the spots on the counterpane of the bed parallel with mine, the door handle suddenly gave a little click. I glanced round and saw that it was being very slowly turned.

Wondering who was outside, and thinking their slowness in entering the room was from a belief that I was already asleep, I watched the slowly moving handle with casual interest. Gradually, very gradually, the door opened, and when at length it had opened perhaps a couple of feet an extraordinary figure suddenly shot into view and, taking up its position against the wall just inside the room, stood and regarded me with the greatest intentness.

It appeared to me to be about six feet high. That is to say, about the same height as a certain tradesman who came regularly every morning for orders, and whom I had heard said was " a good six feet." I also thought the figure looked very strong and powerful, but the extreme length of its arms and the massiveness of its head, which was disproportionately large for its body, gave it a grotesqueness that was considerably increased by its being nude and covered in places with large yellow spots.

Its eyes were yellowish green and sphinx-like. There was nothing in the face to denote the thing's attitude towards me, whether hostile, friendly or merely indifferent. It stood staring at me fixedly for some time, and then turning round, walked out of the room, closing the door noiselessly behind it. It had not menaced me so I was not frightened.

When I spoke about it in the morning to my mother she told me I must have been dreaming. It was not until several years later, after her death, that I learned for the first time that the house was haunted and that other people besides myself had seen strange, inexplicable shapes in it.

My next encounter with a ghost occurred just four years later, in Wales—at the Devil's Bridge, near Aberystwyth. One August afternoon I was descending the steep pathway leading to what is very appropriately known as the Devil's Punch Bowl, when looking behind me I saw a tall, shadowy figure suddenly bound across the track and disappear into the dense foliage.

In shape it closely resembled one of those old-fashioned wooden Dutch dolls. It had the same kind of thin, long arms and legs, which appeared to move all in a piece, and a perfectly round head, somewhat too small for its body. Owing to the shade from the trees and the speed with which it moved, for it simply flashed across the pathway, I could not see its features very clearly, but I was left with the impression of a mere caricature of a human face. It did not seem in any way evil or antagonistic.

Later, when travelling back to Aberystwyth with some friends in the wagonette we had hired for the outing, I mentioned the incident to the driver and asked if he could in any way account for it.

"Well," he replied, "they do say around here as how the valleys of the Rheidol and Mynach are both haunted, more particularly, perhaps, the Punch Bowl and the old Devil's Bridge itself. I can't say that I've ever seen anything there myself, but my father used to say he once saw the Canhywllau Cyrth (Corpse Candles) on the old bridge the night a farmer friend of his in the valley died; and my grandmother declared she saw the Neuaddlywd Toili (phantom funeral procession) cross the new bridge over the gorge the day before one of her sisters was buried."

I had another experience of a Welsh haunting only the following year, in Penmaenmawr, where I was spending the summer holidays. I was awakened one night by the most extraordinary noise. It was like a loud flapping of wings, and was accompanied by a curious croaking and groaning. The sounds seemed to come from the street (my bedroom was in the front of the house), and after continuing for some minutes they abruptly ceased.

In the morning I described what I had heard to our landlady and she said: "It was the Gwrach y Rhibyn, or Hag of the Dribble. My husband and I both heard it, and Mrs. Thomas over the way saw it beating its wings against the window frames of her room and looking in at her. One of her children is ill, and she says she is sure the Gwrach y Rhibyn came for the boy and that he won't last through the day."

She then went on to explain that the Gwrach y Rhibyn was a strange, shadowy form resembling in one part a dreadful old hag with a skull-like face and gleaming eyes, and in the other part, a monstrous bat. She said it only haunted people of genuine old Welsh extraction and never came to them except before a death. If it was heard merely to flap its wings and groan, it portended the death of some more or less distant relative of the family it haunted; but if it was seen looking in at the window or heard calling anyone by name, then it portended the death of the person named, or one of the family in the house.

I asked if it was usual for others than relatives or members of the haunted family to hear it, and she said: "No, unless they have Welsh blood in them." I then told her that I had a strain of Welsh blood in me, and she replied: "Then I've no doubt you did hear the Gwrach y Rhibyn in the night," adding with a look of grim certainty, "That Thomas child will be dead before morning."

And sure enough what she said was true, for late that evening we learned that the "Thomas child," who had been ill for some time, had suddenly taken a turn for the worse and was dead.

I had another unusual experience a few days after this. I was walking one afternoon with my old nurse along a lane near Penmaenmawr, when I noticed a solitary willow growing by a pool on one side of the road, swaying about in a very peculiar manner. Although the day was piping hot and there was no wind, the tree shook as if in the throes of a great storm.

I remarked on the sight to my companion, but she did not reply; instead she turned very pale and quickened her pace. It was not until we had got back to Penmaenmawr that I could prevail upon her to say a word, and then only by much coaxing. However, when the landlady came in to lay the tea, my old nurse's tongue seemed suddenly loosened. She told the landlady of the walk we had taken, and asked her if there was anything wrong with the willow growing by the pool in the lane.

"You mean the lane running in the direction of Llangelynin?" our landlady said. "Because they do say it's haunted. One or two people have from time to time been found drowned in the pool, and there is a story about some old tramp hanging himself on the tree. Anyhow, the spot has got a bad name, and the people round here don't care for passing it after dark, especially if they're alone."

"Well," said my nurse, "I don't need to be told that the tree's haunted, for as sure as I'm alive I saw a skeleton in a winding-sheet sitting on one of its branches, and it was he that made the tree shake. He was swaying to and fro and laughing at us as we went by."

I might state here that, interested as I was in having had, at this early age, perhaps more than my fair share of encounters with the supernatural, I certainly had no ideas of pursuing the subject. Nor was I particularly interested in ghost stories, for I was inclined to be as nervous as the next person of such things.

There was, however, much more in store for me.

From preparatory school in Clifton I went on to spend five years at College. I then went for a time as a pupil on a farm in Scotland; spent two years with an Army crammer in Clifton; and then read for an inspectorship in the Royal Irish Constabulary, at the Queen's Service Academy, Dublin. It was while I was thus occupied, living in rooms in Upper Leeson Street, that I had my first experience of what I might justly term a dangerous ghost.

I had retired one night a little earlier than usual, for I was very tired, and had just got into bed, when I heard a slight noise coming, apparently, from one of the window recesses. Glancing quickly in that direction I saw something stir. I had put out my candle, but the moonbeams filtering in between the folds of the thick plush curtains that hung across the windows illuminated the room sufficiently for me to see, though not very distinctly, any large object in it. And now, as I stared in wonder—and, I admit, not a little fear—I saw something rise from the floor and advance towards me.

In the dim light it was too vague for me to describe accurately; I can only say that it gave me the impression of being something very sinister, something only partly human in form, and wholly antagonistic. It advanced so quickly that before I had time to move or utter a sound, it was gripping me by the throat with long clammy " fingers ", and pressing me backwards—down, down, down, until my head finally touched the pillow.

I gasped, choked, and suffered the most excruciating sensations of strangulation, but there was no relaxation. The pressure from those deadly " fingers " continued until I eventually lost consciousness.

On coming to, I found myself alone. The thing, whatever it was, had gone. But I was far too terrified to move, and it was not for some time that I ventured to raise my head and look around. The dawn had broken, and it was quite light. Just to satisfy myself that no one could have got in from outside, I got up and examined the door and windows. The door was locked on the inside, just as I had left it before getting into bed, and the windows were bolted.

I got back into bed and lay there trembling until I was eventually called. My landlady raised no objections when I asked to be moved to another room, and after much persistent questioning on my part she finally admitted that the house, and particularly the room I had occupied, was haunted. She told me that the house had once been a private home for the mentally afflicted, and that according to rumour, someone, either one of the patients or a nurse, she did not know which, had died in that room under extremely tragic circumstances.

Not surprisingly I was totally unable to sleep in the other room to which I was moved, and so I left the house and found quarters elsewhere.

It might be thought with some justification that such an experience would have cured me of any further curiosity regarding ghosts. But it did not. When I heard that a locality in the Wicklow Hills, near the junction of four crossroads, was reputed to be "fairy haunted ", I took a room in a cottage close to the spot, intending to hold a night-watch at the crossroads.

On my arrival at the cottage, feeling tired after a long cycle ride, I decided to hold my first vigil the following night, and went to bed early. The night was so beautiful, however, that before undressing, I leaned out of the window of my room and drew in deep breaths of the clover-scented air. The view was compelling. Before me, gleaming white in the moonlight, lay the crossroads, silent and deserted, a scene that so fascinated me that it took an effort to tear myself away from it. But I eventually did so, and having got into bed, was soon sound asleep.

I awoke with my heart pounding. No sound disturbed the

stillness of the night, and I was pondering over this and comparing the silence of the hills with that of the city I had just left, when I suddenly caught the sound of footsteps in the far distance. It was someone running with long, even strides, and as the sounds drew near, I became aware of something about them that was both unusual and disconcerting. On they came, sharp and well defined; nearer and nearer still, until they were quite close to the cottage. Then a dog in the yard at the back of the premises set up a mournful howling, and I heard Mrs. Mullins, the wife of the owner of the cottage—the couple occupied a room close to mine—say: " John, do you hear the dog?"

" I should be deaf and no mistake if I didn't," her husband replied peevishly. " What's bothering him?"

" You may well ask that," Mrs. Mullins retorted. " Listen!" And as she spoke, I could hear the footsteps crunching their way up the gravel path to the front door. There they stopped. It then struck me, more forcibly than before, that there was something peculiar about them, something that made them different from any other footsteps I had ever heard; but what exactly that something was I could not for the life of me say.

" John," Mrs. Mullins suddenly began again— " I don't like those footsteps. Who and what can they be? It's the first time I've heard anyone running along the road, past the crossroads too, at this hour. And what can they be doing in the garden? Do get up and make sure the front door is locked."

She had hardly spoken before there came a loud knock, to be speedily followed by a second, and then, after a brief interval, a third.

I heard the husband get up, shuffle his way to the front door and inquire who was there. But I did not hear any reply. Curiosity prompting me, I got out of bed and going to the window, which almost overlooked the front door, peered out. To my astonishment there was no one to be seen. In front of me lay the fields and crossroads, with the gently sloping hills beyond, all sleeping peacefully in the brilliant moonlight. No sign of a caller, and yet I had heard no one go away.

In the morning after I had finished breakfast, Mrs. Mullins asked if I intended staying any longer, and when I said that I had changed my mind and had now decided to leave that afternoon, she showed unmistakable relief.

" Did you hear anything in the night?" she asked.

" Only someone knocking at the front door. There was nothing the matter, I hope?"

" Why, no," she said, with a queer expression in her eyes. " Nothing the matter exactly, but my husband and I didn't like what we heard in the night at all. We have never heard footsteps like those before, and we believe they came for you. I should have been obliged to ask you to go, if it hadn't been that you have said you will go yourself." And she fingered the edge of the tablecloth nervously as she spoke.

" I don't understand," I said. " Who was it that knocked, and what makes you think they had any business with me?"

" It wasn't anybody," she replied, " because when I looked out of the window no one was there. It was a spirit, sir," here she crossed herself solemnly, " and it has something to do with you."

Seeing that she was so very serious, I then told her of my experience with the strangling ghost in Leeson Street, and she expressed the opinion that it was this ghost that had followed me to the cottage.

" In County Galway, where I come from," she said, " they believe that ghosts sometimes attach themselves to people and follow them about. I only hope and trust this one will never do you any harm and that you will speedily get rid of it."

Well, I left the cottage that afternoon. Even if the woman had been willing for me to stay, nothing would have induced me to do so, for whether she was right in her theory about the footsteps or not, I could not endure the thought of another night near those forlorn crossroads.

One other incident occurred during my stay in Dublin. I was very fond of fishing and often spent Saturday fishing either at Dalkey or some neighbouring spot. On the last of these fishing expeditions I engaged a boatman to row me to the Mugglestone rocks, which lie a little beyond Dalkey, and on arriving there told him to row back to shore and come for me again at six in the evening.

It was about 11 a.m. when I first threw in my line, and all the time I fished that day I had the curious sensation that someone was standing at my elbow watching me. I could feel eyes following my every movement, yet when I turned round to look, which I did several times, no one was there. The island consisted entirely of bare rock, affording no cover of any kind, so that had anyone been on it I should most certainly have seen him.

Now as a rule I had no cause to complain of poor sport. But I could not catch a thing that day, and I was glad when the boatman turned up earlier than expected at four o'clock to row me back. I asked him, none the less, why he had come two hours before his time, to which he replied indignantly: " Well, that's a queer question to ask! I came because you signalled me to come."

" But I did no such thing," I said. " Where were you?"

" Why, I was rowing about," he said, " some little distance off, and happening to look in the direction of the island, I distinctly saw you wave your handkerchief at me, which meant you wanted me to come—and all I can say is if you didn't stand up and wave a handkerchief, then the ghost did."

This very matter-of-fact allusion to a ghost struck me as being distinctly comical, and I laughed outright. Consequently it was some time before I could persuade my would-be rescuer to say another word. But he got over his annoyance after a time, and explained to me that some years previously the body of a drowned sailor had been washed up on the island, and that a figure, believed to be his ghost, had frequently been seen there since.

" Have you caught anything?" he suddenly asked. When I told him no, he immediately cried out: " I thought so! When the ghost's about, no one ever does."

It was after this latest odd experience that I resolved to learn more about ghosts and hauntings, purely to satisfy a personal interest. Having failed to pass the medical for the Constabulary I left Dublin to carve out some other career for myself; ghost-hunting would have to be very much a spare-time occupation. But when, after a long working tour of America, followed by spells of acting and schoolteaching in Britain, I gradually became known as a writer, so my activities in the ghostly field increased; until I came to be positively identified as that rarity of the time, a ghost-hunter who did not rest on his own stories alone, but who also went out to investigate and record factually the experiences of others.

THE CRY OF THE BANSHEE

LET ME state plainly that I lay no claim to being what is termed a scientific psychical researcher. I am not a member of any august society that conducts its investigations of the other world, or worlds, with test tube and weighing apparatus; neither do I pretend to be a medium or consistent clairvoyant—I have never undertaken to " raise " ghosts at will for the sensation-seeker or the tourist.

I am merely a ghost-hunter. One who lays stake by his own eyes and senses; one who honestly believes that he inherits in some degree the faculty of psychic perceptiveness from a long line of Celtic ancestry; and who is, and always has been, deeply and genuinely interested in all questions relative to phantasms and a continuance of individual life after physical dissolution.

So much for advertisement. I do not believe that one must necessarily be a professed psychic in order to see a ghost—I have proved far too many exceptions to this assumption. Undoubtedly some people do often see and hear ghostly phenomena, while others never see or hear, but I do not believe the experiencing of such phenomena is dependent on any power within us. I think it is quite a feasible supposition that ghosts can appear

193

to any of us, both when and where they will; in short, that the power lies entirely with the other side.

But the psychic faculty does help, and it does appear that many people gifted with this power tend to inherit it from their parents.

My mother, who came from an old Leicestershire family, had many ghostly experiences when, as a girl, she lived with her parents in a badly haunted house some ten miles from Northampton. Her bedroom in this house was separated from the rest of the bedrooms by a long and gloomy corridor. One night she was awakened by feeling something heavy jump on the bed. Wondering what on earth it could be, she raised herself to look, and in the moonlight saw a huge black cat seated at the foot of the bed, glaring at her.

Very frightened, as she knew there was no such cat in the house, she struck a light, only to find that the cat had vanished. Thinking it must be somewhere in hiding, though she had not heard it jump off the bed, she searched the room thoroughly. But it was nowhere to be found, and the door and windows, it being winter and the weather intensely cold, were shut.

Much mystified and still very frightened, for all was now hushed and silent and there was a strange, eerie feeling in the atmosphere, she got back into bed; but she had not been there long before something sprang on her—and she shrieked. Her parents came running to see what was the matter. They looked everywhere, but there was no sign of any cat, and they went back to their room declaring she must either have imagined it or have been dreaming.

Nothing further happened that night, but subsequently at frequent intervals my mother saw the phantom cat, not only in her room at night, but sometimes in broad daylight, in various parts of the house; and it was a great relief to her when some other members of the household finally saw it too.

On another occasion, this time in the summer, she awoke one night to find the room aglow with a strange, reddish light. On looking around to find the cause of the light, she saw that it came from a fire burning brightly in the grate, and that seated in front of the fire, with his back turned towards her, was a man in a blue tail-coat, peruke and knee breeches, holding a baby in long clothes on his lap. As she watched this man, more fascinated than frightened, he suddenly bent down, stirred the fire into a fierce blaze with a poker and then, springing up, threw the baby into the flames. My mother was so shocked that she fainted.

When she recovered and opened her eyes the room was in darkness save for the moonlight; the grate was black and empty, and nothing whatever remained to remind her of the tragedy she had just witnessed. But the horror of it so unnerved her that she felt she could never sleep in that room again. Her parents, therefore, allowed her to occupy another room, although they did not encourage her in attributing her experience to the supernatural. After this, she had no more disturbed nights, but she experienced a ghostly happening in broad daylight that alarmed her more than any of her former experiences.

She and a maid were left alone in the house one day, when the rest of the family went to a fête in a neighbouring town. The two were walking in the grounds of the house when my mother, discovering she had left something she wanted in her bedroom, ran indoors to fetch it. Having got it, she set off to rejoin the maid, and being anxious to do so quickly, she cut through the housekeeper's room and along a stone paved passage leading to a side entrance that was seldom used, at least by the family.

On crossing the housekeeper's room she heard a noise behind her, and looking back saw that the handle of a cupboard door— an inset cupboard, occupying almost the whole length of one wall —was turning round, as if motivated by someone inside the cupboard who was about to come out. The door being now unlatched, my mother in a paroxysm of terror turned and fled, hearing footsteps coming after her. Fortunately the door at the end of the passage was open and out she flew, without once looking back.

Nothing would have induced my mother and the maid to return to the house alone. Presently however, some of the servants returned from the fête, and in their company my mother again passed through the housekeeper's room. Instinctively her eyes sought the cupboard, and she particularly noticed that its door, which she had last seen open, was now tightly shut.

According to a tradition in the village a murder of a very heinous character had been committed in the house many years previously, and therefore, chiefly at my mother's instigation, boards were taken up and various excavations made, in the expectation of finding bones. But nothing was ever discovered, except a long disused well in the garden, and among the rubbish with which it had been filled in, an ancient blunderbuss. After my grandparents left the house it was partly pulled down and reconstructed. This seemed to put an end to the hauntings, which, it transpired, had been experienced by several other people in earlier years.

My mother was never really happy while she lived in the house, and it was a considerable relief to her when her family moved. However, she had another experience of an even more startling nature at an old country house in Worcestershire, which she was visiting.

She was sitting alone in the drawing-room one afternoon, when something attracted her attention to the floor just in front of her, and she saw the carpet suddenly become violently agitated, as if by a strong gust of wind blowing under it. She glanced up at the window, but the ivy clustering against it hung limp and motionless, and not a leaf stirred. Indeed, the day had been unusually mild for late autumn. Then she looked down again at the floor and was chilled to her bones. Coming up through the carpet was a head, a human head covered with a mass of long, black matted hair, obviously a woman's. Up and up, very slowly it came, until my mother saw a white face with two wide-open, dark, glassy eyes fixed on her. She tried to scream but could not, and as she sat, silent and helpless, the figure kept on rising through the floor, until finally it stood fully revealed before her—the apparition of a woman in an old-fashioned white dress, with a yellow shawl round her shoulders and an infant in her arms. With her eyes still fixed on my mother she turned slightly round, and then glided away in the direction of the antique fireplace, where she eventually vanished, apparently melting into the wall.

The spell then broken, my mother quickly pulled herself together and, springing to her feet, ran out of the room to look for her hostess. The latter expressed great concern.

" I ought to have told you," she said apologetically, " that this house, and the drawing-room in particular, is haunted, but the ghosts so seldom take it into their heads to visit us that I did not think it necessary."

She then added that, according to tradition, a gipsy woman and her baby were once enticed into the house and murdered, their bodies being buried afterwards on the premises.

Naturally this explanation proved a great shock to my mother, who announced her intention of going home the next day—a very wise decision on her part, since only an hour or so before she left, she encountered the same apparition once more in another part of the house.

My object in recounting my mother's experiences is simply to show that if the psychic faculty exists, she undoubtedly had it, and that being so, I most probably inherited it from her as well as from my father.

My father came from County Limerick and belonged to the Truagh Castle O'Donnells. The faculty of his family was never so vividly demonstrated as at his own tragic, violent death, which occurred when I was barely six months old.

As I have already stated, my father's vocation was that of a clergyman of the Church of England, and it was while awaiting preferment from one living to another that he decided to go for a trip with a clergyman friend to Palestine. The two travelled together as far as Alexandria, but there they parted, my father suddenly deciding to go to Abyssinia with a member of a well-known London banker's family, whom he had met on the voyage out.

One evening about three weeks later, my mother was sitting alone in the drawing-room of our old home in Ireland. It was a wild night, the rain coming down in torrents and the wind howling round the house and down the chimney. There was no gas in the house, and my mother, finding the lamplight somewhat trying to the eyes, had given up all attempts to read. Gradually succumbing to the warmth from the fire she relapsed into a gentle doze.

She was awakened by a loud crash. Jumping up from her chair in fright, she found that one of the windows had been burst open by the storm and that a screen standing near it had been knocked over. She was about to replace it, when from the hall outside there came a series of the most appalling screams. She ran to the door and opened it. All the servants were collected in a group, listening.

"What has happened? What is it?" my mother asked, gazing in astonishment at the pale faces in front of her.

"Sure, mum, it's the Banshee," the cook replied. "I know her voice well, there's no mistaking her. Didn't I hear her a'wailing and a'groaning round the house the night the master died, and didn't my mother hear her a'doing of the same the night the Colonel died, seventy-two years ago this very day. Listen! There she is again."

As she spoke there was a repetition of the sounds, only this time they seemed to come from another part of the house.

My mother said afterwards it was difficult to describe the sounds, which seemed to be a strange blending of a woman's voice with something wholly unearthly. Beginning in a low key, the sounds gradually rose to a series of screams of awful intensity and then, as gradually dying away, ended in a heart-rending wail.

At first my mother thought the voice was speaking, and she tried hard to catch the words, but was unable to do so. When she commented on this fact to the cook, the latter at once ex-

198

claimed: "'Tis no wonder, mum, that you couldn't hear what the Banshee said, seeing that you're not an O'Donnell. The O'Donnell Banshee only makes herself understood to an O'Donnell, though it is the likes of us all at this blessed minute that can hear her. She's after letting us know that one of the Truagh O'Donnells will be dying somewhere this very night. Ochone, Ochone."

The sounds continued for some little time longer, and then ceased. Simultaneously the storm abated, and my mother and some of the servants went out into the grounds, but nothing was to be seen, save the long row of motionless trees facing the house, and the long, leaden line of the distant river that formed a boundary to the grounds.

Nothing further happened that night, but the following night, at about twelve o'clock, the whole household was aroused by a loud hammering that seemed to come from the cellars. Then, after a while, the hammering ceased, and footsteps, which were recognized by all who were listening as my father's, ascended the stairs. They came right up, pausing for a few seconds outside each of the bedroom doors, until finally they arrived at the night nursery on the top landing. My nurse, who slept in the night nursery, then saw the door slowly open a few inches, and while a light, that looked like the light from a candle, appeared on the threshold, a voice which she recognized as that of my father, spoke, but so quickly that she could not understand a word of what was said. She was, of course, far too frightened to utter a sound, let alone make herself known to the speaker, and as soon as the voice ceased the light was withdrawn and the door closed. The steps then retraced their way downstairs and nothing more was heard that night.

The following night, however, at the same time, the same phenomena occurred, and they occurred repeatedly every night, without intermission, for a period of six weeks, when they abruptly ceased. After each fresh occurrence of the phenomena, those who experienced them and believed them to be due to the spirit of my father made up their minds afresh to try to overcome their fear sufficiently to speak the next time they occurred, but when the next time arrived, the same thing happened; fear, or something, invariably prevented them from uttering a sound. And so, in this case, as in most cases of bona fide haunting, there was no communication with the ghost.

These nightly disturbances, following on her experience of the Banshee, naturally made my mother very apprehensive for my father's safety, but she heard no news of him, ill or otherwise, till about four weeks after the disturbances began. She then received a letter from the French consul at Massowah stating that her husband, the Rev. Henry O'Donnell, had died at Arkiko, a village on the Red Sea coast, under circumstances that strongly suggested foul play.

In fact, as she later heard from various people in Massowah, there was no doubt whatever that he had met his death at the hands of a gang in that area who robbed and murdered any stranger with money who fell into their hands.

It was established that my father had been killed at about noon on the day after the Banshee had been heard at our home by my mother and the servants

After an interval of eight years the Banshee again demonstrated its presence in the same house, but on this occasion it was a malevolent Banshee, and it was not only heard, it was seen. What happened was this. One winter afternoon, my youngest sister was going upstairs to the top landing, when she was brought to a sudden halt by the appearance of a strangely unpleasant face looking down at her from over the balustrade.

Long and narrow, and crowned with a mass of matted, tow-coloured hair, it emitted a yellowish green light; and as my sister gazed up at it, petrified with horror, its pale, obliquely set eyes seemed to smile evilly. For some seconds my sister was too spellbound to move, but at last, tearing herself away from the spot, she ran helter-skelter downstairs, and as she did so the whole house echoed and re-echoed with loud peals of satanical laughter. As before, the servants assembled in the hall, terrified at the sounds, and it was our nurse who proclaimed them to be due to the Banshee.

The purpose of its advent was soon demonstrated, for a few days after my sister saw it an O'Donnell aunt of ours died, and exactly a week after its manifestation my mother died.

So much for my family hauntings. In the following chapters I now give some of the more interesting cases which I have investigated, and which have come to me, over a period of more than half a century spent ghost-hunting.

THE EYELESS WOMAN

NOT so many years ago the sign "To Let" outside a house in London was a commonplace, far more people renting homes than buying them. Then as now, however, there were some fashionable areas where accommodation was at a premium, and the "To Let" sign never stood outside for very long. If it did, or if it constantly reappeared, then the house was suspect.

Such a house was that in Cheyne Walk, Chelsea, described to me by Mrs. Mary Lulworth, whose family once lived near by. She told me :

"No sooner was a house in our peaceful and comfortable little neighbourhood vacant than it was snapped up at once, so that if you saw one remaining empty for any length of time you knew what to conclude. There was something radically wrong with it—it was haunted. The house in Cheyne Walk was generally in this plight, and I heard my father remark that he would not live in it for all the wealth in London.

"The empty house had a special fascination for me as a child, and I never passed it without thinking I saw some fantastic looking creature peeping down at me from one of the top windows. I used to dare my nurse to venture through the gates, and my young blood would freeze in my veins as I saw her, after going in as far as she dared, come hurrying back to me, her bonnet all awry and her eyes pale with fright.

"Well, Mr. O'Donnell, you can imagine my excitement when I actually met someone who had lived in that house. She was a dressmaker whom my mother used to employ regularly in equipping us for the forthcoming season. Her name was Miss Millward.

"Of course, she was not supposed to waste her precious moments chatting to me, but no doubt feeling a spell of rest would do her good, she would not unfrequently drop her work and launch forth into the most frightening stories. Of course I gave her every encouragement. I can see myself now, sitting in a high-backed chair, drinking in every word she said, my eyes at the same time wandering to the door in guilty expectation of being caught by my mother.

"'Yes, Miss Mary,' I can hear her say, laying down her scissors with a sigh of satisfaction. 'I stayed in that house a few years ago. Mrs. Greene, who occupied it then, engaged me as an extra sewing maid during the busiest time of the season.

"'She was a very nice lady and treated us all most liberally. I was very anxious to remain with her, and as she said she was highly satisfied with my work, I most probably would have done, if the ghost hadn't spoiled everything. It broke up the whole happy household and drove her away.

"'Anyway, I'll start from the beginning. Owing to the number of people in the house, the servants' quarters upstairs were full to overflowing, and I had to make do with a bed in the basement. I can't say this worried me much, for I don't mind where I sleep, Miss Mary, so long as I am in a happy house. It was very lonely though, as I was the only person down there. To be sure, I had a few blackbeetles for company, and they are not at all to my liking.

"'One night after I had undressed and got into bed I heard a peculiar noise in my room, just like someone flapping a duster hard at the floor. It gave me rather a turn, for I knew my door was locked, and I told myself it couldn't be a cat, for Mrs. Greene wouldn't have an animal of any kind kept in the house. What then could it be?

" ' I tried to assure myself it couldn't be anything that would harm me, when I suddenly felt something cold and damp stroke my cheeks. I thought I'd have died with fright, but I couldn't do anything—couldn't move, only lie there and wonder what was happening.

" ' You know how even when your eyes are shut, you can tell if there is a light in the room? Well, I could see one then, through the red lining of my eyelids—a pale glow. I couldn't bear it any longer—I opened my eyes and looked, and—oh, Miss Mary, you can't conceive anything so dreadful. Bending over me was a white face—a hatchet-shaped face, with black hair neatly parted down the middle and caught up in loops over the ears. But she had no eyes—no eyes!—and what was even more horrible, no sockets either. Where they should have been there was only smooth flesh, just like her forehead.

" ' As I watched her she went on stroking my cheeks with her fingers, long yellow fingers with the nails bitten to the quick. I was both terrified and disgusted, my stomach heaving every time she touched me; but her fingers held such a magnetic influence that I was eventually lulled into a heavy sleep.

" ' When I awoke it was morning, and the hideous thing had vanished. I didn't say a word about it to the other servants. I kept my own counsel and tried to persuade myself it had been a nasty dream.

" ' Bedtime came again, and I was once more alone in the basement. I was so nervous, Miss Mary, that I delayed undressing as long as I could—until the candle burned down so low that it went out and left me in the dark. This didn't suit me, I can assure you, Miss, for I was almost as much afraid of the blackbeetles as I was of ghosts, and so, whipping off my clothes like lightning, I popped in between the sheets and tried to go to sleep. But hardly had I settled down when the room seemed flooded with a luminous glow, and on cautiously peering round I saw that dreadful woman crouching in the nearest corner of the room. From the position of her head, which was slightly on one side, I judged she was straining her ears to catch the sound of my breathing, and I watched the twitching of her ugly fingers, which were stretched out towards me. She then began to creep forward.

" ' It was more than flesh and blood could stand. I sprang out of bed, and I have dim visions of the eyeless woman now raised to her full height, very tall, bounding after me, as with frantic screams I raced pell-mell out of the room, along the passage and up the stairs.

" ' What astonishes me most is that I did not break my neck, for during that mad stampede I overturned chairs and tables and cannoned into half a dozen walls. When I got into the hall I was baffled, for I didn't know that part of the house and could no more find the staircase in the dark than I could fly. This was terrible, as the woman was close at my heels, and I seemed to hear the swish of her long fingers through the air each time she made a grab at me and missed.

" ' Oh, how hard I tried to reach those stairs, tugging against the leaden weights that seemed to bind my feet to the floor. Fortunately my shouts had not been in vain, for both guests and servants heard them, and as I fell, exhausted and fainting, in the middle of the hall, help came. I was told afterwards that one of the gentlemen swore he had seen a shapeless something rise from my body and scud away as the lights drew near, but no one knew exactly what to make of it.

" ' Shortly after this had happened, the cook, on entering the larder, almost ran into the ghost bending down and apparently trying to dig a hole in the ground with its hands. In her fright cook dropped the dish she was carrying, at which the figure instantly disappeared.

" ' Master Arthur saw it next. He was Mrs. Greene's second son, a dear young gentleman, passionately devoted to music. He was playing the piano in the breakfast-room one morning.

No one was with him, and it so happened that no one else was in that part of the house. But Mrs. Greene, who was within earshot, noticed that the music stopped suddenly. This would not have worried her normally, but she had been told by the doctor only a week or two previously that Master Arthur's heart was in a weak condition. She became alarmed, and fearing he might have been taken suddenly unwell, she hurried to the breakfast-room. There the most appalling spectacle met her eyes.

" ' Lying on his back on the ground was her son, white-faced and helpless, while crouching over him, her long fingers busily engaged in stroking his forehead, was the ghost woman. Mrs. Greene was held powerless, until she saw the fingers begin to move towards her son's throat. No fear on earth can make a mother silent when her children are in danger. She screamed loudly, and the moment she did so the spectre vanished, but in a curious way. Rising in mid-air, it floated forward, disappearing head first through the wall.

" ' On reviving, Master Arthur told us all—for his mother's cries had brought several of us to the spot—that as he was playing he suddenly felt he was no longer alone, and on glancing behind him, his face all but touched that of the ghost woman, and he fell from his stool in a dead faint.

" ' Nothing would induce Mrs. Greene to keep the house after that. She was not going to risk Master Arthur's life, she said, for all the houses in London. She would send the children away immediately and give up the tenancy at the end of the season. This she did, though not before she had another scare.

" ' It was the day after the children had left, and she had gone to the nursery to see that nothing had been left behind, for Mrs. Green was one of those ladies, who, although she kept a housekeeper, liked occasionally to see that everything was right herself. She was looking around when she saw the door of the wardrobe suddenly begin to open of its own accord. Completely paralysed, she stood glued to the ground, full of the most horrible anticipations. Gradually, inch by inch, the door opened, until she could see the hatchet-shaped head of the eyeless woman protruding through the opening, and the next moment a pair of hands, their long fingers waving to and fro, came lunging forward in her direction.

" ' This broke the spell. With loud yells of terror Mrs. Greene rushed out of the room, and flying wildly down the corridor frantically flung herself into the arms of her startled husband. She must have run hard, poor lady, for the armpits of her dress, which I had to mend afterwards, were saturated with perspiration besides being torn out of the gussets.

" ' A regular panic now set in, guests and servants declaring they could not stay any longer in such a house, so the Greenes, being only too anxious to leave, had the furniture removed and the place shut up.

" ' There now, Miss Mary, you know as much about the haunted house as I do, and certainly more than most people.'

" ' But is there no explanation, Miss Millward?' I asked. ' Nothing that could account for the ghost?'

" ' No,' she replied. ' Only what the " Boots " told us. He had lived round these parts all his life, and had heard it rumoured that a very wicked lady had once lived in the house, and that she was supposed to have murdered her husband and step-child in order to marry again. But instead of marrying she was smitten with smallpox, or some equally terrible disease, which deprived her of sight and led to her committing suicide as the shortest way out of her troubles.' "

Mrs. Lulworth concluded : " And that, Mr. O'Donnell, is all Miss Millward could tell me, and not a very satisfactory explanation at that. But many years later my mother happened to meet Mrs. Greene and obtained from her a full account of the haunting, which although differing slightly in one or two respects from Miss Millward's version, tallied with it very closely in the main.

" As regards the identity of that hideous ghost woman in real life, however, there was no information forthcoming. Every inquiry by Mr. Greene drew a blank.

"Perhaps her poor soul has rested now, though I must confess I often wonder."

THE HIGHBURY HORROR

It was during the summer of 1900, on a warm, bright afternoon, that my artist friend Mr. Stock, who was in his seventies,
told me of the horror he experienced as a young man in a house
in Highbury. It was an odd setting for a ghost story as we sat
eating tea with strawberries and cream, and perhaps all the more
chilling for that. Mr. Stock's memory was clear as a bell as he
described to me his strange encounter of fifty years ago, which
I detailed in my notebook as he spoke on that lazy afternoon.

Since I first wrote of Mr. Stock's experience some embroidered
variations of it have appeared in print. What follows is the
artist's story exactly as he told it to me.

The house in question was in an old square in Highbury. It
bore the ill-omened number 13, and for years had in its tiny
front garden a large board with " To be Sold or Let " in large
lettering on it.

I have called the place in which the house was situated a
square, because that is what the authorities who named streets
in London then styled it. In reality it was just a narrow long
enclosure, where a score or so of melancholy trees cast their
shadows on a wilderness of tall grass and rank weeds, and all

the houses around it seemed to have acquired an air of chronic damp and gloom.

It was not a cheerful spot. The sun rarely seemed to discover it, and at this date—the year was 1849—almost every other house in the square was empty. Number 13 had one great attraction for Mr. Stock, however; it was in a cheap locality and the rent asked for it was small, ridiculously small.

Stock took the house, furnished, employing as his housekeeper a Mrs. Brown who had been strongly recommended by the landlord. She undertook to run the establishment for him with the aid of a charwoman to do the very rough housework. Stock did not work in the house; he shared a studio, not far away, with a fellow artist.

The first night of his stay in the house he arrived about ten o'clock, and being tired after a long day's work he asked Mrs. Brown to show him to his room at once. She went upstairs with him. It was rather a winding staircase, and his room was on the second floor. On the way up to it he had to pass a window, a little above the first landing, just where the stairs took a sharp curve.

Curious to see what the window looked out on to he tried to peer out of it, but the inky darkness outside merely revealed the reflection of his own face, and oddly enough, the reflection of two other faces. One was that of Mrs. Brown and the second face, close beside hers, seemed to be that of a very repulsive looking man. At least that was Stock's first impression, but he concluded afterwards there must have been some curious flaw in the glass, and that both reflections were those of Mrs. Brown, who was certainly far from good-looking, though not exactly ugly.

He found his room quite comfortable, and tired as he was, he slept right through the night without waking.

The following day found him again at work in his studio, but he left early, and after a meal at the restaurant which he usually patronized in Soho, he went home, getting there in time, so he told himself, to do a little reading before turning into bed.

Retiring to his room he settled himself in front of the fire with a bundle of magazines. But he had not calculated on the effects of the fire, which made him so drowsy that before very long he was fast asleep. He awoke with a start to find that the fire had burned very low and that the room, in consequence, was in almost total darkness. Indeed, there seemed scarcely enough glow in the embers to light a candle, in which case, having no matches he would be unable to see to undress and get into bed. But a few skilful touches with the poker soon produced a cheerful flame.

As he straightened up from the fire, intending to get a spill or paper lighter from the mantelshelf to light his candle, his glance fell on his own face reflected in the mirror in front of him—and he saw too another reflection which caused him to stop and stare in astonishment.

Standing at the far end of the room, facing the door, was an elderly woman he had never seen before. That she had not been in the room a few minutes previously he could swear, for he had looked all round the room and, in spite of the dimness of the light, had seen well enough that he was alone and that the door was closed. It was closed now, yet how could she have opened and closed it without his hearing?

It was strange too that she did not trouble either to speak to him or even to glance in his direction. She simply stood still, her face turned towards the door as if listening. That she was someone belonging to the house seemed evident too, since she was wearing a kind of négligé gown of white cambric, with deep frills down the front and at the wrists. Who could she be, he wondered—some friend of Mrs. Brown's who had mistaken his room for her own?

At that moment the fire shot up into a brilliant flame, throwing a bright light on the woman's face and making it startlingly clear. Never in his life had Stock seen such a face before, and never, he told me, would he wish to see one like it again. The woman—she might have been sixty or more—had grizzled hair and her general appearance suggested feebleness. Her face too

211

was lined, but it was her expression that riveted Stock's attention and appalled him. It was an expression of hopeless, utter despair and ghastly, speechless horror. She was concentrated in the effort of listening, and so intense was this effort that it appeared to absorb every nerve and fibre in her body. She was listening to something outside the room, away on the landing or stairs, to something which from her widening eyes and the quivering muscles of her lower jaw seemed to be drawing nearer and nearer. Then, as Stock continued to watch, the door began to open slowly and the woman shrank back, nearer and nearer to the wall, the horror in her face growing more and more fixed.

Suddenly the fire flame died down and the room was plunged again into near darkness. Moments later another spurt of flame revealed to Stock, still standing there unable to believe his eyes, that the woman was gone. The room was once again empty and the door closed. Yet there had been no sound, not even the lightest footfall. The house was wrapped in unbroken silence.

The following morning Stock tackled Mrs. Brown and asked the identity of the elderly lady who had visited his room. The housekeeper eyed him curiously.

" You've been dreaming, sir," she said. " There wasn't anyone in the house but you and me."

" Did you leave the hall door open by mistake?"

Mrs. Brown was indignant. " Why, I'd never think of doing such a thing. The idea of it. It was shut and locked as soon as it grew dark."

But Stock persisted. He said: " An elderly woman in a loose kind of dress of white cambric was in my room at about ten o'clock last night."

Mrs. Brown replied starchily: " Then all I can say is you must have let her in yourself, or been dreaming. It was a dream I expect. Gentlemen who study art or who work in studios often have queer dreams—I've heard them mumbling to themselves at night."

" It was no dream," Stock insisted, but he then dropped the matter.

About a fortnight afterwards he returned home late one night from the theatre. There was no light in the hall or on the stairs, except from the candle he carried; after putting the candle ready for him on a chair, Mrs. Brown had turned out the gas. Stock went upstairs. When he came to the curve and the window he had a sudden impulse to look at the window again, and gazing into it he saw himself reflected at full length—then with a cold shock saw also the head and shoulders of a man apparently coming up the stairs behind him.

Turning sharply round Stock then saw creeping slowly, with stealthy, noiseless footsteps up the stairs, a hunchbacked man in shirt sleeves. His head was slightly bent and at first Stock could only see a mass of coarse, shaggy red hair, not quite long enough to conceal a pair of large, crinkly, mis-shapen ears. Then as the hunchback came on round the curve of the stairs into full view, his face became clearly visible—some strange light other than the flickering flame seemed focused on it.

It was the same dreadfully repulsive face Stock had seen in the window on the night of his arrival. A low, retreating fore-head, a nose that looked as if it had been broken in a fight, loose sensual lips, brutal, wolfish jaws, light eyes, illuminated with an expression of deadly sinister determination. It was the face of some terrible beast of prey rather than that of a human being. In one hairy hand the hunchback held an ordinary table knife, the blade of which, worn to a point like a dagger, had evidently been recently sharpened.

Stair by stair, with a snake-like crawling movement, the hunchback drew nearer to Stock, who, spellbound, shrank back close to the staircase wall. The man, however, did not appear to notice him, but passing by, crept on silently up the stairs towards Stock's bedroom.

Compelled by some power inside him which he could not resist, Stock mechanically followed the creeping figure. When the hunchback arrived at the bedroom door he paused for a few moments and looked at the knife in his hand with a grin of hideous exultation. Then, gripping the handle of the door with

213

his coarse, bony fingers, he slowly turned it.

Inside, the room was full of moonlight, which poured in a broad stream through the open window, and right in its path stood the same woman Stock had seen before, the elderly woman in the loose gown of white cambric. The cause of that look of awful fear in her protruding eyes was now only too apparent. The hunchback's face shone with evil joy as he beheld her terror.

Just as the hunchback entered the room and advanced with devilish slowness on his shrieking victim, a gust of wind blew the door to with a loud bang. Stock, released from his frozen stance of horror, rushed forward and threw the door open, but instead of seeing something terrible, as he had fully expected, he found the room just as usual with no sign anywhere either of the woman or of the hunchback.

Not daring to remain in the room, Stock spent the night downstairs in the drawing-room with the gaslight fully turned on.

A few days later he vacated the house, choosing, despite the desperate state of his finances, to sacrifice a year's rent rather than remain in it.

Now Stock was a really quite matter of fact young man, who had never, before entering the house, seen a ghost or believed such a thing existed. After securing other rooms, he discreetly asked around the neighbourhood seeking to probe the house's dark secret.

Mrs. Brown would not or could not give him any information —she persisted that he had been dreaming, and that there was nothing wrong with the house. She said she had never seen or heard anything, and she had lived in it for several years as caretaker.

All that Stock could discover, after inquiries among neighbours and shopkeepers in the vicinity, was that no one of late years, excepting Mrs. Brown, had ever stayed long in the house, but that years ago, before the present landlord had bought it, the house had been occupied by an old woman and her son, a very ill-favoured hunchback, who were supposed to have gone away somewhat hastily. At any rate no one saw them go. But a year or so afterwards the son returned alone, saying that his mother had died abroad.

The hunchback remained in the house for some months, and then disappeared. No one knew where he went and no one cared. It was after that the house was so often to let and was never occupied for any length of time till Mrs. Brown came there as caretaker.

For some odd reason the strange happenings in the old house did not seem to affect Mrs Brown. She stayed on alone till the end of Stock's year of tenancy. The house was then sold again, but with the same result; no one would live in it.

Its dreary walls kept their dark secret to the end, when the house was finally demolished.

NIGHTS OF A GHOST-HUNTER

I AM frequently asked to describe some of the night vigils I have kept, alone and with others, in haunted places. Such investigations, of course, even when they do produce a phenomenon, do not always provide a ready explanation for the haunting. That is to say, in many instances the ghost cannot be identified and the incident nicely " rounded off " to everyone's satisfaction, as is invariably done in fiction. Therefore a long list of isolated, unexplained incidents of ghostly footsteps, knockings, and fragmentary ghostly appearances would prove repetitive if not tedious; but there are several among my nocturnal adventures which will serve to show the wide scope and interest of my investigations, and I will begin with a notable vigil kept by myself and others in a house near Wells, Somerset.

The house had long borne a widespread reputation of being haunted. It was a low, rambling, medium-sized building, with a fine old oak staircase and a number of equally pleasing oak-panelled rooms. It adjoined a churchyard and confronted a wooded park, where deer wandered at large. The exact age of the house was not known, but I believe it was built about the beginning of the eighteenth century, on the site of an ancient mansion. Among the various stories commonly told about the house was one concerning two brothers.

The elder brother, it was said, visited the other in the house one day and was never seen afterwards, the general supposition being that he was murdered in what was now termed the haunted room, and buried somewhere on the premises. There may, of course, be no truth whatever in the tradition, but some at least of the ghostly phenomena that from time to time took place there were popularly attributed to it.

Another story claimed that long ago, an old woman was crushed to death in a gateway on the estate by some member of the family, the deed being attributed either to revenge or to some sudden act of anger or folly. This again may be pure romance, but it was believed by people in the surrounding villages and her ghost haunted the place periodically.

Having obtained permission of the owners of the property to hold an all-night vigil there, I went to the house accompanied by two friends. Midnight found us in the deep, dark cellars of the building, adjoining the vaults of the old church. Overhead the big clock boomed twelve, an owl in some near tree hooted, and a far-off dog bayed the moon—in the circumstances uncanny sounds all; they nevertheless failed to bring the ghost, and after remaining in the cellars for a few minutes longer we adjourned to the haunted room.

This room, one entrance to which faced a long corridor, possessed some peculiarities. Under the floor, for instance, was a deep cavity known as the priest's hiding hole, which communicated with other secret spots in various parts of the building. Also, in a line with each other across the centre of the floor, some few feet apart, stood two curious pillars, and a second doorway led into what was styled a powder closet.

We had brought chairs with us. I sat facing the window, and one of my companions faced the powder closet, while the other sat about midway between us. At my request one had brought his dog and the other his camera.

The shutters of the room were closed, so as to preclude any

tricks of the moonlight, and we sat in absolute darkness. About 2 a.m. the dog began to whine and snarl, and almost directly afterwards one of my companions cried out. Confronting us, by the doorway leading into the corridor, was a tall, luminous thing, in shape not unlike one of the pillars. It moved very slowly, and passing the door leading to the powder closet, went on at a snail's pace towards the window on the opposite side of the room.

After it had gone some little distance I addressed it, asking it to tell us who or what it was and why it was there. There was no reply. I then asked it to knock on the wall or floor, but again there was no response of any kind. One of my companions also asked it questions, with the same negative result. Continuing to move, the thing kept approaching the window, and when close to it abruptly disappeared. We all three saw the phenomenon simultaneously, and were all so gripped by it that my companion with the camera forgot to use it.

Some months after this visit I went to the house again, accompanied this time by three men, one of whom was a chartered accountant in Wells. It was September. The day had been sultry, and at about eleven o'clock a thunderstorm, accompanied by wind and rain, broke out. As before we had a dog and a camera with us. Having searched the house to satisfy ourselves that no one was concealed in it, we walked to the haunted room and having, as before, closed the shutters, we sat down at some little distance from one another. As on the previous occasion, I faced the window.

The night proved noisy. Outside, the thunder pealed incessantly and the rain beat against the windowpanes, while the wind moaned and whistled dismally down the chimney. Inside, doors and windows jarred and rattled.

During brief lulls in the storm we occasionally heard footsteps, and we got the impression that someone or something was moving about stealthily in our midst. I was so convinced of this that every now and then I switched on my torch. Always, however, with the same result—my companions were all in their

218

seats in attitudes of tense expectation, but nothing was to be seen moving. As time wore on and nothing further happened we gradually dropped off to sleep, to be abruptly wakened by a loud, continuous ringing. For a minute or so none of us could make out whence the sounds came, and then someone suggested it was the front door bell.

We then, in a body, went down the long corridor and the broad oak stairs into the hall, which in the gloom appeared immense, to the front door.

" Who's there?" I called out, and much to my relief a very human voice replied : " It's only me."

It transpired that it was a friend of the accountant, who was so keen on joining in the ghost hunt that he had walked all the way from Bath, a distance of some miles. As he said he was a sceptic and did not mind where he sat, I suggested he should sit in the corridor at the head of the main staircase. He readily agreed, and leaving him there, we retraced our steps to the haunted room. Again a long wait, and then—an excitement. This time it was caused by the man in the corridor suddenly crying out : " Help, help !" We ran at once to his assistance, only to find it was a false alarm. Tired out with his long tramp, the accountant's friend had fallen asleep and had a nightmare.

" I dreamed," he said, " that a tall figure came flying downstairs and leaping over me, went bounding on into the room where I had left you all sitting."

Now this dream struck me as odd, because one of the ghosts said to haunt the house was a tall figure that bounded up and down the stairs and along the corridor in the manner described. However, the young man maintained that it was only a dream, and we returned to the haunted room, leaving him in the corridor.

Another long wait, and then as the clock struck four, the accountant exclaimed : " I shall have to be going. I take it nothing will happen now as it's morning. Besides, I have to be at the office at . . ." Here he stopped short, and then crying out, " Oh, my God, what's that?" began to pant and gasp. Simultaneously the dog with us snarled and then whined, and I saw in front of me a red, rectangular light, about six and a half or seven feet from the floor, and in about the middle of the room. Another of the sitters cried out that he saw something too. I stood up, and addressing the red light, asked who and what it was. There was no reply. I said we had come there as friends, and asked if there was anything we could do for it. Still no reply.

" If you can't speak," I said, " will you knock or rap on the floor or wall?" But still there was no response.

The accountant had now become so agitated that, fearing some harm might come to him, if he was not brought round, I stopped and lighted a candle. The red light then instantly vanished. The man in the corridor, who, hearing voices and seeing the light on in our room joined us, had seen nothing. The accountant, whom we beseiged with questions, described what he had seen thus : " It was a tall, luminous figure which seemed to emit a light from all over it. The body was covered with black and white streaks, possibly it was a check suit. That I cannot say, for it was the face that arrested my attention most. It was very long and swarthy. The skin was drawn very tightly over the bones, which gave it a skull-like appearance. I saw no actual eyes, only large sockets, which appeared to be aglow with light, but it gave me the impression of being intensely malevolent and antagonistic."

The other of my companions who had also seen the figure described it in much the same way; but the third man in our original party, who was present when the phenomena appeared, said he only saw a kind of luminous mist which seemed to move towards the spot where I sat and disappeared behind me.

I asked the accountant if he could bear sitting in the dark again, and on his assenting, I blew out the candle. Almost directly I had done so, the dog growled, and I again saw a red light suddenly appear in the middle of the room. The accountant cried out immediately : " It's there, it's there. I can't stand it. Light the candle !"

I at once switched on my torch, and the light vanished. No

one felt inclined to remain in the room any longer. We now came away, and were not at all sorry to find ourselves once more in the open, rain and all.

Now to a lone vigil. Learning, while in Harrogate, Yorkshire, that there was an alleged haunted house in the town, I sought and managed to obtain permission to spend a night in it. It was a large, tall house, situated about ten minutes' walk from St. James's Hall.

I went there early on a summer's evening, and on entering the premises encountered a stillness which contrasted oddly with the world outside, where all was life and gaiety; only a moment before I had mingled with the streams of ultra-fashionable people heading for the Spa Concert, the theatre, and the Valley Park. The forsaken house was empty of furniture, of everything, save the soft summer evening sunlight, the shadows and my presence. Wandering from room to room and floor to floor, I completed my preliminary search and being tired, sat down on the floor of the hall, took a newspaper from my pocket and started reading.

As the hours passed by and darkness came on I began to be afraid. No amount of experience in ghost-hunting has ever enabled me to overcome the awful fear that seizes me when I see the last glimmer of daylight fade and realize that I am about to be brought into contact with the supernatural, and must face it alone.

Noises in empty houses, I have noticed, usually commence in the basement, and I was not at all surprised to hear a faint tapping proceeding from one of the kitchens. This was followed by a long spell of silence, and then one of the stairs creaked. My heart gave a thump and I gazed expectantly into the darkness before me, but there was nothing to be seen. Silence again, and then more tapping, and more creaking. Something then tickled my hand, and a moment later my fingers touched a blackbeetle. In an instant I was on my feet, and on striking a light I found the whole floor swarming. I wondered very much at this, because beetles do not as a rule frequent houses that have been empty for any length of time, especially in a climate like that of Harrogate. I have since, however, arrived at the conclusion that where there are hauntings, there are, more often than not, plagues of beetles, but whether attracted by the ghost or not, I cannot say.

As I could no longer tolerate the idea of remaining in the hall in the dark I lighted four candles, placed them to form a big square on the floor and sat in the midst of them. It was still only eleven o'clock by my watch and the idea of keeping up my vigil till morning did not strike me as particularly pleasant. I took up my paper and again began to read. Half an hour or so passed, and then I started in shocked surprise. A door opened and shut downstairs, and bare footsteps pattered their way along the stone passage and up the wooden stairs. The nearer they drew, the more intolerable became my suspense. What should I see? I confess I would have given much to be out in the road, but as is usually the case when in the presence of the supernatural, I was quite powerless to move. Then, to my astonishment, instead of anything grotesque and awful, there suddenly appeared before me a little fair-haired girl, clad in a much-soiled pinafore and without either shoes or stockings.

Though not actually crying, the child appeared to be in great distress, and feeling around on all sides, as if anxiously searching for someone, she ran past me and began to ascend the stairs. Picking up a candle I followed her, and as the patterings of her poor, chilled feet spread their echoes far and wide through the deserted house, I thought I had never experienced anything half so pathetic. On and on we went, the little thin legs leading the way, till we reached the top storey, when she ran into a room facing me and slammed the door. I immediately threw open the door and followed, but the room was quite empty. There was no sign of the child; only a particularly vivid beam of moonlight, and an overwhelming atmosphere of sadness.

During the next few days I was told a story that fully accounted for the hauntings. It appeared that about thirty years before my visit to the house a little girl had lived there with her father and stepmother. Her nurse, to whom she was very much attached, being summarily dismissed by her stepmother, she became ill and very soon died, so it was rumoured, of a broken heart. Shortly after her death the house was to let, and no tenant, I discovered, had ever occupied it for very long.

I have often wished that I had spoken to the sad little spirit, but I was too fascinated by it, and too much engaged in watching its movements, to think of anything else. And I have found that this same fascination and preoccupation have prevented me from trying to communicate with the ghost in nearly all the cases of haunting that I have ever investigated. On the few occasions that I have spoken to a ghost I have received no reply, little indication even that it has heard me.

In a very famous haunted house in the West of England, during my investigations which were spread over a period of nine consecutive nights, manifestations took place twice, and on both occasions I stood up and spoke, but in neither case was there any response whatever. This same ghost had been subjected to exorcism by a well-known ecclesiast, but far from being exorcized, the ghost so scared its exorcizer that he all but fainted.

These demonstrations were visual. In a haunted house that I was asked to visit in Sussex I saw nothing but heard knockings, and by means of them tried, though without success, to establish a code. I heard of the case in this way.

Miss Maureen Denning wrote to me. She and her mother occupied a modern and picturesquely situated house at the foot of the Downs, and were very frequently disturbed, she said, between nine and ten in the evening, by sounds, such as might be a muffled hammer, on the wall of her mother's room. Simultaneously the figure of a young man was seen to move noiselessly across the lawn from the direction of the garden swing. He usually approached Mrs. Denning's window and came to a halt immediately beneath it. He had never replied when spoken to. She possessed a revolver and had fired at him several times, but the bullets had had no effect whatever; it seemed as if they had passed right through him, because he still stood there, while the gravel was splattered up immediately behind him.

On one or two occasions, Miss Denning told me, the man shone a bicycle lamp on his face, so that she could distinctly see his features. It was the face of no one she knew, though she fancied it bore a close resemblance to a notorious murderer, whose photos had been in the papers, and who had been executed.

These were not the only manifestations. Stones had been repeatedly thrown at Mrs. Denning, and although the house was being closely watched by the police, the stone-throwing still went on, and so far the culprit had not even been seen, let alone caught. The stones, though, were solid, real and hurtful enough.

In response to the daughter's appeal I visited the house once by myself, and once with a party of men. On the former occasion I hid in a little copse at the farthest extremity of the lawn, and watched the house and swing closely, but I neither heard nor saw anything. Returning to the house, I was told by Miss Denning that both she and her mother had heard the knockings, and that she herself had, at the same time, seen the figure on the lawn.

On the occasion of my second visit, we all heard the knockings on the wall of Mrs. Denning's room, and one of us, who was looking out of her daughter's window, saw what he thought were two shadows of human beings cross the moonlit lawn and vanish in the direction of a hedge. Trickery was impossible, as the garden was protected on all sides by barbed wire, and there were on the premises four or five dogs, including a young bloodhound. We had of course made a thorough search of the house and grounds previously.

One or two other incidents happened during that night. When I was in the hall alone, a light, as from a bicycle lamp, was suddenly shone in my face, apparently from the blank wall; and when we were all seated in front of the dining-room fire we heard heavy footsteps cross the hall—although we ran out at once we could see no one. We were shown the stones that were alleged to have been thrown (none was thrown while we were there). They were a peculiar kind of flint, which certainly did not belong to the neighbourhood. Mrs. Denning had several times narrowly escaped being hit by them, and one had crashed through the bedroom window as she was looking out of it.

I would have liked to have spent more time investigating this baffling case, but this was not possible. Cases of complex haunting, although seldom admitting of any satisfactory explanation, have always attracted me most. Here, for instance, is one I chanced to come upon in Newcastle-upon-Tyne.

A house in D—— Street had stood empty for seven or eight years, and on my making inquiries about its reputedly sinister reputation, I was told to contact a Mr. Black, the last tenant. I did so, and Mr. Black, once assured of my serious interest, gave me a detailed account of what had taken place there during his tenancy. This was his statement :

" A day or two after our arrival I happened to be going up-stairs and as I passed by one of the bedrooms, the door of which was slightly open, I glanced in and saw the figure of a woman I had never seen before. She was dressed in green, and standing in front of the mirror, engaged apparently in putting on her hat. Wondering who on earth she could be, for I knew the room had not been slept in, I spoke to her, and receiving no reply, I was advancing towards her when she suddenly disappeared. I did not know what to make of the affair, but thinking that possibly it was a hallucination, I resolved to think no more of it and to say nothing about it to any of my family or household.

" Some days later, however, when out walking with my wife, I met a friend who asked me where I was living. I told him, and he exclaimed excitedly : ' Good gracious, not in that house ! Why, my dear fellow . . .'

" At a hasty sign from me he then stopped. I had guessed what was coming, and as my wife is extremely nervous I thought it best she should not hear what I knew he was going to say; namely, that the house was haunted.

" That night I went round to see my friend. He made no

bones about it; he told me that the house I had taken was haunted—that he knew it for a fact.

" ' Some months ago,' he said, ' I was thinking of taking it myself, and obtaining the key from the agent went to have a look over the place. It was quite light, not more than five o'clock in the afternoon, and the house seemed bright and cheerful. Closing the front door behind me I began a tour of the premises. I had reached the top floor, and was standing in the centre of one of the rooms, when I heard a slight noise. I started, and turning round in the direction from which the sound came, saw a woman and a little girl standing in the doorway watching me. There was nothing at all remarkable about them. The woman was dressed in green, the child in white—both modern, or at least comparatively modern, costumes. I was so surprised at their being there, however, as I knew I had shut the hall door, that I simply stood and stared at them. Then something much more extraordinary happened—they vanished. It was *not* a hallucination, that I can swear to, and thoroughly scared, I tore downstairs and out of the house. After this I gave up all idea of taking the place, and I can't help feeling sorry, old fellow, that you've taken it.'

" In spite of my friend's warning," (Mr. Black continued) " I did not give up the house immediately. After we had been there a week or so, a cousin of mine came to stay with us, and one evening he and one of my children—my young daughter—were in the drawing-room when they heard a soft, cautious whistle, as if someone were giving a signal, coming from just behind them. The whistle was repeated, and a few minutes later they heard a loud cry, half human, half animal, and wholly ominous. My cousin pretended that it was one of the servants, but my daughter would not be convinced and begged to be taken up to bed at once, as she dared not remain in the room any longer.

" After this, phenomena of all kinds happened. Steps used to be heard bounding up and down the stairs at all hours of the night; one of the maids declared she saw something that was a man and yet not a man come out of the drawing-room with a run, and race up the staircase two or three steps at a time; heavy pantings and sighs were heard, and several of the household were awakened by a cold hand being laid upon their face. But I think the most remarkable thing that happened is this: I was sitting in my study one evening, when the maid rapped at my door and said that a clergyman, whom she had shown into the drawing-room, wished to see me on some very urgent matter. I at once put down the book I was reading, and hastening to the drawing-room found it empty. Wondering what had become of the clergyman, I was about to ring the bell to inquire when I suddenly caught sight of a large eye, human in shape and horribly sinister, glaring at me from behind an arm-chair. I was so frightened that I could do nothing but stare back at it, and then to my intense relief, my wife entered the room with a friend, and the phenomenon disappeared."

" And the parson?" I asked.

" I never heard anything more of him," said Mr. Black. " The maid assured me on her honour that she had shown him into the room, but no one saw him leave the house, so he too might have been a ghost. However, supposing him to have been a living person, his disappearance would not be unnatural. He had doubtless seen the eye and taken to the street through the open window.

" The following day, my children being badly frightened by something in one of the passages, I decided to leave the house at once. I afterwards made every possible inquiry, but could not discover anything tragic in the history of the house. We were the first tenants, so I was told, that had ever complained of disturbances, and it was suggested that we might have brought the ghosts with us. But as none of us had ever seen a ghost before we entered the house, and we had no old furniture—at least none that we had not always had—and not one of us had ever attended a seance or in any way dabbled with spiritualism, I don't think that theory holds water at all."

I would have liked to have sat vigil in this house of the lady in green, but it was not possible at the time. However, I had better luck with a house in Glasgow.

While passing through that city I heard of such a promising case of haunting there that I was unable to resist the temptation of investigating it, and decided to break my journey. The case, as outlined to me in the first instance, was this :

A Glasgow solicitor named James McKaye, desirous of renting a house close to his office, went one morning to look at a likely place in Duke Street. He went there alone, and closing the front door behind him, proceeded to wander from room to room, beginning with the basement.

As he was going upstairs to the first floor he suddenly heard footsteps following him. He turned sharply round, but there was no one there. Thinking this odd, but attributing it to the acoustic properties of the walls, he continued up the stairs. Having arrived on the first landing he went into one of the rooms. The steps followed him. A brilliant notion then occurred to him—he stamped his foot. But there was no answering echo. He turned and went into the next room, and the footsteps once again accompanied him.

It was at this point that he grew frightened. It was broad daylight, the sun shone brilliantly and the birds were singing; but there was something in the house that was wrong. The day was hot, and the sun poured in through the blindless windows, but in spite of this the rooms were icy, and McKaye was deliberating whether it was worth while exploring the house further when he caught sight of a shadow on the wall. It was not his own shadow. It was that of a man with his arms stretched out horizontally on either side of him, and whereas the right arm was complete in every detail, the left had no hand.

James McKaye now yielded to an ungovernable terror and rushed frantically out of the house.

One would naturally think that after all this he would have vowed never to go near the place again. Nothing of the sort. The house fascinated him; he could not get it out of his mind. He even dreamed of it—as having some mystery that he must solve; that only he could solve. Besides, he argued with himself,

228

there was not another house in the city so conveniently situated, nor so cheap. Consequently he took it, and within a fortnight had moved in with all his family and household goods.

For the first few weeks everything went swimmingly, and McKaye congratulated himself on having made such an excellent bargain. Then occurred an incident which recalled sharply the day he had first seen the place. He was writing some letters one morning in his study when the nursemaid entered, white and agitated.

"Oh, do come to the nursery, sir," she implored—"the children are playing with something that looks like a dog and yet isn't one. I don't know what it is!" And she burst into tears.

McKaye sprang to his feet and ran upstairs. On reaching the nursery the blurred outline of something like a huge dog or wolf came out of the half-open door and raced past him, so close that he distinctly felt it brush against his clothes.

Where it went he could not say; he was thinking of the children and did not stop to look. Oddly enough the children were not a bit afraid, on the contrary they were pleased and curious.

"What a strange doggy it was, Daddy!" they cried. "It never wagged its tail, like other doggies, and whenever we tried to stroke it, it slipped away from us—we never touched it once."

Sorely puzzled, McKaye told his wife, and the two decided that if anything further happened, they must leave the house.

That night McKaye happened to sit up rather late. At last he rose from his chair and was about to turn off the gas, when he felt his upstretched hand suddenly caught hold of by something large and soft which did not seem to have any fingers. He was so frightened that he yelled out, whereupon his hand was instantly released and there was a loud crash overhead. Thinking something had now happened to his wife, he rushed upstairs to find her sitting up in bed and talking in her sleep. She was apparently addressing a black, shadowy figure that crouched on the floor opposite her. As McKaye approached the thing it moved towards the wall and vanished.

Mrs. McKaye then awoke and begged her husband to take her out of the house at once, as she had dreamed most vividly that an appalling murder had been committed there, and that the murderer had come out of the room with outstretched hands, asking her to look at them. McKaye, who had had quite enough of it too, promised to do as she wished, and before twenty-four hours had passed the house was once again empty.

These were the bare facts of the case, and as they were given to me by one of his important clients, I had no difficulty in obtaining an interview with Mr. McKaye, who, I was told, still had the keys of the house. It was not, however, so easy to obtain his consent to spend a night on the premises, and he would only permit me to do so on the condition that, for safety's sake, he himself accompanied me, and that I promised to keep the visit a secret from the newspapers.

The evening chosen for our enterprise proved ever memorable. The rain came down in torrents, and the high wind made any attempt to hold up an umbrella utterly impossible. Indeed, it was as much as I could do to hold up myself, while to add to my discomfort, at almost every step I plunged ankle-deep in icy cold puddles. At length, drenched to the skin, I arrived at the house. McKaye was standing on the doorstep, swearing furiously. He could not, he said, find the key. However, he found it shortly after I arrived and we were soon standing inside, shaking the water from our clothes.

This was in the days before pocket flashlamps had become general, and we had to be content with candles. We each lighted one, and at once began to search the premises to make sure no one was in hiding. The house consisted of four storeys and a basement. None of the rooms was very large and I remember the wallpapers were singularly unlovely. McKaye asked me if I could detect anything peculiar in the atmosphere, but I could only detect extreme mustiness, and told him so. He seemed very fidgety and ill at ease, but as he was a much older man than myself, and had some experience of the house, I felt perfectly safe with him. After we had been in all the rooms we went downstairs to the ground floor and began our vigil on the staircase leading from the hall to the first landing.

" I think we stand more chance of seeing something here than anywhere else," McKaye said, " and in the case of anything very alarming happening, we are close to the front door."

He spoke only half in fun and I saw that his fingers twitched a good deal and that his eyes were never at rest.

" Oughtn't we to put out the candles?" I said. " Ghosts as a rule materialize much more readily in the dark."

But he would not hear of it. All his experiences in the house, he said, had taken place in the light. He then began to describe to me once more all that had happened during his occupation of the house. He was still telling me, when there came a loud rat-tat at the door.

" That's a policeman," he said, " he must have seen our light."

He was right, for when we opened the door a burly figure in helmet and cape stood on the step and flashed his dripping bull's-eye lantern in our faces. On hearing McKaye's name the constable's suspicions instantly cleared, and when we mentioned ghosts he laughed long and loud.

" Well, gentlemen," he said, " you won't never be alarmed by an apparition so long as you have that dog with you. I bet he would scare away any number of ghosts, and burglars too. If I may be so bold as to ask, what breed do you call him? I've never seen anything quite like him before," and he waved his lamp towards the stairs.

We both looked in the direction he indicated, and there, halfway up the stairs, with its face apparently turned towards us, was the black, shadowy outline of some shaggy creature, which to me looked not so much like a dog as a bear. It remained stationary for a moment or so, and then, retreating backward, seemed to disappear into the wall.

" Well, gentlemen, good night," the policeman said, lowering his lamp, " it's time I was going."

He turned on his heel and was walking off, when McKaye called him back.

" Wait a moment, constable," he said, " and we'll come with you."

He cast a furtive glance around him as he spoke, then blowing out the lights he caught me by the arm and dragged me away.

" But the dog, sir," the policeman said as the front door closed behind us with a bang " —it hasn't come out . . ."

" And it never will," McKaye responded grimly. " You have seen the ghost, constable, or at least one of them!"

I never had a second opportunity of visiting that house, and for all I know to the contrary it still stands there, and is still haunted.

One lone vigil which I kept at a house near Maidstone, in the late 1920s, produced not the ghost I expected but something uncannily different. The house had a history. About 1812 the owner of it went on a visit to some friends, leaving two women servants in the house to look after it. Fearing burglars and thinking to outwit them if they did break in, the two women hid all the silver in the house in the kitchen oven. However, one of them in a fit of absent-mindedness lit the kitchen fire, and the silver was very badly damaged. They were then, it seems, so fearful of the consequences, servants in those days being treated so severely, that they drowned themselves in a lake in the grounds.

Afterwards a beautiful avenue leading to this lake acquired a lasting reputation for being haunted.

A year or two before my investigations a lady visitor at the house was found lying in the avenue in a dead faint. On recovering consciousness she told a strange tale. She said that as she was walking up the avenue, she suddenly saw a woman clad in a very old-fashioned dress and wearing a kind of mob-cap, approach her. As they drew nearer to one another she saw the woman's face very distinctly, and it was so horrible that she fainted.

After this, various other people saw the same figure, always in the avenue, but not always at the same time. It sometimes appeared in broad daylight. A man who saw it one afternoon

232

preceding him up the avenue, its back to him, thought at first it was merely some eccentrically clad member of the household, but later, when he heard about the haunting, he was convinced from the description given him of it that he had actually seen the ghost.

With these stories fresh in my mind I settled to a nocturnal vigil in the avenue and grounds of the house one autumn evening, and I must confess I did not altogether enjoy it.

Though the weather was fine and the air very sweet and fresh after London, there was a loneliness about the place which I found exceedingly depressing. The feeling of eeriness was worst by the water. There was a ghostly glimmer on it, and I could feel something beside me; something bizarre and evil that had its home there was doing its utmost to persuade me to throw myself in. Indeed, so strong a fascinating did that black, silent pool exercise over me that it took a great effort of will power to drag myself away from it and return to the avenue. On my coming to a part where several paths met, I was deliberating which one of them to take when I heard footsteps pattering along one of the paths towards me.

They came very rapidly, as if someone was in a great hurry, but I could see nothing. When they were close to me I instinctively drew back to let them pass by, but all the same, I felt someone bump into me. The footsteps then went on, and gradually died away in the distance. I walked about the avenue for some time after that, but nothing further happened.

What I had heard and felt was a ghost, there was no doubt of it. But whether it was the same ghost that other people had seen, and which on this occasion had chosen against manifesting itself visually, I cannot say.

I suppose about three-quarters of my night vigils have been held alone. Others I have held with various sitters, ranging from owners and tenants of properties to notable people interested in my investigations; like the late Duke of Newcastle, Lord Curzon of Kedleston, Sir Ernest Bennett, and that fine old actor C. Aubrey Smith. These occasions always produced an assorted

" bag ". One evening in the summer of 1924, for instance, I held watch at a flat in London accompanied by a party which included Miss Myra Smith, a lady bookie, Miss Lucy Shanahan, a skilled dress designer, and Mr. P. T. Selbit of St. George's Hall fame.

The flat was in Redcliffe Square, South Kensington. The woman owner, believing it to be haunted, had invited me to spend an evening there and to bring as many friends as I could with me. Prominent among my companions, besides those mentioned, was Colonel Harvey Wexford, an old friend of mine.

The owner of the flat having also invited several of her friends, including a spiritualist medium, we formed one of my largest ever sittings. For some time we sat listening to the medium, whose efforts were disappointing, and when midnight drew near we all went into the kitchen to see if we could get any better results from table-turning, the most suitable table being in there.

We had been waiting in vain for half an hour or so, and the medium was talking to Mr. Selbit while the rest of the sitters chatted quietly with each other, when Miss Myra Smith, looking startled, whispered to me that she could see a tall figure in the doorway. I looked across at once and there, as she had said, was a tall figure standing in the entrance to the kitchen. It was dressed in long, black, flowing robes, and had something that resembled a top hat on its head. Miss Shanahan, who was sitting near to me, saw the figure too, but none of us could see its face, as there was no light in front of it and only a dim light in the passage behind it. Our seeing this figure caused some consternation, and on some member of the party turning on the electric light the apparition vanished.

Miss Myra Smith said that although she did not see the figure's face very distinctly she was sure it was looking at Colonel Wexford who was sitting next to her.

A few days later, Colonel Wexford died quite suddenly.

Now what makes this case especially interesting is what I learned from Colonel Wexford a few weeks before the sitting at

234

which this strange figure was seen. The Colonel told me that, when he was in Tibet many years before, a lama had prophesied the dates upon which he and a friend who was with him would die. " In my friend's case the prophecy has proved correct," he said. " But," he went on laughingly, " although the fellow hit it off right regarding my friend, I think he'll prove wrong about me, for according to him my time is almost up. I am about to die this year, but I have never felt better in my life!"

The conversation, of course, came back to me the moment I was told of the Colonel's death, and I then asked a friend who had travelled in Tibet and India to give me a description of the lamas' dress. He did so, and commented quite without any question from me that the usual head-dress of a lama was not unlike a top hat. Hence, taking all the circumstances into consideration, I cannot help thinking that the figure that Miss Smith, Miss Shanahan and I saw that night in the haunted flat, was the spirit of the lama who had prophesied Colonel Wexford's death.

Footsteps are a very common phenomenon in hauntings. Some years ago I went to investigate disturbances of this nature said to occur in the top flat of a house near Selfridge's. Several people, including Mr. Arthur Sinclair, the popular Irish actor, accompanied me, and we stood at midnight on the staircase waiting for the ghost. After being there for some time we heard footsteps ascending the stairs. They passed by several of us at very close quarters, and the banisters creaked ominously as if some heavy weight were being pressed against them; but none of us saw anything and nothing further happened. This case sounds trivial enough now, when I come to put it down in writing, but at the time the footsteps, actually heard ascending that long, winding staircase in the darkness of that big, deserted house, certainly awoke a very real sense of fear.

Not long ago I investigated a more complex case in a flat near Theobalds Road, Holborn. The owner of the flat told me that in the dead of night he had frequently heard footsteps ascend the main staircase of the house and halt outside his front door. Sometimes he would hear them cross the floor of his sitting-room, enter his bedroom and approach his bed. Usually nothing further happened, but on one or two occasions he had felt hands on the bedclothes. Beginning at his feet, they felt their way stealthily up his body towards his head. I asked if he ever saw anything, and he said: "No, I was in such a fright that I ducked my head under the clothes and kept it covered up till I heard the steps go away."

Once a friend who was staying with him did see something. Hearing a noise in the sitting-room, the friend got out of bed and on opening the sitting-room door saw a strange man, with a handkerchief bound round the lower part of his face, walk across the room and, without making any attempt to open it, pass right through the front door.

These were the main phenomena. I held several sittings in the flat, but only on one occasion experienced anything I could not satisfactorily explain on natural grounds. I had two friends with me. One had stationed himself in the bedroom and the other, a house agent, on the landing facing the main staircase of the building. I was alone on a bend of the stairs.

We did not begin our vigil till about one o'clock, when the house was absolutely still and everyone in it had gone to bed. After chatting with the agent for some time I was beginning to nod, for I was very tired, when something roused me, and directly afterwards I heard footsteps on the staircase immediately beneath me. They sounded muffled, as if someone in bare or stockinged feet was trying to disguise them. On and on they came, right up to where I was standing, and then halted. I switched on my torch, but nothing was to be seen.

The agent had heard the steps too. He received the impression that the author of them was some very gross person who was muffling them on purpose. He was emphatic that the sounds could not be attributable to the acoustic properties of the house, and he was very much an expert in his field.

I also heard ghostly footsteps in a house in Red Lion Square,

236

W.C., though this was not the result of a vigil. I happened to be sharing the upper part of the house with a friend at the time. He was away, and one summer evening I was sitting in my bedroom, which was on the top floor, quite alone in the house. The two floors immediately beneath the flat were let out as offices, and so were unoccupied after six o'clock; a caretaker, his wife and daughter lived in the basement, but on this occasion, as I learned afterwards, they were out; so I was indeed on my own.

It was a beautiful evening in May. The sunshine came pouring into my bedroom through the open windows, and the square resounded with the discordant shouts of children using the square's garden as a playground. I was listening to them when I suddenly heard heavy footsteps on the uncarpeted stairs outside (the staircase was a very fine one of black oak).

The footsteps came slowly and wearily up, suggesting to my mind some old and decrepit man. I wondered who it could be, as I was not expecting any visitors, and I sat and listened till the steps crossed the landing immediately below me and began to ascend the staircase leading to my room. I then got up and going out of the room, looked downstairs. To my surprise I saw no one.

As I stood there, wondering what had become of the person, the steps suddenly began to descend. I followed just behind them, right down to the ground floor and along the passage to the front door, where they abruptly ceased.

At the time I had no idea the house was known to be haunted, but I afterwards heard that the caretaker's daughter had often seen the ghost of an old man on the staircase, and in various other parts of the building. Also, the people who took the flat after my friend and I had vacated it, told me they several times heard mysterious footsteps on the staircase, and that on one occasion a very strange thing had happened. A young man who was visiting them, seeing a strange old man coming up the stairs, spoke to him and asked him what he wanted. Whereupon the old man replied, " Oh, that's all right," and turning round, walked slowly down. Thinking this rather odd, the visitor followed him, and saw him suddenly and inexplicably disappear in the passage leading to the front door.

As far as I could ascertain, no tragedy was known to have occurred in the house, but as it was probably a hundred and fifty years old, some unknown and undiscovered crime may have been committed there. At the same time, hauntings can arise from a dozen and one causes, and contrary to popular belief, they are by no means always due to acts of violence.

In the case of another haunted flat in Central London I held what might be termed an extended vigil, inasmuch as I promptly rented it and moved in and lived there, in an attempt to probe its mystery. It happened this way.

Two women occupied a flat in Bloomsbury near the British Museum. One of them was in the habit of attending seances, and from hearing or imagining she heard knockings and spirit voices at seances, she took to hearing or imagining she heard them in the flat. She said the voices were those of her friends who had passed over, and that they wanted her to join them on the other side. Eventually, when her friend was away for a time, she did attempt to obey the voices in her own unhappy fashion. She locked herself in her bedroom, and some time later someone staying in the house, smelling gas strongly on the landing outside the woman's room, told the landlord. He went for a policeman and together they forced the door open and found the woman lying dead on her bed.

After this the flat stood empty till I heard of the case and rented the premises. I slept in the room where the tragedy occurred for some weeks, but only occasionally had experiences which I could say for certain were due to ghostly causes.

They all happened while I was alone in the flat. For example, on two successive mornings I awoke at the same hour, about four o'clock, to feel a sharp tug at the bedclothes covering my right shoulder. On both occasions I looked round at once, but saw nothing. Yet I felt sure something was there, close beside me, trying to get into communication with me. Several times when about to enter the flat, in which I lived alone, I heard

238

sounds like footsteps inside, and could have sworn that some presence was on the other side of the door, listening. No one took the flat after I left, and the whole house was later converted for use as business premises.

Oddly enough, it is not always an abundance of phenomena that makes one of my vigils memorable; sometimes the incident has been slight, yet at the time very impressive. I am reminded of what occurred the night before the Delphic Club transferred its quarters from Regent Street to Jermyn Street.

As several of the members declared they had had uncanny experiences in the old quarters, I resolved to do a night's vigil there before the removal took place. Two women members of the club volunteered to join me, and the three of us met there and sat in the hall, or rather on the landing, for the club occupied the third and fourth storeys, and its premises were not self-contained. Our sitting began at about eleven o'clock. In rather more than an hour's time, during an interval of silence (we had been talking), we heard a click in one of the rooms, and the electric light in the room was suddenly switched on. That was all.

In the dead of night, however, and in a building empty save for myself and my two companions, it had a decidedly eerie effect, and brought our vigil to an abrupt end.

As a ghost-hunter one must be sympathetic but sceptical; more vigilant and sceptical, in fact, than the stoutest nonbeliever. Only by working in this way can one reduce extraordinary happenings to the basic evidence, and weigh it accordingly.

I must say here that I sympathize with those people who cannot bring themselves to entertain the very idea of there being such things as ghosts. I am of the opinion that one can learn more from one spontaneous ghostly manifestation in a haunted house than from a thousand lectures, or a thousand books. Experience really is the only medium of conviction. In spite of the widely diverse and complex hauntings in my own files, I have, from time to time, expressed my frank disbelief at a particular incident, only to be corrected later. I give a chastening example of this.

At one time, when as a result of some particular investigation I was getting a flood of letters, a woman in Liverpool wrote to me saying that her daughter, Emily, was tormented by a man coming into her bedroom every night at the same time and walking off with her bedclothes. The man said nothing, merely opened the door, and approaching the bed on tiptoe, caught hold of the clothes and hurriedly retreated with them. Spirit lights, my correspondent added, were constantly seen in the room, and at times figures like angels, and she would be glad if I would visit the house and discover for her, if possible, some explanation of the occurrences.

The nature of the manifestations being somewhat extraordinary I thought it advisable to take a friend. The house was in a crescent close to Clayton Square. We were shown into the drawing-room, where all the family were assembled, and were at once regaled with detailed accounts of all that was alleged to happen. Then we were taken to the bedroom that was haunted, and the young woman whose bed the ghost stripped, sat there with us, at our request.

As soon as the electric light was switched off she began to see spirit lights. But we saw nothing. No man appeared.

On taking our departure, my companion and I agreed that the phenomena were subjective, and that it was simply a case of hallucination. Accordingly I advised the girl's mother to consult a doctor, as in all probability her daughter needed a tonic and a change of air.

Well, I returned to London and thought no more of the matter for a good twelve months, when quite by chance I ran across a young doctor to whom I had mentioned the incident. After the pleasantries he said right away: " Elliott, you remember that Liverpool case you told me about—the case of the girl whose bedclothes used to disappear, and which you thought was a hallucination? Well, you were mistaken. Since I saw you,

I have become acquainted with the doctor who now attends her, and he told me that while he was there one day, the bedroom door opened and in walked a young man. He says the girl immediately exclaimed: 'Here is the man who haunts my room at night— for goodness' sake, Doctor, do something!' Whereupon the man, muttering some words in German, abruptly left the room. My doctor friend immediately ran after him but he had vanished. The house was searched at once, but no trace of him could be found. Now what do you think of the case?"

THE DEAD MAN'S HAND

In the days when, as a young man, I had every intention of pursuing a career on the stage, I at one period found myself at Brixton, paying daily visits to various theatrical agencies in search of work. It was here that I ran across the manager of a fit-up company who wanted a man of about my age and build to play second lead in a melodrama. I closed with his offer, and for the next four weeks, which was as long as his funds held out, I paid three-night visits to various towns in Wales, winding up at Llandudno, no better off financially than when I commenced, and having to pay my own fare back to London.

If, however, my excursion into Wales was unprofitable from the monetary standpoint, it was by no means lacking in other repects, for apart from the experience I gained from playing four entirely different parts at night, with two electric changes, I came across several interesting cases of hauntings, one of which is quite alone in its eerie aspects.

One of my landladies, a kindly soul to whom I had chatted about my interest in ghosts, introduced me to an old man, Clem Morgan, whom she said had a curious experience in one of the neighbouring mines. The incident had taken place some fifty years ago, shortly after a dreadful explosion in which many scores of the miners had been killed and injured.

Clem Morgan was not by any means a fanciful man and it took more than a little persuasion on my part to get him to recount the experience which he had kept mostly to himself for so long; but, once firmly assured of my serious interest, he unburdened himself, becoming all the more stronger in his recollections as he proceeded.

I will narrate the incident, merely tidying up the wording of it here and there, just as Mr. Morgan narrated it to me :

" A thousand feet down, close to the site of that great tragedy which had moved the whole country to mourning, my mate and I were at work. Pick, pick, pick; shovel, shovel, shovel; the sound of our tools must have been heard hundreds of yards away.

" ' George,' I said, stopping work for a breather, ' was it like this before the accident?'

" ' Like what?' George grunted. He was a middle-aged man with a black, stubby beard, and arms like the gnarled and knotted branches of an oak. ' Like what?'

" ' Why, as lonely as this? Were you working with just one other man, or were you with the rest of the gang?'

" ' With one other,' George said, ' and just as soft as you. Why can't you let it drop? I'm sick to death of hearing about it.'

" ' It's a marvel to me how you escaped,' I said. ' Whereabouts were you?'

" ' Just where we are now,' he said—' and that's all I'll tell you, so you'd best shut up !'

" ' You went up them steps with all the hell of the explosion ringing around you?' I said, advancing to the edge of the black shaft close to where we were working, and looking at the slender wooden ladder leading up to the dark vault above. ' It's a wonder to me you didn't miss your footing in the hurry and fall. I would have done.'

" ' I've no doubt you would,' he said, ' but I'm no tenderfoot.

243

I was at this game when you were in your cradle, which you never ought to have left.'

" ' How many feet down is it?' I asked, peering below me, much fascinated.

" ' Fourteen fathoms. We don't reckon by feet here. Done with that way of things in the schoolroom.'

" ' So that you'd be killed outright if you fell?'

" ' Try it and see.'

" ' It's my brother I was thinking of, not myself,' I said. ' Where was he when the explosion took place?'

" ' How can I say, boy,' George said irritably. ' I don't know where half the folk are.'

" ' They told me he was in an adit leading into the main shaft.'

" ' He may have been for all I know.'

" ' Do you suppose it was here he was working?' I said later, going again to the shaft and peering down.

" ' This isn't the only adit on the main,' my companion replied. ' He wasn't here—leastways not when I was.'

" ' I heard he was with a man he unintentionally injured, and who ever after bore him a grudge.'

" ' Oh !' said George. ' So you know as much as that, do you? And what in hell was this man like?'

" ' I can't say, except that he was much older than Dick and very ugly.'

" ' That description would fit in with dozens down here. If he was working with your brother, and your brother was killed, the odds are he was killed too.'

" ' You really think so?'

" ' Seems reasonable enough, don't it?'

" ' He might have escaped, like you did.'

" ' He might,' George laughed, ' just in the same way as pigs might fly. Supposing you get on with your work and let me do the same.'

" ' I had a queer dream about that man,' I said.

" ' Dreams! Who believes in dreams!' George said. ' What was it?'

" ' I dreamed he had something to do with Dick's death and with the accident.'

" ' Then you'd better tell the Inspector,' said George, ' and maybe he'll alter his verdict. You seem to have been very fond of this brother of yours. You've done nothing but carp about him all morning.'

" ' I was fond of him,' I said. ' So we all were. He kept the home going for the last six years.'

" ' Kept the home going! Why, where was you?'

" ' At college, studying for a teacher. I gave it up after his death.'

" ' A schoolmaster! Well, I'm blowed. Then you didn't see much of Dick?'

" ' Only in the holidays.'

" ' And who told you about this fellow who's supposed to have had a spite against him?'

" ' Mother.'

" ' Oh, your mother. Only hearsay after all. Well they're both dead, anyhow—good and bad, bad and good, all went together, boy. What do they call you?'

" ' Clem.'

" ' Well, Clem, get on with your shovelling for mercy's sake. I've had enough of talking to last me to the end of the week.'

" I then took up my spade " (Clem Morgan continued) " and for the next hour there were no other sounds but the steady pick, pick, pick, and scrape, scrape, scrape. Every now and then George sprang aside, there was a crash, and a huge block of coal fell on the rocky floor, amid a blinding shower of dust. A fraction of a second later and he would have been under it, his head a jelly. Yet the narrowness of his escape did not seem to affect him, he treated it with the utmost indifference and wiping away the smuts from his eyes, took up his pick and resumed his hitting. I regarded him in silent wonder. When the·dinner-break arrived I groped my way to one of the big galleries, for the idea of eating alone with George did not appeal to me. When I'd finished my meal I set out on my way back.

" A terrible sense of isolation hung over that part of the mine where I bent my steps. It was so far away from the other adits—so deep down, so dark and silent. Up above in the fields, woods and valleys one is never quite alone, for the voice of nature makes itself heard in the birds and insects. You know you are in the midst of life. But here in the bowels of the earth, encased in the dead vegetation of a long ago forgotten world, there is absolute stillness. As I pressed on, the crunching of my feet on the scattered fragments of coal awoke the echoes of the galleries, and I stopped every now and then to listen in awe to the long reverberating echoes as they rolled round and round me. Once I nearly slipped; another foot and I would have plunged into a labyrinth, the cold draught from which wound itself round me and choked the air in my lungs.

" I drew back in horror, and clinging to the knobbly surface of the black wall by my side, pressed frantically forward. God! Supposing I should ever lose my way down here—be left behind when all the men went home. What would become of me? The sweat rose on my forehead at the bare idea of it. Presently, to my relief, I heard the sound of picking, and an abrupt turn of the passage brought me in sight of George, who had already re-started work. I hurried to his side and, picking up my shovel, began to make a neat stack of the rapidly accumulating chunks, ready for carting.

" ' George,' I said after a while, ' why didn't you tell me it was you who was working along with Dick?'

" ' So you've been asking questions, have you?' he said, still carrying on working. ' Who told you?'

" ' Jim and Harry Peters.'

" ' Well, what of it?'

" ' Why didn't you say so when I asked you?'

" ' What odds if I had? It wouldn't have done you any good.'

" ' Did you have a quarrel with him?'

" ' Did they tell you I had? Because if so, it's no use my saying anything.'

" ' But what do you say?'

246

" ' No! Dick and me never had no quarrel.'

" ' Is that true?'

" ' Gospel.'

" After this we worked on in silence. Then I suddenly cried out and pointed at his cap. It was lying on the ground, some few feet from where we were working, close beneath a projecting block of coal, and it was moving as if being violently agitated by something inside it.

" ' What is it?' I said.

" ' What is what?' said George, resting for a moment on the handle of his pick.

" ' Why, that,' I said, pointing to his cap. ' What makes it move like that?'

" ' The wind, of course.'

" ' There's not enough draught for that. See!' I placed a piece of paper on the ground within an inch or two of the cap and it remained perfectly still. ' Something must be underneath it,' I said, and picked the cap up. But there was nothing there. ' What do you think of it now?' I asked.

" George did not answer. He turned round so that I could not see his face, and plied his pick vigorously. After a few minutes I stopped work again.

" ' George,' I cried, ' what's the matter with your coat? Look! It's doing just what your cap did.'

" At this George threw down his pick with an oath.

" ' What do you want to keep worrying me for?' he said. ' What's wrong now?'

" ' Why, your coat! It's moving—rising up and down as if the wind were blowing it—and there's not an atom of draught.'

" ' It's your fancy,' he said hoarsely. ' The coat's not moving.'

" ' What?' I said. ' Do you mean you can't see it moving?'

" ' No,' he replied. ' It's not moving I tell you.' And picking up his tool he set to work again, even harder than before.

" Some minutes later I again stopped. ' My lamp!' I exclaimed. ' It's burning blue! What makes it do that?'

" George paused, his pick shoulder high, and looked round.

'Nonsense,' he said savagely. 'You are a . . .' Then he left off and his jaw dropped. 'It must be some chemical in it,' he said. 'Let the damned thing be, it'll soon right itself.'

" 'This is a strange place,' I said. 'First of all your cap, then your coat, and now the lantern—all doing something queer. Have you ever known the likes of it before?'

" 'Often,' he muttered. 'Scores of times. Funny things is always happening below ground—you'll get used to them in time.'

" 'And yet you look a bit scared.'

" 'Do I? Well, I'm not. By the saints I'm not.' And raising his pick, he attacked the coal furiously.

" The afternoon was waning. It is a peculiarity of the mines that, however deep down they may be, they yet feel the influence of time, and the departure of the sunlight from above seems to create an immediate increase in the gloom below. On this afternoon I felt the change acutely as the darkness stole down the pit's mouth and permeated adits, shafts, galleries —everywhere.

" My light was still burning blue, but beyond it, down in the great gaping chasm, not ten feet from George, and away along the narrow, winding passage separating me from the rest of the gang, all was dense black. I was staring around, too interested to go on with my work, when something icy cold gripped my fingers, and looking down I saw a big, white hand lying on the top of mine. I gave a yell and dropped my shovel, at which the hand vanished.

" 'What's the matter now, curse you!' George said angrily. 'If you keep on hindering me like this, I'll tell the overseer. See if I don't.'"

" 'The place is haunted,' I gasped. 'A hand caught hold of mine just now.'

" 'A hand?' He cursed loudly. 'What next?' And then started to laugh.

" 'I'm sure it was a hand,' I said, 'and it had a ring on like my brother's.'

248

" ' You've got your damned brother on the brain. In a few days you'll get over it and laugh at your fright. There's no hands here but yours and mine, lad.'

" ' Aren't there?' I said. ' Then what's that just below yours on the pick?'

" George looked down. Instead of two hands—his own two hands—on the pick, there were three, and the third was white and luminous. With a shriek he dropped the pick and sprang away from it as if it had been a serpent.

" ' Do you believe me now?' I said, frightened to hell as I was. ' If that wasn't Dick's hand, I've never seen it. I could swear to his ring among a thousand. And look, have you seen how dark it's been getting?'

" ' I've seen nothing,' George said roughly. He raised his pick and began work again, but his hands shook so much he struck his leg and dropped the pick with a cry of pain.

" ' It's nothing,' he said as I scrambled to his side, ' only the skin grazed. But I reckon I'll sit down a bit—I'm all of a tremble.'

" He had moved nearer to the edge of the pit, and was about to sit down with his back towards it, when I cried out: ' My God! There's Dick! He's just behind you. He's pointing at you, George. I see it all now! George, you devil—you murdered him !'

" George looked round and saw as I did, bending over him, a tall figure with a strangely white face. He threw out his hands to keep the figure off, and as he did so he slipped and fell, with one loud yell of terror, into the pit. I heard him strike the side of the great abyss once, then thud, that was all.

" Sick in my mouth, I reeled back to the safety of the niche where we had been working, and as I did so my eyes fell on the lamp. The flame was now white and normal.

" A rescue party that went in search of George found him in a dying condition at the bottom of the shaft. The fact that he was not killed outright was due to his having fallen in a foot or two of mud and water, which had broken his fall. He lingered

249

just long enough to confess that he, and he only, was to blame for the recent disaster. He said he'd had a violent quarrel with my brother, whom he had hated, and, when Dick's back was turned, he'd struck him over the head with his pick and killed him. Seized with horror, he then dragged Dick's body into the passage, and in order to minimize the risk of discovery had saturated it with paraffin and set fire to it. He'd just time enough to reach the ladder leading up from the shaft, and climb up it, before the explosion took place."

The Welsh miners are at times magnanimous, and on this occasion they agreed to keep George's crime a secret. To give publicity to the affair, they argued, would not give them back the relatives they had lost, and would only do harm to the dead man's widow and family, who were left almost penniless. Thus the matter ended, and to the outside world the cause of the explosion remained, as before, a mystery.

Of course, it may be said of this case that it has no great value from the evidential point of view, no one having witnessed the ghostly happening but Morgan and the man who was subsequently killed. This may be. At the same time much depends upon the character of a witness, and the evidence of one man, who is reliable, is surely worth more than the evidence of several men who are not reliable.

Clem Morgan told his story in a simple, straightforward manner; and I believed him.

THE DEATH BOGLE: AND THE
INEXTINGUISHABLE CANDLE

YEARS AGO, bent on revisiting Perthshire, a part of Scotland which had great attractions for me as a boy, I answered an advertisement in a popular ladies' weekly. It was somewhat to this effect: " Comfortable home offered to gentleman (bachelor) at moderate terms in an elderly Highland lady's house at Pitlochry. Must be a strict teetotaller and non-smoker. F.M., Box—."

The naivety and orginality of the advertisement appealed to me. The idea of obtaining as a boarder a young man combining such virtues as abstinence from alcohol and tobacco was very amusing. And a bachelor, too! Did she mean to make advances to him herself? The sly old thing! She took care to insert the description " elderly " in order to avoid suspicion, but there could be little doubt about it—she thirsted for matrimony.

There rose up before me visions of a tall, angular, fortyish Scottish spinster with high cheek-bones, sandy hair and brawny arms. A daunting prospect. Yet it was Pitlochry, heavenly Pitlochry, and there was no one else advertising in that town. So I decided to write to " F.M."

For once my instincts were all wrong. The advertiser, Miss Flora Macdonald of Donald Murray House, did not resemble my preconception of her in the least. She was of medium height and dainty build, a fairy-like creature dressed in rustling silks, with wavy white hair, bright blue eyes, straight, delicate features, and hands, the shape and slenderness of which at once pronounced her psychic. She greeted me with a stately courtesy; my luggage was taken upstairs by a solemn-eyed lad in the Macdonald tartan; and the tea bell rang me down to fruit salad and cream, scones, and delicious buttered toast.

I fell in love with my hostess—it would be sheer sacrilege to call such a tender creature " landlady "—at once. The food was all that could be desired, and my bedroom, sweet with the perfume of jasmine and roses, presented a picture of dainty cleanliness. It transpired that Miss Macdonald was a Jacobite, and in a discussion on the associations of her romantic namesake, Flora Macdonald, with Perthshire, it leaked out that our respective ancestors had commanded battalions in Louis XIV's far-famed Scottish and Irish Brigades. That discovery bridged gulfs. We were no longer payer and paid, we were friends, friends for life.

A week or so after I had settled in Miss Macdonald's home I took, at her suggestion, a rest from my writing, and spent the day on Loch Tay, leaving again for Donald Murray House at seven o'clock in the evening. It was a brilliant moonlight night. Not a cloud in the sky, and the landscape stood out almost as clearly as in the daytime. I cycled, and after a hard but thoroughly enjoyable ride, eventually came to a standstill on the high road, a mile or two from the first lights of the village of Pitlochry.

I halted, not through fatigue, for I was almost as fresh as when I started, but because I was entranced with the delightful atmosphere, and wanted to draw in a few really deep draughts of it before returning home to bed. My stopping place was on a triangular plot of grass at the junction of four roads. I propped my cycle against a signpost and looked back in the direction from which I had ridden. I remained in this attitude for about ten minutes, and was about to remount my cycle when I suddenly became icy cold, and a frightful, hideous terror seized and gripped me so hard that the machine, slipping from my trembling hands, fell to the ground with a crash.

The next instant something—for the life of me I know not what, its outline was so blurred and indefinite—alighted on the open space in front of me with a soft thud, and remained standing as bolt upright as a cylindrical pillar. From afar off there then came the low rumble of wheels, which grew in intensity until there lumbered into view a wagon, weighed down beneath a huge stack of hay, on the top of which sat a man in a wide-brimmed straw hat. He was deep in conversation with a boy in corduroys who sprawled beside him. The horse, catching sight of the motionless " thing " opposite me, at once stood still and snorted violently.

The man cried out: " Hey! Hey! What's the matter with ye, beast?" And then, in a hysterical kind of screech: " Great God! What's yon figure, Tammas?"

The boy immediately raised himself into a kneeling position and clutching hold of the man's arm, screamed: " I dinna ken, I dinna ken, Matthew—but take heed, mon, it does not touch me. It's me it's come after, na ye."

The moonlight was so strong that the faces of the speakers were revealed to me with extraordinary vividness, and their horrified expressions were even more startling than was the silent, ghastly figure on the roadside. The scene comes back to me as I write, its every detail as clearly marked as on the night it was first enacted. The long range of cone-shaped mountains darkly silhouetted against the silvery sky, the shining, scaly surface of some far-off tarn or river, visible only at intervals because of the thick clusters of gently nodding pines; the white-washed walls of cottages glistening amid the dark green denseness of thickly leaved box trees; the undulating meadows besprinkled with gorse and grotesquely moulded crags of granite; the dazzling white roads saturated with moonbeams . . .

I even counted the horn buttons on the rustics' coats—one was missing from the man's, two from the boy's, and noted the sweat-stains under the armpits of Matthew's shirt, and the dents and tears in Tammas's soft wideawake hat.

I took in all these trivialities and more besides. I saw the abrupt rise and fall of the man's chest as his breath came in sharp jerks, and the stream of dirty saliva that oozed from between his blackberry-stained lips and dribbled down his chin. I saw their hands—the man's, square-fingered, black-nailed, big-veined, shiny with perspiration and clutching grimly at the reins; the boy's smaller, and if anything rather more grimy, the one pressed flat down on the hay, the other extended in front of him, the palm stretched outwards and all the fingers widely apart.

And while all these minute details were being stamped on my brain, the cause of all our terror, the indefinable, mysterious column, stood silent and motionless over against the hedge, bathed in a baleful glow.

The horse suddenly broke the spell. Dashing its head forward it went off at a gallop, and, tearing frantically past the glowing column, went helter-skelter down the road to my left. The wagon's violent passage threw Tammas into a somersault, and he was miraculously saved from falling head first on to the road by rebounding from the pitchfork which had been wedged upright in the hay.

At this moment the suddenly mobile phantom figure, which had followed in their wake with prodigious bounds, began to grope for Tammas with spidery arms. Whether it succeeded in touching the boy I cannot say, for I was so horribly frightened that it would return to me that I jumped on my cycle and rode as I had never ridden before and have never ridden since.

When I told Miss Macdonald of my extraordinary experience she was very concerned.

"It was stupid of me not to have warned you," she said. "That particular spot in the road has always—at least, ever since I can remember—borne the reputation of being haunted. None of the people round here will venture within a mile of it after twilight, so the carters you saw must have been strangers. No one has ever seen the ghost except in the misty form in which it appeared to you. It does not frequent the place every night, it only appears periodically, and its method never varies. It leaps over a wall or hedge, remains stationary till someone approaches, and then pursues them with monstrous springs. The person it touches invariably dies within a year.

" I well recollect when I was in my teens, on just such a night as this, driving home with my father from Lady Colin Ferner's croquet party at Blair Atholl. When we got to the spot you name, the horse shied, and before I could realize what had happened, we were racing home at a terrific pace. My father and I sat in front, and the groom, a Highland boy from the valley of Ben-y-Gloe, behind. Never having seen my father frightened, his agitation now seriously alarmed me, and the more so as my instinct told me it was caused by something other than the mere bolting of the horse.

" I was soon enlightened. A gigantic figure, with leaps and bounds, suddenly overtook us and, thrusting out its long, thin arms, touched my father lightly on the hand. Then with a harsh cry, more like that of some strange animal than that of a human being, it disappeared.

" Neither of us spoke till we reached home—I did not live here then, but in a house on the other side of Pitlochry—when my father, who was still as white as a sheet, took me aside and whispered : ' Whatever you do, Flora, don't breathe a word of what has happened to your mother, and never let her go along the road at night. It was the death bogle. I shall die within twelve months.' And he did."

Miss Macdonald paused, and then after a brief silence went on with all her customary briskness: " I cannot describe the thing any more than you can, except that it gave me the impression it had no eyes. But what it was, whether the ghost of a man, woman, or some peculiar beast, I could not tell. Now, Mr. O'Donnell, have you had enough horrors for one evening or would you like to hear just one more?"

Well, shaken up as I was after my experience, my curiosity now was thoroughly roused, and so I asked Miss Macdonald to continue.

"After my father's death," she said, "I told my mother about our adventure the night we drove home from Lady Colin Ferner's party, and asked her if she remembered ever having heard anything that could possibly account for the phenomenon. After a few moments' reflection, this is the story she told me . . ."

And here I give the story as told to Miss Macdonald by her mother, whose maiden name was Trevor:

There was once a house, known as "The Old White House", that used to stand by the side of the road, close to where you say the horse first took fright. Some people of the name of Holkitt, relations of dear old Sir Arthur Holkitt, and great friends of ours, used to live there. The house, it was popularly believed, had been built on the site of an ancient burial ground. Everyone used to say it was haunted, and the Holkitts had great trouble in getting servants.

The appearance of The Old White House did not belie its reputation, for its grey walls, sombre garden, gloomy hall, dark passages and staircase, and sinister-looking attics could not have been more thoroughly suggestive of all kinds of ghostly phenomena. Moreover, the whole atmosphere of the place, no matter how hot and bright the sun, was cold and dreary, and it was a constant source of wonder to everyone how Lady Holkitt could live there. She was, however, always cheerful, and used to tell me that nothing would induce her to leave a spot dear to so many generations of her family, and associated with the happiest recollections in her life. She was very fond of company, and there was scarcely a week in the year in which she had not someone staying with her.

I can only remember her as a widow, her husband, a major in the Gordon Highlanders, having died in India before I was born. She had two daughters, Margaret and Alice, both considered very good-looking, but some years older than I. This difference in age, however, did not prevent our being on very friendly terms, and I was constantly invited to their house—in the summer to croquet and archery, in the winter to balls.

Like most elderly ladies of that period, Lady Holkitt was very fond of cards, and she and my mother used frequently to play bezique and cribbage, while the girls and I indulged in something rather more frivolous. On those occasions the carriage always came for us at ten, since my mother, for some reason or other—I had a shrewd suspicion it was on account of the alleged haunting—would never return home after that time. When she accepted an invitation to a ball, it was always conditionally that Lady Holkitt would put us both up for the night, and the carriage then came for us the following day, after lunch.

I shall never forget the last time I went to a dance at The Old White House. My mother had not been very well for some weeks, having, so she thought, taken cold internally. She had not had a doctor, partly because she did not feel ill enough, and partly because the only medical man near us was an apothecary, of whose skill she had a very poor opinion. My mother had quite made up her mind to accompany me to the ball, but at the last moment, the weather being appalling, she yielded to advice and my Aunt Norah, who was staying with us at the time, chaperoned me instead.

It was snowing when we set out, and as it snowed all through the night and most of the next day, the roads were completely blocked, and we had to remain at The Old White House from Monday evening until the following Thursday. Aunt Norah and I occupied separate bedrooms, and mine was at the end of a long passage away from everybody else's. Prior to this my mother and I had always shared a room—the only really pleasant one, so I thought, in the old house—overlooking the front lawn. But on this occasion, as there were so many visitors stranded at the house like ourselves, we had to squeeze in wherever we could; and as my aunt and I were to have separate rooms (my aunt liking a room to herself), it was natural that she should be given the largest and most comfortable. Consequently she was situated in the wing where all the other visitors slept, while I was forced to retreat to a passage on the other side of the house, where, with the exception of my apartment, there was nothing but lumber-rooms.

All went smoothly and happily till the night before we returned home. We had supper, and Margaret and I were ascending the staircase on our way to bed when Alice, who had run upstairs ahead of us, ran down again looking very frightened.

" Oh, do come to my room!" she cried. " Something has happened to Mary!" (one of the housemaids).

We both ran up with her and on entering her room found Mary seated on a chair, sobbing hysterically. One only had to glance at the girl to see that she was suffering from very severe shock. Though normally red-cheeked and placid, a very reliable girl and the last person to be easily perturbed, she was now without a vestige of colour, while the pupils of her eyes were dilated with terror. Her entire body, from the crown of her head to the soles of her feet, shook as if with ague.

" Why, Mary!" Margaret exclaimed— " Whatever's the matter—what has happened?"

" It's the candle, Miss," the girl gasped— " The candle in Miss Trevor's room. I can't put it out."

" You can't put it out? Why, what nonsense!" Margaret said.

" But it's true, Miss—true as I sit here," Mary insisted. " I put the candle on the mantelpiece while I set the room to rights, and when I had finished and came to blow it out, I couldn't. I blew, and blew, and blew, but it hadn't any effect, and then I grew afraid, Miss, horribly afraid . . ." She buried her face in her hands, and shuddered. " I've never been frightened like this before, Miss, and I've come away and left the candle burning."

" How silly of you," Margaret scolded. " We must go and put it out at once. Stay where you are, and for goodness' sake stop crying, or everyone in the house will hear you."

So saying, Margaret hurried off, Alice and I with her, and on arriving outside my room, the door of which was wide open, we saw the lighted candle standing in the position Mary had described. I looked at the other girls and saw the unmistakable signs of fear lurking in the corners of their eyes.

" Who will go first?" Margaret demanded. No one spoke.

" Well then," she said, " I will," and stepped over the threshold. The moment she did so, the door began to close. " This is curious!" she cried, retreating before it. " Push!"

We did—we all three pushed. But despite our efforts the door came resolutely to, and we were all shut out. Then, before we had time to recover from our astonishment, it flew open—but again, before we could enter the room, the door came violently to, some unseen force holding it against us.

" Let's make one more effort," Margaret said, " and if we don't succeed we'll call for help."

Obeying her instructions, we again pushed at the door. I was nearest the handle, and in some way—how, none of us could ever explain—just as the door suddenly opened of its own accord, I slipped and fell inside. The door then closed immediately with a bang, and to my unmitigated horror I found myself alone in the room. For some seconds I was spellbound and could not even collect my thoughts sufficiently to frame a reply to the anxious entreaties of the other two girls, who kept banging on the door and imploring me to tell them what was happening.

Never in the grip of nightmare had I experienced such terror as that room now conveyed to my mind. Though nothing was to be seen, nothing but the candle, the light of which was peculiarly white and vibrating, I felt the presence of something inexpressibly menacing and horrible. It was in the light, the atmosphere, the furniture, everywhere. On all sides it surrounded me, on all sides I was threatened in a manner that was strange and deadly.

Something suggested to me that the source of evil originated in the candle, and that if I could succeed in extinguishing the light I should free myself from the ghostly presence. Slowly I advanced towards the mantelpiece, and, drawing in a deep breath, blew with the energy born of desperation. It had no effect. I repeated my efforts, blowing frantically, but all to no purpose. The candle still burned, softly and mockingly. Then a fearful terror seized me and, flying to the opposite side of the room, I buried my face against the wall, waiting for what the sickly beatings of my heart warned me was coming. Constrained to look, I slightly, only very, very slightly, moved round, and there, floating stealthily towards me through the air, came the candle, the vibrating, glowing, baleful candle. I hid my face again and prayed God to let me faint. Nearer and nearer drew the light, wilder and wilder the girls' wrenches at the door. Closer and closer I pressed myself to the wall. And then, when the final throes of agony were more than human heart and brain could stand, there came the suspicion, the suggestion of a touch —a touch so horrid that my prayers were at last answered and I fainted.

When I recovered I was in Margaret's room and half a dozen anxious friends gathered round me. It appears that on my collapse to the floor, the door, which had so effectually resisted every effort to turn the handle, immediately flew open, and I was discovered lying unconscious with the candle—still alight— on the floor beside me. My aunt experienced no difficulty in blowing out the recalcitrant candle, and I was carried with the greatest tenderness into the other wing of the house, where I slept that night.

Little was said about the incident next day, but all who knew of it expressed in their faces the utmost anxiety—an anxiety which, now that I had recovered, greatly puzzled me. On our return home another shock awaited me; we found to our dismay that my mother was seriously ill, and that the doctor, who had been sent for from Perth the previous evening, just about the time of my adventure with the candle, had stated that she might not survive the day. His warning was fulfilled—she died at sunset.

Her death, of course, may have had nothing at all to do with the candle episode, yet it struck me then as an odd coincidence, and seems all the more strange to me after hearing your account of the bogle that touched your dear father in the road, so near the spot where the Holkitts' house once stood. I could never discover whether Lady Holkitt or her daughters ever saw anything of a superphysical nature in their house; after my experience they were always very reticent on the subject, and naturally I did not like to press it. On Lady Holkitt's death, Margaret and Alice sold the house, which was eventually pulled down, as no one would live in it, and I believe the ground on which it stood is now a turnip field. That, my dear, is all I can tell you.

"Now, Mr. O'Donnell," said Miss Macdonald—"having heard our experiences, my mother's and mine, what is your opinion? Do you think the phenomenon of the candle was in any way connected with the bogle both you and I have seen, or are the hauntings of 'The Old White House' entirely separate from those of the road?"

That question still remains on my file, unanswered.

THE ORANGE-HAIRED FOOTMAN

SOME PEOPLE see ghosts when others present at the time do not. Eventually, to these lone witnesses' immeasurable relief, supporting testimony of the haunting is forthcoming from other people who see what they have seen. In some cases, however, such testimony is very slow in coming—or perhaps it never comes at all.

I think there can be no anguish of mind to compare with the mental torture suffered by the lone witness of a haunting. A special case that comes to mind is that described to me a few years before the First World War by my friend Miss Esther Crew, sister of Mr. Rex Crew, the pianist.

Miss Crew was the central figure in the case, which concerned a house in the London suburb of Ealing, occupied by her uncle, Doctor Frederick Garroween, and his family. It was a perfectly ordinary house—but let Miss Crew tell the story as she told it to me then.

"There is nothing in the appearance of the house, Mr. O'Donnell, to distinguish it from dozens of other moderate-sized, detached houses that one sees everywhere in the suburbs. It stands sixty or so yards from the road, the intervening space being occupied by a tidily-kept lawn bordered by copper beeches and pink chestnuts, with a sprinkling of rhododendron and lilac trees. There is an extensive garden in the rear, one end of which is utilized for vegetables, the remainder being kept for a play lawn.

" It has a good coach-house recently converted into a garage for a thousand-guinea motor-car, and you have only to enter the house itself to be immediately impressed with the newness of the paint and paper, the latest designs in dainty frescoes, the clever display of electric lighting, the exquisite workmanship in the overmantels. I tell you all this merely to convince you that the house, bright and cheerful and thoroughly modern—fifty years old at the most—is the least likely place in the world, one would think, to harbour a ghost.

" During the course of two pleasant visits there I saw nothing untoward. It was on my third, most recent visit that I witnessed the phenomenon that brought me such distress.

" I arrived at the house on Christmas Eve, and on entering the hall was startled to see a man—slender, thin and wiry, and dressed after the fashion of a footman in the days of our grandfathers—tiptoeing stealthily from door to door. I was so struck by the strangeness of his clothes and behaviour that I could not take my eyes off him until he disappeared from view. Then, suddenly remembering that I had not returned the greetings of my relatives, I apologized and dismissed the man from my mind.

" I did not see him again that night, but in the morning as I was hurrying downstairs to go to early service at the adjoining church, I almost ran into him coming up.

" I cannot describe to you the awful shock I received on seeing his face. It was not because it was an ugly face. On the contrary, apart from its bloodless pallor it was passably good-looking, round and smooth with tolerably well-cut features. But it was the expression, the wealth of hidden meaning in the tightly-drawn lips and heavily-lidded blue eyes, that seemed to bid me hold my tongue on the pain of instant death.

" I shrank against the wall to let him pass, and as he did so a current of icy air blew through me, causing my teeth to chatter and my legs to totter. He so fascinated me that I gazed after him as he noiselessly mounted the stairs, his bristling, close-cropped hair shining orange in the electric light. Pausing for a second or so on the brink of the landing, he looked down, his eyes shining horribly, and placing the first finger of his right hand on his lips, silently bade me keep his evil intentions secret.

"He then seemed to disappear suddenly, though how or where I cannot say—I found myself facing only a blank wall and balustrades.

"After this I thought I had better approach the Garroweens about the man, so as we were coming back from church I casually said to Muriel, the youngest of the girls: 'By the way, isn't that new footman you have a queer creature.'

"Muriel opened her eyes wide. 'New footman?' she said. 'What on earth do you mean? We haven't a footman, only a chauffeur—and there's nothing odd about him.'

"'What is the chauffeur like?' I asked.

"Muriel was very amused. 'The things you ask!' she said. 'I have never looked at Adams very closely, but he has a large nose, black hair and a jutting chin.'

"'Then it is not him,' I said.

"'Not him?' said Muriel. 'Oh, do tell me the mystery.' So I described to her what I had seen.

"She was greatly interested. 'The house must be haunted,' she said when I had finished, 'and yet it is quite new, without any history—at least, as far as we know. But what a horrid ghost! Do let us hurry, I am dying to tell the others.'

"When she told them my story they were all keenly excited, though none could offer the slightest explanation of what had occurred beyond the rather unkind suggestion that I had been dreaming. I was teased about having too much pudding, about studying too hard, and one thing and another. In short, I had no sympathizers in the household—certainly none in whom I felt I could confide should I see any further phenomena.

"Therefore nothing more was said about the footman, not by

me at all events, during the remainder of my visit. How I suffered! I was always meeting the man, Mr. O'Donnell. Sometimes he would steal quietly upon me as I was crossing a landing and after half scaring me to death would vanish through the walls. At other times he would rap at my door, and on my opening it would glide swiftly away, his malevolent eyes full of devilish glee at my discomfiture.

" On Twelfth Night my aunt and uncle, who made a point of keeping up old customs, gave a party to which they invited more people than their rooms could conveniently hold. I have never been in such a crush. Still, it was fun, many of the guests having devised ingenious costumes for the charades.

" A friend of the family, Doctor Millet, took me in to supper, bravely finding me a seat under difficulties. I was just telling him he ought to be awarded the Royal Humane Society's medal when a bitingly cold current of air made me shiver. I glanced apprehensively at the door, and there was the phantom footman. I can see him now as he stood there, peering at me over the snowy shoulders of one of the prettiest girls in the room.

" Dr. Millet, noticing my tenseness, was very solicitous. ' You look pale,' he said—' let me fetch you a glass of sherry.'

" ' Oh, no !' I cried, trying to remove my gaze from those haunting eyes across the way. ' Please stay. I don't feel well, but I shall be all right in a minute.'

" ' It's the heat,' I heard him mutter. ' Damn these crushes. Miss Crew, are you sure there's nothing I can get you?'

" ' Yes, thank you,' I told him—and then I gasped ' Oh, no !' as the footman, smiling sardonically, began to move in our direction.

" Holding a tray covered with small delicacies in one hand and with the index finger of the other laid jeeringly along his nose, he glided, unseen by all save me, from guest to guest, the atmosphere chilling perceptibly the nearer he drew. I saw the doctor's eyes follow mine as he vainly tried to discover the cause of my alarm, seeing nothing beyond the closely-serried ranks of merrymakers.

" ' I think, Miss Crew,' he said, ' you had better allow me to escort you to another room.'

" ' Oh, no, Dr. Millet,' I said, almost too frightened to open my mouth, for the footman had arrived in front of the third chair to my right. ' Please take no notice of me. I'm simply over-excited—I shall be all right.'

" Two chairs . . . one chair . . . Merciful heavens, I thought, the footman will be at mine next—and almost before I had realized this I saw him leave my neighbour and tiptoe towards me.

" I leaned back in my chair, sick and faint. I shut my eyes to keep the hateful vision out, but I still felt him creeping on. The suspense became intolerable and I felt perspiration burst from every pore. I opened my eyes and there he stood before me. Never shall I forget the horror I went through as our glances met. Bowing derisively he thrust the salver under my very nose, and as I flung myself away from it he burst into mad laughter.

" I fainted. When I came to, Dr. Millet was fanning me and the footman had vanished. How could I explain what I had seen? I could not, so I let it be thought I had merely suffered a dizzy turn.

" My next experience was on the night before my return home. I had gone to bed early as I had a sick headache, and was determined to be well for the journey back next day. I don't think I slept at all, or if I did it was only for a few minutes, as I heard the clock outside sound every hour between ten and two. The thought of travelling next day may have had something to do with this restlessness, but it was also due to a vague uneasiness which I shrank from analysing.

" Two o'clock had barely finished striking before I heard an unmistakable scratching on the valance of the bed just beneath me. I did not dare to look, but trying to reassure myself it was the family's Irish terrier that had wandered into the room, I called out to it. The scratching instantly stopped, but then it re-started, and this time so much like a dog that I was sure it really

266

must be Nip. I turned over on my side and thrusting my hand out of bed, felt for his collar.

" I did not have to grope about long before my fingers came into contact with something very cold and hairy that made my heart beat fast. I raised myself on my elbow and peeped over the edge of the bed, and there, shining up at me, was the face of the footman. I was terror-stricken. His eyes not only chained mine to them but seemed to draw out of my limbs every atom of vital energy—I was powerless to move or utter a sound.

" He smiled, an evil smile, and slowly rose up from his haunches. I noticed with fresh horror that in one hand he held an open razor.

" What would have happened next I dread to think about. Happily, by one of those slender accidents on which the crisis of a lifetime so often depends, his murderous course was interrupted. There was a sudden footfall on the staircase, which loosed the spell upon me and I was able to shriek for help.

" As I did so the footman launched himself on me. With a great bound he almost touched the ceiling, and then, swooping downwards, fell on me with a crash. Something, his hand I thought, collided with my head. It stunned me, and I faded away into blackness.

" I recovered consciousness to find one of my cousins looking at me gravely from the bedside. She had been awakened by my uncle, who told her she had better stay with me for a while as I had had a bad nightmare, and fainted as a result. He had been rung up by a patient, but would look in to see how I was on his return. This he did, and I was relieved to hear him say there was nothing to prevent me travelling home, although he would be glad if I would make my indisposition an excuse to stay. Stay in that house and in that room! Not for a thousand pounds. I was never in my life more glad to end a visit—and I dare say they on their part were somewhat relieved to see me go.

" On arriving home I told my parents everything I had seen. They were very upset, both by my story and my pale appearance. My father, however, was a considerate man and said it would hardly be fair to his brother's family to talk about my experience even to our friends. 'A story like that, once circulated, spreads like wildfire,' he said, 'and would encourage a never-ending stream of newspapermen and others.' He promised he would run up to Ealing some time, ostensibly on an ordinary errand, and if possible seek a solution to the mystery without arousing the family's suspicion.

" Owing to business worries and an attack of appendicitis, my father was obliged to delay this visit for several months, but he managed to go to Ealing at last, and I had a letter from him a week or so after his departure. In this he wrote :

" ' I think I have discovered the origin of the phenomenon that haunted you. Frederick knows absolutely nothing about it, but I got him to introduce me to an old Army surgeon who has probably lived in Ealing longer than anyone else. During a talk with this man, who is in his eighties, I drew him on to the subject of ghosts, and he remarked with a chuckle that he recollected a tale of the house that formerly occupied the site where your uncle's house now stands being haunted.

" ' He told me it was a black sort of building, and that as a boy he had vivid recollections of tearing past it after night-fall for fear of seeing " the man with the orange head." You may guess I pricked up my ears at that, remembering your description of the footman's peculiar coloured hair; so I tried to pump as much information as possible out of him. He said they called the man by that name because he was re-ported to have bristly orange-coloured hair, and added : " I never saw him myself, but I've met plenty of people who took their affidavits they had. Who was he? Why, the ghost of a footman called John Deacon, who they said, once lived in the house but absconded after robbing and murdering his master. Whether the story was true or not I can't say, but at all events the house had to be pulled down as no one would take it—and that is all I know." I could not get anything further from the old man and I think, Esther, you will have to

268

be content with this. After all, it is a very feasible explanation. The phantom you saw must actually have been that of Deacon, returned once again to its former haunts.'

" And that, Mr. O'Donnell, is as far as our investigations could go," said Miss Crew, ending her singular story. " How do you explain it?"

I had to tell her that I agreed with her late father; that it seemed likely enough that John Deacon's ghost had transferred its attentions to the new house, for in dozens of instances it was the ground that was haunted and not merely the building. I also advised her, when next she visited the Garroweens, to let it be in the summer. I explained that ghosts often confined their visitations to certain seasons of the year, so that a ghost which generally appeared at Christmas would not in all probability be seen in July; that if she went to Ealing in this month she might enjoy the society of her uncle's family untormented by the attentions of the orange-haired footman.

What I could not explain to Miss Crew was why one person should see a ghost, be persecuted by it even, while a dozen others should remain oblivious to it. When we have the answer to this we shall in all likelihood possess the key to the ghostly world.

THE HOUSE ON THE CLIFF

I FIND that people are always surprised to hear of ghosts manifesting themselves in new, and comparatively new houses and
buildings. Fictional stories have sent so many ghosts clanking in
armour through Britain's stately homes that there is, perhaps,
some excuse for the common supposition that ghosts must of
necessity have an old house to live in; but of course this is not so.
What often determines the nature of a haunting is not the actual
building, old or new, but what happened on the site years before, or what was already present—perhaps some elemental or
" nature spirit "—at the time the house was erected.

In short, in the case of a fair number of hauntings, the ghost
has been in residence on the spot long before the house was built.

During my years spent in St. Ives, Cornwall, where I lived
while struggling to earn a living as a writer, I once occupied a
new house which was badly haunted. I had seen the house
under construction, high on a cliff, and was so taken with its
delightful position, overlooking a valley, that I secured the letting
and moved into it as its very first tenant.

For some time there was no one else in the house but myself
and Miss Ellie Bolitho, my aged housekeeper. I slept in a room

off the top landing, and very soon found myself awaking, always at about two o'clock, to hear footsteps come up the stairs and pass along the passage outside my room. Sometimes I heard also the sound of heavy breathing and panting.

I thought at first it was my housekeeper walking in her sleep, and to make sure, the next time I was awakened by the footsteps I jumped out of bed and opened my door; but no one was there.

Soon after this, Ellie gave me notice of her departure.

" I am very sorry to leave you," she said, " but I can't remain in the house any longer with those antlers " (I had a pair of old antlers from Ireland mounted on brackets in the hall). " They are unlucky and the creatures they belong to walk about here at night."

" Why, Ellie—what, nonsense," I said. " You surely don't think the house is haunted?"

" I know it is," she replied, " and it's haunted by those animals."

She then described the noises she had heard, and they were very similar to those I heard myself. I pressed her to stay, but it was no use; she left on the hour of expiry of her notice.

I engaged in her place a middle-aged woman, Mrs. Webb. She was a Cockney, very dignified and practical. After she had been with me about a week, I was unexpectedly detained one night in Redruth and did not return home till early in the morning. To my surprise Mrs. Webb was not in the house, but she arrived shortly, carrying blankets and sheets in her arms.

" Whatever's happened?" I asked, looking at the bedclothes she threw down.

" Oh," she said, with a deep sigh of relief, " I'm so glad you've returned, Mr. O'Donnell. I simply daren't stay here alone, so I went to Mrs. Marble's last night, when you didn't return. I might as well tell you, sir," she added, " there's something very strange about this house. When I've been in the kitchen after you've gone to bed, I've had the feeling that something very queer has come into the house, from the valley outside. It's

271

always been about the same time, between eleven and twelve o'clock, and I've often heard it walking about the house all night. I never thought there were such things as ghosts, but I'm quite sure there are now, and I've no hesitation in saying that this house is haunted."

Mrs. Webb left me soon afterwards, and I had to engage yet another housekeeper in her place.

So far the disturbances had been confined to the footsteps and heavy breathing already mentioned, but one night there were new and additional phenomena. I awoke about two o'clock as usual, and heard the footsteps coming up the stairs and into the passage, towards my room. When they arrived at my room they stopped, and after a brief pause, during which I got the impression that something was listening, there was a tremendous bang at the top panel of my door. Then silence.

The noise startled me so much that it was some seconds before I could pull myself sufficiently together to get out of bed and open the door. The passage was flooded with moonlight, and through the open doorway of the room opposite I could see the leaves tapping softly against the window-panes, but that was all; there was no sign anywhere of the author of the disturbances.

The following night I set a trap. I not only sprinkled alternate layers of sand and flour on the floor of the passage, but I tied cotton across it and placed a table in it, with a cupful of water balanced on the edge of it, in such a manner that at the slightest touch it would fall off. Then I went to bed and waited.

At the usual hour I again heard the footsteps. They came unhesitatingly along the passage; there was a crash, as if the cup had been knocked off the table on to the ground, the footsteps continued to advance, then, as usual, stopped at my room.

I got out of bed, and as I did so there was a tremendous bang at the top panel of my door. I threw the door open as quickly as I could, but there was no one, nothing there. The cotton was intact, the cup of water was in its place on the table, and when I examined the flour and sand, I found no trace of any footmarks.

I never heard the bangs again, but the other disturbances went on during the whole term of my tenancy and were heard by quite a number of people, sometimes singly and sometimes collectively.

It was not until I had quit the house that I heard several strange stories in connection with its site. A Mrs. Ashby told me that one night, when passing by the spot upon which the house was afterwards built, she saw a very tall figure with a queer round head rise from the ground, walk across the road in front of her with a peculiar swaggering motion, and disappear abruptly over the edge of the cliff. She added that she did not know it at the time, but only learned subsequently, that the cliff, according to local belief, was, and always had been, haunted.

Another woman, whom I met quite by chance in Plymouth, told me that on a visit to St. Ives about twenty years previously, she too had seen an apparition on the spot now occupied by the house I had lived in, and from her description of what she saw, it was obvious that she and Mrs. Ashby had precisely the same experience; and she, like Mrs. Ashby, assured me that at the time she encountered the phenomenon she had no idea that the place was said to be haunted. She did not then believe in ghosts, but now she had no hesitation whatever in saying she had seen one.

So the cliff haunting appeared to be the work of an elemental spirit.

In two other houses I rented in St. Ives odd things happened, though of a different nature. One house had been occupied by an eccentric old woman, and when her niece showed me over the house she remarked, with a look at the bare and rather gloomy staircase: " I could never live here, I should always be seeing my aunt. She died in one of the rooms overhead, and I can see her now, coming down those stairs."

Well, I took the house, and although during my tenancy I never saw the old lady's ghost, I experienced one or two remarkable happenings. On one occasion a trap door in the ceiling was opened very mysteriously, since the loft to which it had access did not communicate with the house next door, and it was inaccessible from below, while on another occasion I found, on coming out of my bedroom in the morning, a rug spread out very carefully on the landing outside my door. As there was no one but myself and my wife in the house at the time and all the doors and windows in the lower part of the premises were securely fastened, it seemed to us that only a ghost could be responsible.

It was while I was in this house that I was awakened one night by the most appalling screams. If one can compare them to anything human at all, they sounded like a woman in awful physical pain. They lasted for several seconds and then gradually died away.

On getting up and going out on to the landing I found the rest of the household, numbering a good many at that time, collected there, listening. Fear was on every face, and when I told them I felt sure it was the Banshee, all agreed that it must be, since the sounds were not human, and they had never heard anything in the least degree like them before.

A day or two later I received news of the death of my uncle in Limerick. He was the senior member of our branch of the family, the oldest branch of the O'Donnells of the North of Ireland.

THE MIDNIGHT BRIDE

ASSUREDLY ONE of the strangest cases of continuous haunting by a ghost that was both morally and physically harmful, is that of Sarah Polgrain. It has been discussed by several writers in the past, but much of the information which I now give has never before appeared in print. The case is as follows :

In the early part of the last century there lived in the village of Ludgvan, close to Penzance, a married couple named Polgrain. It was the same old story, at least to begin with—that of a rather irritable elderly man, and a wife a good many years younger than himself, who having long lost whatever affection she might once had entertained for him, was now in love with someone else. The pair were always quarrelling. Sarah Polgrain used to fly into violent passions with her husband and was often over-heard to say vicious things to him, and threaten him. There were rumours that she occasionally beat him, and that once, at least, she had jeopardized his life.

Then came the climax. Sarah, very agitated and pale, came running into a neighbour's cottage one morning, crying out that her husband had been suddenly seized with what she believed to be cholera, and was terribly ill. Later on, she again visited the same cottage, this time with the news that her husband was dead. At first no one suspected anything wrong. The doctor, apparently, was satisfied that death was due to cholera, and a certificate to that effect was given.

After the funeral, however, rumours of foul play began to be circulated, and they eventually became so insistent that the local authorities decided to take action. The body of Mr. Polgrain was exhumed, and on examination it was found to contain sufficient arsenic to kill at least three people. Sarah Polgrain was arrested and charged with murder.

Now this being a ghost book and not a work on crime, there is no need for me to go into the details of the trial. It is sufficient to say that Sarah was proved to have had a great hatred for her husband, and to have held many clandestine meetings with her lover, who went by the name of Yorkshire Jack. Some people said Yorkshire Jack influenced her, but in reality there seemed little doubt that she, being by far the stronger character of the two, influenced him. He was a good-looking, gay young spark, and Sarah appears to have firmly made up her mind that no one but herself should have him. The case against her was most damning; it could scarcely have been more so had she been actually caught in the act of murder. She was found guilty and sentenced to be hanged.

So far the case of Sarah Polgrain is ordinary enough; we now come to certain unusual happenings that make it extraordinary. When the time for the execution drew near (executions, in those days, were conducted in full view of the public), Sarah pleaded that Yorkshire Jack might be allowed to accompany her to the scaffold.

In some counties such a request would, doubtless, have been peremptorily refused, but the Cornish being exceptionally tender-hearted where women are concerned, it was acceded to at once; so that when the day of execution arrived, and the procession from the prison slowly approached the scaffold, Yorkshire Jack was seen striding solemnly along at Sarah's side. On and on the execution party came, till at last they had mounted the platform.

Then, when everything was ready, Jack kissed Sarah. As the two stood clasped in each other's arms Sarah was heard to say in slow, measured tones, "You will?" And Jack, after some slight hesitation, responded quickly and nervously, "I will."

He then stepped away from her, but she never took her eyes off him, gazing at him with an expression of awful intensity till the very last. So much for the execution. Now for one of the numerous stories of what happened subsequently.

Close to midnight a day or two later, a resident of Ludgvan, tramping wearily home after a long day's outing in Penzance, was passing the churchyard when, simultaneously with the striking of the church clock, he heard to his surprise the sound of digging. Wondering what could be going on at such an hour, as to his knowledge there was no immediate forthcoming funeral, he stopped, and then entering the churchyard, made for the spot from which the sounds came. He had not gone far before he saw in the cold white beams of the moon, which clearly illuminated every object around him, a tall figure in what looked like a white sheet, with its back to him, busily digging on the spot where Mr. Polgrain had been twice buried. The night was still, and the metallic click of the spade as it scattered the earth sounded loud and clear.

Fascinated beyond measure, the man from Ludgvan continued watching the figure, till suddenly a fit of coughing, which he could not suppress, caused it to straighten itself up and look round. The shock he then received was indescribable, for the white face that looked into his was not the face of the living at all, but of the dead. Feature by feature, though the eyes were fixed and glassy, and the jaw dropped horribly, he recognized it at once—it was the face of Sarah Polgrain. Round her throat, standing out in ghastly contrast to the appalling whiteness of the skin, was the black mark of the rope.

For some seconds he was too overcome with terror to do anything; he remained where he was, staring at the thing, his heart almost at a standstill and his knees on the verge of giving way beneath him. Then, quite suddenly, his faculties seemed to revive, and he turned on his heels and ran, never once stopping till he reached home.

Another incident of a somewhat similar nature involved a stranger to Cornwall. This man was riding along one night in the neighbourhood of Ludgvan, when owing to the wind and rain, for there was a great gale blowing, he somehow lost his way and presently found himself in a lane full of ruts and holes, instead of on the good main road leading from Penzance to Hayle. Riding on as best he could, intending to ask his way at the first cottage he came to, he was making fair progress when suddenly his horse shied, and the next moment started off at breakneck speed. When at last he was able to regain some control of the animal he glanced around and was startled to see a tall figure, swathed from head to foot in white, close to him, and, with apparent ease, keeping up with him, although he was still galloping at speed. He tried to persuade himself that what he saw was due either to an optical illusion, to hallucination, or simply to sheer imagination; but reason asserted itself and he could not.

Arriving at length alongside a churchyard wall, over which he could see the gravestones gleaming white in the moonlight, the thing suddenly turned, strode across the road and approached a gateway. Impelled by curiosity, the stranger then looked back at it, and as he did so it threw off its hood and faced him. In the clear moonlight he could see it distinctly. Its cheeks were white, its wide-open mouth drooped hideously; and as its eyes met his they gleamed and glittered with a baleful light. It had long hair, hanging in disorder about its neck and shoulders, while round its throat there appeared to be a broad black band or ribbon.

Overwhelmed with horror, the rider put spurs to his horse and rode on. Almost immediately afterwards, however, yielding to a sudden impulse, he drew up and turned in his saddle to take a final look at the thing before passing out of sight. It had disappeared; but as he paused, too fascinated for the moment to stir, over and above the moaning and whistling of the wind he heard faint, but quite unmistakable sounds of digging.

Well, these and similar stories produced such panic in Ludgvan and its immediate vicinity that, in the words of a local resident, " no one dared venture near the spot (the burial-ground) after dusk."

There was, in or near Ludgvan at that time, a well with the strange superstition attached to it that no child born in the parish of Ludgvan, and baptized or dipped in the water of its well, would ever suffer the ignominy of hanging. When Sarah Polgrain was hanged, the people of Ludgvan were greatly disturbed, fearing that the superstition, or tradition, had for the first time been departed from, an event which they regarded as a very unlucky omen. Fortunately however, someone suggested that, perhaps, Sarah was not actually born in their parish; and a search being made among the parish records, to the relief of everyone it was discovered that Sarah had been born in a neighbouring village, and therefore was not a native of Ludgvan after all. At which, we are told, " there was universal rejoicing."

Now to return to Yorkshire Jack. After Sarah's death a marked change was seen in this young, gay blade. Gone was all his gaiety and abandonment, and it was not long before he became sour-tempered and morose. His appearance, too, sadly altered. From being healthy-complexioned and well proportioned, he grew miserably thin and ghastly pale, and developed a queer habit of constantly looking over his shoulder, as if he thought he was being followed. A friend met him, so it was said, one wild, rainy night on the beach at Penzance, and asked him where he was going.

" Home," Jack replied surlily, " but it is for the last time."

" Why so?" the friend inquired in surprise.

" Because of her," Jack said gloomily. " She gives me no peace. Wherever I go she follows me. Whenever I turn, I find her at my elbow."

" Do you mean Sarah?" the friend ventured. " Or rather, Sarah's ghost?"

" Aye," Jack said, " you've hit it. Walk along with me a bit, and you won't find I'm gaming you."

The friend acquiesced, and as they paced along side by side in silence, presently there came the sound of footsteps, and the tap, tap, tap of high heels close behind them. They could both distinctly hear these sounds above the breaking of the waves on the shingles and the moaning and howling of the wind. When they left the seafront and footed it along the road leading inland towards Gulval and Ludgvan, the tap, tap, tap still followed them.

" Do you hear it?" Jack declared. " Turn round and look."

The friend was generally considered a reliable man of some courage, but when he got that order he hesitated. There was something particularly unnerving in the tapping and he was afraid of what he might see. At last, however, he steeled himself to turn round, and what he saw was not the figure of a person at all but a peculiar bluish light. It was cylindrical in form, and about five feet or more in height; and as it moved along the middle of the road, there issued from it the tap, tap, tap of high-heeled shoes. Yet there was nothing in its shape suggestive of a woman.

" Well," Jack said, " do you see her?"

" No," replied the friend, greatly disturbed, " I see no ghost at all, nothing but a light, and I'm thinking I'll be leaving you, for I can't stand being followed by it any longer."

He made for a low wall as he spoke, and hastily clambering over it, left Yorkshire Jack to continue the rest of the way home alone; that is to say, alone save for the tapping.

The next day Jack went to sea, and the strange, uncanny presence followed him. His mates used to see him constantly looking over his shoulder at something which they could not see, but at night, when they were lying in their hammocks in the fo'c's'le, they were constantly aware of a strange, unpleasant something standing in their midst. This went on for weeks, all through the voyage, and until they were almost within sight again of Mounts Bay. Then one morning Yorkshire Jack, who had been growing more and more restless and morose, made an extraordinary confession.

Calling aside one of the crew, he told him he doubted very much if he would live to see another sunrise.

"When I was on the scaffold that morning talking to Sarah Polgrain," Jack said, "she made me promise on my oath that on this very day, at midnight, I would marry her. Thinking to humour her, and supposing trouble had unhinged her mind, I agreed. But I know now that she was quite sane and much in earnest. Not being able to wed me in the flesh and blood, she means to bind me to her for ever in the spirit."

He whispered these last words with such emphasis, peering fearfully around him as he did so, that the seaman beside him felt his flesh creep, and was completely unnerved for the rest of the day.

That night, at close to twelve o'clock, the whole fo'c's'le was awakened by the sound of footsteps. They were the steps of someone wearing high-heeled shoes, and they came tap, tapping along the passage leading to midships, and halted beside the hammock in which Yorkshire Jack lay. White as a sheet, his features contorted with terror, Jack got up and without uttering a sound, left the fo'c's'le and made for the deck; and the tapping went with him all the way. Once on deck he walked straight to the bulwarks, and clambering on to them, before his terrified comrades could sufficiently pull themselves together to stop him, he leaped into the sea. Just for a moment or so those on board caught a glimpse of his white face amid the black billows, and then, before any help could be sent to him, he was swept away and out of sight.

According to the statements of certain eye-witnesses of the tragedy, directly Jack disappeared, those of his mates who were leaning over the bulwarks watching, distinctly heard—at least so they declared—coming, apparently from the depths of the ocean, the far-away chiming of bells; a curiously ominous and sinister sound. They were, undoubtedly, wedding bells, but the marriage associated with them was one that could only have been made and sealed in hell.

281

THE PHANTOM DACHSHUND

A HAUNTING can be as much a source of worry as a distressing and puzzling illness. A person with an apparently unusual physical complaint, or one whose symptoms he would find embarrassingly difficult to describe to a doctor, will often keep his condition secret and suffer on in silence for as long as he is able. It is only when he is finally driven to confide in the doctor that he discovers his illness is not at all unique, that thousands of other people have suffered from it and thousands more will.

So it is with a great number of hauntings. The witness involved will keep secret his alarming experience, very often believing that he must have been half out of his mind; until, to his complete surprise, along comes another, absolutely independent witness— or even several of them—to offer personal corroboration of the same ghostly happening.

Over the years, corroboration of hauntings has come to me in a variety of different ways, and one example of this is the case of the phantom dachshund of a street in the West End of London. This began with a letter to me from a correspondent, Mrs. J. Percy, as follows:

" Though I am by no means over-indulgent to dogs, they generally greet me very effusively, and it would seem that there is something in my individuality that is peculiarly attractive to them. This being so, I was not greatly surprised one day, when in the immediate neighbourhood of B—— Street, to find myself persistently followed by a rough-haired dachshund wearing a gaudy yellow collar.

" I tried to scare it away by shaking my sunshade at it, but all to no purpose—it came resolutely on. I was beginning to despair of getting rid of it, when I came to B—— Street, where my husband once practised as an oculist. There it suddenly altered its tactics, and instead of keeping at my heels, became my conductor, forging slowly ahead with a gliding motion that both puzzled and fascinated me. I saw too that despite the heat of the day—it must have been approaching ninety degrees in the shade—the legs and stomach of the dachshund were covered with mud and dripping with water.

" When it came to No. 90 it halted, and veering swiftly round, eyed me in the strangest manner, just as if it had some secret it was bursting to disclose. It remained in this attitude until I was within two or three feet of it—certainly not more—when, to my great amazement, it absolutely vanished—melted away into thin air.

" The iron gate leading to the area was closed, so there was nowhere for it to have hidden, and besides, I was almost bending over the animal at the time as I wanted to read the name on its collar. There being no one near at hand I could not discuss the strange incident, and so came away wondering whether what I had seen was actually a ' ghost ' or a mere hallucination. No. 90, I might add, judging from the brass plate on the door was inhabited by a doctor with an unpronounceable foreign name."

Now this curious little encounter on a hot summer's day would have remained in my notebook along with other interesting single sightings, had I not then been fortunate to hear from another lady—a total stranger to the writer whose letter I have just quoted—about what, without doubt, was this very same phantom dog. Here is Mrs. S. Howard's story as she told it to me:

"I once had a rough-haired dachshund, Robert, whom I loved devotedly. We were living at the time near B—— Street, which always had a peculiar attraction for dear Robert, who, I am now obliged to confess, had rather too much liberty—more, indeed, than eventually proved good for him. The servants complained that Robert ruled the house, and I believe what they said was true, for my sister and I idolized him, giving him the very best of everything and never having the heart to refuse him anything he wanted. You will probably scarcely credit it, but I have sat up all night nursing him when he had a cold and was otherwise indisposed. Can you therefore imagine my feelings when he was absent one day at mealtime? Such a thing had never happened, for fond of morning 'constitutionals' as he was, he was always the soul of punctuality when it came to his food.

"Neither my sister nor I would hear of eating anything. While he was missing, not a morsel did we touch, but slipping on our hats, and bidding the servants do the same, we scoured the neighbourhood. The afternoon passed without any sign of Robert, and when bedtime came (he always slept in our room) and still no sign of our pet, I thought we should have gone mad.

"Of course, we advertised, selecting the most likely papers, and we resorted to other mediums too, but, alas! it was hopeless. Our darling little pet was irrevocably lost. For days we were utterly inconsolable, doing nothing but mope morning, noon and night. I cannot tell you how forlorn we felt. Then came the incident which revealed to us the terrible manner of his death.

"I was out walking one evening when, to my intense joy and surprise, I suddenly saw Robert standing on the pavement a few feet ahead of me, regarding me intently from out of his pathetic brown eyes. A sensation of extreme coldness now stole over me, and I noticed with something akin to a shock that, in spite of the hot, dry weather, Robert looked as if he had been in the rain for hours. He wore the bright yellow collar I had bought him shortly before his disappearance, so that had there been any doubt of his identity that would have removed it instantly.

" On my calling to him he turned quickly round and, with a slight gesture of the head as if bidding me to follow, he glided forward. My natural impulse was to run after him and pick him up to pet but try as hard as I could, I could not shorten the distance between us, although he never appeared to alter his pace. I was quite out of breath by the time we reached B—— Street, where, to my surprise he stopped at No. 90 and, turning round again, gazed at me in the most beseeching manner. I can't describe that look; suffice it to say that no human eyes could have been more expressive, but of what beyond the most profound love and sorrow I cannot attempt to state. I have pondered upon it through the whole of a midsummer night, but have not been able to solve it to my satisfaction.

" I do not know for how long we stood there looking at one another, it may have been minutes or just a few brief seconds. He took the initiative from me, for, as I leaped forward to raise him in my arms he glided through the stone steps into the area.

" Convinced now that what I beheld was Robert's apparition, I determined to see the strange affair through to the bitter end, and entering the gate, I also went down into the area. Robert had come to an abrupt halt by the side of a low wooden box, and as I foolishly made an abortive attempt to reach him with my hand, he vanished instantaneously. I searched the area thoroughly, and was assured there was no outlet save by the steps I had just descended, and no hole, nor nook, nor cranny where anything the size of Robert could be completely hidden from sight. What did it all mean? I knew Robert had always had a weakness fro exploring areas, especially in B—— Street, and in the box where his wraith disappeared I saw a piece of raw meat!

" Now there are ways in which a piece of raw meat may lie without arousing suspicion, but the position of this morsel suggested it had been placed there carefully, and for assuredly no other purpose than to entice stray animals. Resolving to question the owner of the house I rapped at the front door, but was told by the manservant, a German, that his master never saw anyone without an appointment. I then did a very unwise thing—I explained the purpose of my visit to this man, who not only denied any knowledge of my dog, but said that the meat must have been thrown into the area by some passer-by—no one in his household would throw away good meat like that. He asked me to go away at once or his master would be very angry, as he stood no nonsense from anyone.

"I had to leave—I had no alternative. For after all, who would believe my ghostly experience? I found out, however, from a medical friend that No. 90 was tenanted by an Anglo-German who was well thought of at a certain London hospital, where he was often occupied in vivisection. 'I dare say,' my friend added, ' he does a little vivisecting in his private surgery, by way of practice.'

" ' But can't he be stopped?' I asked. 'It's horrible that he should be allowed to murder people's pets.'

" ' You don't know for certain that he does do this,' said my friend. 'You suppose so from what you say you saw—and evidence of that nature is no evidence at all. No, you can do nothing except to be extra careful in future, and if you have another dog make him steer clear of No. 90.'

" I was sensible enough to see that he was right, and did not press the matter. I soon noticed one thing, however: there were no more pieces of meat temptingly displayed in the box. So it is just possible that the occupier of No. 90 got wind of my inquiries and thought it wise to end his nefarious practices."

The stories of ghost dogs which have come my way are many and varied. Here is the strange experience of Mrs. Anna Sebuim.

"One Hallowe'en," Mrs. Sebuim told me, " I was staying with some friends in Hampstead, and we amused ourselves by working spells to commemorate the night. There is one spell in which one walks along a path sowing hempseed and repeating some fantastic words; after which they are supposed to see those people who are destined to come into their life in the near future. Eager to put this spell to the test, I went into the garden alone and, walking boldly along a path bordered each side by evergreens, sprinkled hempseed lavishly.

" Nothing happened, and I was about to give up when suddenly I heard a pattering on the gravel. Turning round I saw an ugly little black-and-tan mongrel running towards me, wagging its stumpy tail. Not at all prepossessed with the creature, for my own dogs are pure-bred, and thinking it must have strayed into the grounds, I was about to drive it out and had put down my hand to prevent it jumping on my long dress, when to my astonishment it vanished—literally melted away into fine air beneath my very eyes.

" Not knowing what to make of the incident, but feeling inclined to attribute it to a trick of the imagination, I rejoined my friends. I did not tell them what had happened, though I made a note of it in my diary. Within six months of this incident I was greatly astonished to find a dog, exactly like the one I have just described, but this time undeniably flesh and blood, running about on the lawn of my house in Bath. How the animal had got there was a complete mystery, and what is stranger still, it seemed to recognize me, for it rushed towards me, frantically wagging its diminutive tail.

" I had not the heart to turn it away, and so the forlorn little mongrel was permitted to make its home in my house—and a very happy arrangement it proved to be. For three years all went well, and then the end came swiftly and unexpectedly.

" I was in Blackheath at the time, and the mongrel was in Bath. It was again Hallowe'en, but there was no hempseed sowing on this night, for no one in the house but myself took the slightest interest in anything to do with the supernatural. Eleven o'clock came, and I retired to rest. My bed was one of those antique four-posters, hung with curtains that shone crimson in the ruddy glow of a cheerful fire. All my preparations complete,

I had pulled back the hangings and was about to slip in between the sheets when, to my unbounded amazement, what should I see sitting on the counterpane but the black-and-tan mongrel! It was him right enough—there could not be another such ugly dog—though, unlike his usual self, he gave no demonstration of joy. On the contrary, he appeared downright miserable. His ears hung, his mouth dropped, and his bleared little eyes were watery and sad.

" Greatly perplexed, if not alarmed, at so extraordinary a phenomenon, I nevertheless felt compelled to put out my hand to comfort him—when he immediately vanished.

" Two days later I received a letter from Bath, and in a post-script I read that ' the mongrel ' (we never called it by any other name) had been run over and killed by a car, the incident occurring on Hallowe'en at *about eleven o'clock*.

" ' Of course,' my sister wrote, ' you won't mind much—he was so extremely ugly, and—well—we were only too glad it was none of the other dogs.'

" But my sister was wrong, for notwithstanding his unsightly appearance and hopeless lack of breed, I had grown to like that little black-and-tan more than any of my rare and choice pets."

Miss Jean Prettyman, whom I met in Cornwall, told me she once lived in a house in Westmorland that was haunted by the apparition of a large dog, enveloped in a bluish glow, which apparently emanated from within it. The dog, while appearing in all parts of the house, invariably vanished in a big cupboard at the back of the hall staircase. Miss Prettyman, her family, the servants, and several visitors to the house all saw the same apparition and were more frightened by the suddenness of its coming than by its actual appearance.

The theory was that it was the ghost of some dog that had been cruelly done to death—possibly by starvation—in the cupboard.

Some other ghost dogs do not make their appearance so startlingly obvious, as may be instanced by the following case in which I was concerned.

A friend of mine, Edward Morgan, had a terrier called Scotch, which was found one morning, poisoned, in its big stone kennel. Soon afterwards Morgan came to me and said: " Elliott, I've got a new dog, a spaniel, but nothing will induce it to enter the kennel in which poor Scotch was poisoned. Come and see!"

I did so, and what he said was true. Mack, the spaniel, when carried to the entrance of the kennel, resolutely refused to go inside it, barking, whining, and showing unmistakable signs of fear. I knelt down, and peering into the kennel saw two luminous eyes and the distinct outlines of a dog's head.

" Edward," I said, " the mystery is easily solved—there's already a dog in here."

" Nonsense!" Morgan cried.

" But there is," I said. " See for yourself."

Bending down, he poked his head into the kennel. He then straightened up, looking at me very suspiciously.

" You're having me on," he said. " There's nothing in there."

" What?" I said. " Do you mean to say you can see no dog?"

" No—because there isn't one!"

" Let me look again," I said, and kneeling down, I peeped in to see exactly the same animal shape and the luminous eyes.

" Do you mean to say you can't see a dog's face and eyes looking straight at us?" I asked.

" No," said Morgan. " I can see nothing." And to prove to me the truth of what he said, he fetched a pole and raked about the kennel vigorously with it.

We both then tried to make Mack enter, and Morgan finally caught hold of him and placed him forcibly inside. Mack's terror knew no limit. He gave one loud howl, and flying out of the kennel with his ears hanging back, tore past into the front garden, where we left him in peace.

Morgan was still sceptical as to there being anything wrong with the kennel, but two days later he wrote me as follows:

" I must apologize for doubting you the other day. I have

just had what you declared you saw corroborated. A friend of my wife's was here this afternoon, and on hearing of Mack's refusal to sleep in the kennel she said right away she knew what was the matter—it was the smell; Mack scented the poison which was used to destroy Scotch. She suggested I should have the kennel thoroughly fumigated and there would be no more trouble. Well, my wife asked her to go into the yard and have a look at the kennel, and the moment she bent down and looked in she cried out like you did— ' Why, there's a dog inside—a terrier.' My wife and I both looked in but could see nothing. Our visitor, however, persisted, and on my handing her a stick, she struck at the figure she saw. To her amazement the stick went right through it. Then, and not till then, did we tell her of your experience. ' Well,' she said, ' I have never believe in ghosts but I do so now. I am quite certain that what I see is the phantom of Scotch. How glad I am, because I am at last assured that animals have spirits and come back to us.' "

That incident happened at a country house. My next case occurred in the heart of London, at the old Motley Club in Dean Street, Soho. This club, sadly no longer with us, was mainly for film artists. One afternoon, a few weeks before the club closed down, a film actor named Dickson as he entered the premises encountered a big yellow dog on the staircase. He threw it a biscuit from a packet he was carrying. Taking no notice of the biscuit, however, the dog walked by Dickson and descended the stairs leading to the ground floor.

The next day, in precisely the same spot, Dickson again saw the dog. As before, he threw it a biscuit, and as before, the dog passed him by without taking the slightest notice of the biscuit. Thinking this rather strange, Dickson turned round to look at the dog, but it had vanished.

Much puzzled, for it was not possible for the dog to have reached the bottom of the staircase, and it could not otherwise get out of sight, Dickson resolved to visit the club at the same hour the following day. He did so, and in the same spot encountered the dog. This time he threw it a small piece of meat, and on the dog taking no notice whatever of the meat, he aimed a slight blow at the animal with his stick. The stick passed right through the dog, which at once faded away into nothingness, leaving Dickson with his hair standing on end.

Dickson told me this story himself and introduced me to another actor who testified to having also seen the dog. I learned from one or two other club members afterwards that, although they had never seen the dog, they had sometimes experienced a very uncanny sensation when ascending or descending the staircase between the first and second floors.

The case is not an unusual one. The ghost was probably that of a dog that had lived and died on the premises, and whose spirit was tied to the spot through some deep emotion. More unusual, and in fact the only case of its kind which I have on record, is that told to me as a boy by an elderly friend of mine, Miss Norah Lefanu.

Miss Lefanu told me she was walking one evening along a lonely country lane when she suddenly noticed an enormous Newfoundland dog following in her wake a few yards behind. Being very fond of dogs she called out to it and attempted to stroke it. To her disappointment, however, it dodged aside, and repeated this manoeuvre every time she tried to touch it. Finally losing patience she resumed her walk, the dog still following her.

In this fashion they went on until they came to a particularly dark part of the road, where the branches of the trees almost met overhead and there was a deep stagnant pool. On one side of the road the hedge was high, but on the other there was a slight gap leading into a thick spinney. Miss Lefanu had never before walked this far along the road alone so late in the day; she had been warned against going as far as the spinney even in daylight. Everything that she had ever heard about it flashed across her mind, and she was more than once on the verge of turning back, when the sight of the big, friendly-looking dog plodding behind, reassuring her, she pressed on.

Just as she came to the gap there was a loud snapping of twigs, and to her horror two sinister-looking tramps sprang out and were about to strike her when the dog, uttering a low, ominous growl, dashed at them. In an instant the expression of murderous intent in their eyes died out, one of terror took its place, and dropping their sticks they fled as if the very salvation of their souls depended on it.

As may be imagined, Miss Lefanu lost no time in getting home and the first thing she did on her return was to go into the kitchen and ask the cook to prepare, at once, a thoroughly good meal for her gallant rescuer, the Newfoundland dog. She had shut the animal securely in the backyard, with the laughing remarks: " There—you can't escape me now!"

But when she returned to the yard the dog had gone. This despite the fact that the walls of the yard were twelve feet high, and the doors had all been firmly shut. It was physically impossible for the animal to have jumped or broken its way out; the only possible explanation was that it was an apparition.

This conclusion was subsequently confirmed by the experiences of various other people who had encountered the ghost animal, and after exhaustive inquiries Miss Lefanu eventually learned that many years before, on the very spot where the tramps had leaped out on her, a pedlar and his Newfoundland dog had been discovered murdered.

THE FLOATING HEAD

I was introduced to the Rev. Joseph Murphy, an Irish clergyman, just prior to World War 1, when researching on some
hauntings in Scotland. The story Mr. Murphy and his wife told
me was outside the compass of my investigations, so I did not go
further with it then. But here it is now, from my notebook; and
in the retelling I see again the earnest faces of the elderly parson
and his wife as they relived for me, after some twenty-five years,
a night they could never forget.

One summer evening early in the 1880s Mr. Murphy and
his wife, who were touring Scotland for the first time, arrived in
Dundee. Not knowing where to put up for the night, and knowing no one in the city to whom they could apply for information,
they bought a local paper and from the list of hotels and
boarding-houses advertised in it selected an inn near the Perth
Road as being the one most likely to meet their modest require-
ments.

They were certainly not disappointed with the exterior of the
hotel they had chosen, for as soon as they saw it they exclaimed
together: " What a delightful old place !" Old it certainly was,
for the many-gabled oaken structure and projecting windows

293

unquestionably indicated the sixteenth century. Nor did the interior impress them less favourably. The rooms were large and low-ceilinged, and the ceilings, walls, floors and staircase were all made of oak. The diamond-lattice windows and narrow passages, and innumerable nooks and crannies and cupboards, created an atmosphere of quaintness and comfort that irresistibly appealed to the couple.

In spite of this welcome atmosphere, however, Mrs. Murphy had certain misgivings as to how the place would strike her at night. Though not nervous naturally, and by no means superstitious, she was not without that feeling of uneasiness which many people experience when passing the night in strange quarters.

The room they engaged—I cannot say selected, as, the hotel being full, Mr. Murhpy and his wife had " Hobson's choice "—was at the back of the house, at the end of a very long passage, and overlooked the yard. It was a large room, and in one of its several recesses stood the bed, a gigantic ebony four-poster, with spotlessly clean valance, and, what was of more importance, well-aired sheets. The other furniture was much the same as that to be found in the majority of old-fashioned hostels, but a fixture in the shape of a cupboard, a deep, dark cupboard, let into the wall facing the bed, immediately attracted Mrs. Murphy's attention.

She poked about in this cupboard for some moments, and then, apparently satisfied that it was a perfectly ordinary one, continued on a general investigation of the room. Her husband did not assist; pleading tiredness, he sat on a corner of the bed munching and reading the *Dundee Advertiser* till she had done. He then helped his wife unpack their suitcase. In doing this they whiled away so much time in conversation that both were startled when the clock of an adjacent church solemnly boomed twelve.

They straightaway prepared for bed.

" I wish we had a nightlight, Joseph," Mrs. Murphy said as she got up from her prayers. " I suppose it wouldn't do to keep one of the candles burning. I am not exactly afraid, only I don't fancy being left in the dark."

She then admitted: "I had a curious feeling when looking in the cupboard. I can't explain it, but I feel now that I would like the light left burning."

"It certainly is rather a gloomy room," her husband agreed, raising his eyes to the black oak ceiling. "And I agree with you it would be nice if we had a nightlight, or, better still, gas. But as we haven't, my dear, and we shall be on our feet a good deal tomorrow, I think we ought to try and get to sleep as soon as possible."

He blew out the candle as he spoke, and got into bed. A long hush followed, broken only by the sound of their breathing, and an occasional ticking as of some long-legged creature on the wall and window-blind. Mrs. Murphy could never remember afterwards if she actually went to sleep, but she is sure her husband did, as she distinctly heard him snore; and the sound, which so irritated her as a rule, was very welcome to her then.

She was lying listening to it, and wishing with all her soul she could get to sleep, when she suddenly became aware of a smell— a most offensive, pungent odour, which blew across the room and crept up her nostrils. The cold perspiration of fear at once broke out on her forehead. Objectionable as the smell was, it suggested something more horrible. She thought several times of rousing her husband, but remembering how tired he had been, she desisted, and with all her senses keenly on the alert, lay awake and listened.

The quiet of the night was disturbed by various intermittent noises—creaks and footsteps, rustlings as of drapery, sighs and whisperings; all very faint and suggestive, though probably attributable to natural causes. But over and above these Mrs. Murphy caught herself—why, she could not say—waiting for some definite manifestation of what she instinctively felt was near at hand.

She could not locate it, she could only speculate on its where-abouts. It was somewhere in the direction of the cupboard. And each time the offensive smell came to her, the conviction that its origin was in the cupboard, grew.

At last, unable to bear the suspense any longer, she got softly out of bed, and creeping stealthily forward, found her way with surprisingly little difficulty (considering it was pitch dark and the room was unfamiliar to her) to the cupboard.

With every step she took the smell increased, until by the time she reached the cupboard she was almost suffocated. For some seconds she toyed irresolutely with the door handle, longing to be back in bed, but was unable to tear herself away from the cupboard. At last, yielding to the demands of some exacting influence, she held her breath and swung open the door. The moment she did so, a faint glow of decay filtered into the room and she saw, exactly opposite her, a human head floating in mid-air.

Petrified with terror and unable to cry out, she stared at it. That it was the head of a man she could only guess from the matted crop of short red hair that fell in disordered entanglement over the upper part of the forehead and ears. All else was lost in a disgusting mass of decomposition. On the thing beginning to move forward, the spell that bound her to the floor was broken, and with a cry of horror she fled to the bed and awoke her husband.

The head was by this time close to them, and had not Mrs. Murphy dragged her husband forcibly out of its way, it would have touched him.

His terror, as he freely admitted to me, was even greater than hers; but for the moment neither could speak. They stood clutching one another in an awful silence. Mrs. Murphy at length gasped out: " Pray, Joseph, pray! Command the thing in the name of God to depart!"

Her husband made a desperate effort to do so, but not a syllable would come. The head now veered round and moved swiftly towards them, its stench causing them both to struggle for breath.

Mr. Murphy, seizing his walking stick, lashed at it with all his

296

strength. But the stick met with no resistance, and still the head continued to advance. The couple then made a frantic attempt to find the door, the head still pursuing them, and tripping over something in their wild haste, they fell together on the floor. The head approached until it hovered immediately above them, and then descending lower and lower, finally passed right through them, through the floor, and out of sight.

It was some minutes before either of them could sufficiently recover to stir from the floor, and when they did move, it was only to totter to their bed, and lie there shivering till morning.

The hot morning sun dissipating their fears, they got up and hurried downstairs to demand an interview with the landlord. When they told him their story he scoffed at it and argued that it must have been a nightmare, but the couple showed the absurdity of this by firmly attesting they had both simultaneously experienced the phenomena. The landlord, however, still stoutly denied there was anything wrong with the room. It was only as the Murphys were about to leave the hotel that he finally approached them—probably because of Mr. Murphy being a churchman. To their surprise he then offered them another room, on any terms they liked, if only they would complete their stay at the inn and not talk about the incident.

" I know every word of what you say is true," he confessed to them, " but what I am to do? I can't shut up a house which I have taken on a twenty years' lease because one room in it is haunted; and after all, there is only one visitor in dozens who is disturbed by the apparition."

The head, he explained, was said to be that of a pedlar who was murdered in the inn more than a hundred years ago. His decapitated body was found hidden behind the wainscoting and his head under the cupboard floor. The murderers were never caught, and were supposed to have gone down in a ship that sailed from the port of Dundee just about that time and was never heard of again.

Mr. and Mrs. Murphy, kind souls that they were, relented and agreed to continue their short stay at the hotel—in another room. In the years afterwards they seldom spoke of their experience beyond the family circle, until, through a friend, I met them and persuaded them to tell it to me.

REBECCA OF BEDLAM

THE HOSPITAL of the Star of Bethlehem was a fine sounding name for London's first lunatic asylum, but it quickly became notorious under the more widely used and chilling slang name of "Bedlam."

The asylum actually began life in a converted priory on the site of the present Liverpool Street Station. In the eighteenth century, however, the still primitively kept and controlled madhouse had moved to Moorfields, and it is there that the opening scene for our next case is set.

It is, perhaps, difficult to imagine a more extraordinary background for a haunting than a lunatic asylum, which is why the melancholy tale of one of its inmates, known as Rebecca, has attracted some writers to offer their fictional versions of it. However, the facts as I was able to investigate them are bizarre enough.

In the year 1780 a handsome young man from the East Indies came to London and took lodging in the house of a City merchant on Fish Street Hill, close to London Bridge. The merchant at this time happened to have in his employ a very plain and shy maid-servant called Rebecca. The girl loved

299

poetry, especially romantic poetry, and often when in bed, used to lie awake thinking over what she had read; she was frequently heard repeating aloud to herself certain lines which she had memorized. Hence it may be deduced that she was both imaginative and impressionable, the sort of girl who might easily fall in love, and fall deeply.

This she did. The new lodger, gay and casual by disposition, possessed in addition much charm of manner, and the kindliness with which he treated Rebecca, who was not accustomed to very much consideration, completely won her heart. In no time at all she became hopelessly infatuated. Instead of repeating lines of poetry in bed at night, she would lie awake repeating his name and, according to witnesses, " conjuring up his image."

Yet so reserved was Rebecca that the young man had not the slightest suspicion she was in love with him. Instead, he scarcely thought of her at all. She inspired no sentiment whatever in him; she was just another domestic—civil, obliging and hard working, but very plain.

Rebecca, however, magnified the lodger's casual, non-significant and ordinary glances into those of ill-concealed latent love and tender admiration. And she was completely shattered to be told one day that he was leaving the house.

To her bitter disappointment not a word of regret at leaving did the lodger utter when she brought him his breakfast on that last much-dreaded morning. He just ate it hurriedly and in silence. Rebecca followed him to the door with some of his luggage, still hoping for some sign of affection. And then came the thunderbolt. Instead of the fond words she had expected him to say, he merely thanked her for the services she had rendered and casually slipped a golden guinea into the hand which was held out for him to squeeze. Then with a brief nod he got into his chaise, and without another word or glance was driven rapidly away.

This was too much for poor Rebecca. The other residents of the house, and neighbours, looked on in bewilderment as the suddenly demented girl, screaming violently and beating the air with her arms, rushed wildly after the vehicle in a vain attempt to overtake it.

It was at this juncture that Rebecca's mind gave way; being given money in lieu of the love she had been hoping for was sufficient to turn her brain. She was overtaken and stopped in her berserk chase, and on its being discovered that she had actually gone mad, she was at once taken to the Hospital of the Star of Bethlehem—still clutching tightly in her palm the golden guinea.

Rebecca remained in the asylum for the rest of her life, dying there an old woman. What makes her case unusually pathetic is the fact that all through her long incarceration she never once parted with her golden guinea. Sleeping and waking, she always held it grasped tightly in one hand. Before dying she expressed a wish that it should be laid with her in her coffin, but she had not long drawn her last breath before an unscrupulous keeper, biding his opportunity, prised the coin from her dead fingers and pocketed it.

Consequently she was buried without the coin. It was then that a new horror in the form of a ghost was added to the frightful lives of the inmates of Bedlam.

Shortly after Rebecca's death strange noises were heard in the madhouse at night, footsteps and the opening of doors, some of which were locked on the inside. And more. Sometimes in the daytime and sometimes at night, the ghost of Rebecca was seen, a lean figure, with ghastly white cheeks and wild eyes, gliding about corridors, in rooms, and up and down staircases, seemingly always hunting with never-abating feverishness for her precious purloined golden guinea.

There were also several reported incidents of cell doors being opened and the apparition standing staring at the inmates, while on more than one occasion a keeper was scared almost out of his senses by Rebecca's wraith suddenly appearing before him and exclaiming in hollow tones: " My guinea! Give me back my guinea!"

Needless to say the guinea was never given back, and the

hauntings continued over a very long period, Rebecca's apparition manifesting itself to patients and staff alike.

It should be borne in mind that, the patients apart, these officially recorded reports came from witnesses of a very certain type. At that time the asylum attendants could scarcely be described as credulous and whimsical in themselves or very considerate of others; they were chosen, generally, for their hard-headedness and brute strength in dealing with the roughest of inmates, and anything of flesh and blood would have received their swift and emphatic attention. If they saw a ghost, then a ghost it most certainly was.

During the time of Rebecca's confinement in the asylum it had moved to a new building at the junction of the Lambeth and Kennington roads, and it was here that her ghostly wanderings caused many an upset. In 1924 the asylum moved again to another home at Denmark Hill, where it amalgamated with the Maudsley Hospital. And Rebecca moved with it, for her white-faced, wild-eyed ghost continued to be seen, still searching for her golden guinea.

When I applied for permission to make a renewed investigation of the hauntings my request was refused. Though the cruel conditions at Bedlam had by then been considerably improved, I cannot honestly say that I was truly sorry at this decision.

THE STRANGE AFFAIR AT SYDERSTONE

AMONG THE countless hundreds of cases I have investigated in a lifetime of ghost-hunting, the curious affair of the old Syderstone Parsonage, near Fakenham, in Norfolk, remains for me one of the most fascinating. Though it occurred so long ago, in 1833, quite forty years and more before I was born, I later had the extreme good fortune to receive first-hand written evidence by the central figure in this now classic haunting, which caused such a great controversy in those days when, for sheer lack of understanding and responsible recording of ghostly happenings, the ridicule-mongers so heavily swayed the day.

In the spring of 1910 the Rev Henry Hacon, of North Kelsey Moor, very kindly sent to me a letter which his father, during those turbulent days, had received from the Rev. John Stewart, the Rector of Syderstone. This old, carefully kept personal letter from Mr. Stewart dealt exclusively with the upsets at his parsonage, and it has the unique value of having been written a full eleven days before news of the hauntings appeared publicly in print for the first time. The letter, which was sent to Mr. Hacon's father at Swaffham, some twenty miles from Syderstone, read as follows:

MY DEAR SIR,

All this Parsonage circle were gratified to learn that you and your family were recovered from the late epidemic. We are very sensible of your kind wishes, and shall be happy to see you at any time your press of business may allow you to leave Swaffham. The interest excited by the noises in our dwelling has become quite intense throughout this entire district of the country. The arrivals from every quarter proved at last so utterly inconvenient that we have been obliged to decline receiving any more. We were compelled to draw the line somewhere, and we judged it could not be more sensibly done than immediately after the highly respectable authentication of the noises furnished last Thursday.

On the night preceding the Thursday morning, four God-fearing, shrewd, intelligent brother clergymen assembled at the Parsonage, and together, with a pious and accomplished lady and a medical gentleman of Holt (of eminence in his profession), joined Mrs. Stewart, my two eldest boys and myself, in watching. The clergymen were those of St. Edmund's, Norwich, of [here the writing is unreadable owing to a tear in the M.S.] Docking, and of South Creake.

At ten minutes to two on Thursday morning the noises commenced and lasted, with very little pause, till two hours after daybreak. The self-confident were crestfallen, and the fancied-wise acknowledged their ignorance as the sun rose high. Within the limits of any sheet of paper I could not give you even a sketch of what has taken place here. The smile of contented ignorance, or the sneer of presumption, cut but a poor figure when opposed to truth and fact—and the pharisaical cloak that is ostensibly worn to exclude " superstition " may secrete in its folds the very demon " infidelity."

Arrangements are in progress to detect the most cunning

304

schemes of human agency—but must be kept profoundly secret until the blow can be struck.

The magistrates, clergy, and surrounding gentry continue to arrive at the Parsonage, and offer us their public and private services in any way that can be at all considered useful. The Marquis of Cholmondeley's agent has gone to town resolved to lay the whole business before his lordship, and to suggest that a Bow Street officer should be sent down. I have likewise written to his lordship, who has been very kind to me.

You may rely upon it, that no human means—at whatever expense—shall be neglected to settle the point as to human agency.

I have already traced the existence of noises in Syderstone Parsonage for thirty-six years back. I am told that Mr. Bullen, farmer of Swaffham (with whom you are intimate) lived about that time at Creake (three miles from here) and re-collects them occurring then. Be kind enough to ask him if he remembers of what nature they were at that period, and how long they continued without intermission. Favour me with the results of your inquiries. I think that but three of the generation then living now survive. The noises were here in 1797. Some ignoramus put the notices of them in the *East Anglian*. In that account some things are correct, mixed up with much that is wrong. However, I have kept a regular diary or journal of all things connected with them, and which in due time shall be published.

Get the solution of these questions from Mr. Bullen for me, and, lest we should be wanderers, when you purpose coming over to see us, let us know by post the day you mean to visit here. On Saturday forenoon there will be a letter for James at Mr. Finch's, and which Claxton is to take.

King compliments from all to all under your " roof tree."

JOHN STEWART

Mr. Hacon, at the time his father received this letter, was a very young boy, but in the way of small boys he was alert to everything that was going on. He recalled for me :

" I can remember my father, when relating some of the fantastic happenings at Syderstone, and seeing my infant eyes expressing delicious terror, I suppose, turning the conclusion into something comic, so that I might not go to my bed in fear and trembling. When older I heard more particulars of the hauntings from one of Mr Stewart's sons.

" Sometimes the noises heard at the Parsonage were like the scratchings, not of a cat, but of a lion or tiger, on the inner walls of the house, while at other times they resembled a shower of copper coins promiscuously falling. One Sunday night, about the time Mr. Stewart came into residence, there were heard in the Parsonage noises like the shifting about of heavy furniture, which caused one who heard the disturbances to remark : ' Well! I do wonder our new Rector should have his house set to rights on a Sunday!' There was not, however, a living soul in the house at that time.

" The Stewart family were, of course, in a way, burdened by curious visitors. But being very hospitable, they were always glad to see their friends, two of whom, Swaffham contemporaries, Mr. and Mrs. Seppings, were passing the day and night there, anxious of course, to witness some of the phenomena. As it was drawing near bedtime, Mr. Seppings, before saying good night, went to a side table to take up a bedroom candlestick, saying : ' Well! I don't suppose we shall hear anything tonight,' when, as his hand was about to grasp the candlestick, there came a stroke under the table like that of a heavy hammer.

" Miss Stewart, the daughter of the house, after retiring to bed, would sometimes sing the Evening Hymn, when taps were heard on the woodwork of the bed beating time to the music. Mr. Stewart, whose wife's health at last became enfeebled under the stress, concluded that the phenomena were evidence of the presence of a troubled spirit, for after every effort was made to ascertain the cause of the disturbance, nothing was discovered that in any way pointed to human agency.

" The Marquis of Cholmondeley, the Patron of the Living,

306

had the ground round the house excavated to see whether there was any vault beneath the house. None, however, was found. Then two Bow Street officers were sent to exercise their skill. They passed the night, armed with loaded pistols, in chambers opposite to one another. In the night, each, hearing a noise as if in the opposite chamber, came out with a loaded pistol with the intention of firing. But a mutual recognition ensuing, the catastrophe of each being shot by the other was averted.

" Other frightening disturbances at the Parsonage included the sound as of a huge ball descending on the roof and penetrating to the ground floor; and the screams as of a human being under torture.

" I think it should be stated that Mr. Stewart was a scholar, and a man of eminent local literary celebrity; while his wife was the daughter of an admiral. Neither, before this affair, had the slightest belief in ghosts or had ever given a moment's thought to such ' superstitions '."

Having all this evidence to hand from Mr. Hacon, I naturally endeavoured to discover more about the Syderstone hauntings, and was successful to a degree. Then came a second stroke of good fortune when I was contacted by Mr. E. A. Spurgin, of Temple Balsall, Warwickshire—the grandson of the Rev. John Spurgin, another key figure in the case. Through the kindness and courtesy of Mr. E. A. Spurgin I was able to add to my notes the full facts as given and attested in the local Press at the time.

The story, which unfolds in report, letter-and-answer fashion, comprises, in my view, one of the finest records we have of a haunting so long ago.

So let us now go back to June 1, 1833—eleven days after the Rev. John Stewart's explanatory letter to his friend—when the following sensational report appeared in the *Norfolk Chronicle*:

" A REAL GHOST "

" The following circumstance has been creating some agitation in the neighbourhood of Fakenham for the last few weeks.

" In Syderstone Parsonage lives the Rev. Mr. Stewart, curate, and rector of Thwaite. About six weeks since an unaccountable knocking was heard in it in the middle of the night. The family became alarmed, not being able to discover the cause. Since then it has gradually been becoming more violent, until it has new arrived at such a frightful pitch that one of the servants has left through absolute terror.

" The noises commence almost every morning about two, and continue until daylight. Sometimes it is a knocking, now in the ceiling overhead, now in the wall, and now directly under the feet; sometimes it is a low moaning, which the Rev. Gentleman says reminds him very much of the moans of a soldier on being whipped; and sometimes it is like the sounding of brass, the rattling of iron, or the clashing of earthenware or glass; but nothing in the house is disturbed. It never speaks, but will beat to a lively tune and moan at a solemn one, especially at the morning and evening hymns. Every part of the house has been carefully examined, to see that no one could be secreted, and the doors and windows are always fastened with the greatest caution. Both the inside and outside of the house have been carefully examined during the time of the noises, which always arouse the family from their slumbers, and oblige them to get up; but nothing has been discovered.

" It is heard by everyone present, and several ladies and gentlemen in the neighbourhood, who, to satisfy themselves, have remained all night with Mr. Stewart's family, have heard the same noise, and have been equally surprised and frightened. Mr. Stewart has also offered any of the tradespeople in the village an opportunity of remaining in the house and convincing themselves. The shrieking last Wednesday week was terrific.

" It was formerly reported in the village that the house was haunted by a Rev. Gentleman, whose name was Mantle, who died there about twenty-seven years since, and this is now generally believed to be the case. His vault, in the inside of the church, has lately been repaired, and a new stone put down.

The house is adjoining the churchyard, which has added, in no inconsiderable degree, to the horror which pervades the villagers. The delusion must be very ingeniously conducted, but at this time of day scarcely anyone can be found to believe these noises proceed from any other than natural causes.

" On Wednesday night Mr. Stewart requested several most respectable gentlemen to sit up all night—namely, the Rev. Mr. Spurgin of Docking, the Rev. Mr Goggs of Creake, the Rev. Mr. Lloyd of Massingham, the Rev. Mr. Titlow of Norwich, and Mr. Banks, surgeon of Holt, and also Mrs. Spurgin. Especial care was taken that no tricks should be played by the servants; but, as if to give the visitors a grand treat, the noises were even louder and of longer continuance than usual. The first commencement was in the bedchamber of Miss Stewart, and seemed like the clawing of a voracious animal after its prey. Mrs. Spurgin was at the moment leaning against the bedpost, and the effect on all present was like a shock of electricity. The bed was on all sides clear from the wall; but nothing was visible. Three powerful knocks were then given to the side-board, whilst the hand of Mr. Goggs was upon it. The disturber was conjured to speak, but answered only by a low hollow moaning; but on being requested to give three knocks, it gave three most tremendous blows apparently in the wall.

" The noises, some of which were as loud as those of a hammer on the anvil, lasted from between eleven and twelve o'clock until near two hours after sunrise. The following is the account given by one of the gentlemen : ' We all heard distinct sounds of various kinds—from various parts of the room and the air—in the midst of us—nay, we felt the vibrations of parts of the bed as struck; but we were quite unable to assign any possible natural cause as producing all or any part of this. We had a variety of thoughts and explanations passing in our minds *before* we were on the spot, but we left it all equally bewildered.'

" On another night the family collected in a room where

309

the noise had never been heard; the maid-servants sat sewing round a table, under the especial notice of Mrs. Stewart, and the man-servant, with his legs crossed and his hands upon his knees, under the cognisance of his master. The noise was then for the first time heard there—' above, around, beneath, confusion all '—but nothing seen, nothing disturbed, nothing felt except a vibratory agitation of the air, or a tremulous movement of the tables or what was upon them.

" It would be in vain to attempt to particularize all the various noises, knockings, and melancholy groanings of this visitation, and each one brings its own variety. We have little doubt that we shall ultimately learn that this midnight disturber is but another ' *Tommy Tadpole*,' but from the respectability and superior intelligence of the parties who have attempted to investigate into the secret, we are quite willing to allow to the believers in the earthly visitations of ghosts all the support which this circumstance will afford to their creed —that of *unaccountable mystery*. We understand that inquiries on the subject have been very numerous, and we believe we may even say troublesome, if not expensive."

*   *   *

SYDERSTONE PARSONAGE

To the Editor of the Norfolk Chronicle

SIR, — My name having lately appeared in the *Bury Post*, as well as in your own journal, without my consent or knowledge, I doubt not you will allow me the opportunity of occupying some portion of your paper, in way of explanation.

It is most true that, at the request of the Rev. Mr. Stewart, I was at the Parsonage of Syderstone, on the night of the 15th ult., for the purpose of investigating the cause of the several interruptions to which Mr. Stewart and his family have been subject for the last three or four months. I feel it right, therefore, to correct some of the erroneous impressions which the paragraph in question is calculated to make upon the public mind, and at the same time to state fairly the leading circumstances which transpired that night.

At ten minutes before two in the morning, " knocks " were distinctly heard; they continued at intervals, until after sunrise—sometimes proceeding from the bed's-head, sometimes from the side-boards of the children's bed, sometimes from a three-inch partition separating the children's sleeping-rooms; both sides of which partition were open to observation. On two or three occasions, also, when a definite number of blows was requested to be given, the precise number required was distinctly heard. *How* these blows were occasioned was the subject of diligent search: every object was before us, but nothing satisfactorily to account for them; no trace of any human hand, or of mechanical power, was to be discovered. Still, I would remark, though perfectly distinct, these knocks were by no means so powerful as your paragraph represents—indeed, instead of *being even louder, and of longer continuance that night,* as if to give *the visitors a grand treat,* it would seem they were neither *so* loud nor *so* frequent as they commonly had been. In several instances they were particularly gentle, and the pauses between them afforded all who were present the opportunity of exercising the most calm judgment and deliberate investigation.

I would next notice the *vibrations* on the side-board and post of the children's beds. These were distinctly felt by myself as well as others, not only once, but frequently. They were obviously the effect of different blows, given in some way or other, upon the different parts of the beds, in several instances while those parts were actually under our hands. It is not true that *the effect on all present was like a shock of electricity,* but that these *vibrations* did take place, and that too in beds, perfectly disjointed from every wall, was obvious to our senses; though in what way they were occasioned could not be developed.

Again—our attention was directed at different times during the night to certain sounds on the bed's-head and walls, resembling the scratchings of two or three fingers; but in *no* instance were they *the clawing of a voracious animal after its prey*. During the night I happened to leave the spot in which the party were assembled, and to wander in the dark to some more distant rooms in the house, occupied by no one member of the family (but where the disturbances originally arose), and there, to my astonishment, the same scratchings were to be heard.

At another time, also, when one of Mr. Stewart's children was requested to hum a lively air, *most scientific beatings* to every note was distinctly heard from the bed-head; and at its close, *four blows* were given, louder (I think) and more rapid than any which had before occurred.

Neither ought I to omit that, at the commencement of the noises, several feeble *moans* were heard. This happened more than once; after a time they increased to a series of *groanings* of a peculiarly distressing character, and proceeding (as it seemed) from the bed of one of Mr. Stewart's children, about ten years of age. From the tone of voice, as well as other circumstances, my own conviction is, that these *moans* could not arise from any effort on the part of the child. Perhaps there were others present who might have had different impressions; but be this as it may, towards daybreak four or six shrieks were heard—not from any bed or wall, but as hovering in the atmosphere in the room, where the other noises had been principally heard. These screams were distinctly heard by *all*, but their cause was discoverable by *none*.

These, Sir, are the chief events which occurred at Syderstone Parsonage on the night alluded to in your paragraph. I understand the *knockings* and *sounds* have varied considerably in their character on different nights, and that there have been several nights occurring (at four distinct periods) in which *no noises* have been heard.

I have simply related what took place under my own observation. You will perceive that the noises heard by us were by no means so loud and violent as would be gathered from the representations which have been made. Still, as you are aware, they are not on that account the less real; nor do they, on that account, require the less rational explanation. I trust, however, Mr. Editor, your readers will fully understand me. I have not related the occurrences of the night for the purpose of leading them to any particular views, or conclusions upon a subject which, for the present at least, is wrapt in obscurity: such is very remote from my object. But Mr. Stewart having requested me, as a neighbouring clergyman, to witness the inconveniences and interruptions to which the different members of his family have been subject for the last sixteen weeks, I have felt it my duty, as an honest man (particularly among the false statements now abroad) to bear my feeble testimony, however inconsiderable it may be, to their actual existence in his house; and also since, from the very nature of the case, it is not possible Mr. Stewart can admit the repeated introduction of strangers to his family.

I have thought it likewise a duty I owed to the public to place before them the circumstances which really did take place on that occasion. In the words of your paragraph, I can truly say: *'I had a variety of thoughts and explanations passing in my mind before I was on the spot, but I left it perfectly bewildered*, and I must confess the perplexity has not been diminished by the result of an investigation, which was most carefully pursued for five days, during the past week, under the immediate direction of Mr. Reeve, of Houghton, agent to the Marquis of Cholmondeley, the proprietor of Syderstone and patron of the Rectory, and who, on learning the annoyances to which Mr. Stewart was subject, directed every practicable aid to be afforded for the purpose of discovery. Mr. Seppings and Mr. Savory, the two chief inhabitants of the parish, assisted also in the investigation. A *trench* was dug round the back part of the house, and *borings* were resorted to in all other parts of it to the depth of six or seven feet, completing a chain round the entire buildings, for the purpose of discovering any subterranean communication

313

with the walls, which might possibly explain the noises in question. Many parts of the interior of the house, also, such as *the walls, floors, false roofs*, etc., have been minutely examined, but nothing has been found to throw any light upon the source of the disturbances. Indeed, I understand the *knockings* within the last four days, so far from having subsided, are becoming increasingly distressing to Mr. Stewart and his family—and so *remain*!— I am, Sir, your obedient servant,

JOHN SPURGIN

DOCKING, *June* 5, 1833.

NORWICH, *June* 5, 1833

* * *

To the Editor of the Norfolk Chronicle

SIR, — The detail of circumstances connected with the Syderstone Ghost, as reported in the public papers, is in my opinion very incorrect, and calculated to deceive the public. If the report of noises heard on other evenings be as much exaggerated as in the report of noises which five other gentlemen and myself heard on Wednesday evening, the 15th May, nothing could be better contrived to foster superstition and to aid deception.

I was spending a few days with a friend in the neighbourhood of Syderstone, and was courteously invited by Mr. Stewart to sit up at the Parsonage; but I never imagined the noises I heard during the night would become a subject of general conversation in our city and county. As such is the case, and as I have been so frequently appealed to by personal friends, I hope you will afford the convenience of correcting, through the medium of your journal, some of the errors committed in the reports made of the disturbances which occurred when I was present. If the other visitors thought proper to make their statements known to the public, I have no doubt they would nearly accord with my own, as we are not, though so represented in the *Bury Post*, "those who deal in contradictions of this sort."

314

The noises were *not loud*; certainly they were not so loud as to be heard by those ladies and gentlemen who were sitting at the time of their commencement in a bedroom only a few yards distant. The noises commenced as nearly as possible at the hour we had been prepared to expect they would—or at about half-past one o'clock a.m. It is true that knocks seemed to be given, or actually were given, on the side-board of a bed whilst Mr. Goggs' hands were upon it, but it is not true they were "powerful knocks." It is also true that Mr. Goggs requested the ghost, if he could not speak, to give three knocks, and that three knocks—gentle knocks, not "three most tremendous blows"—were heard as proceeding from the thin wall against which where the beds of the children and the female servants.

I heard a scream as of a female, but I was not alarmed; I cannot speak *positively* as to the origin of the scream, but I cannot deny that such a scream may be produced by a ventriloquist The family are highly respectable, and I know not any good reason for a suspicion to be excited against any one of the members; but as it is *possible* for one or two members of a family to cause disturbances to the rest, I must confess that I should be more satisfied that there is not a connection between the ghost and a member of the family if the noises were distinctly heard in the rooms when *all* the members of the family were known to be at a distance from them. I understood from Mr. Stewart that on one occasion the whole family—himself, Mrs. Stewart, the children, and servants—sat up in his bedroom during the night; that himself and Mrs. Stewart kept an attentive watch upon the children and servants; and that the noises, though seldom or never heard before in that room, were then heard in all parts of the room. This fact, though not yet accounted for, is not a proof but that some one or more of the family is able to give full information of the cause of the noises.

Mr. Stewart and other gentlemen declared that they have heard such loud and violent knocking, and other strange noises, as certainly throw a great mystery over the circumstance. I speak only in reference to the knocking and the scream which I heard when in company with the gentlemen whose names have been already made known to the public, and confining my remarks to those noises, I hesitate not to declare that I think similar noises might be caused by visible and internal agency.

I do not deny the existence of supernatural agency, or of its occasional manifestation; but I firmly believe such a manifestation does not take place without Divine permission, and when permitted it is not for trifling purposes nor accompanied with *trifling effects*. Now there are effects which appear to me *trifling*, connected with the noises at Syderstone, and which therefore tend to satisfy my mind that they are *not caused by supernatural agency*. On one occasion the ghost was desired to give ten knocks; he gave nine, and, as if recollecting himself that the number was not completed, he began again, and gave ten. I heard him beat time to the air of the verse of a song sung by Miss Stewart—if I mistake not, " Home, Sweet Home "; and I heard him give three knocks in compliance with Mr. Goggs' request.

Mr. Editor, noises are heard in Syderstone Parsonage the cause or agency of which is at present unknown to the public, but a full, a diligent investigation ought *immediately* to be made—Mr. Stewart, I believe, is willing to afford facility. If, therefore, I may express an opinion, that if two or three active and experienced police officers from Norwich were permitted to be the sole occupants in the house for a few nights, the ghost would not interrupt their slumbers, or, if he attempted to do it, they would quickly find him out, and teach him better manners for the future. The disturbances at the Parsonage House, Epworth, in 1716, in some particulars resemble those which have occurred at Syderstone, but in these days we give little credit to tales of witchcraft, or that evil spirits are permitted to indicate their displeasure at prayers being offered for the King, etc,: and therefore I hope that deceptions practised at Syderstone, if there be deceptions, will be promptly discovered, lest that parsonage become equal in repute to the one at Epworth.— I am, Sir, your humble servant,

SAMUEL TITLOW.

(*Norfolk Chronicle,* June 8, 1833)

*   *   *

SYDERSTONE PARSONAGE

To the Editor of the Norfolk Chronicle

SIR, — Having already borne my testimony to the occurrences of the night of the 15th ult., in the Parsonage at Syderstone, and finding that *ventriloquism and other devices* are now resorted to as the probable causes of them (and that, too, under the sanction of certain statements put forth in your last week's paper), I feel myself called on to state publicly that although a diligent observer of the different events which then took place, I witnessed no one circumstance which could induce *me* to indulge a conjecture that the *knocks, vibrations, scratchings, groanings,* etc., which I heard, proceeded from any member of Mr. Stewart's family, through the medium of mechanical or other trickery :- indeed, it would seem to me utterly impossible that the scratchings which fell under my observation during the night, in a remote room of the house, could be *so* produced, as, at that time, every member of Mr. Stewart's family was removed a considerable distance from the spot.

While making this declaration, I beg to state that my only object in bearing any part in this mysterious affair has been to investigate and to elicit the *truth*. I have ever desired to approach it without *prejudging* it—that is, with a mind willing to be influenced by *facts* alone—without any inclination to establish either the intervention of a *human* agency on the one hand, or of *super-human* agency on the other hand :—at the same time, it is but common honesty to state that Mr. Stewart expresses himself so fully conscious of his

317

own integrity towards the public that he has resolved on suffering all the imputations and reflections which *have* been or which may be cast either upon himself or upon his family to pass without remark; and as he has, at different times and upon different occasions, so fully satisfied his own mind on the *impossibility* of the disturbances in question arising from the agency of any member of his own household (and from the incessant research he has made on this point, he himself must be the best judge), Mr. Stewart intends declining all future interruptions of his family, by the interference of strangers.

Perhaps, Mr. Editor, your distant readers may not be aware that Mr. Stewart has not been resident at Syderstone more than fourteen months, while mysterious noises are *now* proved to have been heard in this house, at different intervals and in different degrees of violence for the last thirty years and upwards. Most conclusive and satisfactory affidavits on this point are now in progress, of the completion of which you shall have notice in due time.— I am, Sir, your obedient servant,

JOHN SPURGIN.

DOCKING, *June 7*, 1833.

(*Norfolk Chronicle*, June 15, 1833)

* * *

Following this flurry of correspondence, these declarations were inserted in the *Norfolk Chronicle* of June 22, 1833 :-

SYDERSTONE PARSONAGE

For the information of the public, as well as for the protection of the family now occupying the above residence from the most ungenerous aspersions, the subjoined documents have been prepared. These documents, it was proposed, should appear before the public as Affidavits, but a question of law having arisen as to the authority of the Magistrates to receive Affidavits on subjects of this nature, the Declarations here-

318

under furnished have been adopted in their stead. The witnesses whose testimony is afforded have been all separately examined—their statements, in every instance, have been most cheerfully afforded—and the solemn impression under which the evidence of some of them particularly has been recorded, has served to show how deeply the events in question have been fixed in their recollection. Without entering upon the question of Causes, one Fact, it is presumed, must be obvious to all (namely) That various inexplicable noises have been heard in the above residence, at different intervals, and in different degrees of violence, for many years before the present occupiers ever entered upon it : indeed, the Testimony of other respectable persons to this Fact might have been easily adduced, but it is not likely that any who are disposed to reject or question the subjoined evidence would be influenced by any additional Testimony which could be presented :-

Elizabeth Goff, of Docking, in the county of Norfolk, widow, now voluntarily declareth, and is prepared at any time to confirm the same on oath, and say : That she entered into the service of the Rev. William Mantle about the month of April, 1785, at which time her said master removed from Docking to the Parsonage at Syderstone, and the said Elizabeth Goff further states, that at the time of entering upon the said parsonage, two of the sleeping rooms therein were nailed up : and upon one occasion, during the six months of her continuance in the service of her said master, she well remembers the whole family were much alarmed in consequence of Mrs. Mantle's sister having either seen or heard something very unusual in one of the sleeping rooms over the kitchen, which had greatly terrified her.—This Declaration was made and signed this 18th day of June 1833, before me, Derick Hoste, one of His Majesty's Justices of the Peace for the County of Norfolk.

The mark (X) of Elizabeth Goff.

319

Elizabeth the wife of George *Parsons*, of Syderstone, in the county of Norfolk, blacksmith, now voluntarily declareth, and is prepared at any time to confirm the same on oath, and say : That she married about nineteen years ago, and then entered upon the occupation of the south end of the Parsonage at Syderstone, in which house she continued to reside for the space of nine years and a half. That she, the said Elizabeth Parsons, having lived at Fakenham previously to her marriage, was ignorant of the reputed circumstances of noises being heard in the said house, and continued so for about nine or ten months after entering upon it; but that, at the end of that time, upon one occasion during the night, she remembers to have been awoke by some "very violent and very rapid knocks" in the lower room occupied by them, immediately under the chamber in which she was sleeping; that the noise appeared to her to be as against the stove which she supposed must have been broken to pieces; That she, the said Elizabeth Parsons, awoke her husband, who instantly heard the same noise; that he immediately arose, struck a light, and went downstairs; but that, upon entering the room he found everything perfectly safe, as they had been left upon their going to bed; that her husband thereupon returned to the sleeping room, put out the light, and went to bed; but scarcely had he settled himself in bed, before the same heavy blows returned; and were heard by both of them for a considerable time. This being the first of the noises she, the said Elizabeth Parsons, ever heard, she was greatly alarmed, and requested her husband not to go to sleep while they lasted, lest she should die from fear; but as to the causes of these noises, she, the said Elizabeth Parsons, cannot, in anywise account. And the said Elizabeth Parsons further states, that about a year afterwards at midnight, during one of her confinements, her attention was particularly called to some strange noises heard from the lower room. These noises were very violent, and, as much as she remembers, were like the opening and tossing up and down of the sashes, the bursting of the shutters, and the

320

crashing of the chairs placed at the windows: that her nurse hereupon went downstairs to examine the state of the room, but, to the surprise of all, found everything perfectly in order, as she had left it. And likewise the said Elizabeth Parsons further states, that besides the occurrences hereinbefore particularly stated and which remain fresh in her recollection, she was, from time to time, during her residence in Syderstone Parsonage, constantly interrupted by very frightful and unusual knockings, various and irregular; sometimes they were heard in one part of the house, and sometimes in another; sometimes they were frequent and sometimes two or three weeks or months or even twelve months would pass, without any knock being heard. That these knocks were usually never given till the family were all at rest at night, and she has frequently remarked, just at the time she hoped she had got rid of them, they returned to the house, with increased violence. And finally the said Elizabeth Parsons declares, that during a residence in the Syderstone Parsonage of upwards of nine years, knocks and noises were heard by her therein, for which she was utterly unable to assign any cause.— This Declaration was made and signed this 18th day of June 1833, before me, Derick Hoste, one of His Majesty's Justices of the Peace for the County of Norfolk.

ELIZABETH PARSONS

Thomas Mase, of Syderstone, in the county of Norfolk, carpenter, now voluntarily declareth, and is prepared at any time to confirm the same on oath, and say: That one night, about eleven years ago, while Mr. George Parsons occupied part of the Parsonage at Syderstone, he happened to be sleeping in the attic there; and about midnight he heard (he thinks he was awoke out of sleep) a dreadful noise, like the sudden and heavy fall of part of the chimney upon the stove in the lower sitting-room. That the crash was so great that, although at a considerable distance from the spot, he distinctly heard the noise, not doubting the chimney had fallen and dashed the stove to pieces : that he arose and went down-stairs (it being a light summer's night) : but upon examining the state of the room and stove, he found, to his astonishment, everything as it ought to have been. And the said Thomas Mase further states, that, upon another occasion, about eight or nine years ago, while sleeping a night in Syderstone Parsonage in a room at the south end thereof, the door of which room moved particularly hard upon the floor, requiring to be lifted up in order to close or open it, and producing a particular sound in its movement, he distinctly heard all the sounds which accompanied its opening. That he felt certain the door was opened, and arose from his bed to shut it, but, to his great surprise, he found the door closed, just as he had left it. And finally the said Thomas Mase states, that the circumstances above related, arose from causes which he is totally at a loss to explain.— This Declaration was made and signed this 18th day of June 1833, before me, Derick Hoste, one of His Majesty's Justices of the Peace for the County of Norfolk.

THOMAS MASE

William Ofield, of Syderstone, in the county of Norfolk, gardener and groom, now voluntarily declareth, and is prepared at any time to confirm the same oath, and say : That he lived in the service of the Rev. Thomas Skrimshire, about nine years ago, at which time his said master entered upon the occupation of the Parsonage of Syderstone, and that he continued with him during his residence in that place. The said William Ofield also states, that, as he did not sleep in the house, he knows but little of what took place therein during the night, but that he perfectly remembers, one one occasion, while sitting in the kitchen, he heard in the bedroom immediately over his head, a noise resembling the dragging of furniture about the room, accompanied with the fall as of some very heavy substance upon the floor. That he is certain this noise did take place, and verily believes no one member of the family was in the room at the time. The said William

322

Ofield likewise states, that the noise was loud enough to alarm part of the family then sitting in the lower room, in the opposite extremity of the house; that he is quite sure they were alarmed, inasmuch as one of the ladies immediately hastened to the kitchen to make inquiry about the noise, though his said master's family never seemed desirous of making much of these occurrences: that he, the said Wm. Ofield, was ordered to go upstairs to see what had happened, and upon entering the room he found everything right: he has no hesitation in declaring that this noise was not occasioned by any person in the house. The said Wm. Ofield likewise states, that, at different times during the evenings, while he was in his said master's service, he has heard other strange noises about the house, which he could never account for, particularly the rattling of glass and china in the chiffonier standing in the drawing-room, as if a cat were running in the midst of them, while he well believes no cat could be there, as the door was locked. And the said Wm. Ofield likewise states, that he has been requested by some of the female servants of the family, who had been frightened, to search the false roof of the house, and to quiet their alarms, he has done so, but could never discover anything out of order.—This Declaration was made and signed this 18th day of June, 1833, before me, Derick Hoste, one of His Majesty's Justices of the Peace for the County of Norfolk.

WILLIAM OFIELD

Elizabeth, the wife of John *Hooks*, of Syderstone, in the county of Norfolk, labourer, now voluntarily declareth, and is prepared at any time to confirm the same on oath, and say: That she entered the service of the Rev. Thomas Skrimshire, at Syderstone Parsonage, about seven years ago, and continued with him about four years; that in the last year of her service with Mr. Skrimshire, about Christmastime, while sitting by the kitchen fireside, she heard a noise resembling the moving and rattling of the chairs about the sleeping-rooms immediately over her; that the noise was so great that one of Mr. Skrimshire's daughters came out of the drawing-room (which was removed a considerable distance from the spot in which the noise was heard) to make inquiry about it: that the manservant and part of the family immediately went upstairs, but found nothing displaced; and moreover that she verily believes no member of the family was upstairs at the time. The said Elizabeth Hooks also states, that, upon another occasion, after the above event, as she was going up the attic stairs to bed, with her fellow-servant, about eleven o'clock at night, she heard three very loud and distant knocks, as coming from the door of the false roof. These knocks were also heard by the ladies of the family, then separating for the night, who tried to persuade her it was someone knocking at the hall door. The said Elizabeth Hooks says, that although convinced it was from no person out doors, yet she opened the casement to look and, as she expected, found no one; indeed (being closest to the spot of which the blows were struck) she is sure they were on the door, but how and by whom given she is quite at a loss to conjecture. And finally the said Elizabeth Hooks states, that at another time, after she had got into her sleeping-room (the whole family besides being in bed, and she herself sitting up working at her needle) she heard noises in the passage leading to the room, like a person walking with a peculiar hop: that she was alarmed, and verily believes it was not occasioned by any member of the family.— This Declaration was made and signed this 18th day of June 1833, before me, Derick Hoste, one of His Majesty's Justices of the Peace for the County of Norfolk.

The mark (X) of Eliz. Hooks.

Phoebe Steward, of Syderstone, in the county of Norfolk, widow, now voluntarily declareth, and is prepared at any time to confirm the same on oath, and say: That about twenty years ago, a few days after Michaelmas, she was left in charge of Syderstone Parsonage, then occupied by Mr.

Henry Crafer; and about eight o'clock in the evening, while sitting in the kitchen, after securing all the doors, and no other person being in the house, she heard great noises in the sleeping-rooms over her head, as of persons " running out of one room into another "— " stumping about very loud "— and that these noises continued about ten minutes or a quarter of an hour : that she felt the more alarmed, being satisfied there was, at that time, no one but herself in the house— And the said Phoebe Steward further states, that on Whitsun-Tuesday, eighteen years ago, she was called to attend, as nurse, on Mrs. Elizabeth Parsons, in one of her confinements, then living in Syderstone Parsonage : That about a fortnight after that time, one night, about twelve o'clock, having just got her patient to bed, she remembers to have plainly heard the footsteps, as of someone walking from their sleeping-room door, down the stairs, step by step, to the door of the sitting-room below : that she distinctly heard the sitting-room door open, and the chair placed near one of the windows moved; and the shutters opened. All this the said Phoebe Steward is quite sure she distinctly heard, and thereupon immediately, on being desired, she came downstairs, in company with another female, whom she had awakened to go with her, being too much alarmed to go by herself : but on entering the room she found everything just as she had left it. And the said Phoebe Steward further states, that about a fortnight after the last-named event, while sleeping on a bureau bedstead in one of the lower rooms in Syderstone Parsonage—that is, in the room referred to in the last statement—she heard " a very surprising and frightful knock, as if it had struck the head of the bed and dashed it to pieces " : that this knock was so violent as to be heard by Mrs. Crafer in the centre of the house : that she, the said Phoebe Steward, and another person who was at that time sleeping with her, were very much alarmed with this heavy blow, and never knew how to account for it. And finally, the said Phoebe Steward states, that, during the forty-five years she has been in the habit of frequenting the Syderstone Parsonage (without referring to any extraordinary statements she has heard from her sister, now dead, and others who have resided in it), that she, from her own positive experience, has no hesitation in declaring, that in that residence noises do exist which have never been attempted to be explained.— This Declaration was made and signed this 18th day of June 1833, before me, Derick Hoste, one of His Majesty's Justices of the Peace for the County of Norfolk.

The mark (X) of Phoebe Steward.

Robert Hunter, of Syderstone, in the county of Norfolk, shepherd, now voluntarily declareth, and is prepared at any time to confirm the same on oath, and say : That for twenty-five years he has lived in the capacity of shepherd with Mr. Thomas Seppings, and that one night in the early part of March 1832, between the hours of ten and eleven o'clock, as he was passing behind the Parsonage at Syderstone in a pathway across the glebe land near the house, when within about twelve yards of the back part of the buildings, his attention was arrested all of a sudden by some very loud " groanings," like those " of a dying man—solemn and lamentable," coming as it seemed to him from the centre of the house above : that the said Robert Hunter is satisfied these groans had but then just begun, otherwise he must have heard them long before he approached so near the house. He also further states, that he was much alarmed at these groans, knowing particularly that the Parsonage at that time was wholly unoccupied, it being about a month before Mr. Stewart's family came into residence there : that these groans made such an impression upon his mind, as he shall never lose to his dying hour. And the said Robert Hunter likewise states, that, after stopping for a season near the house, and satisfying himself of the reality of these groans, he passed on his way, and continued to hear them as he walked, for the distance of not less than 100 yards. The said Robert Hunter knows 100 yards is a great way, yet if he had stopped and listened, he, the said Robert Hunter, doubts not he could have heard them to a still greater distance than 100 yards: "so loud and so fearful were they, that never did he hear the like before." —This Declaration was made and signed this 18th Day of June 1833, before me, Derick Hoste, one of His Majesty's Justices of the Peace for the County of Norfolk.

The mark (X) of Robt. Hunter.

We, the undersigned chief inhabitants of the parish of Syderstone, in the county of Norfolk, do hereby certify that Elizabeth Parson, Thomas Mase, William Ofield, Elizabeth Hooks, Phoebe Steward, and Robert Hunter, who are now residing in this parish, and whose Declarations are hereto annexed, have been known to us for some years, and are persons of veracity and good repute.

Witness our hands, this 18th day of June 1833.

THOMAS SEPPINGS.
JOHN SAVORY.

Thus the saga of Syderstone. The old Parsonage, I found from further inquiries, was eventually pulled down and a new one built in its stead. Since when, I understand, there have been no further disturbances.

JANE OF GEORGE STREET

THE POIGNANT story of the ghost of George Street, Edinburgh, was told to me by a friend in the years shortly before World War I. My friend laid no claims to possessing any special psychic powers; his was a very open mind. Here, from my notebooks, he recounts his experiences in his own words:

I was walking in a leisurely way along George Street one day, towards Strunalls, where I get my cigars, and had arrived opposite No. —, when I suddenly noticed just head of me a tall woman of remarkably graceful figure, clad in a costume which, even to an ignoramus in fashions like myself, seemed extraordinarily out of date. In my untechnical language it consisted of a dark blue coat and skirt, trimmed with black braid. The coat had a very high collar, turned over to show a facing of blue velvet, its sleeves were very full at the shoulders, and a band of blue velvet drew it tightly in at the waist. Moreover, unlike every other lady I saw, she wore a small hat, which I subsequently learned was a toque, with one white and one blue plume placed moderately high at the side.

The only other conspicuous items of her dress, the effect of which was, on the whole, quiet, were white glacé gloves, over which dangled gold curb braclets with innumerable pendants; though I also noticed her shoes, which were of patent leather with silver buckles and rather high Louis heels, and her fine, blue silk openwork stockings.

She was a strikingly fair woman with very pale yellow hair, and seemed on a fleeting view to have a startlingly white complexion, a peculiarity which so impressed me that I hurried along determining to get a good look at her. Passing her with rapid strides, I looked back, and as I did so a cold chill ran through me, for what I looked at was the face of the dead! Shocked and bewildered I slowed down and allowed her to take the lead.

It now dawned on me that, startling as she was, no one else seemed to notice her. One or two people appeared to shiver when they passed her, but as they neither slackened their pace nor turned to take a second look, I concluded they had not actually seen her. Without glancing either to the right or left, she moved steadily on, past Molton's the confectioner's, past Perrin's the hatter's.

Once, I thought she was coming to a halt, and that she intended crossing the road, but no—on, on, on, till eventually she did stop and we were both preparing to cross over, when an elderly man walked deliberately into her. I half expected to hear him apologize, but naturally nothing of the sort happened; if there was any doubt left in me that she was not of this world, it was quickly dispelled when she passed right through him.

A few yards farther on she came to an abrupt stop, and then, with a slight inclination of her head as if meaning me to follow, she glided into a chemist's shop. She was certainly not more than six feet ahead of me when she passed through the door, and I was even nearer than that to her when she suddenly disappeared as she stood before the counter. I asked the chemist if he could tell me anything about the lady who had just entered his shop, but he merely looked puzzled, then laughed.

" Lady?" he said. " You're a bit out of your reckoning, sir— this isn't the first of April! What can I do for you, please?"

I bought a bottle of formamints, and reluctantly and regretfully turned away. That night I dreamed I again saw the ghost. I followed her up George Street just as I had done in reality, but when she came to the chemist's shop she turned swiftly round. " I'm Jane!" she said in a hollow voice. " Jane! Only Jane!" and with that name ringing in my ears I awoke.

Some days elapsed before I was in George Street again. The weather had in the meanwhile undergone one of those sudden and violent changes so characteristic of the Scottish climate. The lock-gates of heaven had been opened and the rain was descending in cataracts. The few pedestrians I encountered were enveloped in mackintoshes and carried huge umbrellas, through which the rain was soaking and pouring off from every point. Everything was wet, everywhere was mud. The water, splashing upwards, saturated the tops of my boots and converted my trousers into sodden sacks. Some weather isn't fit for dogs, but this weather wasn't good enough for tadpoles—even fish would have kicked at it and kept in their holes.

Imagine, then, my feelings when amidst this miserably heavy downpour there appeared a spotlessly clean apparition in blue without either waterproof or umbrella. I refer to Jane. She suddenly appeared as I was passing the Ladies' Tea Association Rooms, walking just in front of me. She looked just the same as when I last saw her—spick and span, and *dry*. I repeat the word—*dry*—for that is what attracted my attention most. Despite the deluge, not a single raindrop touched her. The plumes on her toque were splendidly erect and curly, her shoe-buckles sparkled, her patent leathers were spotless, while the cloth of her coat and skirt looked as sheeny as if they had but just come from Keeley's.

Anxious to get another look at her face, I quickened my pace and darting past her, turned suddenly and gazed full at her. The result was a severe shock. The impact of what I saw—the ghastly horror of her dead white face—sent me reeling across the pavement. I let her pass me, but, still impelled by a sickly fascination, followed in her wake.

Outside a jeweller's stood a hansom—quite a curiosity in these days of motors—and as Jane glided past, the horse shied. I have never seen an animal so terrified. We went on, and at the next crossing halted. A policeman had his hand up checking the traffic. His glance fell on Jane and the effect was electrical. His eyes bulged, his cheeks whitened, his chest heaved, his hand dropped, and he would undoubtedly have fallen had not a good Samaritan, in the guise of a non-psychical public-house loafer, saved him as he staggered back. Jane was now close to the chemist's, and it was with a sigh of relief that I saw her glide in and disappear.

Had there been any last doubt at all after my first encounter with Jane as to her being superphysical, there was certainly none now. The policeman's sudden fright and the horse's fit of shying were facts. What had produced them? I alone knew—and I knew for certain—it was Jane. Both man and animal saw what I saw. Hence the phantom was not subjective; it was not illusionary; it was a bona fide spirit manifestation—a ghost.

Jane fascinated me. I made endless researches in connection with her, and at length, in answer to one of my inquiries, I was informed that eighteen years ago—that is, about the time Jane's dress was in fashion—the chemist's shop had been occupied by a dressmaker of the name of Bosworth. I hunted up Miss Bosworth's address and found that she had retired from business and was living in St. Michael's Road, Bournemouth. I called on her at the first opportunity, told her where I had come from, and came straight to the point.

" Can you give me any information," I asked, " about a lady whose Christian name was Jane?"

" That sounds vague!" Miss Bosworth said. " I've met a good many Janes in my time."

" But not Janes with pale yellow hair, and white eyebrows and eyelashes?" I said, going on to describe Jane in detail.

" How do you come to know about her?" Miss Bosworth said, after a long pause.

" Because," I said, " I've seen her ghost."

Though Miss Bosworth hesitated before replying she made no attempt to ridicule my statement. Instead she simply sighed and said: " Is she still there? I thought she would surely be at rest now."

"Who was she?" I asked, adding: "Come, madam, you need not be afraid of me. Who was Jane, and why should her ghost haunt George Street?"

When she saw my earnestness Miss Bosworth thought for a moment, and then began to speak.

"It happened a good many years ago," she said, "in 1892. In answer to an advertisement I saw in one of the daily papers, I called on a Miss Jane Vernelt—Mademoiselle Vernelt she called herself—who ran a costumier's business in George Street, in the very building, in fact, now occupied by the chemist you have mentioned. The business was for sale, and Miss Vernelt wanted a big sum for it. However, as the books showed a very satisfactory annual increase in receipts and her clientele included a duchess and other society leaders, I considered the bargain a tolerably safe one, and we came to terms.

"Within a week I was running the business, and exactly a month after I had taken it over, I was greatly astonished to receive a visit from Miss Vernelt. She came into the shop quite beside herself with agitation. ' It's all a mistake!' she screamed. ' I didn't want to sell it. I can't do anything with my capital. Let me buy it back!'

"I listened to her politely, and then told her that as I had gone to all the trouble of taking over the business and had already succeeded in extending it, I most certainly had no intention of selling it—at least not for some time. Well, she behaved like a lunatic, and in the end created such a disturbance that I had to summon my assistants and actually turn her out.

"After that I had no peace for six weeks. She came every day, at any and all times, and I was at last obliged to take legal proceedings. I then discovered that her mind was really unhinged, and that she had been suffering from softening of the brain for many months. Her medical advisers had, it appeared, warned her to give up business and place herself in the hands of trustworthy friends or relations, who would see that her money was properly invested, but she had delayed doing so; and when at last she did make up her mind to retire, the excitement resulting from so great a change in her mode of living accelerated the disease. Exactly three weeks after the sale of her business she became a victim to the delusion that she was ruined. This delusion grew more and more pronounced as her malady increased, and amidst her wildest ravings she clamoured to be taken back to George Street. The hauntings, indeed, began before she died; and I frequently saw her—when I knew her material body to be under restraint—just as you describe, gliding in and out of the showrooms.

" For several weeks after her death the manifestations continued. They then ceased, and I have never heard of her again until now."

This interview with Miss Bosworth concluded my friend's story, but I then received a letter from him shortly afterwards. In this he stated :

" Since my return to Scotland I have frequently visited George Street, almost daily, but I have not seen ' Jane '. I only hope that her poor distracted spirit has at last found rest . . ."

THE LETTER

In my activities as a ghost-hunter I have met many people who expressed a desire to keep watch in a haunted house, but few who actually carried out this wish, and very few who bravely conducted their night's " sitting " alone. Such a man was Mr. Robert Scarfe, whose story I now tell.

Many years ago now, Mr. Scarfe was spending Easter with some friends of his in Aberdeen. Learning from them that there was a reputedly haunted house in the immediate vicinity of the Great Western Road, he begged them to try and get him permission to spend a night in it. As good luck would have it, the landlord happened to be a connection of theirs, and though at first reluctant to give Mr. Scarfe leave, in case he should then be pestered by other people anxious to watch for the ghost, he eventually yielded. So the following evening at 8 p.m. Mr. Scarfe entered the premises taking with him for company a dog named " Scott ", which had been loaned to him.

" When the door slammed behind me I found myself standing in a cold, dark passage out of which rose a gloomy staircase, suggestive of all sorts of uncanny possibilities. However, overcoming these nervous apprehensions I began a thorough search of the premises to make sure that no one was hiding there.

"Descending first of all into the basement, I explored the kitchen, scullery and larder. The place fairly reeked with damp, but this was not to be wondered at, seeing as the floor was of the very poorest quality of cement, cracked and broken in a dozen and one places, and that there had been no fires in any of the rooms for many months. Here and there in the darkest corners were clusters of cockroaches, while more than one rat scampered away on my approach. Scott kept close at my heel, showing no great enthusiasm in his mission and giving even the rodents as wide a berth as possible.

"I had a very strong feeling that there was some kind of invisible presence in the basement—it seemed to follow me whichever way I turned. I went upstairs and still the presence seemed to follow. In one or two of the top bedrooms, and more particularly in a tiny garret overlooking the backyard, the invisible thing seemed inclined to hover. For some minutes I waited there to see if there would be any further development, but there was none. Obeying a sudden impulse I then made my way once more to the basement. When we got to the top of the kitchen stairs Scott showed a decided disinclination to descend farther. Crouching down, he started to whine, and when I tried to grasp him by the collar he snarled viciously. Deciding it was better to have no companion at all than one so unwilling, I descended without him.

"The stairs terminated in a very dark and narrow passage, into which the doors of the kitchen, larder and storeroom opened; and at the far end of the passage was a doorway leading to the backyard. The presence seeming to be more pronounced in this passage than anywhere else, I decided to spend the night in it, and selecting a spot opposite the entrance to the scullery, I made a seat out of two drawers of the kitchen dresser, placing them one on the other, bottom uppermost, on the floor.

"It was now half-past nine, and the traffic in the street overhead had slackened off. I put out my candle and waited. It was a long, long wait, and when midnight came the only sounds I

335

had heard so far were such trivial noises as the creaking of a board, the flopping of a cockroach, and the growling of the dog. From time to time I felt my pulse and even took my temperature to make sure that I was perfectly normal. At one o'clock I ate some chicken and ham sandwiches, which I helped down with a glass of oatmeal stout.

"As the minutes went by I began to think that perhaps after all there was no more to the hauntings than the presence I had sensed earlier. But at two o'clock Scott gave an extra savage snarl and the next moment came racing downstairs. Darting along the passage and tearing towards me, he scrambled up the overturned drawers and burying his face in my lap, set up the most piteous whinings. A sensation of icy coldness now surged through me, and as I got out my pocket flashlight ready for emergencies, I heard an unmistakable rustling in the cellar opposite.

"At once my whole attention became riveted in the direction of this sound, and as I sat gazing fixedly in front of me suddenly the whole passage, from one end to the other, was illuminated by a low phosphorescent glow. I then saw the scullery door slowly begin to open. Seized by a great fear, I crouched against the wall while the door opened wider and wider.

"At last, after an interval which to me seemed like eternity, a shadowy something loomed in the background of the en-largening space. I felt that another second or so of such tension would assuredly cause me to faint away.

"The shadowy thing, however, quickly developed, and in less time than it takes to tell, it assumed the form of a woman—a middle-aged woman with a startling white face, straight nose, and curiously lined mouth, the two front upper teeth of which projected considerably and were very long. Her hair was black, her hands coarse and red, and she was clad in the orthodox shabby print of a general servant in some middle-class family. The expression in her wide-open, glassy blue eyes as they glared into mine was one of such intense mental agony that I felt the blood in my veins congeal.

" Creeping stealthily forward, her gaze still on me, she emerged from the doorway, and motioning to me to follow, glided up the staircase. I could not help but accompany her, and so up we went, the woman finally entering the garret which I had examined earlier. She noiselessly approached the hearth, and pointing downward with a violent motion of the index finger of her right hand, suddenly vanished. A great feeling of relief now came over me, and yielding to a natural reaction after such severe nervous strain I reeled against the window-sill and shook with laughter.

" Recovering, I carefully marked the spot on the floor indicated by the apparition, and descending into the basement to fetch Scott, left the house and made hurried tracks to my friends' home, where I was allowed to sleep on till late in the day. I then returned to the haunted house with the landlord and one of my friends. It was decided to raise the boarding in the garret, and under it, at the marked spot, we discovered a stamped and addressed envelope.

" As a result of our combined inquiries, we learned that a few years previously the house had been occupied by some tradespeople of the name of Piblington, who, some six or seven months before they left the house, had in their employment a servant named Anna Webb. This servant, whose description corresponded in every way with the ghost I had seen, had been suspected of stealing a letter containing a postal order, and had hanged herself in the cellar.

" The letter, I gathered, with several others, had been given to Anna to post by Mrs. Piblington, and as no reply to the one containing the postal order was received, Anna was closely questioned. Being a nervous woman and highly strung, the inquistion threw her into deep confusion, and her embarrassment being construed into guilt, she was threatened with prosecution. She thereupon took her life, but not before leaving a note. ' As a proof of my innocence,' she scribbled on a piece of paper, which was produced at the subsequent inquest, ' I am going to hang myself. I never stole your letter, and can only suppose it

337

was lost in the post.'

"The mere fact of the accused woman committing suicide seemed to point to her guilt, and as the postal order was never traced, it was generally concluded that Anna had secreted it, and had been only waiting till inquiries ceased, and the affair was forgotten, to cash it.

"Of course, the letter I found was the missing one, and although apparently hidden with intent, the fact of its never having been opened seemed to suggest that Anna really was innocent, and that the envelope had by some extraordinary accident, fallen unnoticed by her through the crack between the boards. Anyhow, its discovery put an end to the disturbances in the house, and Anna—whether guilty or innocent—was never seen walking there again."

THE HEADLESS CAT

THE FOLLOWING case of an animal haunting was related to me by Mr. Robert Dane, of Cheshire, who was at one time the tenant of a house in the Stretford Road, Manchester.

"When we—my wife and I—took the house, no possibility of the place being haunted crossed our minds. Indeed ghosts were the very last things we reckoned on, as neither of us had the slightest belief in them. Like most solicitors I am, I believe, a practical man, while my wife is the most matter-of-fact woman you would meet in a day's march. Nor was there anything unusual or suggestive about the house. It was airy and light, no dark corners or gloomy staircases, and equipped throughout with all modern conveniences. We began our lease in June— the hottest June I remember—and nothing occurred to disturb us till October. I will quote from my diary.

"Monday, October 11th—Brian (my brother-in-law) and I, at 11 p.m. were sitting smoking and chatting together in the study. All the rest of the household had gone to bed. We had no light in the room, as Brian had a headache, save the fire, and that had burned so low that its feeble glimmering scarcely enabled us to see each other's face. After we had sat in thoughtful silence for a time Brian took the stump of a cigar from his lips and threw it in the grate, where for a few moments it lay glowing in the gloom.

" 'Robert,' he said, 'you will think me mad, but there is something very queer about this room tonight—something in the atmosphere I can't explain, but which I have never felt here, or anywhere, before. Look at that cigar-end—look!'

" I did so, and received a shock. What I saw was certainly not the stump Brian had had in his mouth, but an eye—a large, red and lurid eye—that looked up at us with an expression of the utmost hate.

" Brian raised the shovel and struck at it, but without effect—it still glared at us. A great horror then seized us, and unable to remove our gaze from the hellish thing, we sat glued to our chairs staring at it. This state of affairs lasted till the clock in the hall outside struck twelve, when the eye suddenly vanished, and we both felt as if some intensely evil influence had been suddenly removed.

" Brian did not like the idea of sleeping alone, and asked if he might keep the electric light on in his room all night. Tremendous extravagance, but under the circumstances excusable.

" Tuesday, October 12th. I was awakened at 11.30 p.m. by Phyllis (my wife) saying to me: 'Oh, Robert, there have been such dreadful noises on the landing, just as if a cat were being worried to death by dogs. Listen! There it is again.' And as she spoke, from apparently just outside the door, came a series of loud screeches, accompanied by savage growls and snarls.

" Not knowing what to make of it, as we had no animals of our own in the house, but concluding that a door or window having been left open, a dog and cat had got in from outside, I lit a candle and opened the bedroom door. Instantly the sounds ceased and there was dead silence, and although I searched everywhere, not a sign of any animal was to be seen. Moreover, all the doors leading to the garden were shut and locked, and the windows closed.

" Not wishing to frighten Phyllis, I laughingly assured her

340

that the cat she had heard was all right and sitting on the roof of the summerhouse, looking none the worse for its treatment, and that I had sent the dog flying out of the gate with a well-deserved kick. I explained it was all my fault, leaving a door open, and asked her on no account to blame the servants. It seemed a very neat lie and certainly dispelled her worries.

" Friday, October 22nd. On my way to bed last night I encountered a rush of icy cold air at the first bend of the staircase. The candle flared up, a bright blue flame, and went out. Something—an animal of sorts—came tearing down the stairs past me, and on peering over the banisters, I saw, looking up at me from the well of darkness beneath, two big red eyes, the counterparts of the one Brian and I had seen on October 11th. I threw a matchbox at them, but without effect. It was only when I switched on the electric light that they disappeared. I searched the house most carefully, but there were no signs of any animal. I said nothing to Phyllis.

" Monday, November 8th. Thomas and Mable came running into Phyllis's room in a great state of excitement after tea today. ' Mother!' they cried, ' Mother! Do come! Some horrid dog has got a cat in the spare room and is tearing it to pieces.' Phyllis, who was mending my socks at the time, jumped to her feet and flew to the spare room. The door of the room was shut, but proceeding from within was the most appalling pandemonium of screeches and snarls, just as if some dog had got hold of a cat by the neck and was shaking it to death.Phyllis swung open the door and rushed in. The room was empty—not a trace of a cat or dog anywhere—and the sounds ceased. On my return home Phyllis met me in the garden. ' Robert,' she said, ' I have probed the mystery at last. The house is haunted. We must leave.'

" Saturday, November 13th. Sub-let house to Mr. James Barstow, retired oil merchant, today. He comes in on the 30th. Hope he'll like it !

" Tuesday, November 16th. Cook left today. ' I've no fault to find with you, mum,' she took pains to explain to Phyllis. ' It's not you, nor the children, nor the food. It's the noises at night—

341

screeches outside my door, which sound like a cat, but which I know can't be a cat, as there is no cat in the house. This morning, mum, shortly after the clock struck two, hearing something in the corner and wondering if it was a mouse, I sat up in bed and was getting ready to strike a light—the matchbox was in my hand—when something heavy sprang right on top of me and gave a loud growl in my ear. That finished me, mum—I fainted. When I come to myself, I was too frightened to stir, but lay with my head under the blankets till it was time to get up. I then searched everywhere, but there was no sign of any dog, and as the door was locked there was no possibility of a dog having got in during the night. Mrs. Dane, I wouldn't go through what I suffered again for fifty pounds; I would rather go without my month's wages than sleep in that room another night.' Phyllis paid her up to date, and she went directly after tea.

"Friday, November 19th. As I was coming out of the bathroom at 11 p.m. something fell into the bath with a loud splash. I turned to see what it was—there was nothing there. I ran up the stairs to bed, three steps at a time!

"Sunday, November 21st. Went to church in the morning as usual. On the way back I was pondering over the sermon when Dot—she is six today—came running up to me very scared. 'Father,' she cried, catching my sleeve, 'do hurry. Mother is very ill.' Full of dreadful anticipations I tore home, and on arriving found Phyllis lying on the couch in a violent fit of hysterics. It was fully an hour before she recovered sufficiently to tell me what had happened. This is what she then told me:

"'After you went to church I made the custard pudding, jelly and blancmange for dinner, and had just sat down with the intention of writing a letter to mother, when I heard a very pathetic miaow coming, so I thought, from under the couch. Thinking it was some stray cat that had got in through one of the windows, I tried to entice it out by calling to it. No cat coming out and the mewing still continuing, I knelt down and peered under the couch. There was no cat there. Had it been night I should have been very much afraid, but I could scarcely reconcile myself to the idea of ghosts in a room bright with daylight. Resuming my seat I went on with my writing, but not for long. The mewing grew nearer. I distinctly heard something crawl out from under the couch; there was then a pause and then something sprang upon me and dug its claws in my knees. I looked down, and to my horror saw, standing on its hind-legs, pawing my clothes, a large tabby cat without a head—the neck terminating in a mangled stump. The sight so appalled me that I don't know what happened, but nurse and the children came in and found me lying on the floor in hysterics. Robert, we must leave this house at once!'

" Tuesday, November 30th. Left Stretford Road at 2 p.m. Had a great rush to get things packed in time, and dread opening some of the packing-cases, especially those with crockery. Just as we were starting Phyllis cried out that she had left her reticule behind, and I was sent to search for it. I looked everywhere without success and was leaving the premises in full anticipation of being sent back again, when there was a loud commotion in the hall, just as if a dog had suddenly pounced on a cat, and the next moment a large tabby, with the head hewn away as Phyllis had described, rushed up to me and tried to spring on to my shoulders. At this juncture one of the servants, who had been sent to look for me, opened the hall door and called out. The cat instantly vanished, and on my reaching Phyllis she told me she had found her reticule—that she had been sitting on it all the time."

In a subsequent note in his diary a year or so later, Mr. Dane says: " After innumerable inquiries about the history of the house in Stretford Road prior to our inhabiting it, I have elicited the fact that twelve years ago a Mr. and Mrs. Miller lived there. They had one young son, whom they spoilt in the most outrageous fashion, even to the extent of encouraging him in acts of cruelty. To afford him amusement he was allowed to buy rats for his dog to worry, and he on one occasion procured a stray cat, which the servants afterwards declared was mangled in the most shocking manner before being finally destroyed by the boy. Here, in my opinion, is a very feasible explanation for the hauntings, for if human tragedies are re-enacted by ghosts, why not animal tragedies too?

" Mr. Barstow, to whom we sub-let, has now finished his term without reporting anything strange. We hope the next tenants of the house will be as fortunate as he."

HUNTING GHOSTS IN AMERICA

When I worked my way across the United States just before the turn of the century, a hard tour during which I tackled a variety of jobs from freelance journalist to cook on a ranch out West, it was unthinkable to many people back home in Britain that America—being so modern in its civilization—should possess any ghosts at all.

But ghosts there certainly were, and they began to fill my notebook almost as soon as I arrived.

There was, for instance, a good deal of talk going on about a school at Newbury port which was haunted by the phantom of a little boy with golden hair and dressed all in brown. This plaintive ghost was to be seen either peering through one of the windows, with an expression of infinite sadness in its big dark eyes, or wandering disconsolately up and down the stairs.

Pathetic and harmless though it would seem to have been, this poor little phantom had the most alarming effect on the scholars, and as a consequence the school rapidly lost pupils as they were abruptly taken away from it by their parents. Apparently there was no known cause for the haunting.

Another haunting also testified to by a number of witnesses

concerned the driver of an engine on the Syracuse and Bing-hampton railway. The driver suddenly became haunted by the phantom of a woman which, he said, stood by his side on the engine and tried to throw him on to the line.

His mate on the engine used to see the driver engaged in a furious struggle with some, to him, invisible presence, and once this man heard a voice, unmistakably a woman's, say to the driver with a chuckle: " Now, Bill, I've got you and I'll throw you into the water " (the train was crossing a river bridge at the time).

Finally both men became so unnerved that they could not go on any longer, and said that if they could not be transferred to another engine they would quit. They were duly transferred, and were not disturbed by any further hauntings. My informant regarding this curious case told me that the haunted engine was still in existence, and that the last time he had seen it (in one of the sheds of the Syracuse and Binghampton railway) he was told that no one would venture near it at night because of the ghost, which could frequently be heard there, talking and laughing.

Another strange case involving a railway was still very much under discussion at this time. During the 'seventies, great excitement was caused in the railway depot at Newark by a real ghost train. Regularly at midnight on the 10th of every month a train was heard to rush through the depot at express speed. Nothing was ever to be seen, but all who came to experience the phenomena—and as many as six hundred people were gathered together on one occasion in the depot—heard the screaming of an engine's whistle, accompanied by the rattle and clatter of wheels, as the invisible train approached the station and rushed through.

Typical of other recent hauntings was a house in Virginia haunted by the ghost of a human head with wide-open glaring eyes. It peered in through the windows and looked down over the banisters on the landings, always uttering one word only—" Blood ".

I wish I could have stayed and investigated more thoroughly some of these and other hauntings which were brought to my notice as I travelled across the country, but time and money did not allow. I was fortunate, though, to meet in San Francisco the captain of a trader who gave me the background to an extraordinary affair concerning a Norwegian vessel called the *Squando*—a case which must be unique in maritime history. I met Captain Harding at the International Hotel, and in the matter-of-fact way of a sailor he told me the whole gruesome story, which was this.

A few years previously a shocking tragedy had occurred on board the barque *Squando* as she lay in San Francisco harbour. A cry was heard coming from her one night, and in the morning the first mate was found to have vanished, and there were bloodstains on deck. The mate's decapitated body was afterwards found floating in the harbour.

It transpired that the *Squando*'s captain and his wife, for some reason or another, had conceived a strong antipathy to the first mate, and there had been endless quarrels and disputes. In the end the captain and his wife had both attacked the unfortunate mate and murdered him. They first of all plied him with drink, and then when he was too intoxicated to defend himself, the woman held his arms while her husband beheaded him with an axe. They then heaved the body overboard.

Captain Harding told me he had met the murderers on several occasions before the crime, and he described the woman as being " goodish-looking, but with very hard eyes." He said he believed she and the mate had been carrying on together, and that when she feared they would be found out, she rounded on the mate and pretended to the husband that it was all the mate's fault; that he had, in fact, been persistently annoying her.

Soon after this murder, Captain Harding told me, the *Squando* witnessed another tragedy : while at sea the crew mutinied and killed the new captain appointed in the murderer's place. The cause of the mutiny was never made very clear, but there was little doubt that it originated over some heated words with the captain regarding some odd happenings on board which the

347

crew attributed to the murder of the mate. After this second tragedy the *Squando* acquired a sinister reputation, and this was heightened when her next captain was found dead in circumstances that could not be accounted for, and his successor also died in a very mysterious fashion. After this fourth death the hauntings aboard proved too much for the crew, and on the *Squando*'s arrival at Bathurst, New Brunswick, in the spring of 1893, every man aboard her deserted.

All efforts to obtain another crew failed, and the barque was obliged to lie idle until the rumour that she was haunted finally reached the ears of the Norwegian Consul. He at once declared his intention of getting to the bottom of the mystery. With this in view he hired two strong, hard-headed night-watchmen and sent them on board the *Squando* one evening with instructions to hide themselves and lie in wait for, and seize, anyone they suspected of playing tricks.

The two men rowed out and boarded the ship about nine o'clock, and began their vigil in the captain's cabin. For the first hour or so nothing happened, and they were beginning to think the story of the vessel being haunted was all moonshine, when they suddenly heard the most extraordinary noises on deck. They ran for the companion ladder, and on scaling it found the deck in great disorder. When they had come on board everything had been in its place; now the deck was covered with a confused mass of ropes, spars, yards, hand-spikes and other equipment. But they saw nothing to account for the mess. Very puzzled they went below deck again, and feeling tired both lay down in the captain's bunk. They had not been in it long before they felt sharp tugs at their sleeves and trousers; yet when they sat up and looked round, no one was to be seen. But that was not all. The tugs were soon followed by far more unpleasant phenomena. Icy-cold hands were laid on their faces, while the coats and rugs with which they had covered themselves were torn off them and thrown on the floor. Getting up, they lit a lantern, but it was immediately blown out, and as they stood trembling, wondering what was going to happen next, a number of voices, proceeding apparently form all parts of the cabin, whispered in hollow, menacing tones: " Go, go at once!"

Convinced now that they were dealing with the supernatural, and that it would be exceedingly risky for them to remain aboard any longer, they left the cabin and were walking along the passage leading to the companion ladder when they heard a peculiar noise behind them. They turned and received a terrific shock. Coming after them with long strides, from the direction of the cabin they had just quitted, was a tall, grotesque headless figure, surrounded by a pale, misty light.

Up to this point the two watchmen had conducted themselves with great presence of mind, but the sight of the apparition proved too much even for their iron nerves. They made a mad rush for the deck, quickly scrambled overboard into their boat and rowed with feverish haste to shore.

The following night two other watchmen were hired, but they also ran off in terror. The next night it was the same; and the next, and the next; until the *Squando* earned such notoriety that it became utterly impossible to get anyone to set foot on her after dusk.

She was abandoned, and eventually sold, ghosts and all, to the ship-breakers.

What a strangely fascinating city was old San Francisco before the last great fire and earthquake. Street upon street, terrace upon terrace of quaintly irregular buildings. And people then had time to talk. Hearing that I was interested in ghosts, the landlord of my hotel introduced me one day to a Mr. Sweeney, who kept a drugstore in Market Street.

" The only experience I ever had with the supernatural," Mr. Sweeney told me, " took place in this very store. Exactly twelve years ago I engaged the services of a young man called Edward Marsdon. He was very capable, but highly-strung and sensitive. He had been with me about six months when he came into the parlour one evening with a face like a corpse.

" ' I've poisoned someone,' he gasped.

" ' Poisoned someone?' I exclaimed. ' Good God, what do you mean?'

" He went on to say quickly : ' A young fellow came into the store about an hour ago and handed me a prescription. It was signed by Dr. Knelligan, of 111th Street. I made it up and gave it him—but I've just found out I put in salts of lemon instead of paregoric.'

" ' Are you sure?' I asked.

" ' Certainly,' he said. ' The bottle of salts of lemon is on the table in the laboratory with the stopper out—I must have used it by mistake. The young man will die—if he is not dead already —and I am ruined for life.'

" ' We both are !' I shouted at him. ' Ring Dr. Knelligan and ask for the man's address. When you get it, drive round to him— you might still be in time !'

" It was no use scolding him for carelessness, he was upset enough already and a ' blowing up ' just then might, I thought, cause his collapse. All we could do was to hope for the best. He rang the doctor and drove to the patient's address, only to find that the young man had just left. The landlady had no idea where he had gone.

" To Marsdon this was the last straw. He came back in a very distressed state, trembling all over as if he had ague, and after telling me what had happened he went upstairs and slammed his door. I had the police put out an emergency call for the patient.

" About a quarter of an hour later, my wife, the servant girl and I all heard Marsdon, so we thought, come downstairs and go out. The servant then went up to his room to make the bed, and hearing her scream out I ran upstairs to find her standing in the middle of the floor, wringing her hands, while Marsdon was sitting in a chair—dead. He had been dead for some minutes.

" That, Mr. O'Donnell, was the beginning of the strange occurrences here. If it was not Marsdon who we all heard go out, who could it have been? There was no one in the house but we three, and the body in the chair upstairs, so that it must have

350

been Marsdon's ghost. Well, from that day on we had no peace.

"Footsteps which we all recognized as Marsdon's, for he had a peculiar lumping kind of walk, trod up and down the stairs all hours of the day and night, and frequently when I was in the laboratory mixing medicines I was strongly conscious of some presence standing close beside me and watching everything I did.

"One day my wife saw him. She was going out, and wanting some money she called to me. Finding me, as she thought, standing on the hearth-rug of the parlour with my back to her, she touched me on the shoulder. The next moment she discovered her mistake. The person she had mistaken for me turned round and she found herself looking at the white, frightened face of Edward Marsdon. She started back with a loud shriek, and Marsdon walked out of the room—apparently right through the servant, who came running in to see what was the matter. My wife asked the maid if she had seen anything, and the girl said: 'No, only a dark shadow seemed to fall right across me, and just for a moment or so I felt very depressed.'

"A week afterwards Marsdon was seen again, this time by my wife and the maid together. They met him on the stairs. He was quite real and solid and appeared to be under the influence of some very painful emotion as he passed by them at a great rate—so near that they felt his clothes brush against them. He disappeared into the laboratory, but on their entering it immediately afterwards there was no one there.

"Something of this nature, either a visual sighting of him or noises of his walking about now happened pretty well every day, until one morning a young man came to the store to see me.

"'I am the man,' he said, 'to whom your assistant gave that mixture. I have just returned to San Francisco and heard all about it from the police. The medicine was perfectly all right. I drank it directly I left here, and it did me the world of good. There was not even the suspicion of poison in it. If only your assistant had told my landlady about it when he called and found I had gone, she could have given him the glass I drank out of, which he could have examined. They say his apparition has been seen several times since—not that I believe in such things as ghosts.'

" ' Whether you believe in them or not,' I told him, ' it's a fact Edward Marsdon has both been seen and heard.'

" ' Then I hope,' he said, ' my visit here today will put matters to right, and that his spirit, learning I am alive and well, will find rest and trouble you no more.'

" He then bid me good morning, and walked towards the door—but stopped very suddenly.

" ' My God!' he cried—' there he is!'

" I looked, and as sure as I am sitting here, Mr. O'Donnell, there was Edward Marsdon, just as I had known him in life, standing on the pavement with his face glued to the window, peering in at us. The expression in his eyes was one of infinite joy and astonishment.

" I took a step or two towards him with the intention of speaking but he immediately vanished; and from that day to this the hauntings have entirely ceased."

Oddly enough it was also from the proprietor of a store that I learned of a haunting in New York; a particularly evil one, this.

On my stay in New York I lodged in a fifty-cent hotel in West Quay; not a particularly elevating neighbourhood, but one which, I was told, possessed several haunted buildings. I was taken to see one of them, a small store that supplied seamen's kits, by a fellow lodger. The proprietor of the store was a Swede named Jansen. He was at first extremely reticent, but on my assuring him that I was not in touch with any of the New York newspapers and would not connive at his story getting into print, he agreed to tell me what had happened.

Calling his wife, a plain, stolid-looking woman, dressed in a neat and spotlessly clean print gown, Mr. Jansen led the way upstairs to the top landing. There he stopped opposite a closed door, in front of which stood a large oak chest.

" That's the room," he said. " We've barricaded it like that to prevent the children going in. When we first came here my wife and I, and our youngest child, Bertha, slept there. But we none of us liked the room and soon began to have very disturbed nights. I had bad nightmares, and so had my wife."

" And Bertha too," Mrs. Jansen said. " She used to dread being left alone in the room even for five minutes, and would cry till one of us went to her."

" That's right enough," her husband said, " and Bertha's never behaved like that since we moved her into another room."

He continued : " Well, we experienced nothing more disturbing than bad dreams for the first fortnight or so, and nothing happened till we were both woken up one night by hearing Bertha scream in her cot. We lit a candle and got out of bed.

" ' What's the matter?' I asked the child —' are you in pain?'

" ' No, Poppa,' she said. ' I was frightened. I kept hearing the bed creak and I thought one of you was coming out of it to kill me.'

" Of course I brushed it off as so much nonsense. ' You've been dreaming again, child,' I told her. I then said to my wife : ' If she has many more of these nightmares we had better send for the doctor, don't you think so?' My wife made no answer, but suddenly gave a cry and pointed to our bed. ' Otto—look at the clothes! We never left them like that. What's happened to them?'

" I looked. The clothes were all heaped together down the centre of the bed exactly in the shape of a human body, with the face turned towards us.

" We all three stared at it in open-mouthed silence, and the longer we gazed, the more pronounced grew its features, until they at last became so lifelike, so evil, that my wife and I instinctively shrank back against the child's cot and tried to hide the thing from her. My wife declares she saw it move."

" It did," Mrs. Jansen said emphatically. " I saw it distinctly shift nearer to us. So did Bertha."

" I know you were both agreed on that," Mr. Jansen said. " All I can say is I didn't see it move, but I started praying, and

353

whether it was the effect of my prayers or not, the clothes gradually became clothes again, and after soothing Bertha we scrambled back into bed, feeling rather ashamed we had been so frightened.

" The following evening after Bertha had been put to bed, we heard her scream again and ran up to find her quivering under the bedclothes. She said our bed had begun rattling, just as if we were moving in it. On turning to examine it, we found the clothes just as we had seen them on the previous night, with one of the pillows pressed and moulded into the speaking likeness of a face.

" As I looked at it, the features became convulsed with such horrible intent that I backed against the table and upset the light. When I relit it the thing on the bed had disappeared and the clothes were once again normal. The same night, some time after we were in bed, I awoke to find myself being roughly shaken by the shoulders. It was my wife—but perhaps I had better let her go on with the story.

" I shook him," Mrs. Jansen explained, " because a feeling had suddenly come over me that I must kill Bertha. The very first night we slept in the room I became obsessed with a passionate desire to see someone die, a desire that I can assure you was absolutely unspeakable to me, because I am extremely sensitive to seeing other people suffer."

" She is kindness itself," said Mr. Jansen.

" Well," Mrs. Jansen went on, " the feeling became so unbearable, that fearing I should actually be compelled to kill someone, I awoke my husband and begged him to tie my hands together, which after some hesitation he did. Bertha was crying bitterly and told us she had again heard creaks in the room, just as if someone was getting out of bed to murder her. That was the last time we slept in the room. I felt it was a positive danger to spend another night in it, and so we removed to the one we are sleeping in now."

" Has the room not been occupied since?" I asked.

" Yes, for one night," said Mrs. Jansen. She was plainly very upset at the memory of it, but she forced herself to describe it to me. "A niece of mine, Charlotte, came to stay with us, and as we had nowhere else to put her, she had to sleep there. We went to bed late that night, and I dreamed three times in succession that Charlotte was creeping downstairs with some strange weapon in her hand, with which she intended killing Bertha. Bertha was then sleeping alone in the room facing ours.

"The third dream was so vivid that I awoke from it bathed in perspiration. I told my husband, and he said: 'Well, that's curious, for I thought I heard someone moving about overhead. I'll go and see if anything's wrong.' He opened the door, and going on to the landing discovered Charlotte tiptoeing cautiously down the stairs, holding a long, glittering pair of scissors in her hand, and with an expression on her face similar to that on the face in the bedclothes.

"'What are you doing here?' my husband demanded, and Charlotte at once dropped the scissors and began to cry. She told us that no sooner had she got into bed than she felt like another person. It was just as if someone else's soul had crept into her body. All her old sentiments and ideas vanished, and the maddest and most unholy ideas presented themselves in rapid succession to her mind. A blind hatred of everyone in the house possessed her and she was seized with the most ungovernable craving to kill. For a long time she fought against this, until at last, unable to restrain herself any longer, she got out of bed and sought some weapon. Cold hands, she told us, seemed to guide her to the scissors, and armed with them she crept downstairs, just as I had seen her in my sleep, determined to butcher Bertha first, and then, if possible, my husband and myself.

"She pleaded our forgiveness and begged to be allowed to go home first thing in the morning. 'I don't feel I am responsible for my behaviour,' she said. 'I never had the slightest inclination to do anything of the sort before. I am sure it's that room. There's some sinister influence in it, and if I go back to it, I'm certain I shall do something dreadful.'

"She spent the rest of the night on the sofa in the parlour, and shortly before noon returned to her parents. After that we locked up the room and had this chest placed against the door, as you now see it."

" Do you know the history of the house?" I asked the couple.

" Only that before we came here," Mrs. Jansen said, " there were several sudden deaths. I don't think any of them were actually attributed to murder, though they were all due to rather unusual accidents. Originally I think, the house was an inn, kept by a woman with an unsavoury reputation, and we have always wondered if the hauntings had anything to do with her."

" I suppose you couldn't tell whether the face formed by the bedclothes was a man or a woman's?" I asked.

" Not, perhaps, by the actual features," Mrs. Jansen said— " only by the expression. I can't explain how, but it was an expression which at once explained to me its sex, and that sex was not masculine."

The case of the Boston ghost, a haunting of which I had personal experience, came to my notice in very direct fashion. I only stayed in Boston for two nights, and chance led me to put up at an hotel which I learned bore a vague reputation for being haunted. It was in a rather poor neighbourhood, at least poor for Boston, and there were few visitors; indeed, on the landing where I slept, only one. I spent all my first day in town sightseeing and visiting relatives whom I had never met before, and did not get back to the hotel till very late. The place was dimly lit and silent.

" Am I the last in?" I asked the night porter, who rubbed his eyes wearily and yawned.

" Yes, sir," he said. " The other guests have been gone to bed two hours or more. It's close on one."

" What part of Ireland do you come from?" I said.

" County Limerick, to be sure," he replied—" you could tell I was Irish?"

" At once," I said. " What were you over there?"

" I was working on the roads, and before that I was in the Army, in the Inniskillings."

I asked what date, and it transpired he had enlisted in that regiment when one of my uncles was a major in it, and the porter remembered him well. We were talking away and recalling episodes of the long past when I heard a familiar sliding kind of noise and broke off in the middle of a sentence.

" Surely that's the elevator," I exclaimed. " I hope our talking has not disturbed anyone."

" I don't think so, sir," he said. " At any rate, I shouldn't trouble myself about it."

His voice sounded so strange, I thought, and there was such an odd, furtive look in his eyes that I became curious, and walking across the hall, arrived on the other side just in time to see the elevator come slowly and softly down.

To my astonishment there was no one in it.

" How did that happen?" I asked. " No one called it—had they done so we would have seen them."

" I can't say, sir," the porter replied, looking very uneasy.

" Well, it's odd," I said. " Anyway, it's chosen to come down just at the right time," and getting in, I went up.

The following night I again returned late, and entered the vestibule of the hotel just as the elevator stopped.

" Does it come down at the same time every night?" I asked the porter.

" Yes, sir," he muttered. " Every night."

" Why?" I said. " There must be some reason—an elevator can't start off unless someone or something starts it." He was silent. " I see there's some mystery attached to it," I persisted. " What is it? Tell me."

He was very reluctant, but saw that I would not leave him until he gave an answer.

" For goodness' sake don't let on, sir," he said, " because the boss has forbidden any of the staff to mention it, and if he found out I'd told you, he'd sack me at once. This hotel is haunted. Several years ago, before my time, a visitor arrived here late one night and was found by the day porter dead in the lift. How he died was never exactly known, it was rumoured he'd either committed suicide or been murdered. It was never found out who he was or where he came from, and as he had no money on him, he was buried like a pauper.

" Well, sir, ever since then that elevator has taken it into its head to set itself in motion at the same time every night. Sometimes the gates clang just as if someone were getting in and out. At first I usedn't to like it at all. You can imagine what it's like to know you're the only one about in a place like this—and then to hear the elevator suddenly coming down. However, I got used to it, and if that was all that happened, I shouldn't mind."

" What else does happen?" I asked.

" I can't tell you, sir. Would you like a bit of exercise?"

" I don't mind," I said. " Why?"

" Will you try the staircase, then, instead of the elevator? Count the stairs as you go up and note carefully when you come to the forty-first."

Though puzzled, I agreed to follow his instructions. The stairs were narrow and tortuous, the gaslight dim, and I soon began to feel very far from my friend the porter and very much alone in the building. This feeling increased the higher I climbed, until it became so unbearable I stopped. I had conscientiously counted the steps and was at the thirty-ninth. I looked around me. High overhead was a kind of funnel formed of black, funereal, and apparently never-ending banisters; below me was a similarly constructed pit. The flickering gaslight brought into play innumerable shadows. I tried to look away from them, for their gambols were unpleasantly emphasized by the oppressive silence, but they fascinated me to such an extent that I was forced to watch them, and while doing so, I became suddenly aware of a presence. Something I could not see was standing on the staircase, a few steps ahead, barring my way.

I advanced one step, and with a tremendous effort struggled on to the next one. Then the most frightful, the most overwhelming terror seized me, and turning round I tore back downstairs.

"Well," the porter said, "you've come back. Couldn't pass it. No one who's tried to do so at this time of night ever can."

"What is it?" I asked him. "What is the horrible thing?"

"I don't know," he replied. "No one knows. The place was once a madhouse, I believe, and perhaps . . ." He stopped and shrugged.

I did not question him any further. I was suddenly glad I was leaving the place next morning.

"Seeing as it's a choice of two evils," I told him, "I'll go up in the lift."

And I did.

THE VANISHED SECRETARY

THE TOWN of Denver, Colorado, had not been built very long
when I visited it on my U.S. tour. In fact, little more than ten
years previously it had possessed only one orthodox street, so it
seemed the last place in the world where I could expect to come
across a haunted house. Yet I heard of three hauntings at least
while I was in Denver, one of these being so strange that I must
include it here. I call it the case of the vanished secretary, and I
came to hear of it this way.

I had been to the Zoological Gardens and was returning by
tram, when a journalist called Rouillac, who I had met a few
times, came running up to me in great excitement.

"O'Donnell," he said, "I have unearthed something that
will interest you—the case of a haunted office!" He then, on
the spot began to tell me the story.

The office, said Rouillac, was rented by Mrs. Bell, a typist
who employed two girls, Stella Dean and Hester Holt. One day
Hester Holt failed to put in an appearance.

"If Hester is ill," Mrs. Bell told Stella Dean, "she ought to
have let me know. There was nothing wrong with her yesterday,
was there?"

"Not that I am aware of," Stella replied. "When she parted from me, just across the way, she went off in the best of spirits. I expect she'll turn up all right tomorrow."

But next morning Hester Holt did not turn up, and Stella Dean was despatched in the lunch hour to find out what had become of her. Stella returned looking very white-faced and scared.

"Hester's gone away without telling anyone where she was going," she told her employer.

"You don't say," said Mrs. Bell. "What can have happened?"

"She never went to her lodgings after leaving here. At least, that's what the landlady says," Stella replied. "She hasn't written, either—but I think you'd better call there yourself, I don't like the woman." And she burst into tears.

This was the beginning of the mystery. Mrs. Bell called on the landlady, Mrs. Britton, who repeated firmly that she had neither seen Hester Holt nor heard anything of her since she left the house the previous day, presumably to go to the office. There had been no words between them, she said, and Hester had seemed as usual, perfectly happy. She was a very reserved girl and never mentioned her family except when she went away for her annual holiday. On these occasions she asked that all her letters should be forwarded to the address of her married sister.

Mrs. Britton gave this address to Mrs. Bell, who wrote off to it at once. She received an answer by return of post to say that Hester was not there and no news of her had been received for over a month. The married sister, however, made an important statement: she said that one person sure to know of Hester's whereabouts was Pete Simpkins, the young man she was hoping eventually to marry. Mrs. Bell, now most curious, hurried off and spoke to Simpkins. In her own words he seemed "a bright, intelligent young man" and showed great astonishment and concern on learning of the disappearance of his sweetheart.

"When did you last see her?" Mrs. Bell asked.

" The day she left you," said Simpkins. " I had been out in
the country all day, superintending the building of a large farm
some ten miles to the east, and I was cycling home along a
little used road when I met a buggy. Two girls were in it, and I
was surprised to see they were Hester and Stella."

" What?" Mrs. Bell said. " Stella Dean? Are you sure?"

Simpkins replied that he was positive and would swear to it.
It surprised him greatly as he knew the girls had been on very
bad terms. He was engaged to Stella before he met Hester, but
could not stand her temper.

" One day," he said, " Stella was so angry with my dog
because it snarled at her that she seized my walking-stick and
beat it on the head. I found her standing over the dog, white
with fury—and it dead. I felt after this I could never like her
again, so I broke off our engagement. After that I met Hester
at the same house where I had first seen Stella, and we became
friends. Stella did not like it. She took on more than was necessary, and Hester told me there had been some painful scenes
between them. I thought after this that out of business hours
they were not on speaking terms, which is why I was so surprised to see them driving in the buggy side by side."

" It's all very mysterious," Mrs. Bell said. " If Hester doesn't
turn up soon I shall have to inform the police."

The following day Mrs. Bell asked Stella if she had gone for
a drive with Hester the evening of Hester's disappearance, and
Stella made an instant denial. " No," she replied, " the last time
I saw Hester was when she left here that afternoon. She said
good-bye to me as usual on the other side of the road, and I
have not set eyes on her since."

Stella admitted that she had once been engaged to Pete
Simpkins, but strongly denied that Hester's keeping company
with him had led to any disagreement between them.

" Hester and I were always on the very best of terms," she
said, " and it would be downright mean of anyone to say otherwise. Besides, I can produce proof to the contrary."

The next day, as Hester was still missing, Mrs. Bell told the police. They made immediate inquiries, and Pete Simpkins' story about the buggy was corroborated. Someone else had seen the two girls driving towards the outskirts of town that same evening, while a car proprietor also came forward and said he remembered Hester hiring a buggy from him but that she had driven off in it alone. When the buggy was brought back his wife had taken the money for it, but she could not swear to the identity of the girl who had paid her, as it was then dusk and the girl was so muffled up against the cold that practically nothing of her face was visible. The wife could only say that Stella Dean resembled the girl both in build and height.

Stella was now asked if she could produce an alibi, and accordingly her aged mother declared that Stella had come straight home from the office and remained indoors all that evening. To add to the complexity of the affair, another person testified to having seen Hester Holt enter Mrs. Britton's (the landlady's) house with a latch-key late on the night in question, and this made some people suspect Mrs. Britton, but the police could prove nothing and the matter was eventually dropped.

All this had happened about three months before I arrived in Denver.

A week after Hester's disappearance Mrs. Bell took on a new assistant called Vera Cummings, a very practical young lady, the daughter of a farmer near Omaha. The day after her arrival, Miss Cummings was busy typing in the office with Mrs. Bell and Stella Dean when she suddenly exclaimed : " How is it that I get convulsed with shivers whenever I sit next to you, Miss Dean? I don't when I'm sitting next to Mrs. Bell. Ugh! I feel as if the icy east wind were blowing right through me."

" What nonsense !" Stella replied. " You imagine it."

" No, I don't," Miss Cummings retorted. " I'm going to sit somewhere else." And she moved to the other side of the table.

Mrs. Bell made no comment. An hour or so afterwards, Vera Cummings abruptly observed : " My, Stella, what long legs you have !"

" What in the world do you mean?" was the surprised and angry retort.

" Why, there's no one else on your side of the table, is there?" Vera Cummings said— " and someone's feet keep kicking mine."

" You're dreaming," Stella said, but Mrs. Bell noticed she had turned very pale.

Two days now passed uneventfully, but on the third day after this conversation, Mrs. Bell and the two girls were sitting talking —it was close on the interval for tea and work was slack—when Vera Cummings said: " Stella, who is that tall, good-looking girl I've seen following you into the building? I've watched her keeping close behind you till you get to the elevator, and then she disappears. Where she goes I can't imagine."

" A tall, good-looking girl following me to the elevator?" Stella Dean repeated, going very white. " What do you mean? I've seen no one. You've dreamt it."

" What was she like?" Mrs. Bell interrupted.

Vera Cummings gave a minute description of her.

" Are you sure, Stella, we don't know anyone like her?" Mrs. Bell said quietly. " That description seems to tally exactly with someone we once knew. Someone who used to frequent this place. Can she have returned, do you think?"

" I don't know who you mean," Stella said crossly. " I tell you I've seen no one."

The next morning they all three arrived simultaneously and went up together in the elevator. On nearing the office the sound of a typewriter was heard. They looked at one another in open-mouthed astonishment.

" It must be one of the clerks in the building," Vera Cummings said. " She's mistaken our room for hers. She's an early bird anyway, for I reckon there's no one else arrived yet."

" But the door's locked," Mrs. Bell whispered. " See, here's the key!" And she took it from her pocket as she spoke.

" Well, there's no mistaking the sound, is there?" Vera Cummings laughed. " Click, click, click—that's a typewriter, sure enough. Someone must have got in through a window. My, Stella, how white you are!"

Mrs. Bell glanced sharply at Stella—there was not an atom of colour in the girl's cheeks, and the pupils of her eyes were dilating with fright.

Mrs. Bell then put the key in the lock and opened the door. The typewriter was working away furiously, but there was no one at it, the room was absolutely empty. The typing stopped the moment Mrs. Bell crossed the threshold.

That afternoon Stella complained of a headache and went home early. She was in bed for several weeks, and during her absence from the office the strange phenomena there entirely ceased. The morning she returned, Peter Simpkins met her and Vera Cummings just outside the office building. He was bubbling over with excitement.

" She's come back!" he cried. " Come back, and never sent me a word. I am glad though . . . hooray!"

" Come back!" Stella said, drawing herself up stiffly and regarding him with an angry stare. " Who are you talking about?"

" Hester, of course," Simpkins exclaimed. " She's just gone into your place. Didn't you know?"

Stella made no reply. She simply pushed past him and walked in. Vera Cummings, however, dawdled behind.

" What is Hester like?" she asked anxiously.

Simpkins described her.

" Why, that's the girl I used to see following Stella," she said. " Where she disappears to is a mystery, but it's only one of the funny things that have happened since I've been here."

She then told him about the typewriter and the feet under the table. Pete Simpkins repeated the story to his friends. Rouillac got hold of it, checked with the police, and handed it on to me.

Rouillac was most anxious that I should go with him to the haunted office straight away, but I had some work to finish to a deadline and so it was arranged he should call for me one day

365

the following week. He turned up on time, but heavily disappointed.

" I'm afraid it's no use," he said. " The office is closed and it's impossible to get permission to go there. It's come about like this. The day after Stella returned to work Mrs. Bell was away ill, and the two girls were alone. Some time after they had started work, round about eleven o'clock, Vera Cummings got up to get a drink of water and in passing chanced to look at Stella. Stella was leaning forward in her chair and staring horrified at a despatch case on the floor, which was oscillating violently to and fro. Vera noticed that the despatch case was marked on one side with the letters ' H.H.'

" ' That's odd,' she cried. ' What makes it do that—it can't be due to vibration, because there's nothing going by outside. How do you account for it, Stella?'

" ' I don't know,' Stella gasped, making a vigorous attempt to appear unconcerned. ' Perhaps they're shunting something heavy downstairs.'

" ' But we would hear them,' Vera Cummings replied. ' I believe it's Hester Holt. She's dead, and for some mysterious reason her spirit haunts this room.'

" ' Nonsense,' Stella shouted. ' How can you be so silly! There are no such things as ghosts.'

" After a time," Rouillac continued, " the case stopped shaking and the two girls went on with their work. Lunch time came and they both rose to get ready to go out. Vera Cummings had put on her hat and was walking to the door when she heard a sharp cry. She turned round and there was Stella Dean standing in front of the mirror, gazing at the reflection of a pale face with two dark, menacing eyes glaring fixedly at her from over her shoulder. Vera says she recognized the face at once as being that of the girl she had seen following Stella—the girl Pete Simpkins had told her was Hester Holt.

" She was so frightened, for she knew for certain now that the thing she was looking at was nothing earthly, that she ran out of the room, and as she crossed the threshold the door slammed

366

behind her with a terrific crash. Ashamed of her cowardice she tried the door-handle. It turned, but though she pressed her hardest, the door would not open. She called to Stella, but there was no reply. Very alarmed she ran to the elevator and fetched the man in charge of it. They both pushed the door but still it would not open. They were deliberating what to do next when they saw the handle suddenly turn and the door gently swing back on its hinges. They peered in. Stella was lying on the hearth-rug in a dead faint. She died that same night."

" Died !" I said.

" Yes," said Rouillac. " Some people fancy she committed suicide, but her mother says Stella's heart had long been affected. Anyhow, she's dead and the office is closed, as nothing will persuade Vera Cummings to work there till Mrs. Bell is well enough to return. I tried to get permission for us to spend a night there, but Mrs. Bell says she daren't give it—the landlord is furious with her for allowing the rumour to get around that the building is haunted, and he threatens to take action if it doesn't stop."

" That's a great pity," I said. " It's a case I'd certainly like to dig into."

" What do you make of it?" Rouillac asked, though I could see he had reached his own conclusion and was merely seeking confirmation from me. It was risky to build an explanation on circumstantial evidence, yet the facts were so strong that the deduction we had both arrived at seemed glaringly obvious.

" Like you," I admitted, " I feel there can only be one conclusion. Stella was madly jealous of Hester and during that drive in the buggy she killed her. Whether the murder was premeditated or done in a sudden fit of blind passion—you tell me her temper at times was very uncontrollable—of course we cannot say. From your sketch of her, however, I am inclined to think she planned the whole thing."

" But what could she have done with the body?" Rouillac said. " The police searched everywhere."

" Well," I said, " the track Simpkins was on when he passed

the buggy affords countless opportunities for concealing a body. It is full of deep ditches, creeks and crevices, covered with a thick and rank vegetation, and the police would take months—years—to explore it. Besides, I don't think for a moment that Stella Dean was haunted without some poignant reason."

" *Was* haunted?" Rouillac exclaimed.

"What do you mean?" I said. "You said she was dead, didn't you?"

"Yes," he replied. "She's dead right enough. But when Vera Cummings passed by the office this morning, she saw Stella enter it—Stella just as she looked when alive, only very white and in obvious terror. She passed right in through the half-open doorway, and, as usual, Hester Holt followed her."

Shorly after this I left Denver. I never did hear from Rouillac whether he finally obtained permission to hold a vigil in the haunted office, or with what remarks the Denver police closed the Missing Persons file on Hester Holt. If, indeed, it ever was closed.

THE SUDDEN DEAD

I suppose few of the London bridges have witnessed more suicides than the old Waterloo and Westminster bridges, which at
the turn of the century had an especially bad name for these
tragedies. When my wanderings in those years led me across
one or other of the two bridges it was no uncommon thing to
hear a shouting and screaming, and to see a number of people
suddenly rush and peer over the side of the bridge into the brown
depths below.

"What has happened?" someone would ask. "Oh, only
another suicide," would be the reply; and you would probably
see a small paragraph in either the evening or morning newspapers reporting that some poor wretch, thinking to find a way
out of his or her sorrows and difficulties, had jumped into the
Thames. Mainly because of the unemployment situation quite
a large proportion of the suicides in those days were women.

I once talked with a policeman who had one or two strange
tales to tell about Westminster Bridge.

"People say," he told me, "that queer things are seen at times
during the night on this bridge, and I can quite believe it,
because although I've never actually seen anything myself, I've

heard something on several occasions that I could not account for.

"Late one night, exactly two years ago, I was crossing the bridge while off duty, and got about two-thirds of the way over—I was bound for Kennington, where I live—when someone tapped me gently on the shoulder and a voice, which sounded like a woman's, said in very clear, distinct tones: 'This is the spot, this is the spot.' I turned round, but no one was anywhere near me.

"The same thing happened again the next night, and the night after, at the same time and in about the same place.

"Well, the following night I had reached that spot and was fully expecting any moment to hear the voice for a fourth time, when a man suddenly rushed across the pavement in front of me and began to climb the wall, with the obvious intention of jumping over into the river. I was just in time to prevent him. He didn't struggle but behaved quite quietly and naturally, so I did not take him into custody. He told me he was a clerk, that he had been out of work for sometime and had come to the end of his tether.

"I reasoned with him and saw him off the bridge. After I had given him a few pence, all I could afford, and he had promised me he would try again for a job the following day, I left him. I never saw or heard of him again. But I've always wondered what that voice was and whether it had anything to do with his suicide attempt."

"Did you ever hear the voice again?" I asked.

"No," he said. "Never. Though I've crossed the bridge many times since, at all hours of the night and morning."

The constable also told me that the figure of a man with a very white face and a black moustache, wearing a top hat and frock coat, was said to be seen occasionally at midnight jumping off Westminster Bridge.

"A man dressed like that," he explained, "did actually commit suicide off the bridge on the stroke of twelve one night in December, 1889, and as, after that, no more Whitechapel atrocities took place, he was thought by some to be Jack the Ripper. Anyway, whether he was Jack the Ripper or not, it's the ghost of this man which people occasionally see jumping over. But from my own experience it seems pretty clear that the bridge is haunted not by one ghost but by several."

Another Westminster haunting is associated with one of the old ferry steamboats which plied between Greenwich and Westminster. A young man who was travelling on this steamboat, one sunny summer's day, noticed sitting on deck, rather away from everyone else, a woman whose face was hidden by a black veil. Judging by her figure and hands she appeared to be quite young, and the young man consequently took more than a casual interest in her. When the boat was within a few yards of Westminster Bridge she suddenly sprang up and, to his surprise and horror, jumped overboard. In an instant he took off his coat and plunged in after her. Fortunately he was an excellent swimmer, but though he looked around everywhere he could see no sign of the girl. Giving up in despair he swam back to the steamer and was helped on board by several of the passengers and crew. In his exhausted state, his feelings may be imagined when the captain said to him: " You are the third person this week who has jumped in after that creature."

" What!" the young man cried. " Do you mean to tell me she was merely playing a trick? But what became of her—where did she go? I could find no sign of her in the water."

" What becomes of her is more than I or anyone else can tell you," the captain told him solemnly.

The young man eyed him in sheer disbelief. " Are you saying she was something supernatural?"

The captain shrugged. " I don't know how else to account for it," he said. He then told the would-be rescuer that some time previously a girl, the exact counterpart of the one he had just tried to save, had actually jumped off the steamer in that same spot and drowned, and that ever since the steamer had been periodically haunted by what he and others believed to be her apparition.

Yet another elusive ghost of Westminster Bridge, incidentally, is a phantom boat. Two or three men, whose faces are too indistinct and shadowy to be recognizable, are aboard her, and she is seen to approach and go under the bridge, but never to appear on the other side. People have searched for her on the other side but have never yet been able to discover the slightest trace of her.

Away from the river, one suicide that created a very great sensation at the time was that of the Irish Member of Parliament, John Sadleir. This tragedy occurred on Hampstead Heath. His body was found by a labourer at about 8.30 a.m. on Sunday, February 17, 1856 on a mound of grass at the back of the public-house, Jack Straw's Castle. Sadleir lay on his back, his head resting quite peacefully close to a furze bush, and by his side a bottle labelled " Poison " and " Essential Oil of Almonds."

On its becoming known that the body was that of a well-known Member of Parliament, great interest and sympathy were aroused; but the sympathy evaporated when the public learned that John Sadleir had led a " secret life of sin " and was nothing more or less than a common rogue. So much is now mere history, but it is not generally known that for years after the discovery of Sadleir's body the place where it was found was said to be haunted by his ghost. In the autumn of 1898, when having a meal one evening at Jack Straw's Castle, I got into conversation with a retired commercial traveller, who told me of a strange experience he had once had when passing near the scene of Sadleir's death.

It happened in the summer of 1857. The traveller told me he was crossing the Heath alone one evening, and when he was within a hundred yards or so of the place where the M.P.'s body was found twelve months previously, a man in a top hat, whom he described as being well but not smartly dressed, suddenly emerged from some bushes and commenced walking in front of him. As the man's back was turned to the traveller he could not see his face, but from the man's general appearance and the briskness of his walk, he judged him to be about forty years of age. After the man had walked a few yards my informant suddenly became conscious of a stillness in the air, and noticed that although his own steps made a slight noise and awoke a faint echo, he could not hear those of the stranger. This aroused his curiosity, and he next noticed that although his own shadow appeared on the ground by his side, the stranger apparently had no shadow. However, the man looked so material and altogether natural, that to the traveller it seemed impossible that he could be other than a creature of flesh and blood like himself, and so the two of them continued to advance till they came to a clump of bushes. The stranger, then abruptly swerving aside, plunged into the bushes and disappeared.

Immediately afterwards a series of dreadful moans and groans came, so the traveller thought, from the bushes, but on thoroughly searching among them he found no one; there was no trace anywhere of the mysterious stranger—he had completely vanished.

My informant had heard it rumoured that the spot was haunted, and after his fruitless search he came to the conclusion that, for once in a way, rumour was right.

The sinister reputation attaching to this part of the Heath through John Sadleir's suicide and subsequent " appearances " was increased when, about two years later, Mr. Prior, a hosier, likewise took poison there, choosing for the scene of his suicide a spot not very far away from that selected for the same purpose by John Sadleir. I should add that Mr. Prior's ghost too was said to haunt the Heath, appearing, as a rule, near to some fir trees in the vicinity of which his body was found.

If deeds of violence are a cause of haunting, the London district of Blackheath certainly ought to have its phantoms, for it has been the scene of several very grim and gruesome mysteries, some long since forgotten. One rather vivid case that was brought to my notice by witnesses was that of the skeleton of Shooter's Hill.

At Shooter's Hill in the late 1830s, people passing by a certain spot in the neighbourhood at night reported hearing unaccountable noises and occasionally seeing the phantom of a woman in a white dress gliding about the ground. She was always spoken of as the White Lady. Not one of the witnesses was seriously believed, yet after a few years they were vindicated in the most inarguable fashion.

In January, 1844 a labourer working thirty yards from the high road leading to Shooter's Hill, in the allegedly haunted area, unearthed the skeleton of a woman. A terrible fracture of the back of the skull indicated that she had met with foul play, and that she had not been dead very long was suggested by the fact that much beautifully-braided golden hair still adhered to the skull. The hair, however, proved no clue to her identity, and so the remains were properly interred in a churchyard and the mystery relating to her soon forgotten.

But the unfortunate woman's ghost still lingered on. While living in St. John's Park, Blackheath, in 1898 I met several people who remembered the subsequent reappearances of it. One was Mr. Eric Johnson, a man of independent means, then staying in Lewisham. As a boy, he told me, he remembered the following incident being frequently narrated by his father, usually when they had friends to the house.

To be brief, Mr. Johnson, senior, on his way home one night, was walking down Shooter's Hill, which at that time was still a very lonely and deserted locality after dusk, when he heard a cry of such terror and despair that he stopped at once. While he stood listening the cry was repeated, seeming to come from a spot close at hand. He called out, but there was no reply. Then, after an interval of a minute or so, the cry was repeated, and a woman in a white dress rose from the ground, some little way ahead of him. The moonlight being, so it seemed, focused on her, he was able to see her very distinctly, and thinking she was ill and wanted assistance, he ran towards her. To his intense surprise, however, when he was within a few yards of her, she vanished. There was nothing in sight to afford cover, so she

374

could not have hidden.

Mr. Johnson, greatly wondering, resumed his walk home, but he had not covered many more yards before he heard the same cry again, this time very close at hand. Although by no means a timid man, he was now thoroughly frightened; being convinced that what he had heard and seen was nothing earthly and fearing that if he delayed he might see the figure again, he ran the rest of the way home. Mr. Johnson had not heard of the haunting prior to this, and so was very relieved to learn that the phantom he had seen had been seen by others. He never, his son added, passed the place again at night alone.

Nearly thirty years later Shooter's Hill once again came into unpleasant notoriety. The district of Kidbrooke, which lies immediately between Blackheath and Shooter's Hill, was then very thinly populated and one of the loneliest thoroughfares in it was Kidbrooke Lane. At twenty minutes to seven on the evening of April 25, 1871, a pretty servant-maid named Jane Maria Clousen said a laughing good-bye to a girl-friend in Kidbrooke, and was never seen by her again alive.

Some hours later Jane was found lying unconscious in Kidbrooke Lane, having been struck on the head with a hammer dropped at her side. She died shortly afterwards without regaining consciousness. The suspicion of the police falling at once on a young man named Edmund Pook, whose father had formerly employed Jane Clousen as a servant, they arrested him.

A Mr. Lazell declared on oath that he saw Pook in Jane's company at ten minutes to seven on the evening of the murder, close to the spot where she was afterwards found. Dr. Letherby, who examined Pook's clothes, testified to there being blood on the young man's trousers, and the police produced evidence to show that Pook bought a hammer shortly before the murder, at the shop of a Mr. Thomas. All of which testimony seemed, to many minds, convincing; but as Pook was able to produce an alibi to show he could not have been in Kidbrooke Lane at the time the murder was believed to have taken place, he was acquitted; and no one else being arrested, the crime was consigned to the category of unsolved mysteries.

In certain respects the tragedy resembled that discovered in 1844. In each case the victim was a young woman; the skulls of both were battered in, and the places where the bodies were found were very lonely, and not far apart. After the murder, Kidbrooke Lane was claimed to be haunted nightly by cries, and groans, and the apparition of the murdered girl. Such persistent stories, indeed, got into circulation that the lane, for some long time, was shunned by nearly everyone after dark.

Sometimes a haunting following an act of violence will persist for years; over centuries, even, recurring at irregular intervals. More frequently a haunting will occur immediately after the violence and then recur, perhaps, once or twice over a short period of years.

As an example of the more immediate lingering echo of violence, few cases can be stranger than a haunting in Whitechapel at the time of Jack the Ripper. Late one night, about a month after the murder of Lizzie Stride, a Whitechapel tradesman was passing along Berner Street towards the end that leads into Commercial Road, when his ears were chilled by a series of the most harrowing moans and groans. He looked around him everywhere but could not quite locate the sounds. Thinking that the Ripper had been at his work again or that someone was taken violently ill, he ran to tell other people passing by of the sounds, and in less time than it takes to tell quite a small crowd had collected. The tradesman then, although he did not think the moans and groans actually came from it, was about to knock at the door of one of the houses when a woman in the crowd called out: " It's no good knocking there, guv'nor. Them sounds don't come from that house, they're in the street 'ere— we've often 'eered 'em since poor Lizzie was done to death close to this 'ere spot."

I also heard from several sources that the house in Miller's Court, Dorset Street, Spitalfields, where Mary Janet Kelly was murdered was afterwards haunted. A woman in black, said to be the ghost of poor Mary, was often seen entering the house and looking out of its windows, while strange sounds were heard proceeding from it.

The ghosts of violence are, without doubt, among the most pathetic and distressing phantoms we ever do see.

THE BEAUTIFUL SPOILER

MANY ARE the stories that have from time to time been circulated with regard to the haunting of the Pass of Killiecrankie, near Pitlochry, by phantom soldiers, but I do not think there is any stranger story than that told to me, in my early years as a ghost-hunter, by a lady who testified that she had actually witnessed the phenomena. Her account of it I now give exactly in her own words.

Let me commence by stating that I am not a spiritualist, and that I have the greatest possible aversion to convoking the earthbound souls of the dead. Neither do I lay any claim to mediumistic powers. I am, on the contrary, a plain, practical, matter-of-fact woman, and with the exception of this one occasion, have never witnessed any psychic phenomena.

The incident I am about to relate took place the autumn before last. I was on a cycle tour in Scotland, and, making Pitlochry my temporary headquarters, rode over one evening to view the historic Pass of Killiecrankie. It was late when I arrived there, and the western sky was one great splash of crimson and gold—such vivid colouring I had never seen before. I was so entranced at the spectacle that I perched myself on a rock at the foot of one of the great cliffs that form the walls of the Pass, and throwing my head back, imagined myself in fairyland.

I paid no heed to the time, nor did I think of stirring, until the first dark shadows of the night fell across my face. I then started up in a panic, and was about to pedal off in great haste, when a strange notion suddenly seized me : I had a latch-key, plenty of sandwiches and a warm cape—so why should I not camp out there till early morning? I had long yearned to spend a night in the open; now was my opportunity.

The idea no sooner came to me than I put it into operation. Selecting the most comfortable-looking boulder I could see, I scrambled on to the top of it, and with my cloak drawn tightly over my back and shoulders, settled to the night. The cold mountain air, sweet with the perfume of gorse and heather, intoxicated me, and I gradually sank into a dreamy sleep, from which I was abruptly aroused by a dull boom that sounded like distant musketry.

I glanced at my wrist-watch and saw that it was two o'clock in the morning. A nervous dread now laid hold of me, and a thousand and one vague fancies, all the more distressing because of their vagueness oppressed and disconcerted me. I became keenly aware of the extraordinary solitude, which seemed to belong to a period far other than the present, and as I glanced around at the solitary pines and gleaming boulders, I more than half expected to see the wild, ferocious face of some robber chief— some fierce yet fascinating hero of Sir Walter Scott's—peering at me from behind them.

This feeling at length became so acute that in a panic of ridiculous fear, I forcibly withdrew my gaze and concentrated it abstractedly on the ground at my feet. I then listened, and in the rustling of a leaf, the humming of some night insect, the whispering of the wind as it moaned softly past me, I fancied—no, I felt sure I detected something that was not ordinary. I blew my nose, and had barely ceased marvelling at the loud echoes it caused before the piercing shriek of an owl made me jump a mile.

I laughed with relief, but then my blood froze as I heard a chorus of what I tried to persuade myself could only be echoes, proceed from every crag and rock in the valley.

For some seconds after this I sat still, hardly daring to breathe, and pretending to be extremely angry with myself for being such a fool. With a great effort I turned my attention to the most material of things. One of the skirt buttons on my hip—they were much in vogue then—being loose, I endeavoured to occupy myself in tightening it, and when I could no longer derive any employment from that, I set to work on my shoes, and tied knots in the laces, merely to enjoy the task of untying them. But this, too, ceasing at last to attract me, I was desperately racking my mind for some other device, when there came again the queer booming noise I had heard before, but which I could now no longer doubt was the report of firearms.

I looked in the direction of the sound, and my heart almost stopped. Racing towards me, as if not merely for his life but his soul, came the figure of a Highlander. The wind, rustling through his long, dishevelled hair, blew it completely over his forehead, narrowly missing his eyes, which were fixed ahead of him in an agonized stare. He had not a vestige of colour, and in the glow of the moonbeams his skin shone livid. He ran with huge bounds, and what added to my terror and made me doubly aware he was nothing mortal, was that each time his feet struck the hard, smooth road, upon which I could well see there was no sign of stone, there came the unmistakable sound of gravel.

On he came, his bare sweating elbows pressed into his panting sides, his great dirty, coarse, hairy fists screwed up in bony bunches in front of him, the foam-flakes thick on his clenched, grinning lips, the blood-drops oozing down his sweating thighs. It was all real, horribly real, even to the most minute details: the flying up and down of his kilt, sporran, and swordless scabbard; the bursting of the seam of his coat near the shoulder; and the absence of one of his clumsy shoe-buckles. I tried hard to shut my eyes, but was compelled to keep them open and follow his every movement as, darting past me, he left the roadway and, leaping several of the smaller obstacles that barred his way, finally disappeared behind some of the bigger boulders.

I then heard the loud rat-tat of drums, accompanied by the shrill voices of fifes and flutes, and at the farther end of the Pass, their arms glittering brightly in the silvery moonbeams, appeared a regiment of scarlet-coated soldiers. At the head rode a mounted officer, after him came the band, and then, four abreast, a long line of warriors. In their centre were two ensigns, and on their flanks, officers and non-commissioned offices with swords and pikes, more mounted men bringing up the rear. On they came, the fifes and flutes ringing out with a weird clearness in the hushed mountain air. I could hear the ground vibrate, the gravel crunch and scatter, as they steadily and mechanically advanced—tall men, enormously tall men, with set, white faces and pale flashing eyes. Every instant I expected they would see me, and I became sick with terror at the thought of being the target of those eyes. But from this I was happily saved, for no one appeared to notice me and they all passed by without as much as a twist or turn of the head, their feet keeping time to one everlasting and monotonous tramp, tramp, tramp.

I got down and watched until the last of them had turned the bend of the Pass, and the gleam of his weapons and trappings could no longer be seen; then I remounted my boulder and wondered if anything further would happen. It was now half-past two, and blended with the moonbeams was a peculiar whiteness, which rendered the whole aspect of my surroundings dreary and ghostly. Feeling cold and hungry, I set to work on my beef sandwiches, and was religiously separating the fat from the lean, for I am one of those foolish people who detest fat, when a loud rustling made me look up. Confronting me, on the opposite side of the road, was an ash tree, and to my surprise, despite the fact that the breeze had fallen and there was scarcely a breath of wind, the tree swayed violently to and fro, while there proceeded from it the most dreadful moanings and groanings.

I was so terrified that I scrambled down for my bicycle and

tried to mount, but I was obliged to desist as I had not a particle of strength in my limbs. Then to assure myself the moving of the tree was not an illusion I rubbed my eyes, pinched myself, and called aloud; but it made no difference—the rustling, bending and tossing still continued. Summoning up courage I stepped into the road to get a closer view, when to my horror my feet kicked against something, and on looking down I saw the body of an English soldier with a ghastly wound in his chest. I gazed around, and there, on all sides of me, from one end of the valley to the other, lay dozens of bodies of horses and men—Highlanders and English, white-cheeked, lurid-eyed and bloody-browed. Here was the writhing, wriggling figure of an officer with half his face shot away, and there, a horse with no head; and there—but I cannot dwell on such horrors, the very memory of which makes me feel sick and faint. The air, that beautiful, fresh mountain air, resounded with their moanings and groanings, and reeked with the smell of their blood.

As I stood rooted to the ground with horror, not knowing which way to look or turn, I suddenly saw drop from the ash tree the form of a woman, a Highland girl, with bold features, raven black hair and the whitest of arms and feet. In one hand she carried a wicker basket, in the other a broad-bladed, horn-handled knife. A gleam of avarice and cruelty came into her large dark eyes, as, wandering around her, they rested on the rich facings of the English officers' uniforms. I knew what was in her mind, and, forgetting she was but a ghost—that they were all ghosts—I moved heaven and earth to stop her. But I could not. Making straight for a wounded officer who lay moaning piteously on the ground some ten feet away from me, she spurned with her slender, graceful feet the bodies of the dead and dying English that came in her way. Then, snatching the officer's sword and pistol from him, she knelt down and calmly plunged her knife into his heart, working the blade backwards and forwards to assure herself she had made a thorough job of it.

Anything more hellish I could not have imagined, and yet it fascinated me—the girl was so fair, so wickedly fair and shapely.

Her act of cruelty over, she spoiled her victim of his rings, epaulets, buttons and gold lacing, and having placed them in her basket, proceeded elsewhere. In some cases, unable to remove the rings easily, she chopped off the fingers and dropped them, just as they were, into her basket. Neither was her mode of dispatch always the same, for while she put some men out of their misery in the manner I have described, she cut the throats of others with as great a nonchalance as if she had been killing fowls, while others again she settled with the butt-ends of their guns or pistols. In all she murdered a full half-score, and was decamping with her booty when her gloating eyes suddenly encountered mine, and with a shrill scream of rage she rushed towards me.

I was an easy victim, for strain and pray how I would, I could not move an inch. Raising her flashing blade high over her head, an expression of fiendish glee in her staring eyes, she made ready to strike me. This was the climax, my overstrained nerves could stand no more, and before the blow had time to descend, I pitched heavily forward and fell at her feet.

When I recovered, every phantom had vanished, and the Pass glowed with all the cheerful freshness of the early morning sun. I cycled very hurriedly home, none the worse physically for my adventure, but resolved never again to spend another night in the open alone.

THE HAND OF PROMISE

HARMFUL AND vindictive ghosts are, thank goodness, not in the majority, though when they do become active they can cause untold distress. A decidedly harmful ghost is the ghost that tempts one to vice. A house in Chelsea was long haunted by a ghost of this kind, and from accounts given me of the haunting by a tenant who experienced it, I am able to construct the following case.

A Nonconformist minister, the Rev. J. P. Hackett, went to look over the house when it was up to let. He did not go alone, but was accompanied by a boy from the estate agent's office, and it was just about mid-day when they arrived there.

After inspecting the basement and ground floor, Mr. Hackett left the boy in the hall and ascended the stairs. Arriving on the first floor, he was about to cross the landing to one of the front rooms when he heard a noise like the click of a door-handle, and turning sharply round saw the door of a room overlooking the back premises suddenly begin to open.

When it had opened slowly a few inches, a hand, thrust cautiously through the aperture, clutched hold of the door and held it stationary. Though he could see no one, Mr. Hackett now became conscious that someone was closely scrutinizing him. The landing window faced due south, and the sunlight, pouring in, threw the hand into very strong relief. It was obviously a woman's hand, and, just as obviously, its owner was a woman of refinement; for the fingers were white and tapering, and the nails highly polished.

Mr. Hackett was fascinated; he had never seen such beauty in a hand before and found it quite impossible to remove his gaze from it. He was trying to force himself to do so, when there was a whiff of delicate perfume and the hand withdrew, while the door, immediately afterwards, closed noiselessly.

Mr. Hackett supposing the lady to be someone who, like himself, was looking over the house with a view to taking it, but who for some reason did not wish to be seen, thought no more of the matter till he had finished his inspection of the premises and had rejoined the boy in the hall. He then casually remarked that there was a lady upstairs, presumably on the same errand as himself—unless she happened to be the owner of the property. To his surprise the boy did not answer at once, but looking very much alarmed said, after some hesitation: " The owner of the 'ouse is a gentleman, sir. 'E's a widower and besides, 'e's abroad just now, and no one but yourself 'as 'ad the keys today."

Mr. Hackett suggested to the boy that he should go and see who the other person was, but as the boy appeared extremely reluctant to do so, the minister told him to come along and they climbed the stairs together. On arriving at the room in question, the door of which was still shut, Mr. Hackett paused and listened for a moment outside. He could hear nothing however, and when he threw the door open and peered in he could see no one.

" She must be somewhere else in the house," Mr. Hackett said, and at once proceeded to look; but though he searched everywhere in the building he could find no sign of anyone. The mysterious woman had vanished as wholly and completely as if the ground had suddenly opened and engulfed her.

" It's strange," said the minister. " There was certainly some-one in that room, and I can't imagine how they could have got out of the house without our seeing them. There's no back entrance, is there?"

"Only in the basement, sir," the boy replied, "and no one 'as gone down there."

That night, when he got home, Mr. Hackett tried to settle down as usual, after dinner, to write or read; but he could not. A strange restlessness was on him. At last he gave up trying and went to bed. He slept, and in his dreams saw, once again, the delicately moulded hand and inhaled again the fragile perfume.

He took the house, and within a week he and his family were settled in it. Then their troubles began. A few days after their arrival his wife came to him, one morning, very agitated.

"Mary's drunk," she said (Mary was the ' general ').

"Nonsense," said Mr. Hackett, looking up from his work in astonishment.

"It's true," his wife said despairingly. "When I went into the kitchen just now to see her about lunch, she burst out laughing and began talking a lot of rubbish. She simply reeked of spirits."

"And up to now she has been such a pattern," Mr. Hackett said. "Well, she will have to go, that's all."

"I have given her notice," said his wife. "There was nothing else to be done. Do you think there is anything wrong with this house?"

"What do you mean—wrong?"

"I don't know," his wife replied, "but I get impressions. I constantly feel that I am being watched, and this morning after breakfast I had a very odd experience. I was in our bedroom, making the bed, when someone knocked at the door. Thinking it was Mary—that was before I found her drunk—I called ' Come in ', and the door at once opened and someone crossed the room. I heard footsteps most distinctly. They passed close behind me. Yet when I turned round to see who it was, there was no one there. Do you think the house is haunted?"

"Haunted?" said the minister. "Why, my dear, there are no such things as ghosts. You may rest assured it was fancy, sheer fancy. Your nerves are overwrought."

" You may think so," his wife answered. " But you will change your mind if you see or hear something yourself."

Mr. Hackett made no reply. He was convinced that he *had* seen something already, and despite himself he kept wishing that he could see it again, and soon.

A day or two after this incident he came home one evening after holding a service some distance away, feeling more than usually tired and exhausted. His wife and children happened to be out, and there was, apparently, no one in the house but himself.

Sitting on a chair in the hall, he was about to take off his boots—a thing he would not have done had his wife been at home, as he knew she objected to it—when he heard footsteps ascending the stone stairs leading from the basement. They were light steps, accompanied by the tapping of high heels. Up and up they came till they arrived in the hall, where they halted for a moment, and then began to approach him. There was still a certain amount of daylight, enough, at all events, for him to see any tolerably large object in the hall, but though he stared hard in the direction of the sounds he could see nothing to account for them. Yet nearer and nearer came the tapping, and then suddenly there was a whiff of scent, which Mr. Hackett recognized at once. It seemed to arouse within him passions and cravings he had never in his life been conscious of before. He was thrilled right through, and more than intoxicated. The tapping came right up to him and, as it passed him by, it seemed that cool, soft fingers touched him lightly on the forehead, while he felt the clinging folds of a dress pass gently over his feet.

Then all had swept on and left him, and he heard the front door open surreptitiously and close again, after which the air around him suddenly became so cold and chill that his teeth chattered and he was seized with a violent fit of shivering. A wild desire to follow the thing now took possession of him, and springing up from his chair, he rushed out of the house into the darkening street. There was nothing there save the rows of tall,

387

gently nodding trees, and gleaming lamp-posts. Convinced, however, that he would find it again, somewhere, he walked on, and leaving the quiet by-road in which he lived, plunged into the glare and noise of the King's Road. He walked until forced to look round for somewhere to rest. Right at his elbow was a public-house, with the word " Lounge " written invitingly in huge lettering on one of its windows. These was no other refreshment place open within sight.

Mr. Hackett considered the matter. He had the usual Nonconformists' antipathy to public-houses, but it was a question of expedience. He must sit down somewhere, and there was nowhere else for him to go. He approached the place cautiously, and opening a door, was peeping inside when, mingled with the odours of beer and tobacco, came a whiff of something else. It was scent, and fancying, in his overwrought state, that it clearly resembled the scent he had been following with such persistence, he gave vent to something approaching a moan and rushed inside.

An hour or so afterwards he staggered out onto the pavement, at least three-quarters drunk. That was the beginning of it. When he arrived home late his wife was sitting up for him, and there was a harrowing scene. She was, at first, too amazed and dumbfounded to say anything. Her husband drunk ! It was impossible ! She could only sit and gaze at him in stupefied silence. And then, as the truth slowly forced itself upon her, she burst out weeping and flew upstairs to bed.

She fell asleep sooner than one would have thought it possible, after such a shock, but her dreams were nightmarish and she awoke with a start to hear the clock in the hall striking two. Directly afterwards she heard her door open slowly and someone steal softly into the room. With all her faculties painfully on the alert, she at once sat up and looked. There was just enough light from the moon to make certain near objects dimly visible. At first she could see nothing strange, then suddenly out of the blackness came a hand, which she saw, with a start, was not the hand of her husband, nor of anyone in the house. It was absolutely white and slender, the fingers tapering, the nails exquisitely shaped. She could see nothing beyond the wrist. It came nearer and nearer to her, gropingly, as if someone were feeling their way, and finally it rested on her forehead.

Only, however, for one brief second. It was then withdrawn, while immediately afterwards, Mrs. Hackett again heard footsteps, this time retreating in the direction of the door, which opened gently and closed again. Then all was silent.

Somehow Mrs. Hackett was not frightened. On the contrary, she said afterwards, she felt too irritated at being so disturbed to think of going to sleep again. She blamed her husband and attributed it all to him. Had he not come home so late, and in that disgraceful condition, she felt the strange incident could not have happened. How drink degraded a man. In her mind, she again went through her husband's homecoming, and saw him staggering in through the doorway and falling in helpless fashion into a chair. How he had reeked of whisky, and what a dreadfully lost expression there had been on his face.

The more Mrs. Hackett pondered over her husband's conduct, the more the situation magnified itself, until she finally resolved to leave him altogether and return to her parents. With this end in view she immediately dressed, packed some things into a couple of small cases and, as soon as it was daylight, stole downstairs into the street and hailed a passing taxi.

She never returned to the house. When Mr. Hackett realized what had happened he was stunned. That his wife should desert him just at a time when he needed her love and sympathy most, seemed quite incredible, and he felt crushed. Then suddenly, in the midst of his trouble there came to him a memory of that scent, and the exquisite hand, and he actually found himself " revelling " (his own word) in the prospect of being in the house practically alone with them. His two young children, a boy and a girl, did not appear to take their mother's desertion to heart nearly as much as might have been expected, but then the house had wrought a most marked change in them as well.

Up to the time of their coming to it they had been as near

models of obedience as children can be, but now it was the reverse. Hardly a day passed when they did not quarrel violently, and they were most rude and obstructive to their daily governess. But that was not the worst. The girl showed a new and shocking trait in her character. The governess one morning found her deriving the greatest amusement from torturing flies, and a day or two later the girl was discovered in the act, assisted by her brother, of inflicting abominable cruelties on a mouse that had been caught alive in a trap.

The governess was so disgusted that she left the house at once, and the children, having no one to control them any longer, did more or less as they liked. One night, however, they too received a shock. They both slept in the nursery, and after having been asleep for some time, the girl, Emma, was awakened by hearing someone moving about in the room. Thinking it was her brother John, she called out to him to be quiet, and on his taking no notice, she immediately sat up. To her surprise, instead of seeing John, she saw, standing in the centre of the room, in a flood of moonlight, a tallish figure enveloped from head to foot in a long black cloak. The figure remained motionless for some seconds, and then, crossing the floor with a curious gliding movement, advanced towards the door, Emma watching it in breathless expectation.

On its reaching the doorway, which was parallel with her bed, the figure turned round and beckoned to Emma, and the girl noticed its " beautiful white hands ". Wondering who it could be she awakened John, and the two children, slipping out of bed, followed after the cloaked figure. Leading them across the landing, it descended two flights of stairs to the first storey, and then, making direct for their father's door, came to a halt immediately outside it. More than ever puzzled, the children were about to call out to their father, when the figure slowly turned round and confronted them. It remained thus, quite still, for a few seconds, and then, suddenly throwing aside the cloak, which had up to the present concealed its face, it stood fully revealed before them.

To their great horror it was nothing human. The body, beautifully formed, resembled that of a woman, but the face was that of some very grotesque and repulsive animal. In the place of human cheeks were huge collops of white, unwholesome fat, the nose was snoutlike, the mouth a great slit, and the whole conformity of the features suggested the distorted face of a pig, which appeared all the more macabre by reason of the figure's hair, unmistakably a woman's, which fell in a bright gold mass around the neck and shoulders. The children were still staring at the apparition in speechless horror when their father opened the door of his room; and as he did so, the figure slowly faded away, though not before he had caught a full view of it.

Mr. Hackett and his children left the house the following day, and it is pleasant to note that not long after they had been living in a new atmosphere, their life settled back to normal, and a reconciliation between the reverend gentleman and his wife quickly took place.

Many and various tenants in succession occupied the house in Chelsea after the Hacketts, and from my further investigations made as late as the 1940's, there was good reason to believe the house was still badly haunted.

A dozen explanations have been offered for the strange haunting. A popular theory is that the pig-faced apparition is the earthbound spirit of some peculiarly vicious and degenerate woman, who, having lived and died in the house, is bound to it by her earthly desires and passions.

Personally, I think differently. I believe the haunting springs from events which occurred on the site before the house was built, involving as it seems to do a harmful spirit of the elemental kind which never knew human form, and so was unable to manifest itself completely in this guise. The elemental type of ghost is by no means uncommon; the reader will recall that such an apparition was the first I ever saw.

THE HINDU CHILD

I MET Nurse Mackenzie for the first time at the house of my old friend, Colonel Malcolmson, whose wife she was nursing. For some days I was hardly aware she was in the house, the illness of her patient keeping her so occupied; but when Mrs. Malcolmson grew better, I not infrequently saw the nurse taking a morning " constitutional " in the beautiful grounds. It was on one of these occasions that we fell to talking about ghosts, and she told me of her own uncanny experience some ten years earlier, at the turn of the century.

" It happened," she began, " shortly after I had finished my term as probationer in an Aberdeen hospital. A letter was received at the hospital one morning with the urgent request that two nurses should be sent to a serious case near St. Swithin's Street. As the letter was signed by a well-known physician in the town it received immediate attention, and Nurse Emmett and I were sent as day and night nurses respectively, to deal with the emergency. My tour of duty was to be from 9 p.m. till 9 a.m.

" The house in which the patient was located was known as the White Dove Hotel, a thoroughly respectable and well-managed establishment. The proprietor knew nothing about the invalid, except that her name was Vining, and that she had at one period of her career been an actress. He had noticed that she looked unwell on her arrival the previous week. Two days after her arrival she had complained of feeling very ill, and the doctor summoned to attend her diagnosed that she was suffering from an aggravating disease of Oriental origin, one fortunately rare in this country.

" The hotel, though newly decorated and equipped, was in reality very old. It was one of those delightfully roomy erections that seem built for eternity rather than time, and for comfort rather than economy of space. The interior, with its oak-panelled walls, polished oak floors and low ceilings impressed me pleasantly, while a flight of broad oak stairs fenced with balustrades a foot thick, brought me to a seemingly interminable corridor, into which the door of Miss Vining's room opened. It was a low, wainscoted apartment, and its deep-set window, revealing the thickness of the wall, looked out upon a yard littered with brooms and buckets. Opposite the foot of the bed—a modern French bedstead, whose brass fittings and flimsy hangings contrasted strangely with their venerable surroundings—was an ingle containing the smouldering relics of what had doubtless been intended for a fire. There was no exit save by the doorway I had entered, and no furniture except a couple of rush-bottomed chairs and a table strewn with an untidy collection of writing materials and medicine bottles.

" A feeling of depression seized me directly I entered the room. Despite the brilliancy of the electric light and the new and gaudy bed-hangings, the air was full of gloom. I felt it hanging around me like the undeveloped shadow of something singularly repulsive, and on my approaching the sick woman it seemed to thrust itself in my way and force me back.

" Miss Vining was decidedly good-looking. She had typically theatrical features—neatly moulded nose and chin, curly yellow hair, and big, dreamy blue eyes. She was, of course, far too ill to converse, and beyond a few desultory remarks, maintained a rigid silence. As there was no occasion for me to sit close beside her, I drew up a chair before the fire, placing myself in such a position as to command a full view of the bed.

" My first night passed undisturbed by any incident, and in the morning the condition of my patient showed a slight improvement. It was soon after eight o'clock in the evening when I came on duty again, and the weather having changed during the day, the whole room echoed and re-echoed with the howling of the wind which raged round the house.

" I had been at my post for a little over two hours, and had just registered my patient's temperature, when, happening to look up from the book I was reading, I saw to my surprise that the chair beside the head of the bed was occupied by a child—a tiny girl. How she had come into the room without attracting my attention was extraordinary, and I could only suppose that the shrieking of the wind down the chimney had deadened the sound of the door and her footsteps.

" I was naturally very indignant that she had dared to come in without knocking, and getting up from my seat I was preparing to address her and bid her go, when she lifted a small white hand and motioned me back. I obeyed because I could not help myself—her action was accompanied by a peculiar expression that held me spellbound, and without exactly knowing why, I stood staring at her, tongue-tied and trembling. As her face was turned towards the patient, and she wore a very wide-brimmed hat, I could see nothing of her features; but from her graceful little figure and dainty limbs, I gathered that she was probably both beautiful and aristocratic. Her dress, though not perhaps of the richest quality, was certainly far from shoddy, and there was something in its style and make that suggested foreign nationality.

" I was so taken up with watching her that I forget all about my patient, until a prolonged sigh from the bed reminded me of her existence. With an effort I then advanced, and was about to approach the bed, when the child, without moving her head, motioned me back to my chair, and again I was helpless. The vision I had obtained of the sick woman, brief though it was, filled me with alarm. She was tossing to and fro on the blankets and breathing in the most agonized manner as if in delirium, or in the grip of some particularly dreadful nightmare. Her condition so frightened me that I made the most frantic efforts to get to her side. I did not succeed, however, and at last, utterly overcome by my exertion, I closed my eyes. When I opened them again the chair by the bed was vacant—the child had gone.

" A tremendous feeling of relief surged through me, and jumping out of my seat I hastened to the bedside. My patient was worse, the fever had increased, and she was delirious. I took her temperature. It was 104. I now sat close beside her, and my presence apparently had a soothing effect. She speedily grew calmer, and after taking her medicine gradually sank into a gentle sleep which lasted until late in the morning. When I left her she had altogether recovered from the relapse.

" I naturally told the doctor of the child's visit, and he was very angry.

" ' Whatever happens, nurse,' he said, ' take care that no one enters the room tonight. The patient's condition is far too critical for her to see anyone. You must keep the door locked.'

" Armed with this mandate I went on duty the following night with a somewhat lighter heart, and after locking the door, once again sat by the fire. During the day there had been a heavy fall of snow. The wind had abated, and the streets were now as silent as the grave.

" Ten, eleven, and twelve o'clock struck, and my patient slept tranquilly. At a quarter to one, however, I was abruptly aroused from a reverie by a sob of fear and agony that came from the bed. I looked across and there, seated in the same posture as on the previous evening, was the child. I sprang to my feet with a cry of amazement. She raised her hand, and as before, I collapsed back into my seat, paralysed. No words of mine can convey all the sensations I experienced as I sat there, forced to listen to the moaning and groaning of the woman whose fate had been entrusted to my keeping. Every second she grew worse, and each sound rang in my ears like the hammering of nails in her coffin. How long I endured such torment I cannot say, for though the clock was within a few feet of me, I never once thought of looking at it. At last the child rose, and moving slowly from the bed, advanced with bowed head towards the window. The spell was broken. With an angry cry I literally bounded over the carpet and faced the intruder.

" 'Who are you?' I hissed. 'Tell me your name instantly! How dare you enter this room without my permission!'

" As I spoke she slowly raised her head. I snatched at her hat. It melted away in my hands, and to my unspeakable terror I looked into the face of a corpse. The corpse of a Hindu child, with a big, gaping cut in her throat.

" In her lifetime the child had, without doubt, been lovely; she was now horrible with all the ghastly disfigurements, the repellent disfigurements of a long consignment to the grave. I promptly fainted.

" On recovering I found that my ghostly visitor had vanished —and that my patient was dead. One of her hands was thrown across her eyes, as if to shut out some object on which she feared to look, while the other grasped the counterpane convulsively.

" It fell to my duty to help pack up Miss Vining's belongings, and among her letters was a large envelope bearing the postmark 'Quetta'. As we were then on the lookout for some clue as to the address of her relatives, I opened it. It was merely the cabinet-size photograph of a Hindu child, but I recognized the dress immediately—it was that of my ghostly visitor. On the back of it were these words: 'Natalie, May God forgive us both.'

" Though we made careful inquiries for any information as to Natalie and Miss Vining in Quetta, and advertised freely in the leading London papers, we learned nothing, and in time we were forced to let the matter drop. As far as I know, the ghost of the Hindu child has never been seen again, but I have heard that the hotel is still haunted—by a woman."

PHANTOMS FROM MY NOTEBOOK

GLANCING THROUGH one of my notebooks I see the date: " July 24th, 1898." It is a date I am not likely to forget, and this is the story of it, from my pencilled notes.

It was a Sunday, and my rambles that evening took me into Greenwich Park. It was warm and close, the sun still lingering in the west, while the sky in the east was clear and cloudless. Leaving the carriage-drive to the left I stepped on to the grassy walk and, making my way past a score or so of strolling couples, eventually found myself in a narrow avenue composed of magnificent elm trees.

The shade here being so pleasant after the heat of the open park, I looked around for a seat, and discovering one sat down to idle away an hour or so.

Just beneath where I was sitting was a gap in the foliage, through which I had a panoramic view of undulating banks of sun-baked, yellow-green turf, beyond which lay a sea of smoking chimneys of dingy, inhospitable-looking buildings, of slender, lofty masts, and the glistening, winding Thames, now impressively deserted.

I could appreciate all this just then as my holidays were

shortly to begin, when I should be free for a while from the monotony of schoolteaching and able to concentrate on my efforts to write.

The bench on which I sat was directly beneath a giant elm, the base of which afforded an ideal back-rest. I was accordingly leaning against its trunk when a sudden icy cold wind blowing from above made me glance up.

I then noticed that the bark of the tree was not only disfigured by unsightly notches and protuberant gnarls, but bore indications of some malignant parasitical disease. Kneeling on the seat to inspect it more closely, I was examining the trunk with interest, when a dark object seemed to descend from above and something came plump by my side.

I have never been able to describe the awful shock I received when, on turning round to see what it was, my eyes alighted on a figure half human and half animal—stunted, bloated, pulpy and yellow. Crawling sideways like a crab, it made for a bush opposite, into which it disappeared.

I did not wait to see whether it would return, but jumping hurriedly from the seat made tracks for the school—not visiting the park again till the following autumn, when I took care to give that tree a very wide berth.

It was obviously just a common elemental or " nature " spirit, but I don't think any occult manifestation has ever filled me with such unutterable loathing, nor so effectually damped all desire of further investigations.

Some further excerpts from my notebooks may be of interest to the reader, showing as they do the ramifications of a ghost-hunter's activities.

Here, for instance, are brief notes of two odd little hauntings in London which I was unable to follow up. The first came to me from a woman who told me that the house she had recently lived in at Wandsworth was haunted. Day after day, said my informant, she had been disturbed by an old woman who used to chatter outside her bedroom door. She grew so accustomed to the noise that she was not in the least bit nervous, and used to call out to the ghost and bid it be silent—an injunction it sometimes obeyed.

Both my informant and her sister often saw the old woman in various parts of the house, generally on the staircase or flitting about the passages, but she was so entirely harmless and natural that no one paid her much attention.

The second haunting, again described to me by a witness, concerned a thoroughly modern ghost. In a house close to Ealing Broadway, a woman who spent most of her evenings at London night clubs, dancing, died. The night after her funeral, sounds of gay music and dancing were heard coming from the room in which she breathed her last, and the sounds continued to be heard there periodically.

Ghostly music apparently does not affect all animals in the same way, for whereas the dead woman's cat, a large tabby, always ran upstairs directly the sounds commenced and sat on the doormat outside the room, apparently listening with great eagerness to the music and dancing, a dog in the same house immediately began to bark and howl in terror.

Turning the pages again, here is my note of a house I investigated in Whitechapel; an unusual " noise haunting ", this one. Hearing that I was interested in ghosts a man named Andrews, a clerk, told me that the house where he was lodging, in Commercial Road, was haunted, and that he would be glad if I would sit up with him one night and investigate the haunting. When I agreed, he said: " I won't tell you beforehand what happens, because then what you experience can't be put down to suggestion."

The night chosen by me for the investigation was in March, and the weather was bitterly cold. There was absolutely nothing ghostly about the house; it was just a very uninteresting, small and comparatively modern building, crammed full of shoddy furniture and reeking of fried fish and a variety of other living and cooking smells. Mr. Andrews' room was on the first floor, and after everyone in the place had retired to bed, we opened the door of his room and sat facing the little landing.

After we had been sitting there for about an hour in absolute silence—we did not talk, not wishing to disturb other people in the house—I was suddenly conscious of an eerie feeling, and immediately afterwards I heard a jingling and tinkling sound, such as is made by the small bells on a child's harness, and following that, a sound that seemed to have been made by a rubber ball hitting the wall opposite and landing back on to the floor beside me. Andrews immediately lit the gas, but nothing was to be seen. When he had closed the door of the room, he said:

" You heard those sounds? Well, we all hear them every night. They always occur about the same time, and although we are trying hard to find some natural explanation for them, so far we have failed."

I was not surprised. A repetition of this experience on several subsequent nights strengthened and confirmed my impression that the strange sounds owed their origin to supernatural behaviour.

I think I have made it clear that a number of my investigations of alleged haunted houses have produced no result, but that where only one night's sitting can be made, it really is too much to expect everything to happen at once, or anything at all. For various reasons, some of my inquiries have been thus restricted to a single vigil, with negative results. Such was the case with a house in Clifton, Bristol, but the very nature of the haunting, as recorded in my notebook, calls for a mention here.

Lord Curzon, who several times accompanied me most enthusiastically on my investigations, insisted on my taking him to this empty house, which had long borne the reputation for being haunted. It was in a terrace not far from the Suspension Bridge, and dated back to about 1780. The hauntings, however, did not break out until during the last occupier's tenancy.

What happened was this: Before taking the house, the last tenant, on going to view it one day, saw a woman dressed in

400

black standing in one of the rooms. She had her back to him, and obviously unaware of his presence, was arranging her hair under her hat. Thinking she must be some prospective tenant, like himself, come to see over the house, he was about to make his presence known, when to his astonishment she vanished.

Being a very matter-of-fact, practical man, not at all superstitious, he thought it strange, but concluded that he had been the victim of some peculiar kind of illusion. He dismissed the matter from his mind, and continuing his survey of the house, eventually took it.

He and his family had not been in it long, however, before his encounter with the lady in black was vividly recalled to him by certain weird happenings. One evening his wife and little boy, and the wife's sister, heard a strange, ominous cry. It seemed to pass right through the room, leaving them considerably startled. On another occasion, the same boy and his brother saw a woman in black holding a small boy by the hand standing in the doorway staring at them. They yelled out, and on their mother running upstairs to see what was the matter, the woman and boy disappeared.

From the description the two children gave of the woman, it was apparently the same figure their father had seen when looking over the house. She was dressed in black and presented the appearance of just a very ordinary, modern woman.

But there were other, more remarkable phenomena. For instance, every night at about the same hour, footsteps were heard running upstairs from the hall to the landing on the first floor. Sounds like the winding of a big clock were next heard, and when these sounds ceased, the footsteps recommenced and were heard ascending the stairs to the next floor. Arriving there, they ran across the landing to the bathroom, the door of which was heard to open and shut, and then started bounding about on the floor. Once a hospital nurse staying in the house, hearing what she thought was a clock on the landing being wound up, and wondering who could be doing such a thing at such an hour, after everyone had gone to bed, opened the door of her room and looked out. What she saw gave her a shock. A strange looking shadowy figure was in the act of climbing the staircase leading to the floor immediately overhead. Its back being towards her, she could not see its face, but the thing as a whole gave her the impression that it was very evil and grotesque— " more like some huge, horrible ape than a human being ". It went up the stairs two or three at a time, and she heard it open and shut the bathroom door and then bound about all over the floor.

In the daytime, too, the phenomena continued. Footsteps, accompanied by heavy breathing, were heard ascending the stone steps leading from the cellar to the passage on the ground floor, between the morning-room and the kitchen. On one or two occasions an indistinct, shadowy form, which may have been the same thing the nurse saw, was seen to rush along the passage and disappear in the kitchen. At other times a voice calling out " Henry!" was heard proceeding, apparently, from the chimney in one of the rooms. There may have been other phenomena, but this is all I noted down. The incidents were related to me by the man who took the house, his wife, and sister-in-law. It was because the case was so well attested and so well known in Clifton at the time that Lord Curzon chose it for our investigation.

The house certainly looked haunted. It was in a most forlorn and dilapidated condition, being untenanted for some years. The paper in some of the rooms was dropping from the walls, cobwebs festooned the ceilings, windowpanes were broken and doors and floorings were covered in places with huge, repulsive-looking fungi.

We sat waiting on camp stools at the head of the cellar steps, but nothing occurred. As Lord Curzon was too tired to sit up any longer, we came away soon after one o'clock; with regrets, but not, I might add, without considerable relief.

In an earlier notebook I see I have some notes on family ghosts, and particularly those relating to Scotland. Much has

402

been written of the phantom drummer of Cortachy, who was invariably heard playing his drum, sometimes to the accompaniment of ghostly pipes, before the death of a member of the Ogilvie family. There is quite a lot of corroborated evidence on the subject of the Ogilvie family ghost, and I was told years ago, on my first visit to Scotland, that the Ogilvies themselves still firmly believe in it. The family of Grant Rothiermurcus were haunted by the Bodach au Dun; the Kinchardines by the Lhamdearg, or spectre of the Bloody Hand; and the Tulloch Gorms by May Moulach, or the Girl with the Hairy Hand.

All these are families of distinction and according to the popular idea it is only families or clans of distinction that possess family ghosts. Such an idea, however, is quite wrong. There are many ordinary families in the West of Scotland and in the Western Isles that have been haunted for long centuries by spirits of the Glaistig species (in effect, a sort of Scottish Banshee), as well as by spirits of the dead and the more harrowing and alarming types of elementals.

On my second visit to Scotland I stayed with an old school friend, Charlie Campbell, in Argyll. He was a keen sportsman (as I was then) and it was arranged that we should fish one night on Loch Fyne. When the time came for us to set out, however, Campbell was taken ill and could not go, so at his suggestion I set off without him, accompanied by one of his outdoor servants, a rugged, dour-looking Western islander named Neil MacPherson.

The night, though very fine and still, was dark, and ours appeared to be the only boat out. There were plenty of whales, however, and when we had got some little distance from the shore, they began spouting in closer proximity to our boat, so I thought, than was altogether pleasant, though MacPherson assured me they were quite small and absolutely harmless.

We were fishing at anchorage in absolute silence, when quite suddenly I caught the far-off sound of oars.

" Who can they be?" I asked MacPherson, more for the sake of hearing myself speak than for anything else, for we had been sitting in silence for a long time. " Fishermen?"

" I dinna ken, young sir," MacPherson replied, and I thought I detected a trace of anxiety in his voice.

The sound came from the rear. I was sitting facing the bows of the boat, and as the oars drew nearer, I turned round, but could see nothing in the darkness.

" Oughtn't they to carry a light?" I asked.

MacPherson did not answer. The sounds drew nearer still. I could hear the splashing of the water each time the blades of the oars struck it, and the grating of the handles of the oars as they moved to and fro in the rowlocks; but still I could see nothing. On the boat came, and as it passed by us, so close that its oars seemed but a foot or two from our gunwales, I was puzzled by the silence of the rowers (there appeared to be several), none of whom uttered a sound. This silence was extraordinary, as in my experience boatmen, be they fishermen or ordinary sailors, invariably talk.

The night being so still, I could hear the sound of the oars for some time after the boat had passed, and it was not until the sound had died away, to be replaced by the familiar spasmodic spouting of the whales, that I spoke to MacPherson.

" Shall we try somewhere else?" I asked. " It doesn't seem much use staying here. I haven't had as much as a bite."

" You will forgive me, sir," he replied, " if I suggest we go home now."

" Aren't you feeling well?" I said, for there was a tremor in his voice.

" Not very well, sir," he answered shortly.

" All right," I said, " we'll go." Then, before I was really conscious of what I was saying, I added, " It isn't anything to do with that boat that passed us, is it?"

" Yes, sir," he answered, solemnly. " That was the death boat. It has haunted our family for hundreds of years, and is never seen or heard saving before the death of one of us. We all heard it the night before my father was drowned off Portree in the Island of Skye, and again just before the death of my youngest sister. I dread tomorrow, because I am sure I shall get word that my brother Angus is dead."

I tried to calm him. " Surely, Neil," I said, " you could be mistaken? You didn't see your brother, did you?"

" Yes," he replied, endeavouring to steady his voice. " I did. There were four rowers—there are always four—dressed in black, and Angus, my brother, dressed just like them, was sitting in the stern. It is he who is dead."

The sense of finality accompanying this statement seemed to make any further discussion of the subject useless, so after a pause I turned our talk into another channel.

MacPherson's fears, however, proved to be correct, for at noon the next day he received a telegram from his mother saying that Angus had been caught in a sudden squall, and drowned.

While on this subject I ought to make brief reference to the phantom ship that has, from time to time, visited St. Ives Bay, in Cornwall. A fisherman who sometimes took me out in his boat was once called upon to go to the rescue of a ship that had been burning lights as a signal for help to the westward of St. Ives Head. He and his comrades, he said, put off and when they drew near to the vessel, they saw to their astonishment that her masts and riggings were covered with ice, as if she had encountered Arctic weather. Also, no one was visible on deck, and when they hailed her there was no reply. This struck them as being very odd, but stranger things were to follow, for when the man in the bows of the St. Ives boat stood up and tried to clutch hold of the bulwarks of the strange vessel, the latter suddenly and inexplicably vanished, and the St. Ives man would have fallen into the sea had he not been held by one of his mates.

The men now realized that what they had seen was the famous phantom ship, and they lost no time in getting back to harbour. A few hours later a great storm arose and a ship was wrecked at Gwithian, everyone on board perishing.

According to my fisherman friend, the phtantom ship is seldom if ever seen in St. Ives Bay, save before some local maritime disaster.

Now to a summer's day in 1900, and my record of a very unusual animal ghost. I was visiting the London Zoo on this day, and was so struck by the look in the eyes of one of the lions, which seemed to me to be the desperate look of yearning to have just five minutes on the sunny lawn to stretch its cramped-up limbs, that I could not help passing a remark to this effect to a white-haired old man and plainly dressed young woman who stood next to me.

"Yes," the old man said. "It does seem hard on these huge animals to have to pace up and down these little boxes, tantalized by the sight of other creatures enjoying the privileges that are denied to them. But they have one thing to be thankful for, there's a Paradise waiting for all these creatures, just as there is for the lucky ones among us."

"You believe in animals having spirits?" I asked.

"Yes, spirits—ghosts, if you like," he said emphatically. "I've seen plenty of proof of it."

He then stopped himself, feeling he had possibly said too much, but I encouraged him to go on.

He looked at me searchingly, and then said: "I used to be a keeper here some years ago. I was devoted to the animals, and when they died, I often saw their ghosts. So did some of the other keepers. But don't run away with the idea that the Zoo is haunted. It was only to us who had so much to do with them when they were alive that the spirits of these animals appeared.

"I remember one instance in particular, about twelve years ago, just before I left the Zoo. A young lion came here from East Africa. It wouldn't let any of the keepers go near it except myself, and it was generally regarded as having a very uncertain temper. But I never found it so. I knew the reason for its restlessness was its hatred of confinement. I knew it hated its cage, and I used to do all I could to comfort it. There was a sort of mutual understanding between us. When it saw me looking a bit anxious and worried, for my wife was often ill, it used to come and rub its great head against me, as if to cheer me up, and when I saw it looking more than usually dejected, I used to stop and talk to it for a longer time than I talked to any of the other animals.

" One day it fell ill, caught a chill, so we thought, and went off its food. I discussed its case with the other keepers, and they agreed there was nothing to be alarmed about, as it was young and to all appearances healthy. We all thought it would be well again in a few days, so I wasn't unduly worried.

" Well, I had gone home as usual one night, and was sitting in the kitchen reading the evening paper, when something came over me that I must go for a walk. I told my grand-daughter, Mary, here—she was a little girl then, not more than nine or ten—and she begged her mother to let her go with me. We started off with the intention of going to the Caledonian Road, as Mary liked looking at the shops there, but we hadn't gone far before she suddenly said: ' Grandad, let's go to Regent's Park.'

" ' Regent's Park?' I said, ' whatever do you want to go there for at this time of night?'

" ' I don't know,' she said, ' but I feel I must.'

" ' Well now,' I admitted, ' that's odd, because the very same feeling has come over me.'

" We struck off down Crowndale Road—I was living in the neighbourhood of the St. Pancras Road then—and got to Gloucester Gate just about dusk. We had passed through, and were walking along the Broad Walk by the side of the Zoo, when Mary suddenly caught hold of my arm and said: ' Look, Grandad!' I followed the direction of her gaze, and there coming straight towards us from the Zoo walls was a lion. I can tell you it gave me a jump, as I naturally thought one of the animals had escaped. It aimed straight for us, and on its getting close to I recognized it at once—it was the young lion that had been taken ill. To my astonishment, however, there was nothing of the invalid about it now—the expression in its eyes was one of great happiness.

407

"It came right up to us, and I stretched out my hand to touch it, wondering what the passers-by would do when they saw it, and how on earth we should get it back into the gardens. It grieved me to think it would have to lose its freedom again. I stretched out my hand to touch it, and to my surprise my fingers encountered nothing—the lion had vanished. I then realized what Mary had known all along; that what we had seen was a ghost. A ghost, and yet it had been so absolutely real and lifelike."

I turned to the old man's grand-daughter. "How did you know it was a ghost?" I asked her.

"By the curious light that seemed to come from all over its body," she said. "A kind of glow. It was not a bit natural."

"But you saw the figure distinctly?"

"Yes, very distinctly, and I wasn't the least bit afraid."

"Let me tell you the sequel," her grandfather continued. "On my arrival at the Zoo in the morning, one of the men came running up to me. 'It's dead,' he said. 'What's dead?' I said. 'Why, that young lion of yours,' he said—'it died last night.'

"When I went into the lion-house, there was the poor animal lying stretched out full-length. It had died at eight o'clock the previous night, I was told, which was the exact time we had seen it in the park."

The ghosts of animals also figured in two unusual hauntings which I noted as fully as possible from inquiries, but which because of the passage of time I could not personally investigate. They are, in fact, among a handful of absorbing cases which I would have greatly liked to pursue. First, a case from Hampshire.

The sister of a well-known author told me there used to be a house called "The Swallows" standing in two acres of land, close to a village near Basingstoke. In 1840, a Mr. Bishop, from Tring, bought the house, which had long stood empty, and moved into it the following year. But after he had been only a fortnight in occupation two servants gave notice to leave, swearing that the place was haunted by a large cat and a big baboon, which they constantly saw stealing down the staircases and passages. They also testified to hearing sounds as of somebody being strangled, coming from an empty attic near where they slept, and hearing the screams and groans of " a number of people being horribly tortured " in the cellars just underneath the dairy. When they went down to see the cause of the disturbances, nothing was ever visible.

In a matter of days other members of the household began to be harassed by similar manifestations. The news spread quickly through the village, and crowds of people came to the house at night with lights and sticks, to see if they could witness anything.

One night, at about midnight, when several of the watchers were stationed on guard in the empty courtyard, they all saw the forms of a huge cat and a baboon rise from the closed grating of the large cellar under the old dairy, rush past them, and disappear in a dark angle of the walls. The same figures were repeatedly seen afterwards by many other persons. Early in December, 1841, Mr. Bishop, hearing fearful screams, accompanied by deep and hoarse jabberings, apparently coming from the top of the house, rushed upstairs, but as he reached the landing all was instantly silent, and he could discover nothing.

After that he set to work to get rid of the house, and was fortunate enough to find as a purchaser a retired colonel. But this man was soon scared out of it too, and in 1842 the house was abandoned. It was later pulled down and the ground used for the erection of cottages; but the hauntings then transferred to them, scaring people almost out of their wits. The cottages were speedily vacated, and no one ever daring to inhabit them, they were eventually demolished and the site turned over for allotments.

There were many theories as to the history of " The Swallows," one being that a highwayman, known as Steeplechase Jock, the son of a Scottish chieftain, had once plied his trade there and murdered many people, whose bodies were supposed to be buried somewhere on or near the premises. He was said to have met a terrible and decidedly unorthodox end by falling into a vat of boiling tar.

The second haunting of long ago concerns that of a ghost bird, an enormous raven, and it is certainly one of the oddest and most fascinating bird hauntings to have occurred anywhere.

There was much excitement when, about 1749, word spread that the three large vaults under the parish church of West Drayton, near Uxbridge, were haunted. In one vault the family of Paget were interred, and in another the even more ancient family of De Burgh. People passing by the church at night, more especially on a Friday night, swore that they heard knockings coming from the vaults. No very satisfactory explanation of the noises was ever given, but as the remains of a murderer, who had committed suicide, and the remains of his victim were buried together in one of the vaults, many believed that the knockings were thus accounted for; that the spirits of the murderer and the murdered were unwilling that their bodies should lie side by side.

But then events took a different turn. One night some people living close to the church heard dreadful screams coming from it. They hurried off to see the cause, and finding, on their arrival at the church, that the screams came from one of the vaults, they peered into it through the ventilation grating. They then saw, just inside the vault, an enormous raven that pecked at the coffins furiously, and all the while it did so the screaming continued. Among the many witnesses were the sexton and his wife, and a churchwarden.

This story of the raven was confirmed by other people, including the wife of the parish clerk and her daughter, who testified to also seeing it in the church itself.

One evening a youth went to the local bellringers, who had emphatically denied that the bird was a phantom at all, and told them that it was flying about in the chancel. Four of them, taking sticks and a lantern, then ran to the church to try to catch it. On reaching the church they saw the bird, which was just as the youth described it, an enormous black bird, fluttering about the chancel. They at once gave chase, and on one of the men striking it with a stick, it fell down screaming, apparently hurt. Believing that it was at last cornered, the man who had struck it was about to pick it up when, to the amazement of them all, it was found that the bird had vanished.

After that it was often to be seen either perched on the Communion rails of the sanctuary, or flying about in one or other of the vaults. Whenever anyone attempted to catch it, it always mysteriously disappeared.

The villagers firmly believed that the ghost bird was " the restless and miserable spirit of a murderer who had committed suicide and who, through family influence, instead of being put into a pit or a hole with a stake through his body, at the cross-road by Harmondsworth, as was the sentence by law, had been buried in consecrated ground, on the north side of the church-yard." This was also the strong view of a neighbouring squire who saw the phantom bird; he was quite positive that it was the earthbound soul of the criminal, whose family history was known to him.

Mrs. De Burgh, wife of Mr. R. L. De Burgh, a later vicar of West Drayton, stated that in the 1850s she had often heard sounds in the church like the fluttering of some very large bird, and that these strange sounds always appeared to come from the chancel. As late as 1869, two women going into the church one Saturday afternoon, to put some flowers on the Communion table, momentarily saw a huge black bird sitting on one of the pews.

The haunting thus seems to have continued intermittently over a period of more than a hundred years.

Finally, some more animal ghosts, of which I took note while touring Scotland many years ago. These apparently were ghost dogs, but not at all like the usually harmless domestic variety.

The Argyll island of Tiree, I was told, was much haunted. A beach on its northern shore called Cladach a Chrogain, comprising about 1,500 acres of shingle, was at the time of my visit as wild and lonely a spot as one could find in the British Isles, and at night especially, strongly suggested all kinds of horrors. One haunting in particular attracted much attention among the islanders. It was the haunting by a phantom in the form of a large black dog, of a somewhat similar species to the " Thrash " and " Striker " in Lancashire, the " Padfoot " in Yorkshire, and and " Shuck " in Norfolk and Cambridge. Several of the older inhabitants of Tiree, so they declared, had seen this phantom following them, and they believed that if it barked once or twice all was well, but if it barked three times it was a sure sign that it would overtake them, in which case they, or someone very closely connected with them, would die very shortly.

The local folk told me that another ghost dog, very like this one in appearance but not of the same nature, haunted Hynish Hill in the south-west of Tiree, while yet another haunted the rocky shore near Balvaig. My informants, however, assured me that something infinitely more horrible was to be seen and heard on a seagirt rock close to Balvaig known locally as the Grador.

I asked them what it was, and they said : " Something naked, not unlike a human body in form, but with a very grotesque and wholly diabolical face." It was occasionally seen in broad daylight, though more often between 2 and 4 a.m., and its chief characteristic was antipathy to dogs. It was said that a dog belonging to a Tiree fisherman swam one morning to the rock and failed to return, and on a search being made for it, it was found lying on the rock with all its skin scraped off, as if by long nails or talons. It was horribly mutilated and died in great agony shortly after being found.

This hatred of dogs appears to be a striking feature of many of the Western Island and West of Scotland ghosts. On the hills between Loch Tuath and Loch Cuan there is a spot reputed to be haunted by various species of ghosts that exhibit fiendish satisfaction in torturing not only dogs, but animals in general. Many stories declared to be authentic are told of these ghosts. The following is an example :

A man was crossing the hills one day with his dog, a terrier, when he saw a tall woman with long yellow hair standing on the spot that was said to be haunted. At first he took her to be a material being, but on looking at her closely he noticed there was a something peculiar and shadowy about her, something which made him realize that she was no creature of flesh and blood.

When he first caught sight of her, his dog whined and showed fear, but on his approaching nearer it became angry and rushed at her, snarling savagely, at which she snatched it up in her arms and ran off with it, taking cover behind a rock. Being fond of his dog, the man, though frightened, ran after the ghost woman, and on looking behind the rock found his dog lying dead in a pool of blood. Handfuls of hair had been torn from its body, and apparently it had been strangled.

There was no sign of the woman anywhere, nor any place near at hand in which she could possibly have hidden. In the opinion of those who were living in that locality, and whose forebears had lived there before them, the phantom woman was a ghost well known to be inimical to all living things, and who had haunted those hills for generations.

THE RED FINGERS

MANY OF my ghost-hunts, from what promised in the beginning to be a "routine" investigation of a simple enough haunting, held a twist in the tail. A prime example is the case of the Rowlandsons.

I met Mr. and Mrs. Robert Rowlandson many years ago in Perth. They told me they were just quitting a badly haunted house on the outskirts of the city. The name of the house was "Bocarthe". It was their own, and had only been built a year, but they could not possibly remain in it, they said, because of the ghostly disturbances to which they were subjected.

"What strikes us as so extraordinary about the whole thing," Mrs. Rowlandson said, "is that a new house with absolutely no history attached to it—and we can assure you," she added laughingly, "there were no murders or suicides there during our occupancy—should be haunted. Our neighbours say we must have brought the ghost with us."

The couple were just beginning a detailed description of the manifestations when I asked them to stop. I explained that I would like to investigate the case, and that if they agreed, it would be better for me to do so without having any prior

414

knowledge of the nature of the hauntings.

They were quite willing—provided I promised not to discuss the matter too openly, as they wanted to let the house—that I should spend a few nights at " Bocarthe ". They were rather anxious to know if anything unusual still took place there. Thinking, perhaps, that I might not like to go alone, they gave me an introduction to a young friend of theirs, Dr. Swinton, who they thought might be interested to accompany me.

That same day the Rowlandsons went off to Edinburgh, where they told me they now intended living, and the following day at noon I made my way to the house they had vacated. As there was no story connected with " Bocarthe " itself I made inquiries about the ground on which it stood, and it may interest the reader to know my findings—as an example of the exasperatingly negative direction in which these inquiries, though very necessary, often lead.

Instead of learning too little I learned too much. An old minister of about eighty was sure that the ground in question, until built upon recently, had been grazing land since he was a boy, and that it had never witnessed anything more extraordinary than the occasional death of a sheep or a cow that had been struck by lightning. An equally aged and positive postmistress declared that the ground had never been anything better than wasteland, where amid rubbish heaps galore all the dogs in the parish might have been seen scratching and fighting over bones. Another person remembered a pond being there, and another a nursery garden; but from no one could I extract the slightest hint of anything that might account for the haunting.

Then, when I entered the house, I thought I had seldom seen such a cheerful residence. The rooms were light and lofty, and about them all there was an air of friendliness and warmth; there could scarcely have been a more " unghostly " atmosphere.

Dr. Swinton joined me in the evening, but although we sat up till long after dawn, we neither saw nor heard anything we could not account for by natural causes. We repeated the vigil for two more nights, after which we concluded that the house was either no longer haunted, or that the hauntings were periodical and might not occur again for years. I wrote as much to Mr. Rowlandson, returning the keys of the house, and in reply received the following letter from him in Edinburgh:

Dear Mr. O'Donnell,

Many thanks for the keys. No wonder you did not see our ghost! It is here, and we are having just the same experiences in this house as we had in " Bocarthe ". If you would care to stay a few nights with us on the chance of seeing the ghost, we shall be delighted to put you up.

Yours, etc.

ROBERT ROWLANDSON.

I could not resist the Rowlandsons' kind invitation, and just as soon as I could, caught the train for Edinburgh. When I arrived at their house, situated in a pleasant crescent, it was to find the entire household in a panic, the ghost having appeared to one and all during the previous night.

" It was so terrible," Mrs. Rowlandson told me, " that I cannot bear even to think of it, and shall certainly never forget it. One of the maids fainted and was so ill afterwards we were obliged to have the doctor. Now all the servants have given notice to leave."

" Did nothing of the sort happen before you went to ' Bocarthe '?" I asked.

" No," said Mr. Rowlandson—" not a thing. We were then sceptics where ghosts were concerned, but we are certainly not sceptical now."

" Do you think it is possible," I said, " that the ghost is attached to some piece of old furniture? There have been such cases."

" No," he replied. " We have no old furniture. All our furniture is modern and new. At least, it was new when we went to ' Bocarthe '."

" Then if the ghost is neither attached to the house, nor to the ground, nor to the furniture, it must surely be attached to some person," I said. " I suppose no one in the house has gone in for spiritualism?"

" I can tell you I haven't," Mr. Rowlandson said— " and you haven't either, Maud, have you?"

Mrs. Rowlandson flushed. " The only spiritualist I ever knew," she said, " was—you knew, dear, who I mean . . ."

Her husband stared at her. " I don't," he said. " Who?"

" Ernest Dekon."

" Dekon!" he exclaimed. " Why of course. Some years ago, Mr. O'Donnell," he explained to me, " my wife met this Mr. Dekon at a ball given by a mutual friend, and from that time, up to shortly before his death abroad, he persecuted her with his undesirable attentions. I never knew anyone so persistent."

" He resented your marriage?"

" I should think he did!" said Mr. Rowlandson—" though to everyone's surprise he came to the wedding. I shall never forget the expression on his face."

" Mr. Dekon was a spiritualist?" I asked.

" He was very keen on seances," Mrs. Rowlandson broke in to say. " Most keen, and was at one time always trying to persuade me to go to one with him."

" You never told me that," said her husband.

" No," said his wife. " But I never went."

" How did Mr. Dekon die?" I asked.

" Suicide," said Mr. Rowlandson. " He shot himself—and left a note stating that his death was entirely due to the heartless conduct of my wife."

" When was that?"

Mr. Rowlandson thought for a moment. " We have been married not quite eighteen months. About fifteen months ago— shortly before we went to ' Bocarthe '."

" I know what's in your mind," Mrs. Rowlandson said to me. " Do you really think that it could be the spirit of Ernest Dekon that is troubling us?"

I told her it seemed more than likely, and asked when the phenomenon usually appeared.

" At all times, and when we least expect it," she replied. " For example, if I am going upstairs alone, it either springs out at me or peers down at me from over the banisters. Or again, it rouses us in the middle of the night by rocking our bed. Always some alarming trick of that kind."

" Then you would hardly expect it to manifest itself if we all sat here in the dark?"

" Hardly."

I asked if there was a photograph of Mr. Dekon. There was not, but Mrs. Rowlandson described him. She remembered particularly the look of his hands. " The fingers were long and red, and the tips were club-shaped. I am sure I would recognize them anywhere."

This conversation took place in the evening before dinner. After dinner we sat in the drawing-room, discussing plans for the night. We decided that when bedtime came we should retire to our respective rooms and sit there in the dark, waiting and watching. Directly anyone heard or saw anything he would summon the others.

We sat up late and it was close on midnight before Mrs. Rowlandson rose, and we all—there were two guests besides myself, a Colonel and Mrs. Rushworth—took our candlesticks and followed her upstairs. We had mounted the first flight, and had turned the bend leading to the second—the house seemed all stairs—when Mrs. Rowlandson stopped and looking back at us said : " Sssh! Do you hear anything?"

We stood and listened. There was a thump, which apparently came from a room just at the top of the stairs, then another, and then a very curious sound, as if something was bounding backwards and forwards over bare boards with its feet tied together. At a signal from Mr. Rowlandson we immediately blew out our lights. A church clock struck twelve; we heard it distinctly, as the Rowlandsons, being enthusiasts for fresh air, kept practically every window in the house open. The reverberation of the final stroke had scarcely ceased when a loud gasp from someone in front of me sent a chilly feeling down my spine.

At the same moment the darkness ahead of us was lighted by a faint luminous glow. The glow speedily intensified and suddenly took the shape of a cylindrical column of six or seven feet in height, and this in turn developed with startling abruptness into the form of something so shockingly grotesque that I was appalled.

It is extremely difficult to give a very accurate description of it, because like much of the occult phenomena I have experienced in haunted houses it was a baffling mixture of the distinct and yet vague, entirely without substance, and apparently wholly constituted of vibrating light which varied each second in tone and intensity. I can only say that the impression I derived was that of a very gross or monstrous man.

The head, ill-defined on the crown and sides, appeared to be abnormally high and long, and to be covered with a tangled mass of coarse, tow-coloured hair; the nose seemed hooked, the mouth cruel, the eyes leering. The body of the thing was grey and nude, very like the trunk of a silver birch, the arms long and knotted, the hands huge, the fingers red and club-shaped—corresponding exactly with Mrs. Rowlandson's description.

The baleful apparition seemed without doubt to be the spirit of Ernest Dekon.

This was the ghost which could shut and open doors, move furniture, rap, and make other noises; it could also convey the sensation of intense cold, and the feeling of the most dreadful fear.

I found myself wondering if it possessed other properties. Was it sensible? Could it communicate in any way?

While I was deliberating the figure seemed to move forward, then someone shrieked. Mr. Rowlandson struck a light and simultaneously the apparition vanished. The effect it had had on us all was striking, we were all more or less demoralized. Yet no two of us had seen the ghost the same, while Mr. Rowlandson and Mrs. Rushworth had not seen it at all.

We went back to the drawing-room and discussed it. Mrs. Rowlandson was the first to speak. She too had been particularly impressed by the hands, and was sure they were the hands of Ernest Dekon.

" I can say nothing about the face," she said, " as it did not appear to me, but having seen the hands I am firmly convinced that the ghost is Ernest Dekon, and that it is he who is tormenting us. Cannot any of you think of a plan to get rid of him?"

" Cremation is the only thing I can think of," said Colonel Rushworth, who up to now had been silent. " That is the means employed by the hill tribes in Northern India. When a spirit—a spirit they can identify—begins to haunt a place, they dig up the body and burn it, and they say as soon as the last bone is consumed the haunting stops. They have a theory that phantoms of dead people and animals can materialize as long as some remnant of their physical body remains. Where did this Mr. Dekon die?"

" In Africa," said Mr. Rowlandson.

" Well," said the Colonel, " in that case if we can check the cemetery there ought to be no difficulty in arranging for the body to be exhumed. The officials are, as a rule, open to bribery. Anyhow, you might try it as an experiment."

I left Edinburgh next day, but I heard some months later from Mr. Rowlandson. His letter was short and cheery, and in it he wrote : " You may recollect Colonel Rushworth's suggestion. Well, the hauntings have ceased, and I am glad to tell you we are shortly returning to ' Bocarthe '."

From which I gathered that an attempt to exhume and cremate Ernest Dekon's body had been made, and had proved successful.

THE LISTENER

PEOPLE WHO attempt to exchange words with an apparition very seldom succeed in drawing a response, or indeed any recognition at all of their own presence. This is true of most of my own efforts to communicate with ghostly figures. Excluding those of the deliberately harmful and belligerent kind, the majority of ghosts, when addressed, pay no heed but simply continue about their purpose.

In a little case I am reminded of, however, even if the witness drew no response from the figure she saw, her words to it did seem to have an ultimate effect.

I met Mrs. Norah Barrington at a social evening in London, and in the course of our conversation together we touched on ghosts. I happened to ask, just by the way, if she knew anyone who had actually spoken with an apparition, and she replied at once: " Oh, yes!—I have spoken to one myself."

On my pressing her to describe her experience, this is what she told me:

" Some years ago I rented the top flat of a terrace house in a Kensington square. The rooms below me were occupied by a solicitor's clerk and his wife, while the landlady, Mrs. Bowen, lived on the ground floor. My two sisters, Gertrude and Pamela, lived with me, sharing the extra bedroom, and it was not very long before they began to complain that someone came up our stairs at night with very heavy footsteps. Gertrude said she was sure it was a man as no woman could tread so heavily. He always came to our door, and after remaining outside it for some minutes, walked away again.

"Thinking this very strange, I mentioned the matter to Mrs. Bowen, who sympathetically dismissed the idea of there being an intruder. She explained that the acoustic properties of the houses in our terrace were such as often made it extremely difficult to locate sounds accurately. She herself frequently fancied she heard someone about the passages, she told me, when in reality it was merely the people next door.

"Half persuaded that what she suggested was correct, and being anxious to allay the suspicions of my sisters, who are naturally timid, I pretended I was satisfied.

"A few days later our dressmaker, who was at work in the dining-room doing some alterations for Pamela, told me she would like to see Pamela for a minute or so if it would not be disturbing her. 'I know she has someone with her,' the dressmaker explained, 'as I heard a gentleman come up and go into the drawing-room, but I really won't keep her more than a minute.'

"'Are you sure my sister has company?' I asked.

"'Oh yes,' she replied. 'I couldn't help thinking what a very heavy tread he had—it quite shook the table here.'

"Just then Pamela came in, and noticing the intent expression on my face, inquired what was the matter.

"'I was just asking if I might see you, Miss, about this skirt,' the dressmaker said, 'and was apologizing to Miss Norah for disturbing you as I knew you had company.'

"'Company?' exclaimed Pamela. 'Why, whatever do you mean? We don't have visitors at this hour in the morning.'

"The dressmaker was disconcerted, but still quite adamant. 'Begging your pardon, Miss,' she said, 'didn't a gentleman enter the parlour just now? I am sure I heard someone—a gentleman with a very heavy tread.'

" Pamela turned very white. ' You must have heard someone next door,' she faltered. ' At least that is how Mrs. Bowen explains it.'

" ' If you ask me,' the dressmaker said, shaking her head solemnly, ' I'd say this house is haunted.'

" She finished Pamela's dress, but nothing would induce her to come to the house again.

" A day or two after this incident, the solicitor's clerk and his wife, in the flat below us, went away for their holiday. On the night of their departure, at about twelve o'clock, my sisters were awakened by sounds from the vacated rooms—trampings on the stairs and in the passages, the opening and slamming to of doors, and the hustling about of furniture, and much annoyed that the couple should disturb the house by their arriving at such a late hour, my sisters complained to Mrs. Bowen. She was greatly embarrassed, admitted that her tenants had not returned and that the noises could not be accounted for.

" Seeing the look in all our eyes she then added : ' I suppose I ought to have explained to you that the house is said to be haunted, but I delayed doing so, hoping you would get used to the noises. You understand, Miss Norah, that this house is my bread and butter, and if it once got the reputation of harbouring ghosts, I should be ruined. The ghost won't hurt any of you, and—oh, I do beg of you not to mention it to any of your friends.'

" Feeling really sorry for her, though she had tried to deceive us, we promised; and as I was the least nervous of the trio, we changed bedrooms, Gertrude and Pamela going into mine, and I moving to the haunted one. At first I did not dare to sleep in the dark but left the gas burning, taking the additional precaution of locking the door.

" I awoke at midnight to hear the sounds—the heavy tread, tread, tread of a man's step on the staircase and along the passage. All my senses at once became painfully acute, and

423

sitting up in bed, I listened with strained ears. Nearer and nearer they came—the heavy lumbering tread of a big, unwieldy man. I was now so terrified that I felt I must die should the ghost succeed in entering the room.

"Arriving outside the door, it halted, and then the door-handle was gently turned. I was horrified, expecting that the locked door would fly open and that I should see some awful face. Fortunately for me, however, this did not happen. The handle ceased turning and for some seconds there was the sound of heavy breathing; then the same laboured steps slowly strode away.

"I was much ashamed of myself, Mr. O'Donnell, for being such a coward. I ought to have unlocked and opened the door, and at least made an attempt to converse with the ghost, for it seemed quite apparent that it wanted to communicate something, or it would not have walked about like that.

"I worried over this, day after day, until I at last determined I would see the apparition, no matter what risk this incurred. Night came, and I retired to bed as usual, putting out the gas, however, and leaving the door unlocked. I soon fell into a deep sleep from which I was abruptly awakened by the most appalling crash, and on starting up I saw, leaning over the foot of my bedstead and staring at me, the figure of a man—a tall man with black hair, the upper part of his face agreeably handsome, but the lower part disconcertingly brutal.

"His eyes, large and dark, were fixed on mine with the most agonized expression, as of one irredeemably damned. He was immaculately dressed in evening clothes, every detail being startlingly visible from the luminous glow that seemed to emanate from his entire person, in contrast to the darkness of the room. For some moments—to me an eternity—I gazed at him, far too frightened to speak; and then, my courage gradually returning, I moistened my parched lips and with an effort mumbled out a few words. I cannot recollect what I said, but as my one and only thought in those first few seconds of fear was to get rid of the apparition as quickly as possible, I believe I resorted to a wild prayer of exorcism.

"But it had no effect, the ghost remaining silent and motionless. The sound of my own voice reassuring me, and the preliminary shock of the encounter being over, I grew rapidly calmer, and asked the figure a variety of questions, hoping I might be able to obtain valuable information about the future world; but in this I was doomed to disappointment, for he either could not or would not reply.

"Seeing the futility of further questioning I decided on a gentler form of address. I tried to explain to him how absolutely necessary it was for him to overcome his evil ways if he would ever tear himself away from this earth. I begged him to continually pray to Christ to help him, assuring him that there was hope of redemption even for the most debased of mankind—for anyone, in fact, who could once be brought to full recognition of the enormity of their sins. 'When once you begin to repent in grim earnest,' I said, 'the fetters that bind you here will be loosened, and you will speedily rise to the highest spiritual sphere —to Paradise.'

"I continued to talk to him in this manner for a long time, until in fact the clock struck two, when to my great relief he suddenly vanished.

"Well, Mr. O'Donnell, that was not the end—far from it. He kept on visiting me almost nightly for nearly *three months*, and on each occasion I spoke to him in the same strain. Although he always listened attentively, he never replied. Perhaps he could not speak. But his eyes gradually lost their expression of despair, and the last time he appeared to me I was delighted beyond measure to see in his face a look of gratitude and joy.

"He then vanished, and the heavy footsteps were heard no more."

THE LADY IN WHITE

SCOTLAND CLAIMS its share of phantoms in the form of " White Ladies ". According to tradition the ruins of the mansion of Woodhouselee were haunted by a woman in white, presumably (though personally I think otherwise) the ghost of Lady Hamilton of Bothwellhaugh. This unfortunate woman, together with her baby, was—during the temporary absence of her husband—stripped naked and turned out of doors on a bitterly cold night, by a favourite of the Regent Murray. As a result of this inhuman conduct the child died, and its mother with the corpse in her arms, was discovered in the morning raving mad.

Another instance of this particular form of apparition is to be found in Sir Walter Scott's *White Lady of Avenel*, and there are countless others, both in reality and fiction.

Some years ago, when putting up at a friend's house in Edinburgh, I was introduced to a man who had had several experiences with ghosts, and had therefore been specially asked to meet me. After we had talked together for some time he related the following adventure which had befallen him, in his childhood, on the Rownam estate of Sir E. C., near Stirling.

" I was always a lover of nature, and my earliest reminiscences are associated with solitary rambles through the fields, dells and copses surrounding my home. I lived within a stone's-throw of the property of old Sir E. C., who has long gone to rest—God bless his soul! And I think it needs blessing, for if there was any truth in local gossip (and it is said, I think truly, that ' There is never any smoke without fire ') he had lived a very queer life. Indeed, he was held in such universal awe and abhorrence that we children used to fly at his approach, and never spoke of him among ourselves saving in such terms as ' Auld dour crab ', or ' The laird deil '.

" Rownam Manor House, where he lived, was a fine specimen of sixteenth-century architecture, and had it been called a castle would have merited the description far more than many of the buildings in Scotland that bear that name. It was approached by a long avenue of trees—gigantic elms, oaks and beeches which, uniting their branches overhead in summertime, formed an effective barrier to the sun's rays. This avenue had an irresistible attraction for me. It swarmed with rabbits and squirrels, and many are the times I trespassed there to watch them. I had a very secure hiding-place in the hollow of an old oak, where I was often secreted while Sir E. C. and his keepers, without casting a glance in my direction, passed unsuspectingly by, vowing all sorts of vengeance against trespassers.

" Of course, I had to be very careful how I got there, for the grounds were well patrolled, and Sir E. C. had sworn to prosecute anyone he caught walking in them without his permission. Had he caught me, I should doubtless have been treated with the utmost severity, since he and my father were the most bitter opponents politically, and for that reason, unreasonable though it be, never lost an opportunity of insulting one another. My father, a strong Radical, was opposed to all big landed pro-prietors, and consequently winked his eye at my trespassings; but I think nothing would really have pleased him better than to have seen me brought to book by Sir E. C., since in my defence he would have had an opportunity of appealing to the passions of the local people, who were all Radicals, and of incensing them still further against the principles of feudalism.

" I had often heard it rumoured in the village that Rownam Avenue was haunted, and that the apparition was a lady in white—actually Sir E. C.'s wife, whose death at a very early age was said to have been hastened, if not entirely accounted for, by her husband's harsh treatment. Whether he was really as black as he was painted I have never been able to ascertain; the intense animosity with which we all regarded him made us believe anything ill of him, and we were quite ready to attribute all the alleged hauntings in the neighbourhood to his past misdeeds.

" I think my family, with scarcely an exception, believed in ghosts; anyhow, the subject of ghosts was so often discussed in my hearing that I became possessed of an ungovernable curiosity to see one. If only the Lady in White would appear in the daytime, I thought, I should have no difficulty in satisfying this curiosity, but unfortunately she did not appear till night, long after boys of my age had been ordered off to bed. I did not much like the idea of stealing out of the house at dead of night and going alone to see the ghost, so I suggested to a school friend that he should also creep out one night and accompany me to Rownam to look for the Lady. But the risk of being caught trespassing was too much for him, and so I made up my mind to go to Rownam Avenue alone.

" Biding my opportunity, and waiting till my father was safely out of the way—on a visit to Greenock, where a business transaction would oblige him to remain for some days—I climbed out of my bedroom window one night when I judged the rest of the household to be sound asleep, scudded swiftly across the fields, and making short work of the lofty wall that formed the southernmost boundary of the Rownam estates, quickly made my way to the Avenue.

" It was an ideal Sunday night in August, hardly a sound breaking the exquisite silence of the woods. At times, overcome with the delightful sensation of freedom, I paused, and raising my eyes to the starry heavens, drank in huge draughts of the pure country air. I then performed the maddest boyish capers, but finally sobering down, continued on my course. Every now and then, fancying I detected the footsteps of a keeper, I hid behind a tree; but it was only fancy, for I saw no one.

" It must have been fully one o'clock before I arrived at the outskirts of the Avenue, and advancing eagerly, settled myself in my favourite sanctuary, the hollow oak. All was hushed and motionless, and as I gazed into the gloom I became conscious, for the first time in my life, of a sensation of eeriness. Not a glimmer of moonlight penetrated the arched canopy of foliage overhead.

" The loneliness got on my nerves. At first I grew afraid, only afraid, and then my fears turned into a panic to get away from the grim spot. I emerged from my retreat and was preparing to fly through the wood, when from afar off there suddenly came the sound of a voice—the harsh, grating voice of a man. Convinced this time that I had been discovered by a keeper, I jumped back into the tree, and swarming up the inside of the trunk, peered cautiously out.

" What I saw then nearly made me jump out of my skin. Advancing along the Avenue was the thing I had always longed to see, and for which I had risked so much: the mysterious, far-famed Lady in White—a ghost, an actual, bona fide ghost! I thrilled with excitement and my heart thumped till it seemed on the verge of bursting through my ribs. The Lady in White. Why, it would be the talk of the whole countryside! Someone had really—no hearsay evidence—seen the notorious apparition at last.

" I looked at her closely and saw that she was entirely luminous, emitting a strong glow. She wore a quantity of white drapery swathed round her in a manner that perplexed me, until I suddenly realized with a creeping of my flesh that it must be a winding-sheet, that burial accessory so often minutely described to me by the son of the village undertaker.

" Streaming over her neck and shoulders were thick masses of long, wavy, golden hair. Her face, despite its pallor, was so beautiful that had not some restraining influence compelled me to remain in hiding, I would have descended from my perch to obtain a closer view of it. I only once caught a glimpse of her full face, for with a persistence that was most annoying, she kept it turned from me; but in that brief second the lustre of her blue eyes won my very soul.

" Those eyes are still firmly impressed on my memory; I shall never forget them. Nothing, I thought, either on earth or in heaven could have been half so lovely, and I was so moved that it was not until she was directly beneath me that I saw she was not alone, and that walking by her side, with one arm round her waist, his face and figure illuminated with the light from her body, was Sir E. C. But how changed! Gone was the deep black scowl, the grim tightening of the jaws, and the intensely disagreeable expression that had earned him the nickname of ' The laird deil ', and in their stead I saw love—nothing but blind, infatuated, soul-devouring love. Even as a child I could recognize the strong emotion.

" Throwing discretion to the wind, for my excitement and curiosity had risen to the highest pitch, I now thrust more than half my body out of the hole in the trunk. The next instant, with a loud cry, I pitched head first to the ground.

" I don't know how long I lay there, stunned but otherwise unhurt except for cuts and bruises. On coming to, I fully expected to find myself in the hands of the irate laird, who would seize me by the scruff of the neck and belabour me to pieces. Consequently, too frightened to move, I lay still with my eyes closed. But when nothing happened, I picked myself up. All was quiet and pitch dark, with no sign of the Lady in White or of Sir E. C.

" It did not take me very long to get out of the wood and home. I ran all the way, and as it was still far too early for any of the household to be astir, I was able to creep up to my bedroom unobserved. But not to sleep, for the moment I blew the

430

candle out and got into bed, reaction set in and I suffered agonies of fear.

" In the morning, however, my fears had subsided and I went to school bubbling over with excitement to tell the boys what had happened. But I then received another shock. Before I could get out a word of my experiences I was told with a roar and shout that ' the auld laird deil ' was dead! His body had been found stretched on the ground in the Avenue shortly after sunrise. He had died from syncope, so the doctor said, probably caused by some severe shock.

" I did not tell my companions of my night's adventure after all. My eagerness to do so had departed when I heard of the auld laird's death."

FROM THE CELLAR IT CAME

THE WEALTHY Lady Adela Minken (whose yacht at Cowes was the envy of all who cruised in her) was the owner of a considerable amount of house property, much of which, as she freely admitted to me, she had not set eyes on nor had any special desire to do so, having very competent agents to handle her affairs. However, when curious reports kept filtering through to her about an alleged haunting in one of her houses in Edinburgh, she became intrigued and decided to put the haunting to the test.

Lady Adela was a perfectly frank and open-minded woman. Though she had never experienced any occult phenomenon herself, she was not inclined to dismiss as so much rubbish the evidence of those tenants who declared they had witnessed manifestations. Accordingly she proceeded with her " test " in very practical fashion, commencing her occupation of the house, in F—— Road, with a perfectly unbiased mind, and resolving to stay there if needs be for at least a year, so as to give it a fair trial.

Lady Adela took up residence in the house in the early summer of 1908, having been told that the hauntings were generally at their height in the late summer and early autumn.

It is, I think, unnecessary to enter into any detailed description of the house. In appearance it differed very little, if at all, from those adjoining it; in construction it was if anything a trifle large. The basement, which included the usual kitchen offices and cellars was very dark, and to her great puzzlement Lady Adela found that the atmosphere here after sunset on Fridays, and only on Fridays, was tainted with a strong smell of damp earth, together with a sweet and nauseating " something " she and the servants were totally unable to account for. All the rooms in the house were of fair dimensions, and cheerful, except on Friday evenings, when a distinct gloom settled on them and the strangest of shadows were seen playing about the passage and on the landings.

Now as I have said, Lady Adela was a thoroughly practical woman, and so she inclined to put down these " Friday feelings " to mere fancy. And anyway, she told herself, if all she encountered was nothing worse than a weekly menu of smells and easily digested shadows, she was not likely to suffer any harm.

But as the weeks went by, the shadows and the smell grew more and more pronounced, and by the arrival of August had become so emphatic that she could not help thinking they were both hostile and aggressive.

At about eight o'clock on the evening of the second Friday in August Lady Adela was purposely alone in the basement of the house. She had felt that the presence of the servants in the house minimized her chances of seeing the ghost—if ghost it was—and so she sent them all out for a motor drive and for once, unconventionally, rejoiced in having the house to herself. She was not, however, entirely alone, for she had two of her dogs with her; two beautiful boarhounds, trophies of her last trip to the Baltic. With such faithful companions she felt absolutely safe, and ready—as she acknowledged afterwards—to face a whole army of phantoms.

First, she made a tour of the premises. The housekeeper's room pleased her immensely—at least she persuaded herself it did. " Why, it is quite as nice as any of the rooms upstairs," she said aloud, as she stood with her face to the failing sunbeams and rested her strong white hand on the edge of the table. " Quite as nice. Karl and Max, come here !"

But the boarhounds for once did not obey her with good grace. There was something in the room they did not like, and they showed how strong was their resentment by slinking unwillingly through the doorway.

Lady Adela scolded them lightly. Then her eyes wandered round the walls, and struggled in vain to reach the remoter angles of the room, which had suddenly grown dark. She tried to assure herself that this was simply the natural effect of the departing daylight, and that, had she watched in other houses at this particular time, she would have noticed the same thing. To show herself—and the dogs—how little she minded the gloom, she went up to the darkest corner and prodded the walls with a riding-whip. She laughed. There was nothing there, nothing whatsoever to be afraid of, only shadows.

She then walked out into the passage, and whistling to Karl and Max, who contrary to their custom would not keep to heel, made another inspection of the kitchens. At the top of the cellar steps she stopped. The darkness had now set in everywhere, and she reasoned with herself that it would be foolish to venture into such dungeon-like places without a light. She soon found one, and armed with candle, matches, and the whip, began her descent. There were several cellars, and they presented such a dismal appearance that she instinctively drew her skirts tightly round her, and exchanged the slender riding-whip for a poker. She whistled again to the dogs. They did not answer, so she called them both by name angrily. But for some unaccountable reason they still would not come.

Lady Adela ransacked her mind to recall some popular operatic air, but although she knew scores she could not remember one. The only melody that filtered back to her was one she detested, a vaudeville tune she had heard three nights in succession when staying with a student friend in the Latin Quarter in

434

Paris. She hummed it loudly, however, and holding the lighted candle high above her head, walked down the steps. At the bottom she stood and listened. From high above came noises which sounded like the rumbling of distant thunder, but which, she determined after a few moments, was only the rattling of windows.

Reassured that she had no cause for alarm, Lady Adela advanced. Something black scudded across the red-tiled floor, and she made a dash at it with her poker. The sharp noise of the poker striking the floor awoke countless echoes in the cellars, and called into existence legions of other black things that darted hither and thither in all directions. She burst out laughing—they were only beetles! Facing her she now saw an inner cellar, which was far gloomier than the one in which she stood. The ceiling was very low, and appeared to be crushed down beneath the burden of a stupendous weight; and as she advanced beneath it she half expected that it would cave in and bury her.

A few feet from the centre of this cellar she stopped, and bending down, examined the floor carefully. The tiles were unmistakably newer here than elsewhere, and presented the appearance of having been put in at no very distant date. The dampness of the atmosphere was intense, a fact which struck her as somewhat odd, since the floor and the walls looked singularly dry. To find out if this were the case, she ran her fingers over the walls, and on removing them, found they showed no signs of moisture. Then she rapped the floor and walls, and could discover no indications of hollowness. She sniffed the air, and a great wave of something sweet and sickly half choked her. She drew out her handkerchief and beat the air vigorously with it, but the smell remained, and she could not in any way account for it. She turned to leave the cellar, and the flame of her candle burned blue. Then for the first time that evening—almost, indeed, for the first time in her life—she felt afraid, so afraid that she made no attempt to reason her fear. She understood the dogs' feelings now, and found herself wondering how much they knew.

She whistled to them again, not because she had any confidence they would respond, but because she wanted company, even the company of her own voice; and she had some faint hope too that whatever might be with her in the cellar, would not so readily disclose itself if she made a noise. The one cellar was passed, and she was nearly across the floor of the other when she heard a crash. The candle dropped from her hand, and all the blood in her body seemed to rush to her heart.

As she told me: " I could never have imagined it was so terrible to be frightened. I tried to pull myself together and be calm, but I was no longer mistress of my limbs. My knees knocked together and my hands shook. ' It was only the dogs,' I feebly told myself— ' I will call them.' But when I opened my mouth I found my throat was paralysed—not a syllable would come."

She knew full well too that the hounds could not have been responsible for the noise. It was like nothing she had ever heard, nothing she could imagine; and though she struggled hard against the idea, she could not help associating the sound with the cause of the candle burning blue, and the sweet, sickly smell.

Incapable of moving a step, she was forced to listen in breathless expectancy for a recurrence of the crash. Her thoughts became ghastly. The inky darkness that hemmed her in on every side suggested every sort of ghoulish possibility, and with each pulsation of her overstrained heart her flesh crawled. Another sound—this time not a crash, nothing half so loud or definite—drew her eyes in the direction of the steps. An object was now standing at the top of them, and something lurid, like the faint, phosphorescent glow of decay, emanated from all over it; but what it was, she could not tell, except that it was inexpressibly antagonistic and foul.

" I would have given my soul to have looked elsewhere, but my eyes were fixed—I could neither turn nor shut them. For some seconds the shape remained motionless, and then with a sly, subtle motion it lowered its head and came stealing stealthily down the stairs towards me. I followed its approach like one in a horrible dream. Another step, another, yet another; till there were only three steps left between us, and I was at last able to form some idea of what the thing was like.

" It was short and squat, and appeared to be partly clad in a loose flowing garment, which was not long enough to conceal the glistening extremities of its limbs. From its general contour and the tangled mass of hair that fell about its neck and shoulders it seemed to be the phantasm of a woman. Its head being kept bent I was unable to see the face in full, but every instant I expected to have sight of it, and with each separate movement of the figure the suspense became more and more intolerable.

" At last it stood on the floor of the cellar, a broad, horribly ungainly figure, which glided up to and, thankfully, past me into the far cellar. There it halted, as nearly as I could judge on the new tiles, and remained standing. As I gazed at it, too fascinated to remove my eyes, there was a loud, echoing crash, a terrible sound of wrenching and tearing, and the whole of the ceiling of the inner chamber came down with an appalling roar.

" I think I must then have fainted, for I distinctly remember falling into what seemed to me to be a black, interminable abyss. When I recovered consciousness I was lying on the tiles, and all around was still and normal. I got up, found and lighted the candle, and spent the rest of the evening without further adventure, in the drawing-room."

All the following week Lady Adela struggled hard to master a disinclination to spend another evening alone in the house, but when Friday came again she succumbed to her fears and kept the servants at home. She sat reading in the drawing-room till late that night, and when she looked out of the window to take a farewell glance at the sky and stars before retiring to bed, the sounds of traffic had completely ceased and the whole city lay bathed in a refreshing silence.

She put out the lights and got into. bed. It was just one o'clock when she fell asleep, and three o'clock when she awoke with a violent start. Why she had woken puzzled her. She had not been dreaming and there seemed nothing to account for her sudden wakefulness. She lay still, her tired eyes closed again, and wondered. Surely everything was just as it was when she went to sleep? And yet—there was something different, something new. She did not think it was actually in the atmosphere, nor in the silence; she did not know where it was until she opened her eyes again—and then she knew. Bending over her, within a few inches of her face, was another face.

" It was on a larger scale than that of any person I have ever seen. It was long in proportion to its width—I could not make out where the cranium terminated at the back, as the hind portion of it was lost in a mist. The receding forehead was partly covered with a mass of lank black hair that fell straight down into space. There were no neck nor shoulders—at least none had materialized. The skin was leaden-hued, and the emaciation so extreme that the raw cheek-bones had burst through in places. The size of the eyesockets, which appeared monstrous, was emphasized by the fact that the eyes were considerably sunken. The lips were curled downwards and tightly shut, and the whole expression of the withered mouth, as that of the entire face, was one of bestial malignity.

" I was petrified. As I stared helplessly at the dark eyes pressed close to mine, I saw them light up with fiendish glee. The most frightful change then took place: the upper lip writhed away from a few greenish yellow stumps, the lower jaw fell with a metallic click, leaving the mouth widely open and showing a black and bloated tongue, and the eyeballs rolled up and entirely disappeared, their places being immediately filled with the most loathsome signs of advanced decay.

" A strong, vibratory movement suddenly made all the bones in the head rattle and the tongue wag, while from the jaws, as if belched up from some deep-down well, came a gust of putrescent wind tainted with the same sweet, sickly odour which I recognized from the cellar. This was the culminating act. The head then receded, and growing fainter and fainter, gradually disappeared altogether.

438

" I leaped out of bed, put on all the lights, and did not dare close my eyes again until the birds had begun their dawn chorus."

Lady Adela was now more than satisfied that there was not a house more horribly haunted in Scotland, and nothing would induce her to remain in it another night.

Being anxious, naturally, to discover something that might in some degree account for the apparitions, she made endless inquiries concerning the history of former occupants of the house. Failing to discover anything remarkable in this direction, she was eventually obliged to content herself with the following tradition: It was said that on the site of the house there had once stood a cottage occupied by two sisters, both nurses, and that one was suspected of poisoning the other. The cottage, having through their parsimonious habits fallen into a very bad state of repair, was blown down during a violent storm, the surviving sister perishing in the ruins.

Lady Adela, after being assured that only about one in a thousand people seemed to possess the faculty of seeing pyschic phenomena, decided to offer the house for rent again; and once the rumours had begun to fade away, she succeeded eventually in getting a permanent tenant. Apparently, and most fortunately this time, one of the nine hundred and ninety-nine.

THE SIGN OF THE WEREWOLF

IT IS commonly known that long ago, many wolves roamed Great Britain. It is not so widely known that werewolves, too, once troubled these islands in early days.

The authorities for this are many. For example, Halliwell, quoting from a Bodleian M.S., says: "Ther ben somme that eten chyldren and men, and eteth noon other flesh fro that tyme that thei be a-charmed with mannys flesh for rather thei wolde be deed; and thei be cleped werewolfes for men shulde be war of them." And Richard Verstegan, in his *Restitution of Decayed Intelligence*, 1605, says: "The werewolves are certain sorcerers who having anointed their bodies with an ointment which they make by the instinct of the devil, and putting on a certain enchanted girdle, do not only unto the view of others seem as wolves, but to their own thinking have both the shape and nature of wolves, so long as they wear the said girdle; and they do dispose themselves as very wolves in worrying and killing, and eating most of human creatures."

It is, of course, a highly contentious subject, but as a ghost-hunter I have come across much that I believe to be good evidence in support of the testimony of the ancient writers. For instance, in localities once known to have been the favourite haunts of wolves, I have met people who have told me they have seen phantasms, in shape half human and half beast, that might well be the earthbound spirits of werewolves.

Miss Jane St. Denis told me she once stayed on a farm in Merionethshire where she witnessed a phenomenon of this nature. The farm, though some distance from the village, was not far from the small railway station, which had only one platform and a hut that served as waiting room and booking office combined. It was one of those stations where the separate duties of stationmaster, porter, booking clerk and ticket collector were performed by one man, and where the signal always appeared to be down.

As the platform commanded one of the most paintable views in the neighbourhood Miss St. Denis often used to sit there with her sketch-book. On one occasion she had stayed rather later than usual, and on rising hurriedly from her camp-stool saw a figure which she took to be that of a man, sitting on a truck a few yards away, peering at her. She was greatly surprised, because except on the rare occasion of a train arriving, she had never seen anyone at the station besides the stationmaster, and in the evening the platform was invariably deserted.

The loneliness of the place was for the first time brought forcibly home to her. The stationmaster's tiny house was at least some hundred yards away, and beyond that there was not another habitation nearer than the farm. On all sides of her, too, were black, frowning precipices, full of seams and fissures, showing vague and shadowy in the fading rays of the sun. Here and there were the huge, gaping mouths of gloomy slate quarries that had long been disused, and were now half full of foul water. Around them the earth was heaped with loose fragments of rock which had evidently been detached from the principal mass and shivered to pieces in the fall. A few trees grew among the rocks, and attested by their dwarfish stature the ungrateful soil in which they had taken root.

It was not an exhilarating scene, but it was one that had held

441

a peculiar fascination for Miss St. Denis, which she now began to regret. The twilight had come on very rapidly and was especially concentrated, so it seemed to her, round the spot where she sat, so that she could make nothing out of the silent figure on the truck except that it had unpleasantly bright eyes and there was something odd about it. She coughed to see if that would have any effect, and as it had none she coughed again. Then she spoke and said: "Can you tell me the time, please?" But there was no reply, and the figure still sat there staring at her. Miss St. Denis then grew uneasy, and, packing up her things, walked out of the station, trying her best to act as if nothing was wrong.

She glanced back over her shoulder and saw that the figure was following her. Quickening her pace, she assumed a jaunty air and whistled, and turning round again, saw the strange figure still coming after her. The road would soon be at its worst stage of loneliness, cliffs on either side of it making the roadway almost pitch dark. Indeed, the spot positively invited murder, and she realised that if attacked, she could shriek herself hoarse without the remotest chance of making herself heard. To go on with this menacing figure so unmistakably and persistently stalking her was out of the question. Screwing up courage, she swung round and cried: "What do you want? How dare you . . .?"

She got no further, for a sudden spurt of dying sunlight playing over the figure showed her it was nothing human, nothing she had ever conceived possible. It was a nude grey thing, not unlike a man in body, but with a wolf's head. As it sprang forward, its light eyes ablaze with ferocity, she quickly felt in her pocket and seized a small torch which, thankfully, she had carried to find her way if in difficulty. As she switched on the torch the effect was magical; the creature shrank back, and putting two paw-like hands in front of its face to protect its eyes, faded into nothingness.

Miss St. Denis afterwards made many inquiries, but could learn nothing beyond the fact that, in one of the quarries close to the place where the ghost had vanished, some curious bones,

442

partly human and partly animal, had been unearthed, and that the locality was always shunned after dark.

Another " werewolf " haunting related to me at first hand involved a whole family in an alarming way.

A young married couple of the name of Anderson acquired through the death of a relative, a snug fortune. They promptly decided to retire from business and spend the rest of their lives in the country. They bought some land in Cumberland, at the foot of some hills, far away from any town, and built on it a large two-storeyed villa.

They soon, however, began to experience trouble with the servants, who left saying that the place was lonely and that they could not put up with the noises they heard at night. The Andersons took little notice of these complaints by the servants, but when their children began to remark on the night noises they viewed the matter more seriously.

" What are the noises like?" they asked.

" Wild animals," said William, their eldest child. " They come howling round the window at night and we hear their feet patter along the passage and stop at our door."

Much mystified, Mr. and Mrs. Anderson decided to sit up with the children and listen. Between two and three in the morning they were startled by a noise that sounded like the growling of a wolf—Mr. Anderson had heard wolves in Canada —immediately beneath the window. Throwing open the window, Mr. Anderson peered out. The moon was fully up and every stick and stone was plainly discernible, but there was now no sound and no sign of any animal. After he had closed the window the growling at once restarted, yet when he looked out again nothing was to be seen. After a time the growling ceased, and they heard the front door, which they had locked before coming upstairs, open, and the footsteps of some big, soft-footed animal ascend the stairs. Mr. Anderson waited till the steps were just outside the room and then flung open the door, but the light from his acetylene lamp revealed a passage full of moonbeams— nothing else.

443

He and his wife were thoroughly disturbed. In the morning they searched the grounds but could find no trace of footmarks, nothing to indicate the nature of their visitant.

It now drew close to Christmas, and when the noises were not heard for some time it was hoped they would not occur again. At this festive time there were the usual exchanges between parents and children; the three children challenging the existence of Father Christmas, and the parents replying with " Wait and see—he will come into your room on Christmas Eve laden with presents !"

William and his younger brother and sister took all this with a pinch of salt, threatening to lie awake and explode the myth.

Christmas Eve came at last, with heaps of snow on the ground and frost on the windowpanes and trees. In the Andersons' warm and comfortable house, while the children were busy on other things, Mr. Anderson rehearsed in full costume his role of Father Christmas. He had a sack full of presents and meant to enter the children's room with it on his shoulder at about midnight.

It was ten o'clock when the children went to bed, and exactly two hours later their father shuffled softly down the passage leading to their room. The snow had stopped falling, the moon was out, and the passage was flooded with a soft glow that threw into strong relief every minute object. Mr. Anderson had got half-way along the passage when he suddenly heard a faint sound of yelping. His whole frame thrilled and his mind reverted to the scenes of his boyhood—to the prairies in the far-off West, where time and again he had heard these sounds, and his Winchester rifle had stood him in good service.

As he listened the yelping came again. Undoubtedly it was a wolf, and yet there was an intonation in the yelping he had never heard before, and which he was at a loss to define. Again it rang out, much nearer this time, much more trying to the nerves, and he broke into a cold sweat of fear. Then there sounded close under the wall of the house a moaning, snarling, drawn-out cry that ended in a piercing whine.

One of the children, the little girl he thought, stirred in bed and muttered: "Father Christmas! Father Christmas!" and Mr. Anderson, with a desperate effort, staggered on under his load and opened their door. The clock in the hall below began to strike twelve. Mr. Anderson, striving hard to appear jolly and genial, entered the bedroom, and a huge, grey, shadowy figure entered with him. A slipper thrown by William—lying awake as he had threatened—whizzed through the air, and, narrowly missing his father, fell to the ground with a clatter. There was then a puzzled silence as the other two children, raising their heads, saw two figures standing in the centre of the room staring at one another.

The one figure was that of Father Christmas, but with a very white face and frightened eyes. The other figure was something very tall, far taller than their father, nude and grey—"something like a man with the head of a wolf, with white pointed teeth and horrible, light eyes."

They understood why it was that Father Christmas trembled, and why William stood by the side of his bed, white and silent.

It is impossible to say how long this state of things would have lasted, or what would eventually have happened, had not Mrs. Anderson, anxious to see how her husband was faring, and wondering why he had been gone so long, resolved herself to visit the children's room. As the light from her candle appeared on the threshold of the room the thing with the wolf's head vanished.

"Why, whatever were you all doing?" she began. Then Father Christmas and the children all spoke at once, while the sack of presents tumbled unheeded to the floor.

Every available candle was soon lighted, and mother and father and all three children spent the remainder of that night in close company. Next day the Andersons decided without any argument that the house should be put up for rent immediately. This was done straight after the holiday, and suitable tenants were soon found. Before leaving, however, Mr. Anderson made another and more exhaustive search of the grounds, and dis-

445

covered, in a cave in the hills immediately behind the house, a number of bones. Among them was the skull of a wolf, and lying close beside it a human skeleton, with only the skull missing.

He burnt the bones, hoping that by so doing he would rid the house of its unwelcome visitor; and as his tenants afterwards made no complaints he believed the hauntings had actually ceased.

A woman I met in Tavistock told me she had seen a ghost which she believed to be that of a werewolf, in the Valley of the Doones, Exmoor. She was walking home alone, late one evening, when she saw on the path directly in front of her the tall grey figure of a man with a wolf's head. Advancing stealthily forward, this creature was preparing to spring on a large rabbit that was crouching on the ground, apparently too terror-stricken to move, when the abrupt appearance of a stag bursting through the bushes caused it to vanish.

Prior to this occurrence my informant had never seen a ghost, nor had she, indeed, believed in them; but now, she assured me, she was quite convinced they existed, and felt that what she had seen was the spirit of one of those werewolves referred to by Gervase of Tilbury and Richard Verstegan—werewolves who were still earthbound owing to their incorrigible ferocity.

Another account of this type of haunting was told to me by Mr. Andrew Warren, who at the time he saw the phenomenon was staying in the Hebrides.

" I was about fifteen years of age," Mr. Warren said, " and had for several years been living with my grandfather, who was an elder in the Kirk of Scotland. He was much interested in geology, and filled the house with fossils from the pits and caves round where we dwelt. One morning he came home in a great state of excitement and made me go with him to look at some ancient remains he had found at the bottom of a dried up tarn.

" ' Look!' he cried, bending down and pointing at them, ' here is a human skeleton with a wolf's head. What do you make of it?'

446

" I told him I did not know, but supposed it must be some kind of monstrosity.

" ' It's a werewolf!' he exclaimed, ' that's what it is. A werewolf! This island was once over-run with satyrs and werewolves. Help me carry it to the house.'

" I did as he bid me, and we placed it on the table in the back kitchen. That evening I was left alone in the house, my grandfather and the other members of the household having gone to the kirk. For some time I amused myself reading, and then, fancying I heard a noise in the back premises, I went into the kitchen. There was no one about, and becoming convinced that it could only have been a rat that had disturbed me, I sat on the table alongside the alleged remains of the werewolf, and waited to see if the noises would recommence.

" I was waiting in a listless sort of way, my back bent, my elbows on my knees, looking at the floor and thinking of nothing in particular, when there came a loud rat, tat, tat of knuckles on the window pane. I immediately turned in the direction of the noise and saw a dark face looking in at me. At first dim and indistinct, it became more and more complete, until it developed into a perfectly defined head of a wolf terminating in the neck of a human being. Though greatly shocked, my first act was to look in every direction for a possible reflection—but in vain. There was no light either without or within, other than that from the setting sun—nothing that could in any way have produced an illusion.

" I looked at the face and marked each feature intently. It was unmistakably a wolf's face, the jaws slightly distended, the lips wreathed in a savage snarl, the teeth sharp and white, the eyes light green, the ears pointed.

" The expression on the face was so malignant as it gazed straight at me that my horor was as intense as my wonder. This it seemed to notice, for a look of exultation crept into its eyes, and it raised one hand—a slender hand, like that of a woman, thought with long curved fingernails—menacingly, as if about to dash in the window pane. Remembering what my grandfather

447

had told me about evil spirits, I crossed myself; but as this had no effect, and I really feared the thing would get at me, I ran out of the kitchen and shut and locked the door, remaining in the hall till the family returned.

" My grandfather was much upset when I told him what had happened, and attributed my failure to make the spirit depart to my want of faith. Had he been there, he assured me, he would soon have got rid of it; but he nevertheless made me help him remove the bones from the kitchen, and we reinterred them in the very spot where we had found them, and where, for aught I know to the contrary, they still lie."